MW00966879

# Uncaged
## A Story of Faith and Survival

by

**Deeva Denez**

© 1999, 2001 by Deeva Denez.  All rights reserved.

No part of this book may be reproduced, stored in a retrieval system, or
transmitted by any means, electronic, mechanical, photocopying, recording, or
otherwise, without written permission from the author.

ISBN: 0-75965-841-2

This book is printed on acid free paper.

1stBooks – rev. 09/10/01

# DEDICATIONS

First and foremost, I dedicate this book to my Heavenly Father, who made it all possible; who gave me life, a sound mind, His Son, Jesus Christ, His Holy Spirit, and His Inspirations.

A heartful thanks to my parents, Mr. & Mrs. Ellison Kelly, Jr.. I believe Jesus Christ has a purpose in my life today, that neither of you could have comprehended forty-five years ago. Because of the writing of this book, I can say, today, that I love the both of you.

To Jerome, my husband of twenty years. This book could not have been written without you in my life.

My beloved sons, Jerome and Jeremy. I love both of you very much. Thank you for the time that was taken from you to work on this book.

To my brother, Ellison Bernard Kelly, and his wife, Sharon and their children, Shandria, E.K., and Kayla.

To my sister, Kimberly Harris, and her husband, Exabia and their children, Jawuan, and Keyonna.

In loving memory of Big Mama, Mrs. Carrie Pittman, my great-grandmother, who was always good to me. August 28, 1900 - June 5, 1991.

In loving memory of my maternal grandmother, Mrs. Pealie Porter. You will always be missed and never forgotten. September 10, 1900 - June 20, 1991.

# ACKNOWLEDGEMENTS

If it takes a village to raise a child, then it takes half a city to get your first book published. At least, this was true in my case.

I would like to thank Mrs. Edna Crutchfield, founder of I.B.W.A., International Black Writers and Artists Association, for her organization and all the members who helped me with this work.

A special thank you goes to Howard Livingston, who entered my manuscript into his computer and helped me with the revision process. Howard may God greatly bless you and your work.

I would like to thank my co-workers, Judy Newton, Shaveeta Bonner, and Angela Mosley, who read each chapter as I completed it. Their comments and encouragements were greatly appreciated.

I would like to thank my assistant supervisor, Becky Atha, who gave me time off from work as I needed it, especially when I kept working on "the last chapter."

# PREFACE

Vanessa Grant's tumultuous life was revealed to her by prophecies and revelations. Physical abuse, emotional and mental scars, and an unfaithful husband plagued Vanessa, causing her an early, caged, adulthood.

The first six years of her roller coaster adult life begins with a marriage that was a perpetual honeymoon. It was an excellent transition from the physical abuse at home and the splendid years ahead of the next era of her life—seven golden years.

This era included the birth of her two sons, the purchase of a new house, and two well paying jobs. Life was good and worth living to Vanessa until the golden era ended and the next era began.

The next and last era was plagued with abandonment, depression, financial hardships and a dysfunctional family. It was during this era that Vanessa felt caged up—trapped in a marriage she no longer wanted to be in. She also felt as if life was not worth living. The only thing she had to live for was death, which was on the horizon.

However, the last year of the marriage was a time of healing for Vanessa, who became uncaged or freed from her lifetime of physical and mental abuse. Her greatest obstacle was her indecisiveness to liberate herself and her family to experience a new freedom.

# ONE

You know some people say the truth is stranger than fiction. My name is Vanessa Alisha Grant, and I can tell you first hand, it is. I've been through a storm that ripped my humanity into shreds, and I've lived in the golden light of years full of sunshine and love. Today, I stand at the edge looking for the Bearer of the Sign. I'm getting ahead of myself - aren't I? It is important for you to know what transpired before my birth, so you won't be shocked about what happened later on.

So here's my story, which begins January 1956 before I was born. As a matter of fact, it was just days after my conception when I was just a mess of blood and spirit, in December 1955, in an Atlanta neighborhood called Summerhill.

From what I understand, my mom, Betty, and dad, Xavier, were young and in love and doing the best they could. Under the circumstances, it's no wonder everthing happened like it did. I warn you...it's not pretty, or sane, and sometimes it's downright eerie, but that's life isn't it? Anyway, it's true, every bit of it, right down to the barking at my birth.

# BETTY

Big Mama, with her six-foot, two hundred seventy-five pound frame, sits in her favorite dark brown chair in the front room, cracking walnuts with a hammer. Her legs are spread wide open because that's the only way she sits. Her short, white hair stands straight up on her head. She never combs it. When I ask her why she doesn't comb it, she has no problem telling me.

"It's too much damn trouble, bitch," she informs me with her foul mouth. Big Mama is a curser.

I argue the no-hair combing excuse with her, which I can tell you now, is a big mistake, for Big Mama is quick to pull rank.

"Look here child, this is my hair, and I can do any damn thing I want with it. Right now, I ain't combing it."

She spits in the snuff can on the floor by her chair. That disgusts me because some brown spittle always ends up on the corner of her mouth or on her chin. The accumulating brown stuff doesn't seem to bother her, but it bugs the hell out of me. Big Mama never lets a point be put to rest until its time. So, she continues with her 'no-hair-combing excuse'. And like most old folks, she forgets one point and moves on to another, without any warning.

1

*Deeva Denez*

"I'll be sixty-eight day after tomorrow, girl." Big Mama says this, as my husband, Xavier, enters the room. Upon seeing her grandson, Big Mama smiles, showing more gum than teeth. Big Mama rarely smiles. But when she does, her three gold front teeth sparkle although her five bottom snuff-stained teeth look like they are in need of a bath.

Xavier, who is terrified of Big Mama, smiles nervously as he plants a kiss on Big Mama's snuff-stained cheek.

"Mama, I know it's going to be your birthday soon." Xavier says, with a broad smile, hoping to please Big Mama.

"And your ass best not forget it either!"Big Mama says as she slams the hammer on a walnut.

I can sense Xavier is a bit nervous. Something about the hammer, I suspect.

"Mama, you know I'll never forget your birthday." Xavier walks around in circles, which in the tiny living room gives the appearance that he's turning around in place. A trickle of sweat makes its way down the left side of his face. He obviously has something important to share with Big Mama.

"Mama, I have something to tell you."

"Go on, boy, tell your grandmama what's on your mind."

"Well...ll," stammers Xavier. "Me and Betty are expecting another child."

The hammer, raised to assault the walnut, stops in mid swing. Xavier's eyes dart around the room, looking for cover.

"Boy, you got that bitch pregnant again? I'll just be damn. Y'all having babies like damn dogs and ain't got a pot to piss in. I'm kicking y'all asses out my damn house if ya bring one more child in here. Your first damn baby ain't but seven months old. Don't y'all know bout birth control, boy?"

The pitcher of water on the table shakes from the volume of Big Mama's voice. Xavier shakes too, but for a different reason. His eyes never leave the hammer.

"But, Mama, you know how young lovers are. We didn't plan on having another child so soon. It just happened."

"Goddamn, you, boy. I reckon you best learn how to keep that damn thang in your pants. Big Mama makes a face as if she swallows too much snuff. When she recovers, it looks like the white of her eyes have turned dark brown. Xavier positions himself closer to where I'm sitting, which is right outside our bedroom door. I move out the way. No need being caught in the fall out.

"You know this house ain't big enough for a gnat to turn around in, less alone, any more damn babies. Pretty soon I'll have to hang 'em up on the ceiling to change 'em!"

I would have said something, but Big Mama has made it crystal clear where I stand. Lowered to a female dog, I tuck my tail between my legs and keep quiet. Meanwhile, Xavier's stammering worsens.

2

"M-Mama, I promise y-you we won't be h-having another baby in y-your house."

Now, I really love my man, but I wish you could see the boy. Sweat is pouring down his face; he's turning around in circles; his eyes are darting, and he is talking like one of them crazy folks. He's a sight to behold.

"W-we just made a m-mistake—twice." Xavier puts up two fingers signifying the peace sign.

Peace is the last thing on Big Mama's mind. It's wishful thinking on his part.

Xavier continues, "We'll move out as soon as this s-second child is b-born, I h-hope."

Big Mama starts to imitate Xavier's stammering. "H-hope m-my b-black..." Mama's last word get's tied up between her snuff and her gold teeth.

"You best hope I don't go off in your ass. You either move out or go visit Miss Mattie, the fix-um-woman, down the street. I hear she's good and cheap. Maybe, you and your whore need to visit her real soon. You hear me, boy?"

"Y-yes, Mama." Xavier says, bowing and leaving.

I follow him into our room. Something about being called a whore and a bitch doesn't sit well with me, but I can't express this to Big Mama. I go to Xavier Jr., who is lying quietly on my bed, and pick him up. Sitting on the tiny bed, I gently rock him. Tears fill my eyes as I give Xavier a piece of my mind.

"Xavier, your grandmama never has liked me. Just because I was pregnant before we got married, she considers me a slut. I hate living like this Xavier. I hate hearing her constantly cussing, calling me bitch and whore, and calling you boy all the time. Aren't you a man? Stand up to her. Don't let her disrespect us the way she does!"

"Baby, you know how Mama is? No one stands up to her and lives to take their next breath. Look at me. Mama makes three of me. And you've seen how she beat the shit out of Pop. He's twice the man that I am. To tell you the truth, I'm scared to stand up to her. I can't see getting my ass beat just to make a point."

I put the baby down on the bed and walked over to Xavier while he leaned against the door, wiping the fear off his face.

"Xavier, you are a grown man now, with a family."

"Yeah right! I just turned nineteen two months ago, and I want to live to see my twentieth birthday. I'm not ready to meet my Maker just yet, especially, over some bullshit."

I rub my stomach, stroking the unborn child."So now our baby is bullshit! That's a hell of a name to put on the birth certificate." I shake my head in disgust. "I don't know whether you are man or mouse?"

Xavier walks around me. He looks down at the baby laying on the bed and smiles.

"Right now, I'm neither. I'm chicken." Xavier picks up his son and plays with him. He turns around and faces me.

"You have some nerve! I've never seen you stand up to Mama. Why are you trying to send me to an early grave?"

Watching Xavier play with his son makes the anger of the moment pass. It takes the sting out of me.

"It's not a matter of love Xavier. It's a matter of respect and maturity. You've passed from boyhood to manhood. Look at you with your son. Mama doesn't get to see you like I see you. She doesn't respect you as a man. It has to start with you, Xavier. You have to show her who you really are. Don't you see that?"

Xavier rocks the baby trying to put him to sleep, and I suspect to chew on my last few words. He shakes his head, still confused.

"I don't know, Betty. Maybe, Mama's right. We're having these babies too close together. Maybe, we should consider aborting this child. We're young. We can have more kids later after we get on our feet. Besides, I'm not in a position to feed two children. Hell, I can't even feed us and Xavier Jr. right now. Mama's supporting us all, you know."

"Killing my child is out of the question. Go to hell, Xavier and take your two ton, snuff chewing, no-hair combing grandmama with you! I'll go live with my sister, Marilyn, until our baby is born. I'll find a way to support me and my babies. I'll probably get my license to do hair. Continue being a boy, Xavier. I'll go find me a man." My words have a bite to them that eats away at Xavier. He hangs his head and takes his tennis racket, leaving the room.

After he is gone I whisper, "I need a man, Xavier. Grow up! And I'm not having no damn abortion, either."Gazing at my child brings my worried heart some joy. "You are such a beautiful baby. I'm sorry that you have to be born into such a hellish family. I didn't know it myself until I moved in here. I've never heard so much damn cussing and disrespect for other people in all my life. I guess you are use to it by now. You sleep through it all, somehow. Sleep on little Xavier. I'm gonna get us out of this hell hole soon."

I rub my abdomen again, nurturing the unborn child. "Don't worry little one. I'm not getting rid of you. I don't care what these heathens say. You just continue to grow. You're safe. God has a special purpose for you someday."

\*\*\*

4

## XAVIER

Women! I don't care what you do, you can't please them. I can't please Big Mama, and I can't please Betty either. Might as well go play some tennis and beat the hell outta some balls. At least that way, I can please myself.

"Boy!" Big Mama yells as I get to the front door. "Where the hell do you think you going? Don't you know there are thangs to do round here. All you want to do is screw, make babies and play that cracker ass tennis. You act like you white. One of them damn Rockafellas or something. You forget we black folks. We have to work all day. You don't have time to play no white man's game. Your bitch don't do nothing either, but goddamn sleep and eat. She never lifts a finger round here. What's wrong with y'all?"

My anger gets the best of me. I point my rack at Big Mama. "Mama, I ain't no goddamn boy! I'm a grown man now! Don't ever call me a boy again! And don't talk about my wife either! Don't call her a bitch or a whore or anything else that ain't her name!"

I didn't know the racket was pointed at Big Mama while I was saying my piece until I stopped. The look on Big Mama's face told me I'd better lower it fast and run. I followed my instincts and hauled ass out the door. Something whisked by my head as I ran down the steps.

## BETTY

The baby is almost asleep when I hear Xavier protecting my honor. I put the baby down and go to the door. I step out into the hallway where I have a perfect view of Big Mama hurling the hammer at Xavier. Xavier is always a fast runner when he runs from Big Mama. Big Mama doesn't bother to get the hammer. She pulls out a pair of pliers and cracks another walnut instead. The nut scatters everywhere. I'm not surprised because Big Mama totally loses control when she's angry.

"Goddamn kids, you feed 'em, try to be good to 'em, then they grow up, start fucking, and call themselves damn grown. Damn boy has the nerve to call himself a man. I tell you what. He best not bring his grown-man-ass back in my house tonight."

Pop comes out of his bedroom, slumped over, after hearing all the commotion. He walks as if he is about to fall. I figure it's because he's too tall for the doorway, or it could come from being as old as dirt.

Pop and Big Mama have separate bedrooms. Its been that way for the last thirty-five years of their fifty years of marriage. I remember Big Mama saying she needed the whole damn bedroom to herself because a man in the room takes up too much oxygen. Besides that, Pop snores. His snoring is heard in all the rooms in the house, and from some telling, in some rooms of other folks houses as well. Big Mama says something else about Pop that reminds me of Xavier. She says, all Pop wants to do is screw all night long. After working twelve hours in the fields and taking care of five children, the last thing on her mind is sex. When Pop brought his bent, damn near broke behind out of his room, I should have warned him that it was not the best time to mess with Big Mama.

"Mama, what's going on out here?" Pop asks, rubbing crusted sleep from his eyes. I'm trying to get some sleep, but it's too noisy."

"Oh, shut up fool." Snuff sprays everywhere. "You'd best take your tired black ass back into your room before I beat some damn life back into you." She screams waving the pair of pliers at him.

Pop quickly turns around without saying a word. He returns to his room and closes the door.

***

Xavier finally returns to the house about two the next morning, drunk as a skunk. I find out later that he has been drinking and playing cards with some friends down the street most of the night and morning. When I hear him, he is trying to take the screen off of the window to our bedroom. He quietly taps on the window. I get up quickly, so he won't wake Xavier Jr. I'm half awake anyway wondering where he is. I'm glad he is smart enough not to use the front door. I see, he doesn't want to deal with Big Mama at this hour of the morning, since he is chicken.

"Betty, Betty, let me in," whispers Xavier.

I look at him through the window. That's not correct. I look in his direction and see his white teeth and blood shot eyes. I also smell his beer breath through the window as I raise it up. You know, Mama's mad as hell with you. That hammer missed you, but it knocked the hell out of Butch. She spent the rest of the day burying that damn dog."

Xavier climbs through the window.

"You're drunk! Where have you been?"

"Shhhhhhhhhhh, not so loud. I was playing cards with the guys. I was pretty damn lucky, too. I won nearly three hundred dollars. Look, baby, here it is." He pulls the money out of his front right pants pocket. "You can get that abortion now, maybe tomorrow. We're young. We'll have more kids later, baby."

He reaches to kiss me.

"Kiss my ass Xavier! I'm not having no goddamn abortion! Take this money and get us out of here."

6

Xavier stumbles, and I make the mistake of catching him. He tries to kiss me on the mouth.

"Okay, baby. You're right. We'll talk about it later."

I can feel him stiffening in his pants.

"You know I get horny as hell when I've been drinking. Let's make love."

I could lie and say I pushed him away. Coming in drunk, talking that crazy abortion stuff and now wanting to screw me. I could say it didn't happen. But I would be lying. Before my mouth could say no, my body was saying yes. "Oh, Xavier, don't kiss me there on my neck. You know that is my weak spot."

"I know baby, I know." Before I know it, Xavier ventures south. He kisses me all over.

"Oh, honey, not down there either." I hear myself moan.

Next thing I know, Xavier pulls my panties off. Getting somewhat out of control, he bites my sore nipple.

I hit him on the head. "Ouch! You bit me fool!"

"Oh, baby, I'm sorry," he says as he begins sucking the milk from my breast and kissing the bite place at the same time.

"How's that, baby? Is that better?" I press my body close to the hardness in his pants.

Next thing I know, he grunts, cleans himself off with Xavier Jr.'s blanket, and is fast asleep. I'm sitting up in the bed wondering what just happen or when it is going to happen. Finally, I turn the lights off and fall asleep, too.

# TWO

## BETTY

The next day, instead of going to get an abortion, Xavier takes me to look for an apartment. We found a nice apartment just minutes away from Xavier's job at Zelock Paper Company. It's completely furnished including it's own squad of rats and roaches. After the first night, in the new place, I put a finger on the rats and roaches rotating shifts. The rats come out all night and the roaches come out all night and day. That was okay with me since neither the rats nor roaches could talk, making it possible for me to spend my first day without hearing myself being called an assortment of foul names.

Leaving Big Mama's house was the best birthday present we could have given her. I found this out after Xavier went to visit and found Mama's spirits down right cheerful. He said she even went so far as to say, hello to me. Well, after I heard that, I felt bad about wishing her all kinds of evil. I started planning something special for her birthday. I even talked Xavier into inviting Big Mama and Pop over for cake, ice cream and punch. I was in the 'forgive and forget' frame of mind. I wanted to show my appreciation because she let us live with her for the entire thirteen months of our marriage.

I baked Big Mama a chocolate cake with vanilla icing. I even made her favorite sandwich, ham and cheese, to go with the cake, ice cream and punch. I wrapped red and blue ribbons around the white, wooden, table. Red and white balloons hung from the ceiling in the tiny kitchen. This took the better part of the day, but it was worth it when I thought about how much she had done for us.

Though small, the kitchen is cozy. It is exactly enough room for the small, white, wooden table and three badly chipped white chairs. Xavier Jr.'s high chair takes the place of the missing fourth chair. After covering the cake with plastic wrap, I whistle my way into the living room.

The living room has a tattered, dark brown, plaid sofa; green and yellow stripped love seat; orange coffee table; and a red, white, and blue high back chair with half the back missing. The arms on the sofa and love seat are well worn. The inner wood and cotton stuffing can be seen in all the furniture. I spruce them up by placing old diapers over the worn areas. The dark brown carpet matches the plaid, earth tone sofa perfectly. I bought several large plants to liven it up a little. I couldn't help but laugh thinking, how Big Mama would get her big behind on the sofa.

I was still tickled over that vision when Junior starts crying. I walk down the hall, pass the kitchen to Junior's room. Junior's room has two light-brown, pine wood, twin beds with a matching four drawer dresser. The curtains and bedspread are white, blue, and gold stripes. They are both badly torn and faded, but they will have to do for now until we can afford to buy new ones. I have already figured out how I will secure Junior on the twin bed until we can buy a crib. With a new baby on the way, we need one anyway. The walls are painted white, but they appear gray because they have so many fingerprints on them. I make a note to remind the landlord to paint all the walls soon. Since I am making my rounds, I decide to go into my room.

In my room I go immediately to the bathroom and run some water in the sink. At Big Mama's house there was only one bathroom for a house full of people, so hot water in my place is a delight. I start washing Junior, mindful that we are moving up in the world. Washed and powdered, I lay Xavier on the bed. The bed sags so badly in the middle, that he rolls towards the middle. He starts laughing, so I do it again and watch as he once again rolls over several times to the middle of the bed. I can tell by the expression on Xavier's face that he's having fun.

Though a sagging bed may work well for a six month old, it is not as enjoyable for Xavier and myself. We already tested the bed for sex. And each time we finish my back hurts. I felt at least five bedsprings jab me in the back every time Xavier exerted his body downward. To spare my back anymore jabs, I decided we should try another position. So we tried our old, reliable, stand by, 'doggy style'. That was the ticket.

With the exception of the sagging, jabbing mattress, the rest of the bedroom was pretty decent. I especially loved it's size. It was eighteen by fourteen feet wide. My dresser had a large rectangle mirror with plenty of dresser drawers. The curtains and the bedspread were bright orange. They and the mattress would have to be replaced soon. The walls were painted bright yellow. The wall behind the headboard had a bright yellow, orange, purple, green and white solar wallpaper pattern on it. It had the sun, moon, stars, and planets in the design. I thought, maybe the previous tenants were astrology nuts or something, trying to sex themselves to outer space. They were trying to take-off, land, orbit, and come at the same time.

***

Big Mama and Pop arrived at seven o'clock sharp. I heard the doorbell from the bedroom as I put the finishing touches to my hair. Xavier rushed to the door, obviously excited about showing Big Mama how much of a man he had become after just a couple of days. The baby was asleep in the sag of our bed, which practically smothered him.

"Welcome, Ma and Pop," Xavier says, opening the door as wide as his grin. "This is our paradise. I hope you didn't have a hard time finding us? Happy birthday, Mama."

I meet them once they are in and I give Big Mama a big hug. "Hi, Mama, Pop. Everything is ready." Big Mama's eyes dart around the place, giving it the once over.

"How do you like our new place, Mama?" Xavier asks, grinning. Xavier's face has pride written all over it. Big Mama erases it though when she answers.

Big Mama moves her head up and down and all around. "Paradise! It looks more like hell. This place should be condemned! I've never seen so many roaches under one roof in all my damn life!"

I look over at Xavier whose grin had reverted itself. I was not happy about what Big Mama said either, but I tried to maintain some resemblance of a smile. I catch Xavier looking in my direction. I raise my eyes and smile broadly as a sign that he should do the same. He walks over to where I'm standing and holds me close.

Pop adds some relief to a tense situation. When Big Mama asks him what he thinks about the place; she does not get an immediate response. We all turn to find him standing in the middle of the living room, saluting the red, white and blue chair. Pop's vision is very poor and anytime he sees the flag colors, he automatically salutes. It's a habit he acquired from his army days.

Suddenly, loud, foot-stomping noise brings our attention back to Big Mama. She's about two feet from the front door stomping roaches. In fact, she's stomping so hard and so fast, she looks like she's doing an Indian rain dance.

"Mama, would you like a seat?" Xavier asks squeezing me harder.

"Hell no!" Mama shouts back. "I cant' stop stomping roaches long enough to be still. Pop, get my ass out of here."

Pop turns around after completing his patriotic duties. "Mama, settle down. We came to celebrate your birthday. We're not leaving until we do. I'm sure they went to a lot of trouble for you today." Big Mama looked at him as he spoke and leaned. "Remember, honey, you're suppose to be wiser with age."

Big Mama didn't have a hammer or anything else in her hand, but she wore this look on her face that was not in the best interest of Pop.

"I am wiser. When you see this many damn roaches, the wise thang to do is leave."

Pop begins to get nervous as he watches the roaches marching up and down the walls. Where's the baby?" he asks, nervously.

"Oh, he's asleep in my room." I tell them. "Would you like to see him and the rest of the place?"

Pop puts on airs like some big shot. "Yes, I reckon. That would be nice. Come on Mama, let's go see our great-grandson."

I lead the way to my room. Xavier is just waking up. I pick him up and notice he's wet. Big Mama sits her big behind on the edge of the bed. The bed wobbles. I hold my breath. The legs screech from bending to their breaking point. Xavier closes his eyes. The bed holds.

"Thank you Jesus, I hear Xavier whisper to himself."

I walk Xavier Jr. to Big Mama and place him in her arms. The pressure is too much. The bed legs snap like twigs. Big Mama, holding Xavier Jr. close to her massive breasts, falls backward. The mattress hits the floor with a thump. This all takes place in a matter of seconds, but it feels like an hour. When the dust clears, I look around to find Xavier's eyes covered. Pop has a shit-eating grin on his face as if what he just witnessed was the funniest thing he's seen in years. Xavier Jr. is crying, not from the fall but from being cramped between Big Mama's mammoth breast which are damn near suffocating him. I run over and take my baby. Big Mama gets up, looks around, fixes her dress and walks out the room. After she is gone, Pop slaps his leg and starts laughing. He can't stop. He's just laughing his fool head off. Xavier finally opens his eyes. Seeing Pop makes him start laughing, too. I join in and even the baby gives a few chuckles.

All of this laughing comes to an immediate halt when from another room we hear Big Mama screaming, followed by curse words that would make milk sour. Xavier leads the way to Big Mama, who is standing in the kitchen doorway, her body heaving up and down from her hollering and swearing. When we push Big Mama's big behind from the front of the doorway, we finally see what all the hollowing and cursing is about.

On the kitchen table are three rats eating sandwiches. Roaches are swimming in the punch bowl. Rats have pushed the cake off the table and are sharing it with a village of roaches. Other roaches are crawling over everything, having themselves a grand old time.

Big Mama turns from the sight and heads towards the front door. "That's it, goddamn it. Get me out of this rat and roach infested hole!"

Pop follows close behind.

"Pop, I'm leaving now, with or without your black ass!"

Pop quicken his steps.

"Wait Mama, I'm coming, too." Xavier follows Pop. Before going through the door that Mama left open, Pop turns to Xavier. He has a grin on his face, as wide as his face is long. "Thanks for the party, boy. Best damn fun I've had in years."

Xavier smiles back. "Sorry the rats and roaches messed it up."

"Didn't mess it up none for me," Pop says, laughing. "I suggest you call the exterminator tomorrow though. Get your bed fixed, too." Pop reaches in his pocket and gives Xavier some money. "We'll be back when you do."

I'm standing in the middle of the living room crying when Xavier comes back in.

"It's all right, baby. So what if the rats and roaches took over the party. Look at the bright side. We don't have to worry about them coming back over here."

I stopped crying and smiled. I held the baby out for Xavier. "Take Junior so I can clean up this mess."

"Ah, leave it for the rats and roaches to enjoy," Xavier tells me. "All this excitement is making me horny."

Xavier gives me his, I'm ready for sex smile.

"Everything makes you horny."

I go through the house turning out all the lights. Xavier places his son in his bed with a bottle, then comes to our room. He immediately starts the process of moving the legs and frame from underneath and around the mattress. I start taking off my clothes.

"Xavier?"

"Yes, baby?"

"Do you think Mama is right? Do you think we should move because there are too many rats and roaches?"

"No. I don't. I'm gonna take Pop's advice. I'll call the exterminator tomorrow. Don't worry. This is our paradise, remember."

I lie on the mattress, which has firmed since being laid on the floor. Xavier rolls over to kiss me. I position myself ready for him to enter me.

"Take me to Venus or Mars please Xavier, I whisper in his ear."

"I'll do better than that. I'll take you to the year 2001."

# THREE

## BETTY

At the first twinge of a labor pain, I poke Xavier in the ribs, signifying that it's that time.

"Honey, Honey, wake up! I think I'm in labor. Call Big Mama to see if she will keep Xavier Jr." My urgency is answered with a grunt from Xavier and his hand reaching for my breast. I sit up. Xavier barely moves, so I poke his chest again, only harder. Wake up Xavier, we need to go now!" It takes another well placed poke, with my closed fist, in his chest, to wake Xavier up. Xavier shoots straight up.

"What? Go where? Call who?"

I lower my voice a bit as I get out the bed. "I'm in labor. We need to go to the hospital. But call Big Mama first, so that she can keep Junior," I said, looking back toward the bed.

With one eye half-open and the other eye completely close, Xavier glances at the clock on the nightstand beside him. The face that he makes tells me I might have to resort to throwing cold water on him in order to get him out of bed.

"It's two-thirty in the morning. Can't we wait till eight o'clock?" He pulls the sheet back over his face, mumbling underneath. "You know it takes these babies all damn day to come." He pokes his head from beneath the sheet to share this information with me. "It took Xavier Jr. fifteen hours to get here." The look on my face made him pull the sheets totally off his body. He swings his legs off the bed and rubs his face with his hands.

"I have plans today. Today is Saturday. I'm playing tennis with Marvin from nine to eleven, then I'm taking Big Mama to the grocery store." He stands up and goes into the bathroom where he takes a leak, without closing the door. I listen as he continues to explain his schedule. "I'll be back home about one or two o'clock." The toilet flushes. "By then, you'll be ready to deliver."

He comes back into the bedroom and continues to run off at the mouth. "Unless you want me to drop you off at eight-thirty before my tennis match?"

During his spiel, I didn't move from the middle of the floor. Xavier just continues sharing his plans for the day as if his plans were important at the moment. I double over with birthing pains which only adds fuel to my anger. "Xavier, you must have lost your fucking mind!"

He looks up at me not knowing whether to be concerned over my labor pains or the tongue lashing I'm about to give him. I look at him with disbelief and disgust as I hold my abdomen. I take several short breaths to relieve the pain. I try to sound calm.

"Xavier, I said that I am in labor, with your child! You are taking me to the hospital, right now, not at eight o'clock, not after your tennis match, not at two p.m.. We are leaving as soon as we all get ready. So take your sorry ass over to the phone and call Big Mama, now!"

I make my way to the bathroom. Through the tissue thin walls I hear Xavier talking to himself.

"Kids!!! They always come at the damnest time. Why today? Right before I put a hurting on Marvin? He stops talking about his tennis match when Big Mama gets on the line. He tells her that he is coming over with Junior, explaining, somewhat hastily, about my going into labor. When I walk out of the bathroom, Xavier has a look on his face that tells me that Big Mama is cussing his behind out for calling her so early. They are two of a kind.

I put on my clothes, a slow process under the circumstances. When I finish, I see Xavier standing in the middle of the room with his arms crossed and one foot patting the floor as if waiting for me.

"I'm ready. Let's go!"

All I can do is shake my head. I smile at him.

"I don't know what has gotten into you, but I'm glad to see a change."

***

By running every red light—nine to be exact; exceeding the speed limit by forty miles, killing one dog and putting the fear of God in several others; and barely missing a wine-o attempting to cross the street, we manage to get Xavier Jr. to Big Mama's within twenty-two minutes. When Big Mama comes to the door he throws the baby at her. She mouths a few words at his back. Undoubtedly, all four letter words.

When Xavier gets back into the car and my heart slows down considerably, I tell him off.

"Xavier, slow down! You act like you want me to go to the morgue instead of to the delivery room." I smack the shit out of him to emphasize my point. One of the two makes my point because the remaining trip to the hospital is less hurried.

By the time we reach Hughes Spalding Hospital, at 3:46 a.m., my labor pains are four minutes apart. I'm rushed into a birthing room where Alisha, my mid-wife awaits us. Xavier immediately goes to the crowded waiting room.

# XAVIER

I look at my watch. My face still stings from the smack. Why did she slap my face like that anyway? Hormones no doubt. I read somewhere they always go out of whack when a woman is about to have a baby. I should go in there and tell her I don't appreciate her hitting me. In fact, that's what I'll do. Having a baby or not, she has to know her damn place.

A man sitting next to me looks at me concerned. I verbalize my thoughts out loud to him. "A man has to stand up for himself sometimes. Having labor pains is no reason for a woman to slap her man." Several of the men in the room shake their head approvingly. One rubs his face. I continue.

"Let them get away with a slap and pretty soon they will want to cut you. And I don't think putting a knife in a woman's hand when she is pregnant and about to have a baby is a very good idea."

This time I get a few cheers. A couple of the men cross their legs. I shake my head up and down rapidly and stand up.

"I'm putting a stop to this nonsense now. I'm telling that woman that my face is not there for the slapping." The men in the room cheer me on.

I take three steps toward the door when the door opens. Alisha, the two-ton, mid-wife, waddles up to me.

"Mr. Grant, I've prepared your wife for delivery. If everything goes as I anticipate, your new arrival will be here before eight o'clock."

The good news causes me to forget about my pains. The image of a hand slapping my face disappears completely, replaced by a picture of Marvin running after one of my well placed balls. "That's great! I can still make my tennis match."

I bend down and kiss Alisha on the top of her head. When I step back, smiling broadly, Alisha is shaking her head. The look is very similar to the one I saw on Betty's face right before she struck me. I stumble backward, not knowing if this slapping, yelling thing is contagious.

"Mr. Grant, would you like to join your wife in the birthing room?"

My face shows how distasteful her request sounds.

"No, no, no! No, I think I will stay in the waiting room with the rest of the men. I look back at the rest of the fellahs who obviously share my view. I pull up my pants a bit more, confident about my position on the matter. "A man's place is to be with the woman to plant the seed. A woman has to bring the child into the world by herself."

Alisha turns her stubbly little body around and waddles back toward the birthing room.

"I'll inform you when the baby is born."

I return to my seat.

\*\*\*

## BETTY

Two hours pass. I ask Alisha where my husband is. He promised to be in the room during this birth. Alisha shakes her head.

"Men, without a worm between their legs, are totally useless." I laugh at this because she is right. A pain forces me to stop laughing and concentrate on controlling my breathing. My body experiences another rush of pain. One is barely over when another one starts. Through tears, I see Alisha lift the cover and inspect my progress.

"You're doing great, Betty," Alisha says. "This baby will be born soon."

"That's good. I can't take too much more of these labor pains. They are wearing me out."

A few minutes later, I begin to breathe uncontrollably."It's time! It's time!" I shout.

"You're right. Now, Betty, I want you to pant. Can you pant for me Betty?"

"Pant? What's that?"

"You know, pant, like a dog," she instructs me.

I started barking, "Arf, arf, arf, woof, woof, woof, arf, woof, woof." Within seconds, a baby girl is born. The clock on the wall reads six seventeen in the morning.

\*\*\*

## XAVIER

I'm sleeping. A horrible dream is playing in my mind. A face of a dog pops up as if caught between my headlights. Its red eyes cry out to me. In slow motion, I try to turn the car before it hits the dog. It's too late. The sound of the car's bumper hitting the dog is heard. I jump out of the car. The dog is barking. "Arf, arf, arf, woof, woof, woof, arf, woof, woof." The same sound filters through the dream. The face of the dying dog disappears. I wake up. The man sitting next to me stands up.

"Damn, somebody gave birth to a dog! He looks down at me. I woke completely up.

"What you say?"

"I know it's hard to believe, but someone just had a dog."

Some of the other men start barking.  The man standing goes to the waiting room entrance.

"Don't tell me you didn't here it."

I listen, but the barking stops and all eyes look toward Betty's room.  My  aiting room buddy comes back and takes his seat next to me.

"I think the barking came from that room."  I notice that he points at the  Betty is in.  I sit up alarmed.  The man holding the Bible, sitting across  me, shakes his head looking up towards the heavens.

rd, what is this world coming to?"

en brother," a woman sitting next to him adds.

er woman wearing curlers underneath an Aunt Jemima rag gets up and  iting room.

ng to call my psychic," says a tall and slender woman.  "If a woman  to a dog, then this is a good day for me to find a man."

k at the woman, I'm not really certain what's heading out the  he she, he or it wears a rainbow colored wig of orange, green  jeans covers a body with few curves.  The she, he or it fingernail's  orange polish.  And the makeup on its face looks like it will take a  nove.

eighbor looks at me.  He leans over.

"It's a man.  I was looking at her, I mean him, earlier and almost threw up."

The preacher man sitting across from us shakes his head and hugs his Bible tighter.  "What is the world coming to, men who want to be women and women giving birth to dogs."  The preacher man was obviously shaken by what he was experiencing.

The man sitting next to me starts talking to the room.  "I read once, in the National Enquirer, about this woman who gave birth to three puppies, the paper said, it came from having sex 'doggy style'."

I look at the man.  Beads of sweat pop out on my forehead.  My neighbor continues informing us about the contents of the article.

"The article also said that the puppies were the result of a reincarnated dog that had been killed during the early part of the pregnancy."

The preacher man shakes his head as if giving support to the article.  I scratch.  My flesh begins to crawl.  Sex 'doggy style', a dead dog.  My god!  Betty gave birth to a dog.  I'm in mid prayer with the Lord, asking the Almighty to forgive me for causing Butch to die and for killing the dog on the way to the hospital.

Alisha comes out of Betty's room when I finish my prayer.  All eyes are on the midget mid-wife who makes her way towards me.  She stands in front of me.  The sweat is pouring off me now.  What will she tell me? How do you tell a man he is the father of a dog? I slump in my chair. Alisha opens her mouth. Her words come out in slow motion.

"Mr. Grant, your new arrival is here. Please follow me."

I get up in what seems like slow motion. The man sitting next to me looks at me shaking his head slowly back and forth. This must be a dream, I tell myself.

"I'll be damn, it's your woman in that room where we heard the barking," says the man sitting next to me.

The preacher and the woman sitting next to him shake their Bibles in the air. "Lord, Lord, Lord."

I follow Alisha outside the waiting room. She doesn't appear to be too dam[n] concerned that I am the father of a dog. In fact, she has this shit-eating grin [on] her face. I offer another prayer to God.

"Lord, please don't let my baby be a dog. I promise You, from this [day] forward, I'll never have sex 'doggy style', again. I'll also never cause harm [to] any dog as long as I live. Lord, I also promise to go to church every Su[nday] starting tomorrow. Amen."

Alisha is standing by the door holding it open. I walk into the birthing [room.] I wonder, what do you feed a dog-child? Puppy chow or scraps off the p[late? I] know one thing. It will never sleep between Betty and me. I'm going to h[old my] ground on that point.

Betty is sitting erect on the bed. She's all smiles. Her hair is a mess, but there is a radiance on her face. After giving birth to a dog, she looks exhausted, but happy. How can she smile like that after giving birth to a dog child? Her smile's probably fake. She probably does not know how to tell me. Maybe she doesn't realize that I already know. It really amazes me how a woman can love practically anything. She can love stray animals, give them a home and treat them like royalty. I guess it's true, the love a woman has for her child, even a dog child, is the greatest love there is.

"How are you, baby?" I ask as I bend down to kiss her forehead.

"I'm fine, especially now that it's over. You want to see the baby?"

"Of course." I take a deep breath and close my eyes.

"Look Xavier. Look at your daughter, Vanessa Alisha Grant."

I hold my breath before opening my eyes. "It's a baby! It's a real baby girl! Thank the Lord!" Excitedly, I scoop the bundle up in my arms. I dash pass Alisha to the door. Trays fall making a racket behind me. Alisha and Betty scream after me.

"Come back! Come back with the baby!"

I run over an orderly carrying some hospital garments. Behind me I hear Alisha's bulldog legs trying to catch up.

"Stop him!"

I speed up the pace till I'm in front of the people in the waiting room. I look around bobbing my head proudly.

"So you thought my wife gave birth to a dog?"

I pull the blanket away from the baby's face and body. I bend down and strut before everyone in the room.

"I have a girl, thank you very much. A pretty girl at that. Check them legs out. Those ain't dog legs. Those are legs of a beautiful baby girl."

Alisha finally catches up and reaches for the child every time I bend down to show someone my baby girl. She's too slow and too short. When the she, he, it creature takes a look through her fake eyelashes and moves to touch my baby with its long fingernails, the sight causes me to freeze. Ms. Thing smiles at me with teeth as crooked as an Atlanta street. Momentarily stunned, Alisha has time to move in and take the baby. I follow Alisha back to the delivery room. I have a beautiful baby girl.

In the weighing room I learn that Vanessa Alisha Grant weighed in at six pounds, twelve ounces. Her nineteen inch long, light-brown body had a bunch of reddish color hair on its crown. The hair I could tell was not going to be good, like mine.

Xavier Jr., unlike Vanessa, resembled his mother which meant he is pecan brown. It was good that God decided to make this girl child beautiful like me.

When the baby returns to the room, Betty gives me a puzzled look. I also notice that the orderly I knocked down earlier is following close by.

"Xavier, what's wrong with you? You act like you have lost your mind. Why are you running around with the baby like a mad man? Have you been drinking?"

I didn't have the nerve to tell her straight up that I thought my child was a dog. I sort of beat around the question. However, she wouldn't let it rest.

"I'm waiting for an answer Xavier."

"Well, honey, to tell you the truth, I expected to see a dog." I knew, when I said that, Betty wanted to jump off the bed and smack me one good. Her condition wouldn't permit it though. I step back a little anyway. Talking fast, I try to explain.

"You have to understand, honey, that everyone in the waiting room heard this barking noise coming from this birthing room and this man read this article about a woman who gave birth to puppies. I didn't know what to think." Betty, Alisha and the orderly start laughing. "And I haven't been drinking either, though I intend to do so very soon."

Betty is the first to speak. "Fool, you heard me barking." She goes through another laughing spell. "I told her to pant like a dog and she started barking," Alisha adds. "What I witness giving birth as a mid-wife can fill a book," Alisha says, as she leaves the room, taking the orderly with her.

"Here, baby, hold Vanessa."

I take my new bundle of joy. "Don't worry baby you don't have to worry about eating table scraps," I whisper to her.

"What you say Xavier?"

"Nothing, honey." I make another inspection to make absolutely sure the girl has not changed. I open the blanket and count her fingers and toes. I quickly look down her diaper. I breathe better. "Good. A chip off the old block.

"What you saying now Xavier?"

I look at my daughter's almond shape eyes - a Grant family trademark.

Alisha returns. Some time has passed. I don't know how much, but Betty is asleep, so is Vanessa. Without a fuss, I hand the baby to Alisha and tiptoe out of the room. The large clock in the hallway reads seven-forty-eight. "This day turned out to be okay anyway. I can still make my tennis match with Marvin."

# FOUR

## BETTY

Vanessa was a quiet and happy baby. She rarely cried unless she was hungry. Many days, she played peacefully, for hours, in her crib until someone picked her up. She and Xavier Jr., were different as day-and-night. He fussed and whined, demanding most of my attention. The Lord knew my nerves couldn't take two demanding kids, not coupled with their father's drinking and jealousy.

## XAVIER

I wasn't financially prepared for feeding and clothing two children. Each week I realized my paycheck was spent before I cashed it. The increased responsibilities of the marriage made me drink more to relax. I started taking my frustrations out on Betty and the kids. I am a man, now, but things are happening too fast. Sometimes I long for those days when I was a boy and life was fun and carefree.

## VANESSA

Mama frequently exposed me to the sun. I baked in the sun's rays while she hung clothes to dry, or relaxed outside to smoke a cigarette.

"Vanessa, you're too light to be black," said Mama, puffing away. "But with that nappy, red hair, you'll never pass for white. Child, I have to put you in the sun, so you can get some color."

For hours at a time, I baked. That's why I have a high tolerance for heat now. Mama didn't know about heat stroke or skin cancer. She only wanted her baby girl dark instead of light.

My fondest childhood memories growing up were going over to Big Mama and Pop's house for the weekend. Those were truly weekends that I'll always remember.

"Xavier and Vanessa! Breakfast's ready," shouted Big Mama from the kitchen. "Come eat."

Xavier and I raced from the back bedroom to the kitchen. We loved eating breakfast with Big Mama. The menu was always the same. Three strips of

21

fatback bacon, grits that were oozing with butter, toast with apple jelly, scrambled eggs with cheese, and a cup of coffee.

"Big Mama, I love having breakfast with you and Pop," I'd say, swallowing a big gulp of coffee. "You always give us coffee. Mama says we're too young to drink coffee, since we're only four and five years old."

"Yeah, Big Mama, I love your grits and eggs, too. You put lots of butter in your grits and plenty of cheese in your eggs," said Xavier Jr. as he mixed his eggs with his grits. "Mama uses surplus cheese. She gets it from her friend, Miss Helen. Mama uses just a little bit when she cooks. She tries to make one block of cheese last three months until she gets some more from Miss Helen. Mama says cheese is expensive."

"Yeah, that's right Xavier," I said, chewing on my bacon. "Sometimes, you can smell the cheese in Mama's macaroni and cheese, but you can't see any."

"You two need to do less talking and more eating. Eat your food. It's getting stone cold," said Big Mama as the last portion of her eggs disappeared into her mouth. She licked all ten fingers then reached for her napkin to wipe her mouth.

Pop's head was bent completely down in his plate. He frequently got a hump in his back when he ate. You only saw the whites of his eyes when he held his head up to sip his coffee. And that was only for a split second. If you blinked, sneezed, or farted, you missed it.

"Mama says you're, a hell raiser, from Summerhill," I said to Big Mama after taking another gulp of my coffee. "She says you cuss all the time and beat Pop to a pulp, whatever that is. She says Pop's snoring is so loud it can wake the dead. Is that true?" I asked wiping my mouth. "You're always good to Xavier and me. I've never heard you cuss or seen you hit Pop. I have heard Pop snore. Mama told the truth about that. But his snoring is not as loud as my daddy's. If Pop's snoring can wake the dead, then Daddy's can make then want to be dead."

Pop stood up, reached for his coffee, then walked to the cupboard. He poured Jack Daniels in his coffee. In one quick gulp, it disappeared. He filled his cup again with straight whiskey. When he turned around to face us, the whites of his eyes were brown and bulging. They resembled bloodshot frog eyes. We all knew when Pop looked like that, he'd spend the rest of the day in his room.

"Y'all, excuse me. I'm going to my room now," he said as he stumbled past us, hitting the table, and spilling our coffee while making his exit.

"Finish your breakfast, kids," said Big Mama. "I'll pour us some more coffee." Big Mama poured Jack Daniels in her coffee, too.

"Thanks, Big Mama," we said, eating the rest of our breakfast. "We really do love coming over here because you treat us like we're grown."

Big Mama returned to the table with our fresh cup of coffee. She sat down beside us smiling.

"Kids, I enjoy your visits. Since my arthritis been bothering me, I can't get round too good anymore. When y'all come over, I feel better 'cause y'all help me get my mind off these painful joints in my legs and hands for awhile." Big Mama gave one of her toothless grins and sipped on her Jack Daniels coffee.

***

Over the years, my dad drank more and more. Whenever he drank, he became violent, particularly, when he and Mama played cards with their friends on the weekends together.

SMACK!!! Went the deafening sound of Xavier's hand on Betty's face.

"Stop, Xavier! Stop hitting me," shouted Betty through her tears. "You'll wake the children."

"I don't care bout wakin' up those damn kids. Why did you smile at Fred all night? Do you like him?" Slap, slap went Xavier's hand on Betty's face again, in addition to several punches to the rest of her body.

"No. Stop it! Stop! You're drunk and crazy. I'm not going to fight you. Besides, the kids can hear you," she said while holding her face, wiping the tears from her eyes, and backing away from him. Maybe, if I don't fight, you'll stop."

"I'll stop all right. When I'm good and goddamn ready! Damn you and the kids, too. Do you like Fred?" Xavier asked as he landed another blow to Betty's face.

"No, I don't like Fred. But I do love you. Can't you get that through your thick head?"

Xavier Jr. and I witnessed the whole incident through the crack door of our bedroom. We came out of the bedroom crying.

"Daddy! Daddy! Stop! Don't hurt Mama. Don't hit Mama again," we said in unison, crying.

Daddy turned around to face us. His face was beet red. Veins popped out of his forehead. Sweat dripped down his eyebrows onto the floor. His eyes were ready to leap out of his head.

Slap, came a blow to my face when I extended my arms to my mama.

"Shut up and go back to your room!"

I dashed to my room, crying, holding my face. That was the first time Daddy slapped me, but it wouldn't be his last. Xavier Jr. tried to console me by placing his arms around me, while I sobbed uncontrollably. How I wished his arms reached my heart that ached from the humiliation and pain I felt inside.

Moments later, the fighting stopped. We heard the front door slam and Mama crying. We both raced to her.

"Mama, Mama, are you okay?" I asked, compassionately.

"Yes, I'm fine. Don't' worry about me. Go back to bed. It's late."

"Mama, why don't you leave Daddy?" I asked, while holding her in my arms. "He's always hurting you."

"I won't leave your father because I love him very much. He's been through a lot growing up and nobody has ever loved him, except me. His mother abandoned him when he was twelve years old. She let Big Mama raise him here in Georgia, so she could live in Ohio with her aunt, Bessie. He only saw his father occasionally. Big Mama really didn't have time for him, nor did she give him love. She only gave him material things to keep him out of her hair. Since your dad has never been truly loved, he's very possessive and jealous of me. I really love him and you should, too."

"I love Daddy," said Xavier Jr. as he hugged Mama and wiped the tears from her face.

I didn't say anything. I didn't love my dad. I hated him because he fought my mama and slapped me. My mama amazed me. How could she still love my dad after he beat her up?

\*\*\*

As far back as I can remember, beer has been a favorite beverage of mine. My dad either gave it to me or I helped myself to any can of beer sitting around the house. Little did it matter to me who the beer belonged to. As long as the inside of the can had beer, that was all that mattered.

"Vanessa go get two cans of beer," said Daddy while he reclined on the sofa, watching TV.

Being the baby girl also meant being the family gofer. I skipped to the kitchen, anticipating the delicious beverage in my mouth. I quickly returned with a pair of beer cans, one for Dad, and one for me.

"Here's your beer, Daddy," I said, handing him his beer while guzzling on mine.

"Xavier, why are you letting that child drink a whole can of beer?" asked Mama inquisitively. "You usually let her drink from your can?"

"Lately, she's been drinking the damn can dry. We both agreed two cans are better than one."

"Don't complain to me when you make a beer-head out of her."

"I haven't thought about that. I just want to enjoy my can of beer in peace," said Dad, turning his ice-cold brew up in his mouth. When he finished, he let out a loud belch.

Mama and I fanned our noises because he was facing us and we got the funk in our faces.

"Vanessa, honey, go get me a cigarette, and light it for me."

"You have the nerve to talk about me, Betty. It's okay if you get her addicted to cigarettes," Daddy said as I left the room.

"No, you're wrong. She won't get addicted to cigarettes by lighting my cigarettes. It's perfectly harmless."

I returned with my half-empty can of beer in one hand, a pack of cigarettes in the other and a lit cigarette in my mouth. I'm only eight years old. To my parents, I'm a normal sight.

\*\*\*

At the age of nine, I found out another child was on the way. I had mix feelings about having a little brother or sister. Most of my feelings were negative, such as, jealousy, resentment, and bewilderment. Why were my parents having a baby when I was almost grown? At nine, I was too old to play with babies. Besides, I knew the baby would get all the attention. I never received much attention anyway. Now I won't get any. Xavier was the child who received all the compliments, even when he was bad. All I ever received were slaps and punches to my face.

A few months later, three days before my tenth birthday, Beverly Charlotte Grant was born. Beverly was dark-brown like fudge icing. Her hair was a mix of mom and dad's, neither "good" nor "bad". Her hair and eyes were dark-brown, too. She resembled fudge cookies, dark-brown through and through. No mistake about it, though, Beverly had dad's characteristic, large, Grant eyes.

The Grant kids were different colors, but we all had big, hyperthyroid looking eyes. They protruded forward with three-fourths of the white eyeball portion showing. Mama said, our Grant eyes came from serving the devil. Satan visited each unborn child and scared the hell out of us. Afterwards, we grew up with big bug eyes for the rest of our lives.

Of all the Grant kids, Dad loved Beverly the most. She was spoiled and rotten to the core. She got anything she wanted from him. No one could lay a hand on her without having his wrath to contend with. Xavier Jr. and I kept our distance.

I remember wishing many times she was never born, especially when I was stuck keeping her instead of having fun.

"Vanessa, you have to keep Beverly while your father and I go to the store," shouted Mama from the front door.

"But, Mama, I am going to play basketball in a few minutes," I said as I entered the room.

"I don't care. You'll have to keep her. We're not taking her with us."

"You act like she is my child! I keep her all the time. I'm going to play." Slap, went Daddy's hand on my face. "You're not going any damn where. You'll keep your sister like your mama said."

I didn't say a word, no need to. It wouldn't do me any good, anyway. I just rolled my big Grant eyes at Daddy. They left for the store, without Beverly. "I hate you," I said, very low, behind the closed door.

# FIVE

One hot, Georgia day, in the summer of 1969, I was sitting on my front porch when I noticed this fine specimen of God's great creation come walking up to me, showing his pearly whites.

"Hello, my name is John. I have been watching you from my Aunt Martha's house, across the street," he said, pointing to the beige house, the second one from the corner. "I am new in the area," he said, extending his right hand for me to shake.

"I'm Vanessa. I'm glad to meet you. Welcome to the neighborhood," I said, shaking his hand. I didn't know which was brighter—the sun's rays over head, on this clear sunny day, or his perfect white smile straight ahead. I think it was his smile because he had my undivided attention. I could tell that he liked what he saw too because his eyes focused instantly on my crossed legs.

"Do you mind if I sit down?" he asked with his eyes still on my legs. Once seated, his eyes glanced at the sky momentarily, then back at my crossed legs. "I really like the view from here."

I didn't know if he was referring to the scenery or me. The way his eyes undressed me, I gathered I was the "view". My smoking, blazing, white hot-pants were barely visible. My arms were folded over my white halter top. My chest was definitely not the best part of my body. Therefore, I concealed it as long as possible, exposing only by best features. I wanted to hold his attention indefinitely.

"Where are you from?" I asked, fanning a fly from my face.

"Madison, Georgia, but I am temporarily staying with my Aunt, until I leave for the Air Force."

"Air Force?" I repeated. "How old are you?" I asked, losing some of my composure.

"Eighteen. How old are you?" he asked, trying to figure my age. He eased up one more step which allowed him to sit next to me, eyeball to eyeball.

He was a chocolate ice cream complexioned man (who I wanted to lick all over) with a clear, hairless face (smooth as a baby's behind), a short freshly cut natural fro, even white teeth, thin lips (that I couldn't wait to put on mine), a small triangle nose and beady eyes.

I swung my permanently crossed legs, to distract him from hearing my reply. "I'm thirteen," I said, almost choking on the lump in my throat. "I'm mature for my age," I added.

"I'll say. I thought you were at least sixteen," he said while looking down my halter top, smiling. "I have been watching you for a while. I really like what I see." His eyes gave me the once over, three or four times.

I put my arms behind me, no longer ashamed of my miniature breast. I, now, sat erect, proud as a peacock and happier than a pig in slop. I smiled. He's my kind of man, I thought. We talked about fifteen more minutes before he left. Then I stared at his rear end until it disappeared out of sight. Excited, I continued to sit on the porch, repeating every word that we had said.

My parents met John a few days later when he came by the house to see me. I didn't bother to ask them if I could receive company, beforehand. When the doorbell rang, I answered it. I knew it was John. He had just called and told me he was coming over. I invited John inside.

My parents weren't ready to address the issue of me receiving company, yet. In their minds, they had a few more years left before they crossed that bridge. However, they put their foot down and basically into John's rear end. Their verdict resulted in me not receiving company. I believed it was mainly due to the company that I wanted to receive. Both parents thought John was too old for me. Of course, I didn't expect my parents to understand my dilemma because they were both the same age. They didn't realize I was mature for my age.

Dad and John had a man-to-man talk on the porch. Afterwards, he was allowed to visit, briefly.

John wasn't too old. Besides, I liked him a lot. I knew how to handle myself and his advances. So, I did the only thing a red, hot-blooded, American teenager did under the circumstances. I sneaked out with him every chance I could get.

John was an all American male. He always had sex on his mind. When we sneaked to the neighborhood park and lay on the ground, he tried to roll over on top of me. What did he think? That I was born yesterday. I raised my right leg which prevented him from rolling on top of me. He then gazed into my big, Grant eyes. I stared intently into his beady, Bailey eyes. We both smiled. Mine was the smile of victory. His was the sweet smile of revenge. His smile said to me, okay, you won this time, but I'll win the next time, guaranteed. His victory never came.

The following Valentine's Day John sent me a gigantic Valentine's card, four-feet long by two-feet wide. It had a tiger with a flower in its mouth and a small gray mouse with a pink heart in its hand. The card read: "I Love You Something Fierce." I sure missed him. I wished everyday he was with me. Since he wasn't, his card was a constant reminder. I nailed it on my bedroom wall.

My school, East Atlanta High, had a Valentine's dance. What good was a Valentine's dance without your sweetheart? Rarely was John home. Even if he was home, my parents wouldn't let me go out with him since he was too old. I told myself, whomever I danced with, I'd pretend he was John.

I arrived at the dance at seven-thirty. The crowd was thin. No one was dancing. The music was blasting. All of the wallflowers found there places on the bleachers and the wall so they could sprout.

By eight-thirty, no one had asked me to dance yet. My ass was getting sore sitting on the bleachers. I had begun to sprout, as well. Maybe, twelve students danced on the last ten songs. I wanted to dance so badly; I split my right index finger from snapping to the music. My feet had stomped three roaches and one toe. Daddy would be picking me up at ten. At this rate, I'd have full grown leaves and buds.

As I spotted another roach victim, out of nowhere, a hand reached for mine.

"Would you like to dance?" asked Carl Lewis, the junior I teased with regularly about our fictitious children that he made different excuses for not paying their child support payments.

Hell yes, I wanted to say. But I said only, "Yes," being the lady that I was.

We danced on every record. We laughed and joked about our children as usual. Carl was very humorous. He had a way of keeping me in stitches, laughing.

Pretty soon, the disc jockey announced, it was time for the last song. The last song was slow. We held each other very close, not wanting the dance to end. The pressure of Carl's chest against mine expelled the tissues from my bra which landed on the floor. I felt one piece still stuck halfway inside. I wiggled my chest, hoping it worked its way back inside or fall to the floor with the others. Luckily, the room was dark and Carl had his eyes closed. I kicked the tissues out of sight with my right leg. Carl opened his eyes because I lost my balance.

"Am I holding you too tight?" asked Carl, pulling away.

"Oh, no. I didn't want to step on your toe. So I moved my leg instead," I said, pressing even closer to him because I didn't want him to see the sudden change in my chest size.

Moments later, the song ended. The dance was over. Something magical happened in that last hour and a half. Carl, who I only thought of as someone to laugh and tease with, meant more to me now. I saw a side of him that I hadn't seen before. Our friendship went to a higher level. I liked him and I sensed he liked me, too. "I have to go now. Thanks for a nice evening," I said with my arms locked around my chest rubbing my shoulders.

"Thanks for dancing with me. I really enjoyed your company. By the way, can I have your number?"

"555-7856," I said, quickly. "It's ten after ten. My dad is outside waiting for me. He's punctual at picking me up and turns into a grouch if he has to wait over thirty seconds. I don't need his ill temperament to spoil a perfectly good night. Goodbye."

I left like Cinderella. My fast walk turned into a trot as I rushed to the car. "I'm sorry, I'm late. I came out as soon as the dance was over," I said as I entered the car.

"You know I've been here since ten o'clock. You should have come on out. I'm ready to get home," he said, looking at me with his tired, stern, Grant eyes.

The ride home was quiet. Daddy and I rarely had conversations. The radio entertained us. We both felt very comfortable with the silence. Talking to each other was awkward for us. For the entirety of the ride, I thought about Carl.

When we finally reached our house, Dad exited the car first but waited for me to close my door. He always made sure all the doors were locked before we entered the house. Daddy led the way through the grass and up the six steps to the front door. He never looked back to see where I was. Just knowing I was behind him was good enough. I felt like a baby duck following her mom. I even imitated a duck waddling. When I reached the door, I heard the phone ringing. Daddy was moving in slow motion opening the door. One mind told me to snatch the keys out of his hands and open the door myself. Another mind told me to calm down or someone would have to pick my remains up off the ground. Although I was anxious to get inside, I listened to my second mind. However, my legs wouldn't be still. They moved more now than on the dance floor. Eventually, Daddy opened the door. I heard Mama say, "Oh, wait a minute, Vanessa is at the door." I tried not to knock Daddy over. I barely missed his left hip as I whizzed by him and grabbed the phone.

"Vanessa, I couldn't wait another second to hear your voice. Tonight was very special. Thanks for a wonderful evening," Carl said in a low, sexy voice.

I took the phone in my room to relax on my bed while I talked. Suddenly, my eyes focused on John's card on the wall. I turned the lights off to make the card disappear. "Yes, tonight was wonderful. Carl, you know, we really never said much to each other before except for teasing about our imaginary children and your delinquent child support payments."

"I know. I didn't tell you this earlier, but it was by fate that I was at the dance tonight. I asked to be off my job to attend the dance, but my request was denied. I was scheduled to work, but I felt strongly about being at the dance, so I quit my job to come because it meant that much to me. Now, I'm glad I followed my mind."

My mind and heart raced inside. I held my left hand against my chest to calm down. "I'm glad you came to the dance. Before you came, no one had asked me to dance. Carl, I don't know about you, but I feel like something is developing between us."

"Although you only think of me as someone to joke with, I loved you from the moment we first met in August. I didn't tell you earlier because you didn't feel the same way about me. I was hoping tonight would change how you feel about me."

I was speechless. I had no idea Carl felt this way. The news was overwhelming. "Carl, Xavier wants to use the phone. He's stuck his head in the door twice already. Call me tomorrow."

"Okay, I will. Goodnight."

"Goodnight," I said softly as I put the phone back on the receiver. "Xavier, I'm off the phone," I screamed so that he could hear me.

Xavier ran to the phone. "Thanks Sis. From the way you were looking, while you were talking, I thought I had to wait another hour. I really do want to talk to Carolyn before it gets too late," he said as I left the room. By the time I reached the door, he was comfortable on my bed, ready to make his call.

Xavier and I had this rule: whoever was using the phone, the other one left the room. He slept in the den where the telephone wouldn't reach. This rule allowed us to have private conversations.

I caught a glimpse of John's card as I left. I then remembered the unopened letter he sent with the card. I preferred to read his letters at bedtime. Then I thought about him all night long. My dreams generally were about us, our future, the days when we could be together, forever. I went back to my bedroom to get his letter off my dresser which was right at the door. Xavier's back was to the door. He didn't hear or see me come in. I was in and out in a flash. With the letter in hand, I headed for the kitchen to get a Pepsi and some cookies to have while I read my letter. Since no one was in the kitchen, I stayed there and read it at the table.

*Dear Kitten,*

> *I miss you tremendously. I wish I were with you. Although I am absent in body, my mind is there with you always. I think of you constantly. I include you in my prayers daily. I hasten the days when we can be together without separation. You truly are the joy of my life. I am your man, and I want to make you my woman, one hundred percent*
>
> *Vanessa, right now, you are only my woman ninety-nine percent. The next time I come home we need to go all the way, in order to make our relationship complete. You have time to think about it. I will be home in May.*

> *I hope you are doing well. How are you coming along with your saxophone? The last time I heard you play, you seemed to be improving. I hope you like the card. It describes my feelings perfectly. I will call you soon.*
>
> > *With Love,*
> > *John*

I stared at the letter. I thought of John. I pictured him in my mind. I thought about all the good times we had shared. All of those wonderful moments. He was a good man and I cared a great deal about him. I put the letter down. Folded it up and placed it back inside the envelope. Two cookies were left. I ate them and thought of Carl.

Why am I thinking of Carl? I asked myself. John is my man. I then reminisced the evening with Carl. I surely enjoyed his company. He was a good dancer, too. We had so much fun together.

I'm tired, I thought. I'm going to bed. I hoped Xavier was off the phone. When I opened the door, he was gone. I took off my clothes and got into bed. I jumped out quickly, remembering I forgot to say my prayers.

> *Dear Lord,*
>
> *I am only a teenager. My life is in Your hands. Only You know what direction my life will take. Only You know who is best for me and who I am destined to be with. I pray, Lord, that You make Your decision known to me. That it will be crystal clear in my mind who I am to be with, either John or Carl. In Jesus Christ name I pray. Amen.*

I slept peacefully knowing that it was not my decision to make but the Lords. Tomorrow was a new day. I would wait to see what it had in store.

# SIX

On Saturday's, I routinely cleaned the house. I started with the dining room, where Mama always kept It a mess. She had newspapers everywhere trying to figure the number. It's no telling how many meals were directly contributed to Mama hitting the number. I knew her small salary and tips as a beautician's assistant and Daddy's meager income at Zelock couldn't account for the new car, endless clothes, abundance of food, and other luxuries we had.

Although the numbers were illegal, everybody played. Mama was not good with basic math, but she figured the number, using her own math formulas. Once, Mama got locked up because of the numbers. The police came to the house and escorted her to the paddy wagon. Xavier, Beverly, and I waved goodbye until the wagon was out of sight. We called Daddy at work when we came back inside. The police didn't allow her to make any calls before she left. Mama was back home by evening more zealous than ever to play the numbers. Her trip to the police station only stopped her temporarily. Nothing and no one could make her quit forever.

I finished cleaning by noon. Mama was at work. Daddy was playing tennis. Xavier was, who knows where. Beverly was in our room playing. Unfortunately, I had the double duty of keeping her and cleaning, too. Life wasn't fair.

The doorbell rang as I finished. It was Cynthia from next door. She was three years older than me, and she was an only child. We were best friends. She came over sometimes just to comb Beverly's hair. Although Mama was a beautician's assistant, she put very little effort into combing both Beverly's and her own hair. Their hair was a black version of Phyllis Dillar's. Cynthia felt sorry for Beverly, so she came over periodically to comb it. I didn't feel sorry for either Beverly or Mama. I was used to them looking like two nappy-headed fools.

Cynthia came inside. "Where's Beverly?" she asked as she sat down in the green chair by the door.

"She's in her room playing like a good girl. I've threatened to whip her behind if she gets in my way while I'm cleaning," I replied, looking at her questionably. "Why do you want to know?"

"I'm going to the store, and I want to take her with me."

"Sure, that's fine. She can go. But you know you have to comb her hair first. Don't be too shocked because it hasn't been combed all week. I think Mama only brushed it back a little. You have your work cut out for you, today."

"I expect it. I always do. It won't take me long to get her ready. I'll probably keep her for an hour or two."

"Great! I welcome any opportunity to get rid of her rotten ass."

Cynthia walked past me going into my bedroom where Beverly was. "Vanessa, I see John's letter. Can I read it?"

The letter was on my dresser. That was the first time she asked to read one of John's letters. I was puzzled why she asked. But I didn't question her because she was a big sister to me. She knew John and how much he meant to me.

"No. I don't mind."

Cynthia finished with Beverly in less than twenty minutes. When they came from the bedroom, I didn't recognize Beverly. She was a pretty little girl when she was taken care of properly. Cynthia did a better job of dressing Beverly than anyone in our house. Since Beverly was not my responsibility, I put forth very little effort. Our parents did, too. I waved goodbye, but really I meant good riddance.

The house was clean. Beverly was gone. I was free! I think, I'll go play basketball, I told myself. There's always a game going on at Burgess Elementary. I made sure the back door was locked. I turned off all the lights and headed for the door. As I reached for the knob, the phone rang. At first, I hesitated to answer it. Mama might be calling me to do one more thing. What the heck. I'll do it later if she asks. I answered the phone on the third ring. "Hello?"

"Vanessa, this is Carl. I was going to hang up. I thought no one was home."

"I was getting ready to leave. A second later, you would have missed me."

"I was wondering if you would like to spend some time with me? I have my mothers car and some time to kill."

"How soon can you get here?"

"Two minutes. I'm at the Gulf service station down the street. I thought, it would be better to call first, instead of coming straight over, in case you didn't want my company."

"How do you know where I live?"

"I know where you live because I play basketball with Xavier all the time. I've walked home with him occasionally but never came inside. I didn't know he was your brother. Y'all don't look alike."

"Come on. I'll be waiting outside on the steps."

"Okay. Goodbye."

Two minutes later, a long, forest green, station wagon pulls up and stops at the steps. Carl is driving. I hop in on the passenger side.

"I hope you don't mind riding in a station wagon? You do know there are eight kids in my family?"

34

"No. I didn't know your family was so large. And no, I don't mind riding in a station wagon. I'm glad we can spend some time together."

"Are you hungry? We can go to the Varsity," he said, looking at me smiling.

"Yes, I am. The Varsity will be great! I've never been there before." I suddenly remembered, I hadn't eaten a thing all day.

I looked at Carl while he was driving. He was cola brown with golf ball shaped eyes. His nose and ears were large, but, somehow, they went well together. His teeth were yellow and uneven with some kind of golden-yellow stuff on the front bottom tooth that completely encircled it. If it was plaque, it had been there all of his life. It was definitely not your ordinary plaque build-up.

He was a nice guy, I told myself, a Christian. That counted for something. Carl was a talker. He talked the whole way to The Varsity. He was funny, too. I've never heard anyone put words together the way he did. He had me cracking up the entire time. I've never laughed so much in all my life. Boy, did it feel good. We finally reached The Varsity. He went to the curb service side.

"What do you want to eat?" he asked as he slipped his right arm around my shoulders.

"What's on the menu?"

"Chili-dogs, hamburgers, french fries, onion rings, fruit turnovers, sodas, shakes, and ice cream."

"I'll have one of everything you named," I said to him smiling.

I noticed his smile disappeared after he placed my order. He ordered ice water for himself.

"Aren't you hungry?"

"Not anymore. I suddenly lost my appetite. But yours is big enough for both of us. When was the last time you ate?"

"Everything sounds so good on the menu. I want to try them all. I may be thin, but I eat like a horse."

"You mean a herd of horses. At this rate, you'll be as big as a house, and I'll vanish into thin air."

"I'll let you have some of my food if your appetite comes back. I don't want you to be hungry."

"That's very kind of you, Miss Piggy. Or should I say, Mr. Ed. Monday afternoon, I'll definitely start looking for another job. It takes a weeks wages just to feed your ass for a date."

When the food came, the waiter placed my order in front of Carl. Carl told him only the ice water was his. All the food was mine. The waiter brought the food to my window and looked at me in disbelief.

"When is the baby due?" he asked handing the ice cream to me. I get pregnant customers all the time. They always order ice cream."

"I'm not pregnant. I'm hungry."

He looked at Carl. "More power to you, brother. You must be a good man." He said, walking away to the next car shaking his head.

"I hope I impress you as much as I impress him," Carl said, gazing at me and giving me a golden, plaque smile.

"You don't have to impress me."

"Oh, no? Since that's the case, you really don't think I'm gonna let you eat all that food in front of me, do you?" His long arms reached past my nose to retrieve the food at my window ledge. He centered the food between us.

Before I finished my fries, Carl had eaten the hamburger, onion rings, shake, and apple turnover. When I realized what was happening, I stuffed the chili dog in my mouth whole! A race was on and I was losing. I squeezed the ice cream in my lap, hoping it was not his next target. I put my soda between my seat and the door. I leaned toward the door and turned my head to the window to eat my chili dog in peace. The way he was eating, I wasn't sure it was safe. The only thing that was safe was his ice water which was untouched.

After the last morsel disappeared, I heard a loud burp and an earth-shaking fart. I thought to myself, this Negro is crazy. Not once did he say excuse me or anything. Does he think I'm deaf?

"Aren't you going to say excuse me?" I asked in complete disgust.

"Why? It's only natural to burp and pass gas after you eat."

Totally flabbergasted, I let the matter rest. Carl cleaned up the mess between us by placing the trash on the back seat. Afterwards, his right arm rested upon my shoulders again. Our eyes met. No one spoke. Our bodies drew to each other like magnets. His lips touched mine. His arms pulled me closer to him. My breasts touched his chest. I knew it was February, but if felt like the Fourth of July. The fireworks in my head exploded. Rockets took off throughout my body. Our bodies became one, completely enmeshed with the other. I felt his heart beating next to mine. His embrace felt awesome. His hand slipped down to my breast. The fireworks stopped. The rockets ceased. An alarm went off in my head. I straighten up. I was ashamed of my small breasts. I stuffed my bra with tissues to make them appear larger or shall I say normal.

"What's wrong? Did I do something to upset you?" he asked concerned.

"Yes. But I can't talk about it now. Just take me home, please."

"No. Let's finish where we left off," he said, trying to kiss me.

"I said, take me home, right now!"

"Okay, okay. Don't get bitchy. You must be having indigestion from all that Varsity grease."

He cranked the car and took me home. The ride home was very uncomfortable. The long periods of silence made it seem twice as long. Carl attempted to break the silence, but his efforts were futile. I didn't want him to know I had microscopic breasts. The fact that he almost found out unnerved me.

Daddy's car was in the driveway when we arrived. Carl parked behind his Buick. I opened the door to get out.

"Would you like to go to church with me tomorrow?"

I looked back at him. "Yes. I would love to go to church with you tomorrow. What time?"

"Eleven o'clock."

I closed the door and walked to the house. No one had ever asked me to go to church with them before. My family didn't go to church. Naturally, the kids went on Easter morning. That was the extent of church for us. Mama said, every Sunday she was made to go as a child. She hated going so much, she swore when she was grown, she would never go or force her children to go either. She kept her word.

Daddy was at the door and saw Carl drive off.

"Where have you been?" he asked sternly.

He slapped me before I opened my mouth to speak. Another slap landed across my face, followed by several punches.

"You have no business being in any car with a boy," he said when he finished using my face for a punching bag.

"Yes sir," I said, looking in his eyes. I wanted to roll my eyes at him and curse him out, but I resisted the urge. I knew the less I said or did, the better off I'd be. After he cooled down, I went to my room. I didn't cry when Daddy slapped or punched me. I'd grown accustom to his assaults. They didn't have the sting they once had.

"Where's Beverly?"

"She's with Cynthia. They should be home," I said before I closed my bedroom door.

John's letter was facing me from my dresser. I reached for it to read his words which were always comforting. I also stared at his card on the wall. "John, please, deliver me from this nightmare called life," I said aloud.

"Vanessa, the telephone is for you," Dad said after answering the ringing phone.

I went to the phone, "Hello?"

"Hello, Vanessa? This is John. How are you doing, Kitten?"

"John. It's so good to hear from you. I was just re-reading your last letter and looking at your card." My hand touched my ear and felt the diamond post earring he gave me for Christmas.

"I have some good news. In my letter, I said, I'll be home in May. But, I will be home next week. I miss you, sweetheart, and I can't wait to put my arms around you."

"I miss you, too. What day will you be here?"

"Friday or Saturday. Have you thought about what I said in the letter about being my woman, one hundred percent?"

"No I haven't. I'm already your woman, one hundred percent. That one percent that's missing is for your wife, not your woman. I'm not your wife yet."

"We will discuss it later. I am running out of change for the phone. I will see you next week. Goodbye."

"Goodbye."

I called Cynthia's house to see if she was home. The house felt awkward with only Daddy and me in it. I needed to go somewhere to relax. Cynthia answered the phone on the first ring. "Hello, Cynthia, I'll be right over. I need to get out of the house."

"Daddy, I'm going over to Cynthia's to get Beverly," I yelled as I left.

Cynthia met me at the door with a fork in her hand. She didn't want the doorbell to wake Beverly, who was asleep, because the slightest noise wakes her up. Cynthia escorted me to her room. Beverly was asleep on the spare, twin bed.

"I'm eating dinner. Do you want me to fix you a plate?"

"No thanks. I've eaten already. I'll stay in here with Beverly in case she wakes up."

"Suit yourself," she said as she left to finish her dinner.

I sat down on the other twin bed watching Beverly while she slept. How could she be a perfect angel asleep and be a total hellion awake? I stood up, and quietly paced back and forth. I went over to Cynthia's dresser to look at her pictures. My eyes instantly focused on an envelope. The handwriting was familiar. It was from John. I opened it and read the letter inside.

*Dear Cynthia,*

> *I hope you are doing well, You know that I love you and not the baby next door. I savor the thought of your body next to mine. You put me in shear ecstasy. I will be home soon to be with you and not Vanessa. My relationship with Vanessa is over. You are my love. My one and only love...*

There was more, but I heard Cynthia coming. I quickly put the letter back into the envelope and returned to the bed. Cynthia gave me an inquisitive glance, then looked at her dresser, the letter. She removed it by placing it in her front pocket. We chatted for a few minutes until Beverly woke up. I immediately grabbed Beverly and left. But, I left my heart behind, folded up in Cynthia's right pocket.

# SEVEN

I canceled going to church with Carl on Sunday. After discovering John's devious ways, I was in no mood to hear about God. He was not listening to me, and I was not talking to Him. I felt God had let me down this time. The one person who meant anything to me had now been taken away. I was pissed off with God, and He knew it.

In my depressed mood, the days passed quickly. Friday came and so did John. He appeared at my door more handsome than ever. His arms were overflowing with presents. It was not Christmas, or my birthday, or any other special day.

"Are those for me?"

"Yes they are. May I come inside? I am cold and these boxes are heavy."

"All those presents took me by surprise. Come on in."

He placed the presents on the sofa. With his empty arms he gave me a very passionate kiss.

"How are you, Kitten? I missed you so much. You look terrific!"

I always melted in his presence. Cynthia's letter completely escaped my mind. My man was home. That was all that mattered at the moment.

"What's in the boxes?" I asked, wanting to rip the paper off each one.

We sat on the sofa. I sat near the presents. There were five boxes of various sizes, colors and shapes. I chose the biggest box first.

"What is the purpose of these gifts?" I asked as I tore the paper off.

"When I went shopping yesterday, I saw these things and wanted you to have them. I wanted to show you how special you are to me."

A full length, black leather coat was in the first box. It had a hood with black fur inside. I tried it on and modeled for John. Then I laid it on the sofa and reached for the second largest box. The paper was off in one second flat. It contained a pair of black boots that matched the coat. I stood them up on the floor by my feet. Next, I selected the navy oblong box. Inside was a white silk, long sleeve blouse. It had a high collar and six buttons down the back. I took it out of the box, put it to my chest then landed a very wet kiss on John's right cheek.

"These are beautiful! I can't believe you bought these lovely things for me. What's the occasion?"

"I don't need an occasion to show you how much I care for you. I know I am gone a lot. This is my way of making up for it."

I reached for the next to the smallest box. Inside was a bottle of Spirit cologne. I put a little on my neck. It smelled heavenly. I placed it on the coffee

39

table in front of me. As I reached for the last box, the smallest, John grabbed my hand.

"Have you thought about what I wrote in my last letter and our last conversation, about you being my woman one hundred percent?"

Suddenly, I remembered Cynthia's letter. A picture flashed in my mind of them having sex. At that point, I totally lost my mind. I picked up the gifts and threw them at him.

"Get out! Get out of my house right now!" I shouted as I continued in my rage.

I took the unopened smallest box and threw it at him. It barely missed his left eye. The coat landed on top of his head. The boots hit his groin. The blouse was on his lap, and the cologne flew past his left ear. If it had been any closer, that Spirit would have taken him to heaven. I pushed him to the door and kicked his ass out with all his gifts dangling off him. He was too bewildered to say anything. All he knew was he was out in the cold in more ways than one.

The door slammed so hard, the window shook. I stood with my back pressed against the door to reassure myself he was not getting back inside.

"What's going on in here?" asked Mama, looking at me pressed against the door.

"John came by to see me but had to suddenly leave."

"When did he come into town? It's been awhile since he's been by," said Xavier, noticing the mess on the floor. "Where did the wrapping paper come from? It looks like wrapping paper hell in here."

"Boy! Watch your mouth!"

"Sorry, Mama."

"John brought me gifts, but I decided not to accept them. Let me clean up this mess," I said, moving toward the pile of paper, hoping they would leave and stop asking questions.

"What did he buy you? It looks like Christmas with all this wrapping paper everywhere. Here, let me give you a hand," volunteered Mama.

Xavier disappeared. He always did when it was time to clean up.

"Oh, he gave me a full length, black leather coat, black boots to match, a long sleeve, white, silk blouse, and Spirit cologne."

"And you let that man leave here with all those nice gifts? You know you need a new coat. And you can always use boots. Even I look good in silk. Spirit cologne is very expensive. What's wrong with you? You're not using your head. Go and apologize now before he takes all those nice clothes back to the store. Sometimes, even when men are wrong, we have to say, I'm sorry. Seems to me, this is one of those times."

"Mama, you don't understand."

"I understand, you are crazy as a bessy bug. I must have fried your brains when you were younger."

"Vanessa, telephone," yelled Dad from his bedroom.

"If that's John, give me the phone. I'll apologize for you. I love Spirit cologne. A white silk blouse will go good with my new red pants."

Dad left the room as I answered the phone.

"Hello."

"Vanessa, what happened? What did I do to you?"

"Dearest, John, I'll tell you what you did. Last week I read the letter you sent Cynthia. I'm very hurt, knowing the two of you are lovers. And you spoke of me as the baby."

"I have no idea what you are talking about. I never wrote Cynthia any such letter. When can I see you again?"

"NEVER!" I screamed as I slammed the receiver down.

The telephone rang instantly after I slammed it down. I let it ring five more times. Xavier came to answer it.

"Vanessa, what's wrong? Answer the phone!" He screamed as he reached to answer it.

I moved out of his way.

"Hello, Carolyn, I was getting ready to call you."

Xavier talked on the phone in my room. I went in the den with Beverly, Dad and Mama. Beverly's big head was blocking my view of the TV. She was blocking everybody's view because she was sitting directly in front of the TV. She had her favorite doll, Candy, perched on her shoulders. Dad and Mama were glad that she was still and out of their hair. They didn't care if they saw the program or not. I didn't say anything. I was not in the mood for talking. I stared at Beverly's head and Candy's butt until Xavier finished talking on the phone.

When Xavier came in the den, I made my exit. My eye caught a glimpse of an object on the floor in the living room. What is that? I asked myself. It was three steps away. I went closer to pick it up. As I reached down to retrieve it, I recognized what it was. To my surprise, it was the smallest present. If I had seen it earlier, I would have aimed it at the back of John's head when I threw him out. But, now, what do I do with it? I carried it to my room.

The box was wrapped with gold paper and a white bow. I placed it on my dresser and pretended it was not here. But the box was so beautiful, and my curiosity was getting the best of me. I gently picked the box up, sat on my bed and ripped the paper off. Inside was a stunning, diamond engagement ring. The stone was the shape of a diamond and was as big as my head. What was John thinking about? He hadn't left the United States, so I knew he didn't have one of those foreign diseases.

I remembered his letter and conversation about being his woman one hundred percent. Was he crazy? I was not even a woman, one percent. I was one hundred percent child. Granted, I liked to be kissed and hugged, but he was taking our relationship too far. I was not ready for what was on his mind. If Dad found out, John would be attending my funeral, instead of our wedding. If Dad got mad enough, it would be a double funeral.

I slipped the ring on my finger. It was beautiful! Absolutely, beautiful! After admiring it for several minutes, I put it back into the box. I knew I couldn't keep it, nor could I continue my relationship with John. I would not marry a man who two timed me. How could I trust him? I knew our relationship was over. Although he denied the letter he wrote to Cynthia, I knew what I saw with my own eyes. Tomorrow, I would return his ring.

John called early the next morning. He wanted to see me. He suggested we sneak to the park to talk in private. The arrangement suited me perfectly. In case I got ugly, my family didn't have to witness me making a scene. We met in our usual spot below the ball field at the big oak tree. John was there when I arrived. His hands were in his coat pockets His head was bent so low it appeared to be growing out of his chest. Was this my man? Was I the cause of his distress? Or did he have something else on his mind? Time would tell.

"Vanessa, Kitten, after last night, I thought I would never see you again." He reached to hug me but I stood colder than the winter air that was bringing tears to both our eyes.

"John, it's over between us." I searched my pocket for the ring. "Here is your ring back. I can't keep it under the present circumstances. For you to two-time me for Cynthia, my best friend, my play sister, is too low. Our relationship will never be the same. I will always have the two of you together, forever, branded in my mind. That's a scar I will bear the rest of my life." I took his left hand out of his pocket and placed the ring in the palm of his hand.

"Vanessa, you are wrong about this. Let me explain."

"There is nothing to explain. I know what I read with my own eyes. I'm leaving now. This is our goodbye." I turned around to go home.

As I started running, I heard him call my name, alternating between Vanessa and Kitten. When I arrived at the busy intersection of Memorial Drive and Clifton Street, I heard a car horn. I looked behind me. It was Carl blowing at me. I ran to the station wagon, both glad to get out of the cold and to distance myself from John. I opened the passenger door and hopped inside.

"Take me somewhere, anywhere but home," I told Carl between breaths.

"How about the Varsity?"

We both looked at each other and laughed. Carl was always good for a laugh.

"Wherever you want to go has to be close by. I don't have much gas and this station wagon uses a gallon a mile. Unless you have gas money."

"I have gas money. Let's ride. I just want to ride around. No place in particular."

"Okay," he said then put his right arm around me as he drove.

We were like two peas in a pod. Our bodies were so close together, we appeared as one person instead of two. From that day on, Carl and I did everything together. We went to church every Sunday. He walked me home from school, carrying my alto saxophone. He attended the varsity football games to see me perform as drum majorette. After running the four-forty race for track, Carl was usually on the sidelines waiting for me to finish. I sat on his lap and watched the remainder of the track meet. He attended the varsity basketball games where I played first string guard. He was present at all my activities if he was not working. He was my personal fan club.

Life, finally was great! I had a companion whom I loved and who loved me. Carl was the warmest person I had ever known in my life. I was a cold empty shell in comparison. The previous years of slaps from Dad left me hollow inside. The close relationship with Mama, however, kept some semblance of normalcy in my life.

God had given me the right person, Carl. Carl supplied the things that were lacking in my life, such as, joy, warmth, humor and love—pure uncut love. The kind of love that mended years of hurts. My prune size breasts were no longer a concern either.

Later, I discovered, Carl had scoliosis. For a long time, I didn't see the prominent hump in his back. When God did open my eyes, I was in love, and it didn't matter. I was able to love my own body, including my miniature breasts, after I discovered Carl's scoliosis. The size of my breasts seemed insignificant in comparison to his obvious humped back. His scoliosis was a plus not a minus. Seeing how he dealt with an outward abnormality, that the whole world saw, made me love him more. I knew my defects were internal, apparent to God and me. They were basically hidden from the rest of the world. His predicament made me think less about me and more about him. He was the most wonderful person I knew!

# EIGHT

Now that John was out of my life, my relationship with Carl blossomed to maturity. As the day of my high school graduation approached, so did my desire to become Carl's wife. There were only two obstacles in my path: finances and Carl's stern objection on the subject.

I brought up the subject of marriage twice to Carl in the past. He said, he was not ready financially, nor was he ready to give up his bachelorhood. He was at the prime of his life and enjoying every minute of it. After several no's, I got the message loud and clear. Why should he be tied down with a wife? He had his own crib, a job, oodles of friends, and plenty of sex from me.

Yeah, he thought he was making it now. Although his cribs got progressively worst, than better, he was a very happy man. His new place, his third since he left home over a year ago, was a real loser. It looked like a slave's quarters. It had two rooms and a bathroom with a tub that was at least one hundred years old. It was located behind a big plantation looking house. How he found this place in the middle of the city, I'll never know.

The last time I brought up the subject of getting married was March of seventy-four. We had just left Carl's crib after making love all day. We generally spent our Sunday's now at his place instead of going to church. He came by my house bright and early, Sunday morning, dressed in his church attire. I was dressed in mine as well. We caught the bus and went straight to his crib. We returned to my house in the evening.

"Carl, I'm ready to get married," I said, waiting for the number eighteen bus to pick us up to go back to my house from his crib. My eyes were focused on his although the March wind made it difficult by stirring the air with debris. My hands were embedded in my coat pockets. His right hand reached for mine. But I didn't budge before I heard his reply.

Carl reached inside his coat for his cigarettes. The subject of marriage always made him nervous. Cigarettes calmed his nerves. He lit one and took a long, hard drag. Looking at the cloud of smoke, he replied.

"Like. Vanessa. Baby."

He paused between each word. He took another drag and held it for what seemed like eternity.

"I'm not ready for marriage. You know my ends ain't meeting. Shit, they don't even see each other," he said, moving his hands and shoulders as he talked with his head bent to the side. His skullcap was completely covering his head which made his large ears appear to be talking, too. "I know you want to live a certain way, baby. But I can't afford your lifestyle. Right now, I can't afford any lifestyle. I'm barely making it now. I'm catching hell trying to survive." He flipped the cigarette on the ground and pulled me close to him.

"I don't care about living a certain lifestyle," I said, embracing him. "I just want us to be together as man and wife."

"You know I'm your man. And Baby-Doll, I know you're my woman. We don't need to be married to prove our love. Okay?" He pulled me back to look into my eyes. "We have everything except a piece of paper telling us we are one. Doll, we are already one. We don't need a piece of paper telling us that."

"You don't understand Carl. I'm tired of going back home after we've been together the whole day. I want to be with you always without separation." He embraced me as the tears trickled down my cheeks. I rubbed them off on his coat. I didn't want the other people at the bus stop to see me crying.

He whispered in my ear, "I love you, Doll. Give me more time."

In other words, Carl had his pussy on a string. He knew I would never leave him. So what difference did it make if we were married or not, he had a leash around my neck already. He didn't need to be married to have his bed warmed.

Within seconds, the bus arrived. We boarded the bus last. Carl paid our fares. I trailed behind him with my eyes glued to the floor, holding his hand. He found seats in the rear of the bus. We would arrive at my house in fifteen minutes.

Carl put his arms around me, but they didn't soothe the hurt I was feeling. He continued to defend his position about not needing a piece of paper to proved our love. I was his, and he was mine. I truly loved Carl, but his position on marriage told me I needed to go on with my life. Our relationship was a dead-end. I stared out the bus window looking at the streetlights fluorescing in the darkness. Carl was still talking. His words were like echoes. Finally, our stop was next. I reached for the line. Carl and I stood up and positioned ourselves at the middle door. The crisp night air greeted us as we exited. Luckily, my house was only a few feet away.

December of the same year, I knew I must move on. I didn't tell Carl how I felt. I didn't know how to tell him. Besides, he probably would not have believed me anyway. By this time, Carl's "ends" not only didn't see each other, they were no where in the same vicinity. He was now breaking into his own crib to live. Whenever he didn't have his weekly rent money, which was often, his landlord padlocked the front door. Carl left the front window unlocked and entered through it. Sometimes he was inside when the landlord came by. Since the front door was still padlocked, he figured Carl was not there. Needless to say, he was wrong.

New Years' 1975 rolled around. Carl came to visit. When the doorbell rang, I was in my room reading.

"Vanessa, Carl is here!" shouted Mama from the living room as she opened the door.

Because my room was adjacent to the living room, I heard every word.

"Happy New Year! Come on in Carl."

"Happy New Year! Miss Betty."

"Have you eaten? Dinner will be ready in a few minutes."

"No, I haven't. I was hoping to eat over here. What did you cook?"

"I cooked collard greens, so we can have some dollar bills in our pockets this year. And some black-eye peas for change. I'll give you an extra helping of collards and black-eye peas, so you'll have more money this year."

"In that case, I need to eat the whole pot of greens. As broke as I was last year."

"I know, son. It wasn't a good year for me either. Maybe '75 will be better for both of us."

"I hope so. Surely to God, it won't be any worst.

"I got ham, too. It's suppose to keep the hanks off."

"Give me a double portion of that, too."

"I..."

"Hi Carl," I said, cutting Mama off as I entered the room.

"I'll leave you two alone. I need to get back to the kitchen. I don't want our good luck to burn."

"Me neither, especially the ham and greens," chimed Carl.

To our surprise, when we turned to sit down, Beverly had positioned herself on the sofa. She loved Carl and often sat between us. I learned a long time ago, it was futile to tell Mom and Dad to get her. They were glad to get the break. She only left when she was good and ready and not a second before. Although this scene had occurred a thousand times, this afternoon, I was not in the mood for her shenanigans.

"Beverly get up and go back into the den," I said, pulling on her arm yanking her little butt off the sofa.

"Stop Nessa, I'ma tell Daddy you're hurting me. He won't like it either," Beverly said, snatching her arm from my grip.

"Mama! Come and get Beverly. She won't leave so Carl and I can be alone."

"I'm cooking. Can't you watch her?" Mama shouted from the kitchen.

"No. I have company."

"Leave her alone, Vanessa. She's okay sitting between us," Carl said, smiling at Beverly.

She quickly smiled back at him.

"Oh! Did you come to see her or me?" I said with my hands on my hips in hot indignation.

"I refuse to answer that. Come here," he said, patting his legs. "Sit on my lap."

Beverly beat me to his lap. I ended up sitting on her. We were a three-layer cake, Carl, Beverly, and me. I was livid. I pinched her arm so hard a knot appeared the size of a grape. She left the room crying.

"I'ma tell Daddy on you. You're trying to kill me."

With her out of the room, Carl and I snuggled up close together. Dad stormed in the room with Beverly while we were embracing.

"Daddy, Nessa tried to kill me," she said, pointing her finger at me while holding her pinched arm. The pinched spot was so red, it glowed in the dim lit room.

"Vanessa, what did you do to Beverly? She said you tried to kill her."

"Daddy, I just pinched her arm."

"She's your sister. Don't pinch her anymore. You're more than twice her size."

He walked towards me. "How would you...," Slap! went his hand on my face before he finished the sentence.

"Dinner's ready!" yelled Mama.

Dad walked out of the room towards the kitchen. Beverly licked her tongue at me then ran out of the room, too. I leaped to get her, but Carl held me back.

"Don't worry about her. Leave her alone," he said, restraining me. "Let's eat before the food gets cold. Just pretend nothing happened."

"That's easy for you to say. You're not the one that's just been humiliated. I am so tired of being slapped. I can't pretend it didn't happen. I can only believe that one day it will end."

"I'm sorry. You're right. I didn't know what else to say."

I held his hand. "I'll live. Let's go eat."

We went to fix our plates. The other three were in the den eating. Carl and I ate in the dinning room where we found peace and privacy at last.

Carl hung around for two more hours. The incident with Beverly and Dad earlier put a real damper on my disposition. I was bitchy the remainder of the evening. Carl tolerated me for as long as he could. Finally, he said, he had to leave.

After he left, I went into the den. The trio were watching Star Search on TV. For some reason, I suddenly remembered the lime sherbet ice cream in the freezer. I left without saying anything then returned to the den with the almost empty ice cream carton.

"Nessa, gimme some," said Beverly, pointing to the carton.

"No. I'm not giving you any. I haven't had any yet, and this is all that's left," I said, eating a big spoonful.

"Vanessa, give Beverly some of that ice cream," demanded Dad. "I'm sick of you treating your sister like dirt. I'm not going to let you mistreat her."

"Here. Have it all!" I said as I threw the carton at Beverly and stormed out of the room.

Dad ran behind me. "Come back here! Don't throw anything at your sister," he said as he landed a blow to my face.

For the first time in my life, I returned blow for blow.

"Don't hit me! Stop hitting me!" I said with each blow. I broke free from the punching match and ran to my room. Dad ran behind me.

"Stop Xavier!" I heard Mama scream. "Don't hurt her. Leave her alone!"

I was surprised to hear Mama come to my defense. Usually, she observed his assaults without defending me or stopping him.

Xavier Jr. was no help either. Once he jumped on Dad's back when Dad punched me. Dad discouraged any future attempts by flinging him off his back like a sling. Xavier Jr. never made another attempt to come to my rescue again.

"Leave me alone," I screamed, repeatedly, as I kicked Dad with every ounce of strength I had in me. The tears were flowing, my feet were kicking, my fists were swinging. I couldn't and wouldn't take anymore. I lay on my bed fighting back as long as he kept up his end of the battle. Dad was saying something, but I was too busy fighting to decipher what he said.

Mama came and pulled him away from me.

"That's enough! Stop it the two of you, right now!" she said, pulling on Dad.

"I'm leaving! I'm leaving this house tonight!" I said when Dad left the room. I began packing my belongings to prove my point.

That was not the first time I wanted to leave. I had thought about running away many times before. My only problem was, where would I go? I never was able to answer that question in the past. Tonight, was different though, God reminded me of a conversation I had with a co-worker, Jennifer. One day at work, Jennifer mentioned a spare bedroom in the house she rented with two other roommates. God brought this conversation to my mind. Coincidently, I had Jennifer's number. I never called her before, but God knew I needed the number tonight.

I called Jennifer and inquired about the spare room. It was obvious I was very upset and had been crying. She gave me the address and directions from the bus stop. She said the bedroom was still available, and I was welcomed to have it. I thanked her and hung up.

By now, it was late. Mama informed me I could not leave tonight since it was past ten o'clock. I obeyed her. But early the next day, I got up, took all my belongings, boarded the bus, and went to Jennifer's. When I reached the house, Jennifer let me in. After I put my things in her bedroom, we both caught the bus to Georgia State University.

January 2, 1975, at eighteen, I was suddenly on my own. I went through my normal routine of classes and work. Carl called my house that morning. Mama told him what happened last night. He called me at work and wanted us to talk later. I gave him Jennifer's number and address. Coincidently, his crib was down the street from Jennifer's.

That evening he came by. We preferred talking at his place, so we walked to it. He wanted to know what happened; I told him.

"Vanessa, what are you going to do?"

"I don't know. I guess I'll live with Jennifer until I'm able to live on my own. Making only one dollar and seventy-six cents an hour, I'll probably be with her for the rest of my life."

"Why don't we live together? It doesn't make any sense for each of us to pay rent. What do you think?"

"I think you're crazy if you think I'm living here."

"Vanessa, listen baby, we can get an apartment together."

"Do you mean...get married?" I asked not believing my ears.

"Ahhhhh, that's not exactly what I had in mind, but under the circumstances, that seems like the right thing to do. Yes. Let's get married."

He held me close. His arms locked our bodies together. His warm breath against my ear whispering, "I love you", sent cold chills down my spine.

"I love you Vanessa. I really do. Tomorrow, we will find out what we need to do to get married. Tonight, I'm going to fuck your brains out. Okay?"

"Okay."

# NINE

Telling my parents was the hardest part of getting married. Xavier Jr. married his high school sweetheart, Shelia Carson, four months prior, in September. Mama always said we did things at the same time. To them, my sudden engagement to Carl appeared as an imitation of Xavier instead of the truth—the incident with Dad.

The next day, I made several inquires on how to get married. I discovered the Health Department had neighborhood clinics that gave free, pre-marital, blood tests. The results were ready in seven days. Carl and I made plans to get our blood tests then go to the courthouse to get married when the results came back. With everything happening so fast, it was still hard to believe I was finally getting married. Under the circumstances, I didn't have time to get nervous because I had too much to do.

Luckily, everything fell into place. I found affordable housing on the bus line. Our apartment was on Welika Street, in Decatur, near the Avondale Mall. The monthly rent was the same price Carl was paying to live in his slave quarters, one hundred dollars. Since January is traditionally the month for sales, I was able to buy everything on sale. Our complete bedroom suit—mattress, boxspring, dresser, chest of drawers, and headboard—was one hundred and ninety-nine dollars. It was a bargain even though it was made of genuine plastic. But it had a real wood look.

The only furniture Carl owned was a small metal table with four plastic chairs. Our one bedroom apartment was three-fourths furnished with the table and bedroom suit. Purchasing a living room suit was out of the question. Besides, it was not considered a necessity but a luxury. Being married to Carl didn't allow for luxuries. A wedding band was another luxury. We had our piece of paper. We didn't need rings to say we were married. I was so glad to get the paper, a wedding ring seemed insignificant.

The time came to tell Dad and Mama about our plans to get married. We went to the house the third day after I left home. Mama greeted us at the door. "Come on in Carl and Vanessa," Mama said as she gave me a hug. "How are you doing? I haven't seen or heard from you since you left."

Carl remained by my side. He took his hat and coat off.

"Miss Betty is Dad here?" asked Carl, grinning like a cheshire cat.

Mama and I looked at him in unbelief. That was the first time he addressed Dad as "Dad". Usually, he called him Grant.

"Yes. He's in the bedroom. Honey!" Mama shouted. "Vanessa and Carl are here. Let me go get him. Sometimes he's so glued to the T.V., he doesn't hear anything else."

When Mama left, Carl and I debated about who was going to break the news to them. We went into the den discussing the matter. We heard Mama and Dad coming our way. I pushed Carl out the door since I was not ready to confront Dad. I couldn't tell him and Mama I was getting married. The words wouldn't come out.

Carl stumbled out the door before they came into the den. I sat motionless on the revolving bar stool near the door.

"Mr. and Mrs. Grant, me and Vanessa are getting married. We took our blood tests today. We plan to get married next Friday at the courthouse after the blood tests come back."

"Are you getting married 'cause of what happened?" questioned Mama.

"No, Miss Betty," he lied. "We were planning on getting married anyway. It has nothing to do with her leaving home."

Carl always was a good liar. Lie-Lie was his nick name. He certainly was living up to it now. I began to tremble in my seat. Hearing those words coming from Carl gave me the jitters.

"Where is Vanessa? Why isn't she telling us, too? Are you sure about this?" asked Dad.

"Yes sir. I love your daughter very much, and I want her to be my wife. Do you object?"

"No. I don't. If that's what you want to do. But I want Vanessa to tell us to our faces," retorted Dad.

I knew that was my cue to leave my twilight zone and enter the real world. I went to the doorway. Carl's back was to me. Dad and Mama were facing me.

"What's this about you getting married? Is it true?" Dad asked, looking me dead in my eyes.

"Yes. It's true. Carl and I are getting married. We've been together five years. Don't you think it's time?"

"I don't know. I never heard you say anything before. It seems all-of-a-sudden to me."

"No, Dad. It's not all-of-a-sudden. We discussed it before."

"Vanessa, be sure to wear something old and new. Something borrowed and blue," said Mama, easing the tension in the room by adding her superstitious comments. Only my mama would say something so irrelevant at a time like this.

"Grant do you have anything to drink? I can sure use a hit right now," Carl said, pulling me close to him. His hands were cold and shaking. I sensed he was just as nervous as I was.

"Let's go to the bar. I'll fix you up. What's your pleasure? I have Johnny walker, Jack Daniels and..."

Mama walked over to me and gave me another hug after Dad and Carl walked into the den to celebrate with a drink.

"Vanessa, are you sure you're doing the right thing? What about school? Do you plan to finish?" asked Mama still hugging me and looking me in my face at the same time.

"Mama, you know I love Carl, and he loves me. I don't know if getting married is the right thing to do or not. But I'm going to do it. Don't worry about school. I plan to finish. It will probably be easier to finish being married than being single," I said, removing myself from her embrace.

"Don't be having no babies before you finish. Are you pregnant?" Mama asked looking at my stomach. Her expression told me she had discovered the missing piece to the puzzle.

"No. I'm not."

"Vanessa and Betty come in here with us and have a drink. This cause for a toast," yelled Dad from the den.

Mama didn't drink alcohol, but I sure could use a good strong drink. The way our conversation was going, I was expecting Mama to ask me when the first time Carl and I had sex.

"Come on Mama. Let's join Carl and Dad in the den. You can have a Pepsi. I'll take Dad up on a drink."

"Vanessa, you're not getting married because of what happened between you and your dad, are you?"

"No." I lied too. No sense in telling the truth at this point. What was done was done. My life at home was over. My new life with Carl was on the horizon. I'd drink to celebrate that!

Friday, January 10, 1975, Carl and I exchanged vows at the Decatur Courthouse. Remembering what Mama said, I got married in a white, long sleeve blouse and sky blue pants. I bought a new pair of white pearl earrings for the occasion. I borrowed ten dollars from Xavier Jr. to buy our wedding cake, a German Chocolate cake from Rich's bakery. Everything else I had on was old; therefore I fulfilled Mama's request. Carl had on a loud, orange, sweatshirt and checkered, navy blue, orange, and white pants. He thought he was sharp as a tack. If I wasn't getting married, I would have cussed him out for looking like a clown. But, it's a time and place for everything. I reminded myself that those were our school colors. Maybe, he was being sentimental.

We said our, "I do's" before the judge. Carl was so happy he gave him a ten dollar tip. Judges are public servants and therefore not suppose to receive money for their services. But who can turn down a tip? This judge didn't. So our wedding cost ten dollars plus the cost of the cake. Finally, I was Mrs. Carl Lewis. My new life had begun.

Our bedroom suit would not arrive until Saturday, therefore we spent our first night together on Carl's old mattress. We borrowed Xavier's car to move our meager belongings into the apartment. We were very happy. The things we didn't have didn't take away from the joy we experienced by just being together, as man and wife.

By late February, we were able to buy a mint condition, canary yellow, 1972 Chevrolet Impala for two thousand dollars. It seemed as though we accomplished more together, than apart. Being man and wife worked for us.

In July, we took, a belated honeymoon trip to Disney World. It was wonderful! Life was grand! Our marriage was a perpetual honeymoon.

Over the course of time, we took many trips in Nellie, our beloved car as we affectionately named it. We went to Look Out Mountain and Ruby Falls in Tennessee, Calloway Gardens and Lake Lanier in Georgia. Although the sky was the limit on the things we hoped for, our finances kept us here on Earth. Of course, we wanted to go to Hawaii, California, and the Carribbeans, but our finances said Tennessee, Georgia, and sometimes Florida.

We were able to purchase both living room furniture and silver wedding bands by December. The furniture was a dark-brown and beige, plaid sofa and love seat with a hint of green. We bought a dark brown oak, coffee table and bookshelf to accompany them. We felt like a king and queen in our fully furnished apartment. Also the addition of our wedding bands made our marriage complete. We were coming up in life, slowly but surely.

We moved to Tall Oaks, a nicer complex of apartments, the following month when our one year lease expired. They were located on Memorial Dr., near the police station. For the first time in our lives, we had enough money to buy the things we wanted. We had happiness. We had each other. Life was truly good. But...during this time, there was one black day.

Carl was sitting in the living room when I came home with pills sprawled across the coffee table.

"Hi, honey, I'm home," I said as I rested next to him on the sofa. He sat lifeless with a forlorn look on his face. Something was up. But what?

"What's wrong with you?"

"I have VD," he said in a low audible whisper. He lifted his head up slightly and pointed to the pills on the table.

"You have what?" I asked, shocked not believing what I thought I heard. This must be a joke or a very bad dream. Certainly, this was not the truth, not my reality.

"You heard me right. You need to go to the clinic to be tested." He buried his guilt-ridden face in his hands.

"How did it happen? Who was she? Why Carl? Why!!!" I demanded as tears flooded my eyes.

"She was some white women I met walking down the street." He stood up with his back to me and walked to the sliding glass door.

"I'm sorry Vanessa. It just happened," he said facing the curtains.

"It just happened! Bull-shit Carl! Some white whore was walking down the street, your dick smelt pussy, and y'all started fucking? Is that what happened? Mother fucker start packing your shit now!" I screeched as I scattered the pills everywhere with a quick swipe of my hand.

He turned towards the bedroom. "I'm sorry. I'll start packing. It won't take me but a few minutes, and I'll be out of your life." With his head still hung, he walked to the bedroom. I heard drawers opening and closing. Finally, he came out with one suitcase and a bag full of stuff.

"Goodby, Doll. I didn't mean to hurt you." The tears streamed down his face. "I love you," he said as he reached for the door knob.

"Wait! Don't leave," I said, running to the door to close it. "Don't go. I love you so much. Please don't leave me." I wrapped my arms around him and his things.

He dropped the suit case and emptied his arms. We embraced. No words were spoken. Only the sound of our hearts beating in rhythm was heard. We both cried, holding each other, not wanting the other to let go.

"I love you Vanessa. Please forgive me," he whispered between tears that choked his words.

"I love you too, Carl. I forgive you. I love you too much to lose you. You mean too much to me. Although this whole incident hurts like hell, the thought of losing you is more painful."

We kissed. The passion flowed. The realization of almost losing each other enhanced the lovemaking that followed. He was mine, and I was his. We were one. When we exchanged vows, we took each other for better or worst. This was the worst, so it had to get better.

# TEN

When Carl made love to me, I thought about her. My man had been with a dirty, disease-laden, white slut. The same dick he put in me, he rammed in her white ass. Was it good? Did she give him head? Hell yes. I felt extremely violated. I went to the clinic the next day. Innocent me. All I did was make love to my husband. I gave him his conjugal rights, and he gave me mine. As I waited on the table to be examined, my thoughts reverted to them. Why Lord? Why me? Why?

I never told Carl how I felt about his fling. We didn't discuss it. I think we were both trying to forget it ever happened. I tried not to tense at his touch or throw up when we kissed. Sometimes were better than others. Fortunately, the tests were negative. I didn't have VD. But, I did have a bad case of "vapid depression". Somehow, I must lick it before it licks me. I must not think of him and her. I must think of me, of us. If only the hands of the clock could be turned back to before it happened, my life would be great again.

In two days, Saturday, our club, OUI-7, would be having another disco. We had them once a month. It was a time of dancing, drinking, and fellowshipping. Usually, the same people came. We had built a large following in the past ten months of our existence. Preparing for the discos kept me busy. Trying to squeeze time from my studies and work was difficult. I was the only female in the club, so naturally, I was responsible for the refreshments. I was also the treasurer and barkeeper. Carl bought the liquor, beer and wine, but I kept track of the inventory.

By Saturday morning, my "v.d." had disappeared. I didn't have time for it. I was happy thinking about the music, the old and new friends, the food and the fun. I had my disco boog-a-loo down to an art. Certain records, like Car Wash and Super Freak, made my pressed hair go back to a fro. I went looking like Farrah Fawcett and left looking like Godzilla. The more drinks I consumed, the more fun I had. Since the bar was free to me, I had plenty of both.

The time for the disco to begin had arrived. We opened the doors to Misty Waters Clubhouse promptly at 8:00 p.m.. On a good night, a moderate line formed at 7:30. Tonight, a large crowd was ready to enter. This was our pre-Memorial Day Jam. The DJ, Dr. Death, was known for giving at least six, healthy, young brothers, heart attacks. He had a reputation of killing his audience. Of course, no one thought they would be his next disco fatality. He especially loved it when the party animals begged him to slow the music down. He stopped the music. Stand in his long, black, doctor's coat with Dr. Death emblazoned on the back in big, bold, red letters. He asked his assistant to bring his black bag. All eyes focused on him and the bag. Old timers knew what it contained—a death wish. Although his black Dr. Death hat and black shades covered his face, you felt the evil lurking in his eyes. His hand slowly retrieved the eight-track tape from the bag along with his stethoscope, which he placed around his neck. This maneuver always made the crowd scream to the top of their lungs. They knew what was coming up—death, uncut, uncensored, and UNCAGED!

The weak hearted took a seat. The disco demons remained on the floor. It was not uncommon for couples to snatch the other one off the floor. When those who dared to continue were asked by Dr. Death if they were ready and gave a thunderous "yes", he played the tape. One-by-one the floor cleared. Dr. Death did it again. He came out of his bag with the most awesome disco jams to be heard. Intermission always followed the tape.

"Look at the bar. It's packed!" said Ronnie, the president of the club, to Carl who was helping me at the bar. "Dr. Death knows how to draw a crowd and keep 'em thirsty."

"I know, man," replied Carl. "I stayed on the floor one time after he went into his bag. I told myself, never again. I drunk so much water when it was over, I nearly drowned. If the music don't kill you, quenching your thirst will."

"Yeah, man. I'm like you. I tried it once myself, too. When I got home, my dick was shaking so hard, I couldn't fuck for two days. I said, "Fuck this shit. Can't no music replace fucking."

"Yeah, man?"

"Yeah. I ain't lying either."

"Ronnie, can you take over for me. I need a break," I said. "This bar has been busy all night. I just need fifteen minutes to regroup." I handed one customer two drinks, trashed the dirty cups that were on the bar, and took another order.

"Sure, Vanessa. Take twenty minutes. I like the sound of money ringing up at the bar."

"Watch out for wolves. You look irresistible," shouted Carl from the bar.

I must admit. I did look rather attractive in my tomato red, tight, silk pants and red, black and white, short sleeve, stripped blouse. A wide black belt accented my twenty-two inch waist. My hair was flipped in the front and swinging in the back. I looked like a black Farrah Fawcett without the Angels.

"I will," I shouted back as I headed for the patio outside.

Ah, the outside air was refreshing. The inside air was hot and musty. Some who didn't die from the music were killing the rest of us with their Dr. Death-jam-funk. There is funk. And there is Dr. Death-jam-funk. Dr. Death-jam-funk is indeed the funkiest. You can smell asses that haven't been washed in days.

My eyes scanned the apartment complex. The darkness of the night engulfed everything, including me in it. I gazed into the sky. My eyes focused on a speck of light. Is it a star? A galaxy? I was mesmerized by it.

"I think it's Pluto," a voice said out of the darkness.

I turned my head quickly to the voice. "You startled me. I thought I was alone." He moved from his position. No wonder I didn't notice him. I only saw him vaguely in the moonlight. He was wearing a black suit and black shirt, with no tie. His complexion was midnight black. Even the whites of his eyes were black because he was wearing black shades. His slender six-foot frame, every black inch of it, now captured my attention.

"What are you doing out here alone? That can be dangerous," he said, lighting a cigarette and moving closer to me.

"I'm taking a break. I thought some fresh air would be nice."

"Let me introduce myself," he said, exhaling a perfect ring of smoke and extending his hand. "My name is Rocket."

His very large diamond ring sparkled in the moonlight. His hand felt hard. "My name is Vanessa Lewis," I said, shaking his hand. "Rocket. That's an odd name. It suits you to a T."

"That's what my ladies say, too. I live my name."

"Are you enjoying the disco? Don't you just love Dr. Death?" I said, trying to change the direction of the conversation.

"I own this complex. I came by to inspect a work order I gave my maintenance man today. Lately, he hasn't been doing his job. Everyday I have to go behind him and check his work."

"Why don't you hire someone else?"

"He's blood," he said, blowing smoke into the air again. "You sure look stunning tonight."

"Thank you. I think my break is over. I better get back inside. It was nice meeting you, Rocket." I said as I turned toward the door. His hand grabbed my hand and twirled me into his arms. His lips gently kissed mine. The expression on my face said it all.

"I live my name." He grinned and released me.

I ran back inside, past Leonard, my brother-in-law, at the patio door. I couldn't believe what just happened. Intermission was over. The floor was packed. As I was making my way to the bar, Gary, a regular, asked me to dance. While dancing with Gary, my mind was on Rocket, the kiss, the excitement, the explosion inside. Gary and I departed after our dance. All of a sudden, I felt a hand hold mine. It was Rocket.

"May I have this dance?"

"Yes. You may." To my delight, it was a slow song. The one and only one that Dr. Death would probably play. I closed my eyes and rested my head on his chest like I had known him for years. Halfway through the song, "Do Right Woman", a hand tapped Rocket on the shoulder. It was Leonard.

"I hate to cut in, but I would like to dance with my sister-in-law. Do you mind?"

Rocket did mind, and so did I. Neither one of us said anything, though. Rocket stepped aside. Leonard took his position. Rocket vanished. Leonard and I danced until the song ended.

"My break is over. I need to get back to the bar. I told Leonard as I left the dance floor.

"I was getting ready to look for you. I didn't see you anywhere. I sent Leonard to find you when he came to the bar," said Carl, with a smile of relief, holding a drink.

"I guess I lost track of time. I was on the patio getting some fresh air, then I danced on a couple of songs," I said, opening the swinging gate of the bar. "I saw Leonard." I wondered how much Leonard saw, I thought to myself. Leonard approached the bar. The look he gave me said, he saw too much.

"Good work Leonard. I see you found Vanessa in one piece. What can I fix you to drink?"

"I'll have a double screw driver with a peppermint twist."

He looked me dead in my eyes then glanced at my blouse. I got the message. I hoped to God, Carl didn't.

"Peppermint twist? Man what have you been smoking? We don't even have lemons for lemon twists," laughed Carl.

"If you look around, you can find one lemon."

"Here's your drink, man."

Leonard took his drink and disappeared in the crowd.

"Hey Ronnie! Come and keep the bar. I want to dance with my lovely wife," shouted Carl, waving his hands, from behind the bar.

"No problem. Go have a good time. We set a record tonight at the door," he said, entering the swinging bar door. "From the looks of the cash box, you set a record here, too. Take the rest of the night off and enjoy yourselves."

"Thanks man. Come on Vanessa. Let's party!"

We partied down for the remainder of the disco. I totally forgot about Rocket and Leonard. I was too busy enjoying my man. The world always stood still when Carl and I were having fun. Nothing else mattered and no one could come between us, no one.

The disco was a success according to the comments, turnout and bottom line. We cleaned up, packed the car with the bar inventory and called it a night. The night was only a prelude to an action-packed weekend.

As life would have it, all good things must come to an end. The Tuesday after Memorial Day it was back to the same old grind, work and school I was glad my school days were coming to and end. In less than two weeks, I would graduate from Georgia State University with a B.S. Degree in Medical Technology. Carl couldn't wait until I started making decent wages. My job as a library assistant increased thirty cents in the two years we had been married. He worked two jobs to make ends meet and pay for his brand new, gray and burgundy, 1977 Charger.

Tuesday evening, at five o'clock, I heard the telephone ring as I entered the empty apartment. Since Carl was in transit to his second job, he was probably calling to see if I made it home safely, I thought. I grabbed the phone on the fourth ring, in the bedroom.

"Hello."

"Vanessa, can you talk?"

"Who is this?"

"Rocket."

"How did you get my number?"

"Carl gave it to me. I asked him after the disco if he knew where I could find a good maintenance man. He said he might be interested. I told him I was hard to reach, but I would take his number and call him when I was ready to fill the position. Is he there?"

"No."

"Good. I don't want to talk to him anyway."

"I can't believe you deceived my husband to get my number."

"Believe it. I've been watching you for sometime. I've been wanting to talk to you but could not find the right moment, until Saturday."

"Why are you interested in a married woman? There are plenty of attractive single ladies you can have. I'm sure you can have your choice."

"You are my choice. I want you. You being married has nothing to do with it. Besides, what Rocket wants, Rocket gets, and I want you Vanessa."

"I'm hanging up. This whole conversation is ludicrous!" When I said those words, my eyes saw the VD pills on the dresser. A picture flashed in my mind of Carl and her. The hurt resurfaced.

"Vanessa wait! Don't hang up! Meet me at Grant Park Zoo."

The thought of her and the explosion I felt Saturday prompted my response. "What time?"

"In thirty minutes, at the Boulevard entrance, near the tower."

"Okay."

"Wait for me if I am not there."

I heard the click and stared at the receiver before putting it down. Oh my God! What am I doing? I saw the pills again and thought to myself, if he can do it, I can do it, too. I looked at my watch. In twenty-nine minutes, I'll be with Rocket.

Traffic was heavy. I arrived five minutes late. My eyes scanned the parking lot. I had no idea what type of car he drove. I parked my car and walked toward the tower. I saw someone walking towards me. It was Rocket. He didn't look so black in the daylight. He was still black but not black-black. He had on a dark brown shirt and matching pants. Upon closer inspection, it was a maintenance uniform, he smelt musty, too. He definitely didn't have that, "I've been sitting at a desk all day", look and smell. As a matter-of-fact, he had that, "I've been working like hell", smell. His Right Guard had taken a left turn hours ago. I didn't get too close. I didn't want his B.O. on me. I tried to hold my breath but was forced to inhale the rancid fumes.

"Excuse my appearance. My maintenance man didn't show up today. Being the owner of my complex, I have to do whatever needs to be done. I have a very small crew."

"You must have a crew of one—you."

"We did not come here to discuss me. Let's go sit down."

That's a good idea, I thought, before I passed out. "I won't be able to stay long. I need to study for an exam."

In the light, he looked like a slim version of Willie B., the gorilla at the zoo. Wait a minute. He looked like Willie B.. He smelled like Willie B.. Maybe, he was Willie B.. That's probably why he choose Grant Park to meet at. This was his home.

As we approached the bench nearby, he held my hand. We talked for twenty minutes. He talked about his business ventures, his Eldorado, his vacation home in St. Petersburg, Florida, and how much he liked the color of my chestnut brown eyes. We talked about everything except his wife and real J.O.B..

At the end of our two-week, sex-less, affair, I found out the truth about both. He was not the owner of Misty Waters but the bonafide maintenance man. He was the son of a preacher who owned a restaurant on Moreland Avenue. I found that out accidently. I called the restaurant that "he owned". The voice on the other end was his mother. When I asked to speak to him, she told me never to call that number again. His wife worked there and sometimes answered the phone. I politely hung up the phone. I didn't know he was married. I also didn't know he was a compulsive liar. He made Carl look like a saint.

Speaking of Carl, I confessed the whole thing when it was over. I was so guilt stricken. I began to loose my appetite and jump every time the phone rang. I was a nervous wreck.

I learned a valuable lesson. When you meet a Rocket, shoot his lying, black ass to the moon. You'll save yourself a lot of heartaches and grief.

# ELEVEN

After I graduated from Georgia State University, I was offered a position in the Hematology laboratory at Saint Joseph's Hospital where I trained as a student. Being out of school provided two major advantages: I had a lot of time to kill and extra money to blow.

One evening, soon after graduation, Carl was sitting at the table doing his usual end of the day routine of getting high. While I was in school, I never smoked marijuana. But this particular evening, I decided to try it, just once, out of curiosity.

Carl rolled a couple of joints. He lit one. I watched him as he inhaled it and held his breath. In slow motion, he exhaled. His mood changed instantly to a mellow state. He took another drag. His eyes turned red.

"Let me try it."

"Here. Inhale slowly, hold it in, then release it," he instructed me as he handed me the lit joint.

I followed his instructions. I'd lit Mama's cigarettes in the past. I'm sure it was the same thing. I inhaled and attempted to hold it in, but I choked instead. I coughed violently. Carl laughed.

"Maybe, you need to stick to studying. And leave the smoking to me. You obviously can't handle it."

Nothing gets my blood boiling quicker than an old fashion challenge. Does he know who he's talking to? I'm Vanessa Grant Lewis. I can do anything I set my mind to do. Didn't I just complete four years of college? A first for both of our families. I'm certainly not going to let a lifeless joint defeat me. Not now. Not ever! "I can handle it. Watch." I took the joint, inhaled, held it inside and exhaled without coughing. "You better light this up," I said, handing him the other joint. "I'm going to finish this one myself."

"Oh, I see you got the hang of it. Go ahead and knock yourself out. I'll save this one for later. You might want more." He put the joint down and watched me indulge in mine. His eyes had a strange glimmer, a glow.

Sure enough, I wanted more. We smoked the second joint together. The feeling in my head was different than any alcohol high I ever experienced. And believe me, I had experienced a great deal.

We moved from the table to the living room. Carl played some nice, mellow, love songs. The music sounded different. Carl's music, in the past, was an irritation because he played it at an eardrum breaking volume. Tonight, the volume didn't bother me, nothing did. I heard every note on every instrument being played. When Carl kissed me, I felt an instant reaction. Suddenly, I

61

needed a fire extinguisher between my legs. Carl quickly came to the rescue. He put the fire out when he entered me. I never knew love making could be so good. After that first night, every evening ended the same way—reefer, alcohol, music and sex.

St. Joseph's Hospital moved from downtown to Peachtree Dunwoody Road, in 1978. Carl and I decided we needed a change also. We moved into a two bedroom townhouse in August of 1979 that was ten minutes from the hospital. We especially liked the steps that curved from the bottom to the top. By all indications, we were really making it now. We had a very nice townhouse, two cars, and two decent incomes. With the exception of children and God, we had everything.

Carl and marijuana were my gods. I worshipped both. I didn't have time for the real God. I had placed Carl on His pedestal. When trouble arose, however, I got my Bible that I took when I left home, closed my eyes and pointed my finger to the first scripture "God" directed me to. Sometimes, I tried to read the Bible but couldn't get past Genesis with the he begot him and him and him. I usually fell asleep in the attempt. I'd ask myself, why would God be interested in a pothead like me anyway?

Although we didn't have a child, my desire for a child increased. I told Carl it didn't matter when the subject came up. He never knew how depressed I became, and how I fought back the tears of disappointment when my menstruation started. Maybe next month will be different; I'd console myself.

For the time being, the drinking and marijuana increased. My new white supervisor and good friend, Adrianne, supplied me with marijuana. Every payday I bought a thirty-five dollar bag from her. She and her husband, Lucas, came to our place to get high, and we went to theirs. Life was one high after the other.

It was also during this time a desire came over me to write a book. I began my book but never completed it. My poor spelling, broken grammar, and weak writing skills made the task impossible. One day, I put it aside and never picked it back up.

Shortly after the hospital moved, we acquired a new pathologist, Dr. Stevens. The old pathologist, Dr. Griffin, was old and very frugal. For Christmas, Dr. Griffin brought a box of oranges and apples to the lab. He told each employee to help themselves because the fruit was our Christmas present. Dr. Stevens was younger, in his late forties. He treated us differently. Our Christmas present included money, twenty-five or fifty dollars depending upon our status, and dinner with our spouses at Gene and Gabe's, an upscale dinner club. The food was delicious. The entertainment was superb. I was sitting at the table with Carl, Leonard, and Gloria, Carl's oldest sister and Leonard's wife. Gloria worked at St. Joseph's, too. At intermission, Carl and Leonard went to get drinks. Gloria went to the ladies room. I was at the table alone. Adrianne came by and sat next to me club.

"Vanessa, I have something for you. It will help you enjoy the show better."

"What is it?"

"A Quaalude."

"What's a Quaalude?"

"It's a horse sedative. But it gives you a high. Here's one." She placed a small foil package in my hand. "Take only half of it at a time. If you like it, I have more." She said, standing up to leave.

"Okay. I'll try it." I took the round white tablet, that resembled an Alka-Seltzer tablet, out of the foil and broke it in half. I popped one-half into my mouth, washing it down with the last of my third mixed drink. The other half, I put away in my purse.

Everyone returned to the table at the same time. Gloria, obviously, had reapplied her make-up. Her fat yellow cheeks and lips were fire-red. Either Leonard had been slapping her around or she accidentally stuck her face in some cheap, red paint. She looked like a big yellow bear ready for war.

The Quaalude had unquestionably taken affect. I experienced a high, higher than any marijuana had taken me. My head was swimming. I was acutely aware of my surroundings. Everyone was staring at me, I thought. I couldn't keep my eyes open, so I put my head down on the table. Carl thought I was extremely tired. He let me sleep.

When everything was over, Carl woke me up. So much for a night out. It wasn't a total lost though, I did get both high and drunk in the short time I was awake. Carl was accustomed to carrying me out of functions. He took it in stride that his wife was an alcoholic and druggie.

My whole life evolved around the next high. I couldn't wait to get home from work to get high. I kept plenty of liquor and marijuana at the townhouse. Sometimes Gloria came home with me after work instead of waiting for Leonard to pick her up at the hospital. We both enjoyed a good high. It was not uncommon for us to begin in the hospital parking lot lighting up a joint. When we reached my place, we fixed a drink to accompany the high.

I knew I had an addiction when I came home from work one day and couldn't find a joint. I emptied the "roach" container and began smoking one roach after the other. I fixed a drink and lit a cigarette, something I had never done before. The cigarette boosted the high to outer space. I was in euphoria, in paradise. I was stoned out of my living mind. I was happy in my world of nothing. My wonderful world of not.

One day when Carl and I were lighting up a joint, we discussed the possibility of owning a house. The next day, I scoured the newspaper for available homes. I saw nothing affordable. With no savings, it seemed impossible. We both agreed that we wanted to move back to Decatur. Buford Highway was a nice change, but we needed to go back to Decatur where both our families lived.

I called a real estate agent to show me some homes in Decatur. Carl had to work and couldn't go with me. I think the real estate agent had a serious communication problem. I distinctly said "houses", not ruins, not shacks, and not condemned holes-in-the-wall. One neighborhood she took me to, I thought, I had to fight somebody to get out alive. The neighborhood was very run down. I felt like I needed an AK-47 rifle to get out of the car. I didn't see anyone, but I anticipated a grenade to land at my feet any second.

The "house" was a small brick structure with a carport. The grass was in patches scattered throughout the front yard. A young black girl answered the door.

"Hello, I'm Carla Butler from Homestead Realty." She showed the girl her real estate badge she was wearing. The young girl looked at the badge. I looked, too. It had to be fake ID, I thought. "I have an appointment to show this house today. Is your mother home?"

"Ma. Some folks are here to see the house," shouted the girl with the front door opened and the screened door locked.

"Let 'em in Nikki. I'll be'se thar in a minit," said a voice in a back room.

I thought to myself, never mind, I'll be gone in a second. If only I was driving my car, my feet would have left a trail of smoke. I really don't want to go inside or meet the body to that voice. Nevertheless, we went inside. Everything looked old. The sofa was draped with a blue flower bedspread. The antiquated dark-brown, end table was supported with phone books. The two red high back chairs had more yellow stuffing hanging out than in. There was no carpet.

"This is the living room," said Carla, standing in the middle of this nightmare, smiling.

"Come on'se back to thar kit'ch. I'm cookin suppar."

We went to the kitchen. This tall, dark-brown, burly woman stood there with a brightly colored rag on her head. she was the closest person I've ever seen who looked like Aunt Jemima.

"I've seen enough," I told Carla. The woman had a king-size frying pan in her hand and a miniature smile on her face. Her mannerism clearly said we were not welcomed. The For Sale sign in the yard should have included the words, Over My Dead Body. I thanked Carla afterwards for her time, shredded her business card into a million pieces, and I forgot about being a homeowner for a while.

Two months later, I found an advertisement for a brand new house in Decatur. I called the number. They had one lot left in one subdivision and several in another. Carl and I went the next day. We liked the subdivision with only one lot left. We wrote a five hundred dollar check for the earnest money and filled out credit applications along with release forms for our credit reports.

We went home excited about the house. The price was cheaper than the older homes we had seen. Everything felt right. When we turned on the wide street going to the lot, I knew we were going to get the house. The finances, somehow, would be worked out. I gave it to God.

The next day, Uncle Mark, my mama's youngest brother, called and asked us to live with him. We hadn't told anyone about the house. But I knew it was God who prompted him to ask us. We accepted his offer and moved out the following weekend. It's a good thing because someone tried to break into our apartment two days before we moved.

# TWELVE

Adrianne and I both wanted a child. Before Carl and I moved into my uncle's house, Adrianne came up with the idea to do a semen analysis on our husbands. Neither one of us were using birth control, nor were we able to conceive. We felt like the time had come to find out why. Adrianne came up to me, at the Coulter Analyzer, while I was sampling blood specimens through it.

"Vanessa, let us collect semen from our husbands and do a semen analysis on them tomorrow. Lucas and I are beginning to think something is wrong with one of us."

"I know Adrianne. I'm beginning to think the same thing about Carl and me. I haven't used any birth control in three years. You'd think I'd be pregnant by now," I said, putting the last sample through. Adrianne grabbed the profile sheets and laid them on the table beside Norma, who was doing differentials, counting the different white blood cells.

"You two oughta leave well enough alone," said Norma, talking to us while looking through the microscope counting diffs.

Norma was white, in her mid-fifties, talked constantly, and was nosy as hell. She made it her business to keep track of everyone else's business. Usually, we didn't say anything personal in her presence. This time was a regretted exception.

"Children are a big responsibility," she continued. "I have three of my own. They are quite a handful, especially, Roger, the baby boy. He's seventeen and is nearly driving both Sam and me crazy. He can't make up his mind whether he wants to be good or bad, stay in school or drop out, date girls or guys. I don't know how many gray hairs I have because of that boy. When you have children, you never know how they will turn out. Now the oldest two, Beth and Sam Jr., never gave me a bit of trouble a day in their lives."

Adrianne and I looked at each other from our microscopes. We'd heard this same spiel, verbatim, at least ten thousand times. We rolled our eyes at each other saying, oh no, not again.

"It requires a lot of love, patience, and money to raise kids. If I didn't have kids, I wouldn't be working today."

You're NOT working today, I thought. You need to retire. The little work you manage to do, I don't trust it. How Adrianne continues to let you come back day-after-day is beyond me. Don't blame your kids for having to come to work. You need a roof over your head even if they weren't born.

"Norma, I am twenty-nine. I am not getting any younger," said Adrianne, putting another slide under the microscope. "I have done a lot of things in my lifetime. I am ready to have a child. I feel a child will add joy to my life and my marriage. I can't think of anything more positive than having a child."

"Adrianne, if you know what I know, you're better off without one," said Norma, checking the time on her watch and getting up. "It's time for my break. The cafeteria closes in fifteen minutes. I think I'll grab a bite to eat before they close. If you two will excuse me," she said, giving her wide mouth smile as she left the table.

One thing about Norma, she never misses a meal, and she never completes her work. Good riddance, I thought, you always find an excuse to leave when their is work to do. Adrianne never says anything so I can't either. "Adrianne, Norma gets on my nerves big time. Maybe, she got pregnant by accident and didn't want her children like so many people do. But, if the Lord ever opens my womb and gives me a child, I'll love it until the day I die."

"I agree with you Vanessa. People who have children take them for granted. Don't they?"

"Yeah. Some even abort them or abuse them once they are born. They don't realize what a precious gift God has given them to love and to cherish."

"I know, Vanessa. I would love mine too much if I ever have one."

"Me too. You know Adrianne, it doesn't seem fair. Some people who have children don't want them. And people like us, who can't have a child, want one and would love it. I think about those people who want to adopt. They would give anything, like us, to have a child. Would you consider adoption?"

"I don't know. I would try to have my own first. Speaking of own. Are you going to bring a semen specimen tomorrow?"

"Yes. Most definitely! That's a good idea you came up with. It's time we get this baby ball rolling."

"Good. I'll have mine tomorrow, too. Don't forget to take a urine cup home today. Lucas won't mind collecting this specimen."

"Neither will Carl. Especially since he doesn't have to jerk himself off to collect it. It's just a matter of pulling out and squirting the semen into the cup. I don't think Carl can jerk himself off anyway," I said, laughing.

"We better concentrate on this work. Look at the counter. It's full again," said Adrianne, looking at the front counter where we received specimens. Several phlebotomist had dropped off their morning run while we were talking.

Norma came back as we finished the diffs. She logged in the new samples. Adrianne and I gave her a hand. I ran the new samples through the Coulter, Adrianne ran the coagulation specimens, and Norma went to the ladies room.

The next day, we came to work with our husband's semen. Adrianne examined Lucas's semen first under the microscope. His semen was normal in sperm count, appearance, and motility. By all indications, his semen analysis was normal. Therefore, Lucas was ruled out for having the problem with infertility. Adrianne knew, now, she needed to make and appointment with her gynecologist to undergo the numerous tests for females.

When she finished, I examined Carl's semen under the microscope. To my utter surprise, there were no sperms, absolutely none! I couldn't believe it! I examined more semen after mixing it up. This could not be right, I thought. The second sample tested the same. Oh my God! Carl is sterile. We will never have any children. Somehow, I managed to fight back the tears, but I was relieved at the same time. Now, I knew what our infertility problem was—Carl.

It wasn't easy telling Carl that night. We were at the top steps heading downstairs to the living room. After hearing the news of his sterility, he sat on the top steps, put his hands over his face and cried.

"I asked God not to let you get pregnant while you were in school. I wanted you to finish first. I never wanted our child to interfere with your education."

"You never told me that."

"I know. I didn't have to. I knew God answered my prayer. But I didn't know how He answered it, until now."

We were both silent. His response totally surprised me. If only there was a way to reverse the prayer. If a prayer made him sterile, can another prayer make him fertile?

Monday, I inquired about what to do to correct his sterility. I was given the name and number of a urologist, Dr. Harvey, who was on staff at the hospital. His receptionist scheduled an appointment for early September, a month away.

A lot of things happened at this time. We were in the process of possibly solving our infertility problem and possibly becoming homeowners, soon. I worked part-time as a waitress at Pizza Hut to help save for the down payment on the house since St. Joseph's didn't have any overtime. And we were moving in with my Uncle Mark. Life was somewhat insane but exciting. The possibility of having a child and owning a house made the zaniness tolerable.

Moving into my uncle's house turned out to be a blessing for all of us. My uncle was in the process of getting a divorce after thirteen years of marriage. He needed us to help him with his monthly expenses. He only charged us one hundred and twenty-five dollars a month. That was a lot cheaper than what we spent to live in the townhouse. The arrangement made saving for our house and paying off bills easier.

My Uncle Mark and my mama often did things together. Like the time mama wanted to go to Bessemer, Alabama to see Madame Lee, a seer, who foretold the future. Mama asked Uncle Mark to take her because she didn't want to go by herself. Plus, she wanted him to drive. I happened to be off the day they went, so I tagged along.

It took three hours to reach Madame Lee. She lived in a poor, rundown section of town, the houses were very old. Most needed a lot of repair. They were framed houses with large screen porches. Madame Lee's house was black with a dozen blood red steps that led to the front porch. The yard was filled with parked cars. We parked our car on the street in front of her house and walked toward the steps. I felt like I was walking into hell with each step I took.

An old humped back woman opened the screen door. She led us into a corridor lined wall-to-wall with sickly people. No one spoke. Everyone had dazed looks on their faces. Most seemed to be over forty. All of them seemed down and out. I asked myself, what have I gotten myself into? Coming here was not a good idea.

"You may have a seat here." The old woman pointed to three vacant seats in a room at the end of the crowded corridor. "Madame Lee will be with you as soon as possible. Please make yourselves comfortable. I must go and attend to Madame Lee's mother. She is very ill. Someone will escort you from here when it is your time to see the Madame." She slowly turned and exited from a different door.

There were eight other people in the room. They looked just as forlorned as the other people in the corridor. Their blank stares were directed to the floor. After two hours of waiting, I'm sure my countenance resembled theirs. Finally, a tall, thin, skeleton looking man came to us. His head was bald with several large black spots. His black nub teeth were grossly decayed. Red suspenders held up his black baggy trousers. His red and black sweater smelled like moth balls. He looked like death warmed over again and again and again. In other words, death fully done. He must have a coffin in here somewhere, I thought, looking around.

"The Madame is ready to see one of you now," he said in a very stiff manner.

My uncle and I both volunteered Mama to go first.

"Betty you go first. This was your idea."

"Yeah, Mama, we'll go next."

"Are you sure? I can wait," she said leaping from her chair.

"No. You go right ahead. You're keeping the Madame waiting," said Uncle Mark.

"Okay. If you both insist." She disappeared out of sight.

My uncle and I looked at each other. "This will be the last time I let your mother talk me into anything. I should have known better," he said, leaning his head back and closing his eyes.

I did the same. That way, I could pretend I was someplace else, anyplace but here.

Twenty minutes later, the skeleton man reappeared. "Next please," he said with the door opened.

"Well, I guess it's my turn. I wonder where Mama is," I whispered to my uncle as I stood up.

"I don't know. I'm trying very hard not to think about it," he whispered back.

The skeleton man slowly closed the door once I was completely inside. The door needed to be oiled. It squeaked loudly with each movement. He escorted me to a chair in front of the Madame.

"Madame Lee, here is your next client. May I be of any further assistance to you before I depart?"

"No. Thank you, Sylvester. You may leave."

He bowed and left the room.

"I am Madame Lee," she said, sitting erect, moving her hands in a circular motion. "How may I assist you?"

Her complexion was a caramel brown. When she smiled, three gold teeth, with a star in each, sparkled. Although she was sitting down, she appeared to be tall, over six feet. She was a heavy woman, built like a man, with big wide hands that mesmerized me because they were constantly moving in a circular motion.

I glanced on her desk for a crystal ball but didn't see one. I didn't want to take my eyes off of her too long, thinking she might put some voodoo spell on me. Other objects in her room did catch my attention. I looked at them through the corner of my eye. To my left, a large white Bible was opened on a tall, slender, wooden podium. Two tables in the back were filled with candles, oils, powders, large roots, small sticks, and an assortment of unfamiliar objects. The walls were forest green. There were no curtains, only heavy shades that prevented any light from coming into the room. The few candles burning on her desk were the only source of light. Her desk was clear with the exception of the candles, notepad, and an ashtray with burning incense.

The voice of someone moaning broke the silence in the room. The person obviously was in a great deal of pain or was being tortured. I didn't know which was the case. I did know I was ready to go because the sound unnerved me to no end.

"That's my mother you hear. She is very sick. I hope she doesn't bother you," Madame Lee said, sensing my uneasiness.

"No. She doesn't bother me, now that I know what the sound is," I lied.

"Good. Lets' get started."

"Okay."

"I see you are a kind and gentle person. You've had difficulties in your life, but you have been able to triumph over them. God has been with you from the very beginning of your conception. You don't yield to Him whole-heartily now, but you will later. You have more hard days ahead, but they will pass. The end of your life will be better than the beginning. Continue to follow the path you are taking. Soon, you will be directed to a different path, one that is more fulfilling and God centered."

She stopped talking and added more incense to the ashtray. She pushed her chair back and walked over to the Bible on the podium. Her mouth moved as she read Scriptures to herself. She walked over to the tables with the candles and other things. Several of the powders, she mixed together. Her back was to me, so I couldn't see clearly what else she did. After several minutes, she returned to her desk with several things from the table.

"I see a house," she continued. "You are having trouble with the financing, but you will get it anyway. Here, take this and sprinkle it in your yard." She said handing me a small plastic sandwich bag one third full of a powder mixture.

"What is this?" I asked, examining the bag.

"It is a cinnamon mixture. Make sure you put it in the back and front yard. Here is an oil." She handed me a vial from across her desk. "Put this on you to make your husband madly in love with you."

I took the oil and placed it beside the sandwich bag. The vial was two inches high with a red and yellow oil combination inside.

"Take these and chew on them." She handed me several small twigs. "These will help change the course of your life."

I took the twigs and held them in my hand. "Madame Lee, what about children? Will I ever have any?"

"Oh, don't worry about children. You will have four, two boys and two girls. You will leave your husband. Eventually, you will get tired of him." She began writing on her notepad. When she finished, she tore the paper off and held it up for me to see. "Here are some initials of men who will play a significant role in your life." She handed me the paper. There were six initials in a vertical column. They were: B.C., L.C., Z.A., H.L., D.J. and R.M..

"Is there anything else you want to discuss?"

"No."

"Well then, this concludes our session. You may leave through the door behind you. I hope this session was profitable to you."

"Yes it was." I lied again. I was sick to my stomach about the whole thing.

"Please come again," she said, smiling showing her gold star teeth.

I exited from the door behind me. Mama was sitting in a chair close to the door with two other people. The moaning was even louder now than before. We both waited in silence until Uncle Mark finished. Since I didn't know if the room was bugged, I didn't want to risk saying the wrong thing and end up like the person in the other room. Instead, I kept reliving my session, not believing what I heard. Mama was probably doing the same, too.

Each session lasted twenty minutes. Uncle Mark had the same look on his face as we did on ours when he finished. Since we were seated near the outside door, we let ourselves out and walked to the car like zombies.

The ride home was basically quiet with a few interruptions of conversation. I made one thing perfectly clear. I will NEVER, EVER, do this again! My uncle agreed. Mama didn't. If she ever goes back, it will be without us. During the ride home, I repeated Madame Lee's words over and over in my mind. Here I was twenty-four with no children, all I wanted was one or two. The thought of having four children made me ill. The thought of leaving Carl made me even sicker. How could I ever leave someone I loved so much. Madame Lee had to be a phony. Surely, there was not truth in what she said.

My uncle revealed to us Madame Lee told him he will re-marry and he will have a child. Uncle Mark was thirty-six and fatherless. He was hoping she told him, he would get back with Martha. She didn't. Madame Lee said the opposite, that they will never get back together. I believe Uncle Mark was sick like me of what he was told. He laughed at the thought of being a father at his age or older. He felt the time for a child had passed him by. He didn't want a child. He wanted Martha back.

Mama only said, Madame Lee told her she would own some property. That her life was one of giving. She was an asset to her family and community. Her warm loving nature made others flock to her like bees to honey. Her life would be full all of her days.

When I returned home, I threw the list of initials away, along with the oil, cinnamon mixture, and twigs. I don't need any oil to make Carl love me. I don't need any of this stuff. Never, ever, again was all I could say. My conclusion to the matter was, sometimes it doesn't pay to know what lies ahead. The present woes are sufficient.

# THIRTEEN

The day finally arrived to visit Dr. Harvey. His receptionist, Cathy, greeted us as we signed in.

"Dr. Harvey will be with you shortly. Please have a seat in the waiting area." The waiting room was occupied with one other couple. Carl and I held hands as we waited.

"Vanessa, what do you think Dr. Harvey will do?"

"I don't know, probably, an examination and ask a lot of questions."

"Suppose after he finishes, we still can't have children?"

"I guess that means I'll be stuck with just you, and you'll have some serious pampering to do. I'll expect you to spoil me rotten."

"What do you mean? You're already rotten."

"No. I'm slightly putrid. I'm not rotten yet."

"Mr. and Mrs. Jacobs, Dr. Harvey will see you now. Please come this way," said a woman, in white, opening a door in the waiting area.

Carl and I thumbed through the magazines on the table in front of us while we continued to wait. We knew we were next.

"Are you nervous?" I asked, feeling nervous myself.

"Kind of. I'm not looking forward to him handling my meat."

"Men. You are such babies. You could never be a woman. We have our breasts examined. We have Pap Smears performed where our whole ass is exposed and doctors put instruments inside of us to get a specimen. We loose all sense of modesty for the sake of our health."

"You're right. I could never be a woman. I thank God, I'm a man, every coward inch of me."

"Mr. and Mrs. Lewis, Dr. Harvey will see you now," the receptionist cheerfully announced.

We held hands going to the door. The woman in white led us through a short passage, passed three examining rooms, to Dr. Harvey's office. Dr. Harvey sat behind his solid oak desk in a brown leather, high-back chair. He had a stocky build, a full blond-brown beard, and Vitalis slicked back hair. The wet-look made him resemble a just washed dog, complete with large pointed ears to match. He peered at us over his thick, black, granny glasses. We sat in the two vacant chairs in front of his desk.

"Dr. Harvey, this is Mr. and Mrs. Lewis," the nurse said before she laid a file on his desk and left the room.

"Thank you, Sandy. Mr. and Mrs. Lewis, I am Dr. Harvey," he said, extending his right hand to us.

"It is nice to meet you," we both said after shaking his hand.

He opened and read Carl's file. "I see you had a semen analysis performed, and it was negative for sperms. Is this correct?"

"Yes, Dr. Harvey, that is correct. I did the analysis myself. Carl has no sperms in his semen."

"I will examine Mr. Lewis in a few minutes. The examination should shed some light on Mr. Lewis's problems. Depending on the nature of his problem, different procedures exist that can make a sterile man, fertile."

"That's good news, Dr. Harvey. My wife and I are ready to have a child. I will do whatever it takes to make it possible."

"Good, Mr. Lewis. Let's get started with the examination. Are there any questions before I begin?"

"What exactly will the examination involve?" asked Carl with visible chicken feathers coming out of his back.

"Mr. Lewis, first I will look for any physical and physiological abnormalities. Then, I will feel your genitalia for the presence of any lumps or obstructions. The whole process is painless and quick. It will let me know if more extensive tests need to be performed."

Carl's feathers shed to the floor when Dr., Harvey said, "painless". I actually heard a sigh of relief.

"Are there any other questions?"

"No," we both said.

"Mrs. Lewis, you need to return to the waiting area while I examine your husband. Mr. Lewis, I will escort you to your examining room. Undress from the waist down and drape the sheet around your waist. After the examination, Mrs. Lewis, Sandy will bring you back into my office to discuss the results."

Thirty minutes later, I was summoned into Dr. Harvey's office. Carl and Dr. Harvey were sitting, leaning forward, in their chairs talking to each other as I entered the room.

"Have a seat Mrs. Lewis. This will not take long." He waited until I was seated before continuing. He leaned back into his chair, positioning himself so he could talk, eye-to-eye, over his glasses.

"Mr. Lewis has two problems. The first problem involves his scrotum. It is positioned too high in his body cavity. Therefore, elevating the temperature of his testicles where sperm production originates. Wearing loose fitted underwear will help correct this problem. However, the second problem is more complicated. It will require surgery to correct. Even with surgery, Mr. Lewis has less than a five percent chance to father children. His examination revealed he has a varicose seal. That's the same as having a varicose vein in the scrotum, which blocks sperm from leaving the testes. No sperms are being transported by the vas deferens during ejaculation. If, indeed, any sperms are being produced." He paused, looking into both our eyes, "Do you have any questions?"

"What will the surgery do?" Carl asked, putting his hands between his legs.

"Surgery will open the sealed or blocked area, thereby making it possible for sperm to mix with the semen during ejaculation. The varicose seal is acting as a barrier, preventing the release of sperm into the semen."

"Why such a low percentage rate of success even with surgery to correct the problem?" I asked, feeling like our case was hopeless.

"Due to the nature of Mr. Lewis' problem and the size of his varicose seal, which is quite large, the success rate is next-to-nil. I still recommend surgery. He needs this problem corrected whether he wants to father children or not."

Carl and I looked at each other. His eyes searched mine. "How soon can you do the surgery?" Carl asked, grabbing my hand.

"I can schedule the surgery in three weeks, on October 28," Dr. Harvey said, checking his calendar on his desk.

"Yes. That day is just as good as any day," Carl replied. "I'm willing to have the surgery, Vanessa. What choice do we have?" Carl squeezed my hand as he spoke.

"I agree with you, Carl. Less than five percent is greater than zero."

"Do you have anymore questions or concerns?"

"No."

"No."

"In that case, Cathy will give you all the information you need before the surgery. Trust me. You are doing the right thing."

"Thank you, Dr. Harvey. We hope so," I said, leading the way out of his office.

"Thanks man," Carl said, shaking his hand as we left.

We held hands again going to Cathy's desk. She gave us a packet of information and confirmed the surgery date. When we left, we were more discouraged than when we first arrived. Our high expectations of Dr. Harvey being able to correct the wrong and make it right had been reduced to a less-than-five-percent chance, nearly-nil.

Adrianne called me at home that night. She wanted to know the outcome of Dr. Harvey's visit. I told her what he said. She wished me good luck with the surgery. Her doctor wasn't able to find anything physically wrong with her so far. He was beginning to think her problem was psychological. She thought, he was full of it and had the psychological problem instead. She knew of another doctor in Kentucky where she and Lucas planned to move in three weeks. She gave her two weeks notice, today, on the job. Since I was off today, this was all new to me.

"You have to keep in touch after you move to Kentucky. Let me know how you come out with your new doctor. You and Lucas will have to visit us when we move into our new house."

"Aren't you having trouble with the financing?"

"Yes, but I know in my heart it will be worked out. The mortgage lenders want to deny us financing because we have two car notes. They even suggested we take one of the cars out of our names so the loan can easily go through. We refused to do that. Carl and I both feel we don't want the house if we can't afford it. We will not lie to get it either. If it is meant for us, we will get it by telling the truth."

"That's right, Vanessa, you'll probably get it. Don't you think?"

"I hope so. I just know the house is ours."

"Well, when do you expect to move?"

"Possibly the beginning of February."

"We have to notify each other when we get pregnant."

"That's a deal. Give me your new number."

"I don't have it yet. I'll have to call you when I get it later."

"Make sure you give it to me when you get it."

"I will...I won't see you tomorrow, though. I'm off. That's why I called you tonight. I wanted you to know what was going on. I didn't want you to hear it from Norma. I have to go. Lucas is calling me. I came in the kitchen to get us a beer. I decided to call you while I was by the phone. I'll see you Monday."

"Okay. Have a nice weekend. Goodbye."

The telephone rang as soon as I put it down on the receiver.

"Hello."

"Mrs. Lewis, this is Ronald Stewart of Lovely Homes, Inc.. I have great news. Your loan has been approved. We need you and Mr. Lewis to come by our office Monday to sign some papers and choose your interior and exterior colors. Is Monday convenient?"

"What time?"

"Whatever time is best for you. Our office hours are from ten to six."

"We will be there unless something comes up. If so, I'll give you a call. Thanks, Mr. Stewart, for the good news."

"My pleasure, Mrs. Lewis. I look forward to seeing you and Mr. Lewis, Monday. Congratulations!"

I put the receiver down again. "Carl, Carl," I shouted from the kitchen to our bedroom and racing up the three steps in my uncle's house. "Our loan has been approved!"

Carl met me at the entrance of the bedroom door.

"Our loan has been approved. That's no surprise to me. I knew we were going to get the house. Didn't you? I had that feeling."

"Monday, they want us to sign papers and choose our interior and exterior colors. How is your schedule Monday?"

"Anytime after four-thirty is fine with me."

"That's a good time for me, too. I'm off at Pizza Hut. This calls for a celebration. I'll go fix us a drink," I said, heading back to the kitchen.

"Wait! Let's celebrate the old fashion way."

"What way is that?"

"Sex, followed by more sex."

"Don't you mean, have a drink, then sex?"

"No. With your crazy schedule and long hours at Pizza Hut, I don't need a drink. What I need is some loving and plenty of it." He reached into his right pants pocket and pulled out a joint. "This joint is just right for the occasion," he said, holding it between us admiring it.

He lit it, took several tokes and passed it to me. It was one of those fat, Jamaican joints that go straight to your head and between you legs. We spent the rest of the evening in the bed, fulfilling his desire.

Monday, we went to the builder's office. After being shown different samples of colors, we decided on gray with burgundy trim for the exterior. For the interior, we choose gold wall-to-wall carpet, avocado green kitchen appliances, green floor tile in the kitchen, gold tile in the hall bathroom and blue tile in the master bedroom and off-white paint throughout the house.

The house was tri-level. The top level had three bedrooms and two full bathrooms. We especially liked the size of the master bedroom. The other two bedrooms were considerably smaller. Their size didn't matter since they would be used as a spare bedroom and den. The middle level had a great-room and small kitchen. This was the level you entered into. The third level had a laundry and storage room. The rest of the area was unfinished. When completed, it will serve as the den. The builders wanted twenty-five hundred more dollars to complete it. We opted to finish the third level later when our financial picture improved.

Carl had his surgery as scheduled. According to Dr. Harvey, everything went as anticipated. He successfully removed the varicose seal. I did not perform a post-op semen analysis. Carl and I both felt the proof would be in the pudding. If he was producing sperms, I would become pregnant.

On February 13, 1981, we moved into our brand new house. We were the fifth and last house built in the cul-de-sac. Bobby Freeman, a high school underclassman and fellow band member, lived two houses across from us. Bobby and I were good friends in high school, and he lived one street over in the neighborhood I grew up in. Sometimes he came to me for tutoring when we were in school. Bobby was now married and lived with his lovely wife Monique and son Cory.

My days at Pizza Hut were coming to an end. I had only one more week to work. The extra income was no longer necessary since the down payment had been paid on the house. One night, I noticed a small group of young, white people who came to the Pizza Hut regularly. The group consisted of four to eight people. Without exception, they only ordered coffee and hot water. At first, I didn't pay them much attention. They were more of a nuisance than anything else. They never tipped. They never ordered food. They drank their coffee or made tea and talked.

Three days before my last night to work, one of them said something to me as I approached their table to take their order.

"Do you know Jesus?" asked a short, brown-haired woman with oversized brown eyeglasses sitting on the end seat.

The others looked at me waiting for my reply.

"Yes. May I take your order, please," I said with my pad ready to take their order. I was tired and not in the mood for games.

"Do you love Him with your whole heart?" a pale, freckled guy asked with fire-red short hair and piercing green eyes.

"What do you want to order? I'm very busy. If you are not ready to order, I'll come back later."

"We are ready. We will have four coffees and two cups of hot water," said another pale guy with a large bald spot in the top of his head and a smile that seemed to be plastered on his face.

Haven't you heard of Greshen formula? I thought. You are too young to be bald. This whole group is weird. Maybe, if you ate food sometimes, you wouldn't be so pale. Eat! People eat! I took their order and returned to their table. "I have four coffees and two hot waters," I said, placing them in the middle of the table. "Can I get you anything else?"

"Would you like to worship with us? We believe in Jesus Christ and worship Him with our whole heart," said the bald guy.

"I'm busy right now. If things slow down, I might come back and talk."

The dinning room became empty before they left. They were my only customers. They usually had several refills of coffee while they talked for hours. I joined them later. I learned a lot about Christ. Their religion seemed a little off-centered, at first, but the more they talked, the more they made sense. They invited me to their home to worship. I accepted the invitation. I went to five meetings before discontinuing.

At the third meeting, I told them about Carl's infertility and the obvious failure of the surgery. Four months had passed without conceiving. Sherry, the short brown-haired woman with oversized eyeglasses, prayed over me. She had me to stand in the middle of the room. The others surrounded us. She placed her hands over my head and prayed the most beautiful and awe-inspired prayer I had ever heard. She asked God to open my womb and correct whatever problems Carl and I had. I felt a surge of heat go through my body as Sherry prayed.

My cycle was due on March the tenth, but it didn't come. My breasts were swollen and sore. Ten days later, my cycle still had not arrived. The urine pregnancy test required me to be two weeks late. Otherwise, it may give a false negative result. I planned to test my urine in four more days, but that night, I awoke out of my sleep doubled over in pain. My first thought was to go to the toilet. Within seconds after I sat on the toilet, I felt something leave my body. The pain ceased as this thing passed through. I got up and inspected what it was. There was a red and white tissue mass inside. I cried. Although I had not taken a pregnancy test, I knew I was pregnant. Now, I had to flush my long awaited offspring down the toilet.

"Lord, why allow me to conceive, then take my baby away? Why Lord? Why?" I moaned in the dark still hours of the night.

# FOURTEEN

The lab wasn't the same without Adrianne.  In addition, the drive from Decatur to Dunwoody was taking its toll.  The thirty minutes of driving like a maniac on I-285 with Atlanta's reckless, brake tappin', no signal using, bird giving drivers made me a nervous wreck by the time I arrived at work.  Something had to be done and soon.

I felt like I needed a change, a fresh start to go with my new house.  I searched the classifieds for another Medical Technologist position, hopefully, one that paid more money.  I found an ad at Grady Hospital, located downtown.  I called the next day, Monday, to schedule an interview.  That night, I called the midnight supervisor, my former Georgia State classmate, confidant and very close friend, Reginald Franklin, Reg for short.  I told Reg to put in a good word for me to the Chief Technologist, Peggy Morganstein.  He said he would, and he did.

Monday morning when I called Mrs. Morganstein, she knew who I was and was looking forward to our interview Friday at two o'clock.  She had an immediate opening in the Hematology lab.  The supervisor was Samantha Foster.  The interview went well.  They offered me the job at the conclusion of the interview.  I accepted.  The pay was fifty cents more an hour than St. Joseph's paid.  My starting date was Monday, April 6.  This date allowed me to give St. Joseph's two weeks notice, which I insisted upon giving.  Mrs. Morganstein agreed.

I reported to work at seven-thirty on April 6.  Ms. Foster introduced me to the Hematology staff, of eleven people, who seemed very pleasant during my introduction.  The ratio was sixty-to-forty, with the majority being white.

Grady's Hematology lab was five times the size of St. Joseph's, with four times the people.  Their workload was awesome.  Grady did more work on one shift than St. Joseph's did in one month.  The lab was broken down into workstations to handle the volume.  Each person was responsible for doing certain tasks.  I liked that method because it eliminated having people with the Norma syndrome, people who refused to complete their work.  Although, I discovered later, there were Normas in every work place, some were more noticeable than others.

Toward the end of the week, I brought plenty of sanitary pads with me to work.  My cycle was due Friday, April 10.  However, Friday came and went without my cycle starting.  Two weeks passed, still no cycle.  My breast were swollen and sore like last month.

Carl knew I was late again this month. We didn't want to get our hopes up too high, only to experience another disappointment. The ordeal was too emotionally devastating. I told him I planned to take a pregnancy test and would tell him the results when he picked me up after work. He worked at Georgia State University in the Maintenance Department. We car pooled since we worked the same hours and worked only one block away from each other's job.

I gave my urine specimen to Phyllis in the Immunology lab who performed the pregnancy tests. She said my results would be ready in one hour. One hour and one minute later, I called Phyllis for the results. She said, my test was positive. I was pregnant! I told everyone in my department. I was so excited! It had finally happened. I was pregnant!

I didn't say anything to Carl about the results of the pregnancy test when he picked me up in front of the hospital. I wanted him to ask me first. Several yards away, at the intersection of Butler Street and Decatur Street, he couldn't take the suspense any longer.

"Did you take the test?"

"Yes," I said, nonchalantly looking straight ahead at the light.

"Well...what's the results?" he asked, looking at me instead of the oncoming traffic. The traffic light had just turned green and he was making a left turn.

I turned toward him and said, "Positive."

"Positive? Are you sure?" he said, nearly wrecking the car.

"Yes. I'm sure. You'd better concentrate on driving before you kill us all. Keep your eyes on the road."

"I can't believe it," he said, taking his cigarettes from his shirt pocket and removing one to light.

"Well believe it, Dad. It's true."

"I know." He exhaled a cloud of smoke. "It takes a minute for it to sink in."

I rolled my window down to breathe. "Dad, how about taking your pregnant wife out to dinner? I'm eating for two now, and we are ready to eat."

"Don't psych yourself out and get fat on me. Having an increased appetite is all in your head. You just found out you're pregnant today. Now, all of a sudden, you want to eat like you're crazy."

"That's right. And it's not all in my head."

"Okay, okay. Whatever you say. I'm not marking my baby. I'll be glad to get y'all something to eat, provided you're paying for it. I spent my last dollar buying cigarettes."

"I'll pay for it. I always do. You just take us to get some food."

"I see, it's going to be a long nine months. You're already snapping at me. That's all right. I've waited a long time for this. I'll do whatever it takes to make you happy and my child normal," he said, exhaling another super could of smoke into the car.

"Good. We should get along just great! Now, how about dinner? We're right at Mrs. Winner's," I said, pointing to the entrance a few feet away.

He turned into Mrs. Winner's entrance. "Mrs. Winner's it will be for Mrs. Lewis and my baby."

I called Sherry that night to tell her the news. She told me, she knew I was pregnant, and I was having a son. I was dumbfounded by her response, but I knew she was telling the truth.

I called Adrianne as soon as I hung up from Sherry. She was excited about my news. However, she had news of her own. She was two months pregnant. She hadn't called me earlier because she wanted to be absolutely sure before she spread the word.

Becoming pregnant changed my life. No longer did I smoke marijuana. By the power of God, I gave it up cold turkey. Since God had blessed my barren womb, I owed Him my life for the life of my unborn child. Life for life. My life to know and serve Him as a sacrifice for the life of my child. As a result, I was miraculously cured of my alcoholism and drug dependency. No longer did I crave them. They lost their power over me, and I lost my desire for them. My life belonged to Jesus Christ, The Creator of all things, from the crown of my head to the soles of my feet.

Carl Lewis, Jr. was born Monday, December 14, 1981 at 3:10 a.m.. He weighed nine pounds, six ounces and was twenty-one inches long. He was born vaginally after twenty-one hours of labor. Although he had his father's name, he was the spitting image of me with his bright yellow complexion, large brown eyes, and head full of brown hair.

During his birth, Carl Jr. swallowed his first stool which developed into pneumonia. Consequently, he was hospitalized an additional nine days before being released from Grady Hospital's Intensive Care Nursery.

The birth of Carl Jr. ended six years of a perpetual honeymoon. Our marriage became golden, wall-to-wall like our carpet, with the birth of our son. Golden. Golden. Golden. Everything in my world was golden. Carl Jr. added an extra dimension to our marriage. Watching him mature was the joy of our lives.

But with the joy came the reality of the obligation of raising a child, physically, financially, and spiritually. This new sense of obligation, prompted me to read my Bible. Carl Jr. was here by a prayer and by the Grace of God. I wanted to teach him about God, but first I had to teach myself.

We started going to church regularly. The three of us went every Sunday. We church hopped from Pentecostal, Methodist, Baptist and Holiness. We were looking for a church home, but none of these satisfied us. Something was missing. But what? I couldn't quite put my finger on the answer. All I knew was, I had not found the right church for me. The search resumed as I continued to read God's Word.

Crystal Flowers, who worked in the Radial Immuno Assay lab, told me about a group called Women in Christ. They met every other Saturday at 10:00 a.m.. I went to the next meeting and loved it. One meeting I attended, Laura Sims, a good friend of Crystal's and the guest speaker, started prophesying.

"Please stand up, young lady in the navy blue dress," Laura demanded, pointing to me.

I stood up.

"I see you with another child. A young girl from out of town will live with you." She started waving her right hand. "I see a room in your house that is unfinished. I see it being finished. You will get a promotion on your job. I see where you will be greatly blessed financially." She ended and went to someone else, a woman in a red and white suit.

I sat down and pondered her words in my mind. I loved little Carl, who was six months old, but I wasn't ready for another child. Carl and I still did not have the funds, a year later, to finish the third level. Financially, we were broke, or as my Chinese friend, Dee, would say, broken. Broke or broken, it amounted to the same thing, we didn't have any money. Being, somewhat, new at Grady, I was considered the low woman on the totem pole. Advancement for me was slim to none. I didn't have a clue what she meant by young girl from out of town living with me nor being greatly blessed financially. I stored it all in the back of my mind. I did think it was interesting that she only said, another child and not four like Madame Lee.

An arrangement had been made for me to work the midnight shift in Hematology for six months when I returned from my twelve week maternity leave. Toni Caldwell, who worked the shift, was due to start her maternity leave when I returned from mine. After working the midnight shift, I realized how much I hated working the day shift. I was accustomed to working with fewer people which meant fewer personalities, less conflicts and less headaches. The midnight shift only had two people who worked Hematology.

When the six months were almost up, I noticed an opening for a day shift Immunology position posted on the employee bulletin board. Unlike the Hematology day shift lab, the Immunology lab had three employees, including the supervisor, Robin Fuller. I applied for the position and got it. Later, I discovered, I was the only applicant.

Being able to change labs so smoothly, strengthened my relationship with God. I knew He answered my prayers concerning the transition. As I continued to read His Word, He taught me more.

In my Bible study, Christ taught me, Saturday, the seventh day of the week, was the Sabbath. My conviction was very strong on this point. I knew in my heart it was right because the Apostles, who wrote the Scriptures after Christ's death, observed the Sabbath. It was distinguished from Sunday, the first day of the week.

As the end of the year drew near, I was scheduled to work Christmas Eve and Christmas Day in the Hematology lab. I worked weekends and holidays in Hematology because the Immunology lab didn't have weekend and holiday rotations. I prayed fervently to get out of working the holidays since it was little Carl's first real Christmas. No one wanted to switch with me, so I was stuck working it.

On Christmas Eve, Violet Hightower was our clerk. She was a phlebotomist, who worked every fifth weekend as a clerk in Hematology. Violet was short and overweight. She kept a "don't-bother-me and I won't-bother-you" expression on her face at all times in neon lights. The extent of our conversations were to speak as we passed each other in the hall.

Since it was Christmas Eve, I was full of the Christmas spirit. Maybe, her neon lights were out today, I reasoned.

"What are you doing for Christmas?" I asked as I picked up my three spinal fluids from the accesioning desk.

"I don't celebrate Christmas," she replied not looking up from the computer terminal.

Her answer struck me as odd. I'd never met anyone who didn't celebrate Christmas. She probably doesn't believe in Jesus Christ either. While I was counting my fluids under the microscope, I kept thinking, why Violet didn't celebrate Christmas. The suspense proved to be too much. I had to ask why. I completed my fluids then returned to her desk to retrieve more fluids.

"Do you believe in Jesus Christ?" I asked, picking up more fluids off the desk.

"Yes," she said never looking away from the terminal again.

I walked away more baffled this time than the first time. She believes in Jesus Christ but doesn't celebrate Christmas. I'm really confused. I must find out why. Each time I picked up specimens, I'd ask another question. Finally, Violet suggested we eat lunch together. I agreed. We went to lunch twenty minutes later. I think I was beginning to wear her down with my questions.

When we were seated at the cafeteria table, I had one very important question to ask her that I had saved. The answer to this question would let me know if her religion was true or false. If she gave the wrong answer then I would not be receptive to anything else she said.

"What day do you worship?" I asked once we were seated with our food.

"Saturday."

"That's the right day."

She smiled. I sensed a calmness come over her. I asked questions until our lunch was over. She offered me books to read on different Bible subjects. I took her up on her offer.

My life after that encounter became a first love for God. I read and read and read. I couldn't read enough about Him, His Kingdom, His great plan of salvation, Jesus' ministry, and His grace and love for all mankind, even for a wretch like me.

# FIFTEEN

I started attending Violet's church in February of 1983. At first, I had a conflict between the Women in Christ meetings and the weekly church services. Eventually, the church services prevailed although it wasn't easy giving up my Women in Christ meetings. My knowledge and thirst for Jesus Christ grew. The church gave me the spiritual nurturing I hungered. I felt whole. My spiritual void had been filled with Christ. My search for a church home had ended.

Carl attended a few services before discontinuing. Although I had found my church home, he felt this church was not for him. Worshipping on Saturdays was not the problem because we worshipped at the Seventh Day Adventist Church together before attending Violet's church. On Saturdays, little Carl and I went to church while Carl hung out with his friends. The church glued me together, but it separated Carl and I. For the first time in our courtship and marriage, we did not worship together. This disturbed me at first, but then I learned to accept it.

One thing I especially liked about my church was it took annual trips. Each member was responsible for saving enough money to pay the expenses for his family to attend the annual Holy Days. Carl didn't attend the services, but he traveled with me to the annual trips.

One year after the Women in Christ meeting when Laura prophesied about a promotion, Robin summoned me into her office. A note was strategically placed on my work station when I returned from lunch. It said, come to my office as soon as possible. Signed, Robin. I took the note and went to Robin's closed office door. The updated procedure manual was due in two weeks. Robin was working feverishly to make all the revisions by the deadline.

I knocked on the door. "It's me, Vanessa."

"Come in. It is not locked." She motioned for me to sit in the chair by the door as I entered. "Have a seat."

"Thanks." I said moving toward a comfortable chair.

The office was small. It had Robin's desk and chair and a vertical gray file cabinet to her left. A long black counter, the length of the office with a microscope and a chair lined one wall. I sat in the chair by the door.

"I'm sorry I took an extra three minutes for lunch." I said, nervously. That was the only thing I could think of that I had possibly done wrong. Or maybe I had verified the wrong results. I was known for being fast on the computer. Maybe, I had accidentally typed in the wrong answer code. Whatever the case, being called into Robin's office meant something was wrong. But what?

"I am not concerned about the three minutes. You usually work through your breaks anyway."

I sighed a breath of relief.

"I guess you are wondering why I want to see you."

"Yes. The thought has crossed my mind." Actually, this whole scene was driving me crazy, I thought. I was trying hard to look cool and collected on the outside while I was falling apart on the inside.

"Today, Frankie found out she was chosen to be the new supervisor for the fifth floor lab. Since she is the teaching technologist, I need to find a replacement. Frankie recommended you for the position. I feel you are an excellent candidate.

"Will I get a raise?"

"No. There is no increase in pay involved, neither will your position change."

"What's in it for me?"

"Extra work. You will be a great help to me. Will you take the position?"

"Okay. I'll take it." Robin was a wonderful supervisor. I'd do whatever I could to help her.

"Thanks, Vanessa. I really appreciate you taking on the extra responsibility."

"When will the students be here?"

"In three weeks."

"I need some time to get ready."

"I will take you off a station next week in order for you to prepare for the students. Frankie will work with you to get ready. If you need more time, let me know."

"Okay." I left the office and Robin continued working on the procedure manual.

I told Carl about my new position. He didn't get excited since there was no increase in pay. He called it slave labor. Increase work without increase pay is slave labor even in 1983. That's okay. At least this slave had a job.

Carl put in numerous applications over the past five years to Lockheed of Georgia. He was hired in November on the swing or second shift after passing the physical and drug test.

When Carl started working the swing shift, the sole responsibility of taking care of little Carl was suddenly dumped in my lap. Arriving home, I cooked, washed clothes, cleaned the house, entertained, fed and bathed little Carl, listened to him whine for hours, read to him, and tucked him into bed. Afterwards, I dragged myself to bed only to start the process all over again the next day.

Carl didn't understand why I wasn't interested in sex anymore. Why I was lifeless at 12:30 in the morning when he came home from work ready for sex. Sex was the last thing on my mind. I was exhausted. I needed a full night's sleep, undisturbed.

The combination of my religion and his job deteriorated the marriage. Taking care of little Carl by myself was overwhelming. Not spending time with Carl was devastating to our marriage. The months that followed were filled with one argument after the other. The division of the church and the second shift was creating a void in the marriage that widened daily.

Three and one-half years into our golden age, the brilliance of the gold was beginning to fade—just like the gold, wall-to-wall carpet in our house was becoming soiled from neglect and proper care.

For the first time, Carl and I made basically the same salary. We paid bills according to what we made. Whoever made less, paid less. With overtime, Carl brought home close to five hundred dollars a week. I asked Carl for a fifty dollar a week raise after he had been working at Lockheed for awhile.

"Carl, I need you to start giving me $150 a week instead of $100. You're making more money so an increase shouldn't be a problem," I asked while he was sitting at the kitchen table. I was standing at the edge of the table next to him.

"You're trying to take all my damn money," he snapped back, and who do you think you are? In a you little piece of shit, tone. "I ain't giving you no mo money. You've been managing this long with $100. Why do you need any mo?"

"How can you sit here and not contribute more to this household? I'm not asking you anything unreasonable."

"Nag. Nag. Nag. All you do is nag me to damn death. You don't tell me what to do," he said in a nastier tone. He reached in his shirt pocket, pulled out his cigarettes and lit one.

"Ever since you've been at Lockheed, you think you are Mr. Big Shit. I'm not going to beg you for more money. God will take up your slack."

"Why should I give you mo money when you give all your money to the church? I ain't giving you shit! You don't need my money if you give all yours away."

"Oh. So that's it. You're upset that I tithe. I'm not giving my money to the church. The tithe is God's money. I'm giving what belongs to Him. God gives us everything. Don't you think it's only right to give Him something, a tithe, like He asks?"

"Salvation is free. All you tithe paying saints are gonna bust hell wide open. All you're doing is leaving more room in heaven for good Christians like me who would give the shirt off my back to help somebody. All you tithe paying saints are too busy paying them devils in church your tithe, you don't have any money left to feed a hungry soul."

"You're missing the point."

"No, I'm not. The point is, ever since you've been in that church, you've been giving all your money away. I'm keeping mine. I'm not giving you any mo money to give to that church. You can pay these bills the best way you can with the hundred dollars a week I give you."

I ran up the steps to our bedroom and slammed the door. I heard the front door slam almost simultaneously. He's gone again. He's been leaving a lot lately, hanging out with his single friends. He's with them more than he's with us. Carl wanted to be single. All indicators pointed to it.

Little Carl awoke from his nap at the sound of the slamming doors. He opened my door and ran over to me crying.

"Mama, Mama, hold me," he said with his arms outstretched.

I held my son in my arms and kissed his head. "Do you feel better now?"

"Where's Daddy, Mama?" he asked, looking into my eyes with his large, sad brown eyes.

"He's gone son, but Mama will never leave you," I said, rocking him back and forth.

"Will he be back?"

"Yes, son, he'll be back. He needed to get some fresh air. Go get a book. I'll read to you."

He dashed to his room and returned with several books. I read to him until he went back into his room to play.

The marriage continued to splinter. I was involved in my church and Carl was involved with his single friends. The more I did things with the church; the more he did things with his friends. As the months passed, we grew further and further apart.

Everything wasn't bleak. Our financial picture had improved. With our income tax money, we finished the basement. We made arrangements with Mitch Simpson, my father's best friend who did odd jobs on the side, to finish it.

March of 1985, my Uncle Mark called with the good news that he was going to be a father in November. He and his second wife, Lila, just found out two weeks ago.

Since, our financial picture was at an all time high, we planned to take our first airplane trip to the Caribbean in September for the annual Holy Days of my church. Our destination was St. Lucia, a small island close to South America. In the past, for the Holy Days, we traveled to Biloxi, Mississippi and Jekyll Island, Georgia. Little Carl went with us on our two-week excursion.

I can still picture the ocean and surrounding mountains from my hotel window. Crystal blue water bordered the hotel. Clear white sand separated the two.

During services, the ocean was the minister's background while he preached to the congregation of seventy people. It was the most awe struck sight I've ever experienced. The sunrays glistened on the water creating a breathless view. I truly felt the presence of God. The beauty of His creation made me think of the splendor of His heavenly home.

At the conclusion of this paradise trip, I was jolted back to reality. We returned from our trips-of-trips to find the lights off in the house. Carl used the money for the electric bill as his spending money on the trip.To come home to no lights after having a paradise trip pissed me off. I was tired of him being irresponsible. The no lights killed my good disposition. He sent a message, loud and clear. Paradise is over. Welcome back to the REAL world, Dear.

April of 1985, my intrauterine device expired, but I never had it replaced. I kept putting it off and eventually forgot about it. Each month my cycle came, so I didn't give it much thought. However, in February of '86, my cycle didn't come. I waited a couple of days before taking the pregnancy test. If I was pregnant, I needed to know quickly because I needed the IUD removed as soon as possible. Since I was working in Immunology, I did my own pregnancy test.

The Immunology lab used a white, cylinder, urine pregnancy test procedure. A blue dot appeared for positive samples. Nothing happened for negative ones. I followed the directions and waited the specified time. To my utter surprise, a blue dot appeared. I was pregnant again. This pregnancy was not a joyous as Carl Jr.'s. Both Carls were getting on my nerves. Little Carl with his constant whining, getting into everything, constant spills, the numerous demands for my time and dwindling energy. I went ninety miles an hour doing things for him and the house. I had zero time left for myself. Consequently, my personal battery became critically low. I needed recharging but didn't have the time, nor knew quite what to do. Carl had reduced me to a sex object; no longer did I feel like a wife or the love of his life. Unfortunately, thick, barrier walls of communication formed between us. He rarely took me anywhere. I was either at home, work, or church. We did nothing together except sleep in the same bed.

I thought maybe this child will mend some of the things that were broken in this marriage; maybe it will be a miracle glue from God. Whatever the case, I was pregnant and this baby was due in October. Carlos Carlton Lewis was born November 7, at 8:20 a.m. after five hours of labor. He weighted eight pounds and nine ounces. He was twenty inches long. Carlos was the image of Carl with his medium brown complexion and dark brown curly hair. He should have been called Carl Jr..

The day after Carlos's birth, Dr. Barrett came into my room with papers to get my tubes tied. I declined. I was young, only thirty years old. I knew I didn't want anymore of Carl's children. But I wasn't absolutely sure I didn't want anymore children.

The addition of Carlos neutralized our differences. Carl and I were one again. Our relationship was back on track. We all took delight in watching Carlos. Little Carl liked the idea of having a playmate. The two of them became very close, almost inseparable. We were a happy family again. Sometimes, babies have a way of buffering acidic relationships.

# SIXTEEN

In December of 1987, Carl noticed a lump on his chest. It was in the same place where another one had grown years ago. He had the first lump removed, but now it had grown back. Eventually, he thought the lump would disappear. But months had passed, and it was getting larger and becoming sore. We were lying in bed early one Saturday morning when Carl pulled up his T-shirt and showed me the lump on his chest at his left breast.

"Vanessa, look at this knot."

"How did you get that?"

"Someone hit me playing basketball this summer. I thought it would go away, but it hasn't. It's beginning to hurt when I touch it. It's also getting bigger."

I examined the one-inch lump. It was darker than the rest of his body. "Why don't you make an appointment with Dr. Barrett so he can look at it. If it's bothering you, you need to get it checked out."

"I think I will. This is the same spot where I had another knot removed. I wonder why it keeps coming back?"

"I don't know. But you need to find out," I said, hugging him, being careful not to touch the spot he was guarding.

"Will you call to make me an appointment with Dr. Barrett?" He pulled his T-shirt down and stared at the bedcovers.

"Sure. He'll probably see you next week. I'll call today as soon as his office opens."

"Thanks. This will be one less thing to worry about."

"How about some breakfast? What would you like?" I asked, attempting to cheer him up and get his mind off of the lump. I jumped out of bed.

"Eggs, grits, bacon, toast, and coffee." He watched me go into the bathroom. "Bring me my cigarettes when you come out." His cigarettes were on the ironing board near the bathroom door.

I gave him his cigarettes then went back into the bathroom to turn off the light. "Breakfast will be ready in a jiffy. I'll bring you your coffee first to go with your cigarette," I said, after washing up.

"I think I left my book on the table. Bring it up with my coffee if you see it."

When I left the room, his spirit seemed lifted. Cigarettes and food always had a way of cheering him up.

Dr. Barrett, our general practitioner, was booked for the year. He had an opening the first week in January. Carl took the appointment. After examining

Carl, Dr. Barrett felt the lump was serious. He referred Carl to an oncologist, Dr. Rosenfield, who promptly scheduled Carl for a biopsy.

Two weeks later, the results of the biopsy proved Carl needed surgery to remove the lump. The surgery was scheduled for March 17.

Carl wasn't happy about having another surgery. He hated doctors. He associated doctors with knives and pain. He didn't want his body cut on again, but he knew he didn't have a choice. The knot was not leaving on its own. It was getting bigger and sorer. This time the growth was different than the first time. Hopefully, this surgery will be the second and last time he would have to deal with the knot.

Before his surgery, Carl suggested we take out a third mortgage on the house to get caught up on his bills. He knew he would be out of work for awhile and wanted everything squared away before the surgery. We went the following week to take out a third mortgage of two thousand dollars. The second mortgage was for five thousand dollars. We took it out when I went on six months maternity leave with Carlos. Carl and I never have been big savers. It seemed as if our living expenses took all that we made, but our house proved to be a gold mine, an easy way to get extra money when we needed it. Having three mortgages on the house didn't bother us. Debt was a way of life. We believed tomorrow will take care of itself. Today, we needed the money; that's all that mattered.

Carl's surgery went well. The lump was removed. Dr. Rosenfield cut out all the flesh surrounding the lump, down to the ribs. If the lump grew back, there was nowhere else to cut. Carl required seven radiation treatments after the surgery. The lump was a tumor called a sarcoma or cancer. His prognosis was good with the radiation treatments to kill any remaining cells left from the surgery. Carl was reassured he should have no future reoccurrences of the tumor. He was young, thirty-four, with the remainder of his life to be cancer free.

Although Carl had a good prognosis, he thought he was dying. The thought of cancer cells invading his body made him freak, mentally. Unfortunately, I wasn't aware of how he felt until later. Carl concealed his feelings. Even though he appeared fine on the outside, his inside was in turmoil.

Carl's radiation treatments began one week post-op. I accompanied him to some treatments, some he attended alone. The treatments left a dark brown, almost black discoloration on his chest. It was quite noticeable without his shirt. The treatments didn't make him physically ill, only mentally unstable.

Family and friends came in droves during his convalescence which lasted for a short while. Afterwards, it was back to the rat race of work and every day life, or so I thought.

On Wednesday, April 6, I received a call at work from a fellow church member, Pamela Benson. I was surprised to hear from her, especially, since we never talked on the phone before. We only spoke to each other in passing at church.

"Vanessa, you have a call on line two," announced Robin from her desk.

I was sitting at the computer terminal, near the second telephone, entering results. "Hello," I said, picking up the receiver.

"Hello Vanessa, this is Pamela Benson from church."

"Pam. What a surprise. How did you get this number?"

"You gave it to me last year when you tried to sell me life insurance, remember?"

"Oh yeah. I forgot about that. Are you ready to buy life insurance?"

"No. I called because I need a place to stay. I was wondering if you have room for me at your house?"

"I'm sorry, Pam. My house is small. It is full with just my family. Most of the times, we get in each other's way. No. I don't have room for you or anybody else."

"Do you know anybody in the church who has an extra bedroom that they want to rent?"

"No. I can't think of anyone at the moment. Maybe, you can ask around this Sabbath."

"Well...thank you anyway. Goodbye."

"Goodbye." It was odd of her to ask me that, I thought as I hung up the phone. My house was full with the four of us. The boys shared one bedroom. The other bedroom was a den. I couldn't believe she called me at work to ask to live with me. I was not the one. I soon forgot about the call and continued my work.

April 8, was a Holy Day for me which meant being in church all day. The boys and I went to services while Carl went to work. When we returned home at 7 p.m., Carl greeted us, took the boys, entertained them, bathed them, and put them to bed by 9:00.

"Vanessa, I want to talk with you after I put the boys to bed," Carl said, marching them into their bedroom.

"Okay. I'll wait for you in the living room," I told him. Minutes later, Carl joined me in the living room. I was sitting on the sofa, facing the steps. My right arm was behind my head, propping it up. He walked down the steps with an envelope in his hand and his rust colored jacket on.

"I'm leaving you," he said, handing me the envelope. He walked towards the door, opened it, went outside, and locked it. He was gone. He never looked back. He didn't say anything else.

I stared at the locked door. I must be dreaming. Lord, wake me up, please! Tell me, Lord, this is not really happening. My husband of thirteen years just walked out on me, our sons, the three mortgages, and all these other bills. I sat motionless in a daze. Suddenly, I remembered the letter in my hand. I examined the outside. It read: To Vanessa From Carl. I ripped it open and removed the one page letter inside. I read it. It said:

*Dear Vanessa,*

*I know this letter will come as a shock to you. I am leaving you and our sons. I have taken everything out of the house which belongs to me. Everything left is yours.*

*I am sorry to break your heart. I can not explain why I am leaving in this letter.*

*We have gone through a lot together. I never thought it would end this way.*

*Forget me. Go on with your life. Explain to Carl and Carlos the best way you can. Tell them, I love them very much. Kiss them for me when you do. I wanted to tell you to your face, but felt this way was best. I am leaving so I can be happy at last. I was not happy with you. And if you think about it, you were not happy with me. You can have the boys and the house.*

*Carl*

When I finished reading the letter, I was stunned. The days of living at home with Dad conditioned me not to cry when my feelings were hurt. I kept my emotions locked up inside. I stared at the letter and the door for ten minutes, thinking he'll be back. He'll walk through the door any minute now. I was wrong. The minutes turned into hours, without him returning. Reality set in. I went to my bedroom, fell down on my knees and cried out to my heavenly Father, and elder brother, Jesus Christ:

*Oh, loving and merciful Father.*
*I know Thou art with me. Please*
*put Your loving arms around me*
*and comfort me. Please help me*
*through this dark, dark hour.*
*Give me the strength to carry on.*
*I don't understand what is*
*happening, but You do. You said,*
*You will never leave me or forsake*
*me. Tonight, Your words are truly*

*encouraging. Everything*
*happens for good to those who*
*love You and are called according*
*to your purpose. I don't understand*
*the good in this, but I*
*believe Your Word.*
*I know I am not able to pay all the bills of*
*this household which have been*
*suddenly placed on my shoulders.*
*I give them to You. They are*
*Your burden, not mine.*
*Father, I pray You open a door*
*to me for overtime at work.*
*Monday morning, I will ask*
*Samantha if I can work overtime*
*in her lab. I pray You grant*
*me favor in her sight.*
*Give me the courage and wisdom to*
*raise my sons. Father, they are*
*not mine but Yours. You have*
*granted me the opportunity to*
*share them with You. They and*
*I belong to You. Keep us in*
*Your fold. Embrace us with*
*Your love. Let our lives*
*glorify You. I will praise*
*You no matter what happens,*
*in the good times and the bad.*
*My faith will not be moved.*
*In Jesus Christ name I pray. Amen.*

The boys woke up bright and early the next morning. They came running into my room, jumping on my bed.

"Mama. Mama. Wake up! Wake up!" shouted little Carl, pulling the covers off my head.

Carlos was helping Carl. "Ma. Up. Up. Ma."

I stuck my head out from the covers, not wanting to get up. I looked at my babies. "Good morning, sons," I said, sitting up.

"Mama. Where's Daddy?" Little Carl asked sitting on his dad's side of the bed.

"Da da, da da," chanted Carlos.

I embraced my babies. "Your dad is gone. He doesn't live here anymore. He left last night after putting you to bed."

"Why he leave? Is he coming back?"

"That's a good question, Carl. Only God knows. Mama doesn't know. He still loves you. He even wanted me to give you a kiss." I kissed their cheeks. Carl started crying. He loved his dad. I held him closer and wiped his tears away. Carlos wasn't really clear on what was going on. I held them as long as they wanted to be held.

"Mama, where's my daddy? Why he go?" Carl asked with his head on my breast.

"I wish I knew, son. We must pray God will give us the answer."

"Eat. Mama. Eat. I wanna eat."

"Okay, Carlos. I'll fix breakfast. Y'all have to help me make it."

"Let me get my car and truck first, Mama."

"Ball. Ball."

"We don't have much time to waste. We have to get ready for church," I shouted as they ran out of the room.

They ran into their room for their toys. They asked more questions. I was able to answer some, most were unanswered.

That morning, I saw Pamela Benson in church. I asked her if she still needed a place to stay? She said, "yes." I told her she was welcomed to stay with me. She accepted. She wanted to move in the first of May.

Pamela was in her early twenties. She loved wearing hats to compliment her stylish outfits. At church, she was dressed to kill. Her coca brown complexion and Chaka Khan build, heavy on the top and bottom, made her stick out like a sore thumb. Pam lived in Newnan, Georgia with her parents and four sisters. She was offered a job in Atlanta and needed to relocate. I charged her two hundred and twenty-five dollars a month for rent. The arrangement worked well for both of us.

Pam living with me was definitely God sent. God knew Carl was leaving when Pamela called me at work, two days prior. He sent her to me for spiritual solace and financial help. God knows everything. God is good! Pam moved in the first week in May. She proved to be a blessing. She kept the boys while I worked overtime shifts in Hematology. Her favorite pastime was reading church literature and The Bible. It felt so good to talk about God at home. Religion was a taboo subject with Carl and I because it generally led to an argument.

Carl came by periodically and called occasionally. I never knew when I would see or hear from him. As a result, the kids became emotionally disturbed. It was very painful for little Carl to be separated from his dad. He cried and asked for him constantly. He loved his dad so much. At home, he was solemn and despondent. The only thing that perked him up was being with his dad. The minute they separated, he returned into his depressed cocoon. Carlos screamed to the top of his lungs when Carl departed. It took every ounce of strength in me to restrain him. He cried with his arms stretched towards his dad. He didn't want Carl to leave because he didn't know when he was coming back. He loved his dad very much, too. Carlos began to stutter. His speech became incoherent.

Witnessing the destruction of my children shattered my broken heart even more. How could any man abandon his family who loved him so much? The cancer wouldn't kill Carl, but his actions were killing us. We died a slow death, daily.

I felt my husband, whom I loved, died on the operating table. In my opinion, Carl rose from the operation table a new man. The Carl who came up was cold, indifferent, and angry with God. His body was free of cancer, but he was riddled with anger. I felt he was angry with God for allowing him to have cancer. How could he serve a God who allowed such a thing to happen to him?

When Carl turned from God, he gave Satan the opportunity to have dominion over him. The mind coupled with Satan and his demons can destroy a healthy mind, body, soul, marriage, and family. The devastation is REAL! It can be IRREVOCABLE!

Carl lived in the heart of the slums near the Atlanta Fulton County Stadium, it was adjacent to Summerhill, where my dad lived with Big Mama and Pop, who were now deceased. Summerhill was known as Crack County, home of the crack cocaine addicts. The way he was acting, I thought he was an addict, too. His place reminded me of how he lived before we were married. I couldn't believe he would return to living that way. An eerie feeling came over me when I entered his neighborhood and saw his house.

The houses were small, wooden framed and set on a parcel of land which was separated by a driveway with a stone's throw of yard in the front. Carl's slum house was white with two levels of steps, four steps led to the sidewalk and eight steps led to the house. The tiny yard and walkway to the driveway separated the two levels. The driveway was bordered with chain linked fences on both sides.

Carl's house had a living room, kitchen, one bathroom, and two moderate size bedrooms. The two bedrooms had double beds and long mahogany dressers with mirrors. A small gas heater was in the front guest bedroom, adjacent to the living room. The remainder of the house was heated electrically. The rectangular living room was furnished with a very used pre-antique sofa and chairs. They looked so bad, if they had been on the street, no one would have taken them, even in his neighborhood.

The Saturday before Memorial Day, Carl had a party without inviting me. However, he volunteered to keep the boys since I had to work and Pam had plans. That Saturday night, a bright idea came to me. I was going to the party, uninvited and unannounced. Boy, was that a bad idea.

I parked my car on the street in front of Carl's house and went to the back yard where I heard music. It was 9 o'clock, two hours before my shift started at work. I entered the fenced yard by opening the unlocked gate. Five people were sitting in green folding chairs, talking, clustered around the back steps and barbecue grill. Their backs were facing me and no one heard or saw me enter the yard because of the loud music.

Smoke ascended from the grill carrying a burnt meat aroma. Carl was famous for burning food. When he said he could burn in the kitchen, he meant it literally. As I drew closer, I saw plates of black chicken, blistered wieners on burnt buns, blacken corn in the husk, straight from the can pork and beans, and white bread smothered in Carl's not so famous mustard and vinegar barbecue sauce. He said it was his mama's secret recipe. I felt everyone would be better off if they both knew how to keep a secret. Whatever the secret was, I damn sho' didn't want to know it. The sauce was totally disgusting.

The five people resembled living zombies. They were the closest thing I've ever seen to death this side of the grave. They had to live in the ground and come up at night. They were razor thin in weight. Their faces looked like clay replica's of a starving Cheeta on Tarzan. They were just as ugly, too. The five consisted of three ladies and two men.

Carl came from the kitchen unto the back porch as I reached the end of the patio where a vacant chair was.

"What are you doing here? Carl asked me with a Colt 45 in one hand and a pan of raw chicken in the other. "I thought you had to work tonight."

Carl didn't make a scene, but I knew I wasn't welcomed. I was an uninvited party-pooper. His friends were so out-of-it, they didn't have a clue who I was or who they were.

"Hello, everyone," I said to the group before I answered Carl.

"Hi, hello, hey, yeah, what's happening," were the replies.

I know you didn't invite me to your party, Carl, but I thought I'd surprise you and come. I didn't think it mattered, one way or the other, "I said, walking toward him.

"No. I guess it doesn't. Hey, everybody this is my wife, Vanessa," Carl shouted to his living-dead guest.

They mumbled a few inaudible sounds. Their attention was focused on their plates and the music.

"Do you want something to eat?" Carl asked, putting the chicken down on the table next to the grill.

"No thank you. I'm not hungry."

He opened the grill, exposing more black chicken.

99

"I thought this chicken was done. Looks like it will be another fifteen minutes before it's ready."

I couldn't believe him. If that chicken cooked another second, it would make The Guinness Book of Records for having the most burnt areas on a food item without being completely burnt-up. Carl added a new dimension to being burnt-to-a-crisp in his cooking.

"Carl, I think the chicken is ready. It looks done to me."

"There you go, telling me what to do. This chicken will be ready when I say it is ready. And I say it has fifteen more minutes." He closed the hood, grabbed his Colt 45 and finished it off. "Hey does anybody want anything from the house?" he shouted to the group. "What about you Lewis? Can I get you another brew?"

"Nah, man. I'm straight. I haven't finished this one." He lifted his beer up and gulped it down.

The others did not respond. They were looking at us, drinking their beer, eating their burnt food.

"Gimmie mo chicken, man," said the other man, licking his fingers then wiping his mouth with the back of his hand. "Gimmie a suds, too. Ain't nothing in this one." He threw the empty bottle in the trash can next to him. His cut-off jeans and black T-shirt reeked of a nauseous body odor.

"I want another hot dog, but I can get it myself," said the tall, thin dark woman with skin tight, black pants and dark brown blouse. Her hair was a combination of short fro and a curl which needed re-doing. The roots were very, very nappy. The ends had one-half inch of curl. Her hair was matted down to her head. She either needed a super perm kit, or a pair of hedge clippers to get it back right.

"Where are the boys?" I asked Carl. "I want to see them before I leave. I don't feel welcomed, so I won't stick around any longer. I'm sorry for intruding on your party."

"The boys are inside, but I don't want you to go inside."

"Why not? What are you hiding? I have a right to see them." I ran up the steps into the house. What is he doing to my kids over here? What is he hiding? I thought to myself.

"Stop! Vanessa don't...," he said, running after me.

He was too late. I was inside. I walked through the empty kitchen. I heard noises coming from the adjoining living room. I entered the room. My boys were watching TV with six other kids their ages. Carl was sitting on the sofa and Carlos was sitting on the floor in front of the TV. Two women, who looked just as strange and deranged as the others, were chaperoning the children. Carl snatched me from behind and ushered me out the front door.

"You must leave, NOW!" he commanded. "Come on Carl and Carlos, we are taking your mother home."

"Ah, Dad, we're watching a movie. It's not over yet," chimed little Carl.

"I don't care. Come on, less go!" He grabbed Carlos while still holding on to me. We left his house with his guests inside.

"Let go of me!" I said, releasing myself from his firm grasp. "What are you doing? Why are you leaving your party? What is wrong with you? Are you on drugs?" Carl made no attempt to answer any of my questions. He was too busy walking to the car.

"Look. I don't want you around this." He stopped abruptly and turned me to face him.

"Around what?"

"Around this?" He waved his free arm through the air, pointing to the neighborhood.

We continued to walk toward the car. When we reached the car, he opened all the doors with his key. He put Carlos in the back seat. Carl and I got in on the other side. Carl cranked the car and sped off.

"What's going on? What are you doing?"

He didn't answer me. He drove with a troubled expression.

"Daddy, daddy. Where are we going?" asked little Carl.

"I don't know son. Sit back and enjoy the ride."

"Carl, where are you taking us? Talk to me. What are you doing?"

"I don't want you around that. You shouldn't have come."

He drove completely around I-285. He drove and drove and drove. He wouldn't talk. He just drove.

I didn't know what was going on with him. Something was terribly wrong with my husband. But what? What did he want to hide from me but didn't mind exposing his sons to? Why did his new friends look dead? Why? Why? Why? Carl refused to answer any of my questions, therefore, I had to draw my own conclusion: my husband was strung out on drugs. He left me to live his life with his crack-head friends. Why Carl? Why?

We returned to his house by 10:30. Everyone was gone. The party was over. I had enough time to get to work on time. I left the boys there with Carl. I couldn't believe what had transpired. Lord, please wake me up. I must be dreaming.

# SEVENTEEN

Carl refused to answer my questions no matter how much I pleaded. Therefore, I spent many nights in my room searching The Bible for answers to my unanswered questions. In God's Word, I found peace and comfort for my troubled mind. The most comforting Scripture I read was at the end of Hebrews 13:5, "I will never fail you nor forsake you." When the man of my life walked out on our children and me, the reassurance that Jesus Christ, The Almighty, will never leave me meant so much. I knew I was abandoned but not alone. My God was with me. He would be with me all the days of my life, guaranteed.

Internally, I felt like my insides were coming out. I felt torn in two. The oneness I had while married was now being torn asunder. Marriage makes you and your spouse one. It doesn't matter how good or bad the relationship is, the two of you become one. I began to experience the removal of our oneness bond. I was becoming a separate entity again, and the process was very painful.

Emotionally, I couldn't cope with the anger and hurt.They were both turned inward to cause a severe depression. Sure, I appeared normal on the outside. No one but God knew how much I hurt on the inside. My physical consolation was a bowl of ice cream. After I put the kids to bed, I relaxed on the love seat in my bedroom with my Bible and a bowl of ice cream. I was comforted by both before I went to sleep.

In June, Carl experienced a turn for the worst. First, he received a letter from Lockheed stating he was due to be laid off at the end of the month. Lockheed was a great place to work. It had excellent benefits and pay. But their only downfall was frequent layoffs. This was the first layoff that affected Carl since he started working for them. His seniority was nothing compared to the countless other people who worked at Lockheed for eons. Second, one week after he was laid off, his house caught on fire.

Two o'clock in the morning, the door bell rang. Someone kept pounding on the door before I answered it. I peeped outside, it was Carl. I opened the door. He rushed inside.

"My house just caught on fire," he said, excitedly. He had on a pair of white, soiled, painter's overalls that had a peculiar odor.

"What happened?" I said, sitting down on the sofa.

"I was in the kitchen cooking. Then I heard something go "pop" in the front of the house. I left the kitchen and went to the living room to investigate the noise. I saw smoke coming from the front bedroom as I stepped into the living room. When I looked inside the bedroom, I saw flames leaping from the walls, setting the curtains on fire. I ran out the room, dialed 911 and got the hell out of there."

"What started the fire?"

"I didn't stay long enough to find out. The fireman said the gas heater in the bedroom started the fire. When he told me that, I thanked God for not allowing the fire to happen while the boys were there. You know, that's where they sleep when they stay with me. They slept in that room yesterday."

"God is so good, isn't He? He spared our sons from a tragedy."

"I know. He spared my ass, too. I escaped in my pajamas."

"Where did you get the overalls?

"When I saw those flames, I didn't care about nothing but getting my ass out of there. I ran across the street to Blade's house. He gave me these overalls. Everything else burned up. The house burned to the ground."

"How long did it take the fireman to come?"

"At least fifteen minutes. You know, they take their sweet time for us. We don't have much to begin with, and the little bit we do have they figure it ain't worth saving anyway."

"You're lucky you didn't burn up, too. You could have been asleep."

I've thought about that. I thanked God that didn't happen either. I know I'm no saint, but I see He still loves my black ass."

"Can I get you anything?"

"Yes. I came by to get some blankets and bed covers." He remained standing, pacing back and forth with his head hung down and his hands in his pockets.

"Is that it? That's all you want? Do you have a place to stay?"

"Yes."

"Are you okay?"

"Yes, I'm okay. I didn't get burned, and I was running too fast to inhale any smoke."

"Something's wrong. You don't look right."

He stopped pacing, reached into his shirt pocket and pulled out his cigarettes. He took one out and lit it. The cigarette calmed him down. He sat down on the adjacent loveseat.

"It seems like everything is happening to me, right now. First, being laid off, now this." He took several puffs. "I'll make it though. God will see me through," he said, exhaling a cloud of smoke into the air.

"Yes, He will. He always does."

Suddenly, he stood up and extinguished the cigarette butt in the ashtray on the end table between us.

"I'll get the covers. I don't want to keep you up. You have to go to work in a few hours."

"Are you sure that's all you need?"

"I'm sure." He walked up the steps to the linen closet in the hallway, took the blankets and bedcovers out, and came back down the steps. "I'm gone. Thanks for the covers." He opened the door and left.

Carl was in like lightning and out like the wind and just as unpredictable. I thought about his house, thanked God the kids were safe at home and returned to my bed. It felt as though the alarm went off as soon as I fell asleep. Today would be routine for me. But for Carl, with no job, no home, and no possessions, how would his day be, certainly not routine.

The next night, a salesperson called with a good deal on carpet. I made an appointment to meet with him at the end of the week. The gold carpet was badly soiled, thin in areas, and overall in very poor condition. It needed replacing. The golden years were unquestionably over. A new era in our marriage had begun.

The salesperson came at his appointed time. After examining the different swatches of carpet, I selected baby-blue for the great room, hall, steps, and master bedroom. For the kids room, I selected burnt-brown. I chose off-white for Pam's bedroom. Since I had not purchased carpet before, I wasn't sure how much it cost. The salesperson quoted me a price of seventeen hundred and fifty-seven dollars. Of course, what I selected was not the best they had to offer, but it was the best I could afford. The carpet was installed the following week.

Another salesperson called the week the carpet was installed. He had a good deal on vinyl siding. I'd wanted siding for several years but could never afford it. This salesperson gave me a deal I couldn't refuse. I chose baby blue. He paid the balance of the second mortgage and refinanced a new one. I signed a contract with the company, making them the new second mortgage lenders. The payments were only thirty-five dollars more. With the addition of the carpet and siding, the house received a much needed facelift. My spirits were lifted as well.

As life would have it, with ups, come downs. I received a letter from GMAC a few days after the siding was installed. Carl was two months behind on the 1985 Grand Prix I leased in my name. They wanted to repossess it as soon as possible. Unfortunately, since the car was in my name, I was responsible for the four thousand dollar balance after it was auctioned. I explained my situation to GMAC. They agreed to let me pay twenty-five dollars a month without interest or penalties until the balance was paid.

I needed the wound of my broken marriage closed. The new carpet and siding worked only as band-aids. The pain of losing Carl was too great. I needed to be healed. By the end of July, I realized I needed to get on with my life. I made an appointment with Ronald Smith, a lawyer in Lithonia. He was the same lawyer Beneficial Finance used to collect five thousand dollars from Carl when he defaulted on their loan. I figured if he was good enough for Beneficial, he was good enough for me.

The cost of the divorce was two hundred and fifty dollars. I paid the full amount before I left. The divorce settlement included custody of the kids and the house, nothing else mattered. I was tired of hurting and trying to figure out what was wrong with Carl. It was obvious, he was happy without us. I had come to grips with that fact. The same Friday I went to Mr. Smith, Carl came by. He wanted to take us for a drive. The kids and I piled into my Camaro. He drove. During the course of the drive, we talked.

"I went to Ronald Smith today to file for a divorce. I asked for custody of the kids and the house," I said, facing him.

"I don't want a divorce. I love you. I want to come back home," he said with one eye on the road and the other eye on me.

"I'm getting a divorce because you won't tell me anything. You keep me guessing and wondering what's going on with you. You seem to be happy without us."

"That's not true. I'm not happy. I realized I made a mistake, a big one, when I left you."

"Why do you insist on keeping me in the dark? You won't tell me what's going on."

"I'll do whatever it takes to get us back together. Go ahead, ask me anything you want to know. I'll answer all your questions."

"Are you on drugs?"

"The only drug I use is marijuana. I'm too smart to do crack and cocaine. They're a fool's drug. You know, I ain't never been no fool."

"Explain what happened Memorial Day weekend."

"I didn't want you in that environment. I charged crack addicts a fee to use my house to get high. It was all business, baby. I used my head to make money. It was my way of making ends meet."

"Why did you leave home?"

"I was involved in some illegal shit. I didn't want any harm to come to you and the boys. I love y'all too much."

"If it was so bad that you left us to do it, I don't want to know what it is. But what puzzles me is, what made you get into something illegal in the first place?"

"For the m-o-n-e-y, baby. I wanted a better life for us. I know, I haven't been much of a provider in the past. There have been many times I've wanted to buy you and the boys something but didn't have no money. Since I thought I was leaving this world soon, I wanted my last days to be prosperous. I wanted you to have everything money could buy."

"Money can't buy love and happiness. Instead of making our lives better, you made it worst. Your leaving us turned our world upside down. We are all emotional wrecks. Satan dangled a golden carrot in your face, and you fell for his trap. He didn't tell you the whole story, how it would destroy your family and eventually cause you to loose that which you wanted to improve. There are no winners with Satan. His purpose is to kill, steal, and destroy. I'd say he did a pretty good job. He is a master at it."

"You're right. I never thought about it that way. I only saw the money and what it could buy."

"Carl, you know, I'm not a material person. I could care less about money and what it can buy. You mean everything to us. We rather have you any day than all the money in the world with your broke, homeless, carless, jobless ass."

"I don't want a divorce. Will you forgive me and take me back? I love you. Please, let's get back together. I've made a terrible mistake."

He pulled the car over and parked it on the side of the road. He then pulled me over to his side of the car. We kissed, embraced, and cried together.

"Look Carlos. Mommie and Daddy are kissing." I heard Carl say. They both were giggling in the back.

"Why day cry?" asked Carlos.

"I don't know. Parents act crazy sometimes. You'll find out as you get older."

"I'll call Mr. Smith, Monday, to cancel the divorce," I said, wiping the tears from my eyes.

"Good." He wiped his eyes, too. "Let's eat to celebrate." He turned around to face the boys. "Sons, I'm coming home."

"When?" asked little Carl.

Carl looked at me.

"Today," I said, smiling at them.

"Yippee! Yippee!" they thundered in the back. "Daddy's coming home. Daddy's coming home," they sang.

"Now that that's settled. Do you have any money so we can eat?"

"Yes, I do. Welcome back Carl. Somethings never change."

"That's my wife," he said, cranking up the car.

"That's my Carl," I said, laying my head on his shoulders as he drove off.

# EIGHTEEN

Monday, I contacted Mr. Smith. I told him I had changed my mind about the divorce. Carl and I had reconciled our differences. Our marriage was intact. He informed me his services cost fifty dollars. His secretary would send me a two hundred dollar check. The call to Mr. Smith made it a done deal. I was done with the whole divorce business. It was time to rekindle a smoldering fire.

Now, I was faced with telling Pam, Carl was moving back in. Pam and Carl got along like polyester pants and a silk top—they clashed. I broke the news to Pam when we returned from our drive. Carl dropped me off at the house. He took my car and the kids to get his belongings. Pam was in the kitchen eating dinner when I entered the house.

"Hi, Pam. What are you eating? It must be good whatever it is," I said, walking toward her.

"Texas chicken wangs, tater fritters, and stuffed cabbage rolls." She was smacking on the wangs as she spoke, swinging a naked bone in the air. "Where's the boys?"

"I want to talk to you about that." I sat down in the chair I was standing near. Pam stuck her fork in the cabbage roll. Something green, yellow, and brown oozed out. I almost lost my train of thought when I saw the gooey concoction. "What's in that cabbage roll?"

"Minced yellow and zucchini squash and peanut butter. It's delicious, here try some," she said, scooping up more on her fork and pointing it at me.

"No thank you. I'll pass."

"What did you want to talk about?" she asked, popping a whole tater fritter in her mouth the size of a biscuit.

"Carl is coming back home. We reconciled."

Pam choked on the fritter then spit it out in my face. I jumped from the table and ran for a paper towel a few feet away and wiped white, yellow, green and brown slime off my face. I grabbed more paper towels, added water and dish washing liquid. I scrubbed my face so hard skin came off.

"I'm sorry. I'm sorry," Pam said over and over.

I felt so nasty; I ran upstairs, filled my tub with hot water and soaked for an hour. By then, Carl and the kids were home. After that incident, I learned never to talk to Pam while she was eating.

Carl came into the bedroom with the kids. They were all loaded down with Carl's stuff. Carlos carried his dad's record collection. It consisted of three tapes. The fire destroyed the other four hundred tapes and albums.

Pam came from her room when she heard the commotion and stuck her head out of her door.

"Hey Miss Bidson," said little Carl on his way downstairs.

"What you doing?" she asked.

"Helping my daddy move back home. He has more things in the car for me to get. Miss Bidson, why you ain't sleepin? Why you ain't readin? My Mama says all you do is sleep and read."

"Is that right. What else did she say?"

"Mama say you eat strange food and you eat with your fingers. My mama tells me not to eat with my fingers. Your mama must didn't tell you not to eat with your fingers?"

"My mama told me a lot of things, especially not to repeat what she said."

"My mama never told me that."

"I know."

I came out of the bedroom. "Carl you don't have time to talk. Go finish helping your dad."

"Okay Mama," he said as he ran down the steps.

"Is he disturbing you? Did he wake you up?"

"No, he didn't. I was reading and licking my fingers while eating a bag of parsley flavored carrot chips," she said as she slammed the door.

"What's wrong with her? She must have eaten a bad chip." I let the matter rest and helped Carl get settled in.

It felt good being a family again. The boys wouldn't let Carl get out of their sight. Everywhere he went, they went, too. Carl took up a lot of time with them. He spoiled me with attention as well.

Everything was sailing smoothly until the second week in August when he received a separation check from Lockheed. I was standing in the kitchen, going through the mail, when I came across an envelope, for Carl, from Lockheed. "Carl, you have a letter from Lockheed. It looks like a check," I screamed from the bottom of the steps.

"A check! I'll be right down." He ran from the bedroom and jumped down the steps.

"Wow! I haven't seen you move that fast since that big, black dog chased you up a six foot fence."

"Where's the check?"

"Here it is," I said, waving it in the air.

He snatched it from my hand and ripped it open. He took the check out. His eyes lit up. I examined it. My eyes lit up, too. The check was for $5,857.92. I instantly thought of all the bills I would pay.

"Yes! Yes!" He shouted and danced around the room. "Payday is here! Vanessa, let me use your car. I want to cash this check."

"Sure. My keys are in my purse, upstairs."

"Baby, things are going to turn around. This check is the answer." He kissed me and ran up the steps. Within seconds, he had gotten the keys and left the house like a whirlwind.

Hours passed before Carl returned home. I had my list ready of the bills I wanted to pay and the things I wanted to buy with my portion of the check. When I heard the key in the door, I ran down the steps.

"What took you so long?"

"I had a lot of errands to run," he said walking past me to go into the kitchen.

"Did you cash the check?"

"Yeah." He opened the refrigerator, took the cold water out, opened the cabinet, retrieved a glass, and poured himself a glass of water.

"How much are you going to give me?"

He reached in his pants pocket and pulled out a fat roll of dollar bills. He took two bills from the roll and put the rest back into his pocket. "Here you go. You can have this." He gave me the two bills.

I took the bills. They were two fifties. "Is this all I get? One hundred dollars."

"That's all. You better be glad I gave you that," he said in his nasty, you little bitch tone. He walked past me and headed for the den, downstairs.

Motionless from shock, I remained in the kitchen. I was too shocked to cry and too hurt to argue. He made me feel like a dumb, used fool. Hours later, after I had gotten over the shock, I asked Carl for money to register little Carl for private school. He was still in the den watching T.V., reclined on the sofa, drinking a beer. When I entered the room, his eyes never left the screen.

"Carl, I need $250 to register Carl next week for school."

"Why are you telling me?"

"Because you have money."

"I swear!" He jumped up from the sofa, reached into his pants pocket, pulled out the roll of money, quickly counted $250 and threw it at me. "You're trying to take all my damn money. I can't have nothing without you trying to take it." He returned to his position on the couch. His eyes once again glued to the T.V..

I left the room $250 richer but more hurt than before. Later that evening, his brother, Egghead, picked him up. Carl returned, driving a light-gray Ford Mustang.

Carl found a job, welding, by the end of the week. He contributed it to having transportation. Carl said, jobs were more available off the bus line. He felt, everything was beginning to work out for him. He, now, had a car, a job, a place to stay, and his family back. Everything was working except our relationship. It was not the same—an unquestionable distance was between us.

The rose colored glasses had been removed. I saw Carl for who he was. He no longer was the man I wanted him to be or mistakenly thought he was. The scales and blinders were gone. My naiveness was also gone. I read his opened mail. I made it my business to know as much as possible about Carl without appearing to pry or be nosy. My man left me once without warning. The next time, I would know. I would be aware in advance.

I knew, financially, I could never depend on him. I always had to be prepared for the "next time" he walked out. When a person leaves once, they will probably leave again. I prepared myself financially, mentally, spiritually, emotionally, and sexually. I knew, I must separate myself in all these areas while he was with me. I made strategic defensive moves with every offensive blow.

Carl gave me fifty dollars from his first pay check. He said, he needed to catch up on his bills. The second check, he gave me twenty-five dollars.

"Carl I need more than twenty-five dollars. You know we have three mortgages, private school, and day care. Not to mention, utilities, car notes, car insurance, groceries, and other bills. What is twenty-five dollars?" I asked with my hand still out as we stood in the kitchen.

"Twenty-five dollars is all you get. You better ask Christ to bless it and multiply it like He did the fish and loaves of bread. That's all the bread you'll get from me."

"Is that so. No bread. No bed. You got to go. If this is all the money you can contribute, I'm better off by myself."

"Well. That's all you damn get."

"Hit the road, Jack, and don't come back! See ya," I said, pointing to the door. The new him had met head-to-head with the new me.

Carl went upstairs. He threw his meager belongings together. Little Carl and Carlos were sitting in the living room, watching him depart. Tears streamed down little Carl's face.

"Come and hug your daddy goodbye." Carl kneeled down in front of the opened door with his arms stretched out. "Come on. Come on," he said, waving his arms.

Carlos ran into his arms and buried his head into Carl's chest. "Da da. Luv voo."

Little Carl broke the bond between them and sat on his bent knee, wiping the tears from his eyes. "Daddy, don't go. Stay with us."

"I must go son, but I'll be back. I'll be around to play ball, to ride you on my back, to take you to get ice cream, to watch you run and play, and to see you grow up to be a man." He kissed them on their foreheads. "I love you both. Be good. Don't give your mama any trouble. I must go now," he said, removing their clutches on him and standing up.

I grabbed them and held them close to me. "Your daddy has to leave. You will see him again." I reached down to pick Carlos up. He started crying. They cried as Carl walked out the door. Two hours later, they were still crying, begging for their daddy.

"He'll be back," was all I said. I was at a loss for other words.

Although I told the kids, "he'll be back." I had no intentions of ever getting back with Carl. My Carl died on the operating table. I didn't get along with this "new" Carl. Our relationship was one upheaval after the other. Good riddance, Carl. And don't come back! I thought to myself.

Carl, eventually, moved into an apartment close to the airport on Camp Creek Parkway. His new car was repossessed in December. I thought to myself, what happened to all that money? I knew Carl couldn't manage money but to blow nearly six thousand dollars so quickly was absurd. It has been said, a fool and his money will soon depart. Carl, certainly, proved that saying to be true.

Support from Carl was erratic, fifty dollars here and there. Most of the times, I received nothing. The Lord truly was my source of help, strength and support. He delivered me through this financially lean time. We never missed a meal. All my creditors were eventually paid—although my credit suffered because I couldn't pay them all on time. Those days weren't easy. They were very hard, financially, emotionally, mentally, and physically.

Spiritually, I was strong because of the strength of Jesus Christ. He carried me during this time, like in the Footprint in the Sand poem. I virtually had no strength of my own. I relied on Him completely, for everything. My relationship with Christ grew to an unprecedented level, to a new dimension. No longer was Christ someone I read of in The Bible. He literally was snatched from the pages of The Bible and placed into my heart. He became REAL. He became the LIVING CHRIST, my Lord, my Savior, my confidant, my supplier, my EVERYTHING!

I thanked Jesus Christ daily for His presence in my life. I thanked Him for the opportunity to know Him face-to-face, one-on-one. I thanked Him for allowing Carl to leave so that we could become one. Carl had been my god. I worshipped and loved him. Now that he was gone, I was granted a lasting relationship with Jesus Christ—one that will never end.

March 1989 rolled around. I was seriously contemplating divorcing Carl. Although I was married, I didn't have a marriage. They way things looked, I never would have one again. I loved Carl, but he wasn't right. I felt like, he equated love with using me. I didn't want to be used. I wanted to be loved.

Carl came by the house after I had made up my mind to file for divorce again. We were talking in my bedroom. "Carl, I've been thinking about filing for a divorce," I said, sitting on the loveseat, facing him as he sat on the bed.

"I don't want a divorce. I love you," he said with tears swelling up in his eyes.

"You have a funny way of showing your love. You don't love me. You love yourself. You love your single friends. You love the single life."

"No. You're wrong. I love you. I love my sons. I love our home, our family. I want to be a family again. I don't want a divorce." He moved from the bed and sat beside me on the loveseat. He placed my hand in his.

"I'm tired of living apart. We don't have a marriage. We don't have anything. The Carl that I loved died on the operating table," I said, removing my hand from his clasp.

"You're wrong again. I'm not new. I'm improved. I want to show you how I'm a better husband. I've been doing a lot of thinking and soul searching since we've been apart. I want our relationship to be the best its ever been."

"I don't believe you. You don't love me. You just want to use me." I stood up and sat on the bed.

He rushed over to the bed and put his arms around my shoulders. "I love you, Doll. Let me prove it to you. I don't want to use you. I love you too much. Don't you want to experience the improved me? I've changed, Baby. You'll love the difference." He kissed me on my lips. His hand slid down to my breast. He kissed my neck.

"Wait," I said. "Lock the door."

He locked the door and finished what he started. Afterwards, he moved back in. I did not file for a divorce. I loved Carl, and he loved me. I never found out about the other things, but his love making was definitely new and IMPROVED. Amen.

# NINETEEN

I was too embarrassed to inform Pam that Carl was moving back in again. Of course, I didn't care what she thought of my roller coaster marriage with its on-again, off-again ride. That night, Carl stayed over. I rose early the next morning and made breakfast for him and the boys. Pam came into the kitchen half-asleep but became wide-awake at the sight of Carl.

"What are you doing here?" Pam asked Carl as she suddenly stopped in her tracks a foot away from the kitchen. She wiped her eyes with both hands then stared at Carl.

"I live here. I ain't no ghost either. Do you have a problem with me being here Miss Buffalo Butt?"

Carl always got a rise out of Pam whenever he referred to her behind which stuck up and out. It swayed when she walked. Her small waist accented it even more.

"I guess not, Mr. Penniless Lewis. It's none of my business what you do. But if I were Vanessa, I would keep your deadbeat behind out of this house. I am sure she has her reasons for you staying here. Only Christ really knows," Pam said, walking towards the refrigerator. She opened its door and reached inside for her mango-peach juice, star fruit and prune chestnut bread. She poured herself a glass of juice, sliced a piece of bread and cut her star fruit into bitesize pieces on a plate.

"You two behave yourselves. You're acting like preschoolers. Why can't y'all get along?" I asked while sipping on my coffee at the table.

"Vanessa, Pam is your roommate, but this is my house. These are my kids," Carl said, pointing to the boys. "This is my family, my domain. I belong here, Miss Organic Breath."

"You're the one that walked out of your domain. Leaving your sons and wife behind, Mr. Crab. Oh, I mean Carl."

"Now. Now. You two stop it this minute!" I said, standing up spilling my coffee on the table.

"No, Mama. Don't stop 'em now. The good part's comin when they start throwin food at each other like they do at school," added little Carl while he was eating the last of his cereal.

"F-fight! F-fight! Da da fight," Carlos said, splashing milk on the table and floor as he banged on his highchair.

"Stop Carlos! You're making a mess, child," I shouted as I ran to get some paper towels to wipe both our spills.

113

"Da da fight. Ma ma clean. Car Car eat." Carlos looked at Pam and asked. "Wha wha you do?"

"She get the hell out of my house. That's what she do," answered Carl.

"This is not your house. It's Vanessa's. I can stay here as long as she wants me to. Isn't that right Vanessa?

"That's right. As long as you pay your rent. Speaking of which was due yesterday. You can pay me before you leave for work today."

"I am not going to work today. I lost my job last week, so I don't have all my rent money either. I was going to tell you yesterday, but you had company all night," Pam said, glaring at Carl.

"Damn right! I stayed all night. And I'll be here every night from now on. That's more than I can say for you. What did you tell me last fall, Vanessa, "No bread. No bed." Start packing Pam. Your time is up at this house."

"You don't have the right to put me out. I am Vanessa's tenant. What do you say Vanessa?"

All eyes focused on me. I stood up from wiping the milk off the floor. "Well Pam, Carl is right. You are renting your room and the use of the house. If you can't pay, you can't stay."

Pam looked bewildered and betrayed. "You don't have to do me this way Vanessa. You can let me stay without paying." She poured the last of her mango-peach juice and held the bottle firmly in her hands. A piece of bread-fruit mixture fell to the floor from her mouth.

By reflex action, I ducked under the table. When I thought the coast was clear, I came from underneath the table peeking at everyone. After positioning myself in my chair I said, "Pam, when you came, we made an agreement that you stayed here for two hundred and twenty-five dollars a month. If you can't live up to your end of the agreement, then I don't have to let you stay. I did not agree to let you stay with me for free or anything less than the two hundred and twenty-five dollars."

"I see, but I don't have anywhere to go," Pam said, looking sorrowful. "Besides, I plan to work temporary jobs to pay my rent. I start one tomorrow."

"Good. I don't care how you pay your rent. As long as you pay the full amount, you can stay. That's the agreement we made, and I will honor it."

"In that case, I will call my dad and ask him for the rest of this month's rent money. I am fifty dollars short." She breathed a sigh of relief then ate more bread and fruit.

"I'll take what you have, today, until you get the fifty dollars from your dad."

Pam reached in her long, beige housecoat and pulled a wad of money from her right pocket. She walked past Carl and handed it to me.

"Here is one hundred and seventy-five dollars. I should have the rest by tomorrow."

"Thank you. I'm sorry you lost your job. I hope the temporary job works out."

"God will supply all my needs. If this job doesn't work out, He will provide another one. Excuse me. I am going back to my room to read." She turned, walked to the living room and went up the steps.

I looked at my watch. "We have ten minutes to get out of here. Carl help them brush their teeth while I get their things together. Little Carl, wipe your mouth with your napkin. Carlos, stop making a mess!"

"Come on boys. Let's get moving." Carl helped Carlos get down from his highchair. Little Carl scooted from his chair.

"I don't wonna go to school. I wonna see Dad fight."

"F-fight. F-fight," Carlos repeated.

"The only fight you'll see is me fighting traffic if we don't hurry up," I said giving the three of them a good swat on the rear.

"Okay. Okay. We get the message," said Carl. "Let's go boys. We don't have much time."

"Dad, I'll race you and Carlos to the bathroom. The last one in is a rotten egg!" exclaimed little Carl.

"Let's go!"

The trio ran to the bathroom. I cleared the table then grabbed our things. By that time, we were all ready to go. Off to work and school we went leaving Pam behind.

For the entire month of April, Pam was in-and-out of temporary jobs. She didn't earn enough to pay her rent again; therefore, she borrowed more money from her father. He was living on disability and had four younger daughters to raise at home. He told Pam the second time that he was in no position to help her anymore with her rent.

May came and the job market completely dried up for Pam. She worked two days the whole month. Rent time rolled around. I knocked on Pam's door. It was six o'clock in the evening on a Friday. Pam opened the door wearing her PJ's, hair in rollers, face not washed, and teeth not brushed. Her breath and body odor made me take three steps back when she opened the door. Every since she lost her regular job, she had neglected her hygiene. Her total lack of interest in her appearance, which she was meticulous about before, was a sign of depression to me. Her life was crumbling before her, and she didn't quite know what to do about it.

"What do you want?" Pam asked with a doped expression.

I held my head down because her breath was kicking. It smelled too bad to be breath. It smelled more like ass.

"It's time to pay rent," I said, holding out my hand.

She turned around, went to her purse, took out some money, came back to the door and put the money in my outstretched hand. "Here's what I have."

I counted the money. It was fifty dollars. "When will you have the rest?"

"That's all I have. I won't have anymore. I only worked two days this month."

"Call your father so he can give you the rest of your rent money."

"I've called him already. He can't help me pay my rent this month. He said he doesn't have any extra money."

"In that case, call him so he can pick you up. You can't stay here if you can't pay your rent."

"Why? You can let me stay. You don't have to put me out."

She slung the door wide open. A roller fell to the floor. She put one hand on her hip and pointed the other one in my face. "You never put Carl out if he doesn't pay rent."

"Get your finger out my face, Pam." She looked at it as though she did not realize what she was doing. When she put her finger down, I continued. "That's different. Carl is my husband. Besides, what applies to him doesn't necessarily apply to you. We made an agreement that you pay two hundred and twenty-five dollars a month to stay here. If you don't pay, you can't stay."

"But Carl stays without paying. You're not being fair to me." She shook her head in disgust. "And I thought you were a Christian. When I first moved in here, I thought you were a very nice person. Now, I don't know what to think about you."

"I am still a very nice person. My being nice or not has nothing to do with this. Let me explain the difference between you and Carl. I made a marriage covenant with Carl to take him for better or worst. Unfortunately, I am experiencing the worst, right now. I must admit, you're absolutely right. He should pay to live here and he does most of the time.Granted he doesn't contribute like he should, but he pays something. He also should be the head of this house and do a lot of things he doesn't do. But that does not give me the right to put him out. He's my husband who's sitting on the fence that divides this relationship between marriage and divorce. One day, something will happen to knock him off the fence. He'll either be totally committed to this marriage or we will be divorced."

"I am on the fence, too. I am between being employed and unemployed. I just need more time."

"I'm sorry, Pam. I can't give you anymore time. Call your father today, so he can pick you up tomorrow. And, yes, I am a Christian. In Second Thessalonians 3:10-13, Christ says, *"...If anyone will not work, let him not eat. For we hear that some of you are living in idleness, mere busybodies, not doing any work. Now such persons we command and exhort in the Lord Jesus Christ to do their own work in quietness and to earn their living. Brethren, do no be weary in well-doing."* Christ, himself, tells me I'm not responsible for you. You are responsible for yourself. Call your father. I'm sorry Pam. I know you don't understand, but I'm doing the right thing." I kept the fifty dollars and walked off. The door slammed behind me.

Pam gathered her belongings, called her father later that evening and left the next day. She had stayed with me for a year. She could have stayed longer if she was able to pay her rent. I interpreted her unemployment to mean her time was up with living with me. Christ could have easily kept her employed. Obviously, her mission had been accomplished. It was time to move on.

Carl remained on the fence. Our marriage kept him rocking back-and-forth. I threatened to put him out several more times in the months to follow. Little Carl put an end to my threats, however, when he went downstairs in the basement after I had a blowout with Carl. Little Carl was sitting on the sofa crying.

"What's wrong, baby? Why are you crying?" I asked as I put my arms around him and sat next to him.

"I don't want my daddy to leave." Tears streamed down his face.

"Your dad's not leaving. We just had an argument. That's all." I held him closer.

"Anytime you argue like that, he leaves."

"Look at me, son." I lifted his face and wiped his eyes. I promise you, I'll never put your daddy out again. He'll always be with you. Okay?"

He looked up at me. The tears stopped. He smiled. "Promise, Mama."

"I promise. You can count on it. I cross my heart and hope to die." I crossed my heart with my hand.

"I love you Mama. I love Daddy, too. I hate for Daddy to leave. I hate it!" He snuggled up to my breast.

I held him close. "I love you, too." I stroked his thick, short hair." I won't hurt you anymore,baby."

He soon ran off after being assured his daddy would be with him forever, without interruption. I knew from that point on I was stuck in this disintegrating marriage, whether I liked it or not. From now on, I had to take the short end of the stick. I had to take whatever Carl dished out for the sake of our sons. We were destroying them with our actions. They had had enough. I wouldn't send them through anymore changes. I would suffer, not them.

I kept peace in the house for the sake of our sons at all cost. Carl was recalled to Lockheed by June. Although he made over thirty thousand dollars a year, he only gave me one hundred dollars a week. I didn't argue with him. I gladly took whatever he gave me.

I worked more overtime to make ends meet. Since I no longer had Pam's rent money to help with the expenses, I worked every weekend to compensate. It never mattered how much I worked to Carl. As long as he had food to eat and a roof over his head, he didn't care. He kept the boys while I worked seven days a week, week-in, week-out. The boys were happy because he kept them while I worked. They loved spending as much time with Carl as possible. They didn't miss Mama because they had Daddy. I missed them. But I knew I couldn't be in two places at one time. It was my responsibility to make sure the bills were paid.

I felt overwhelmed with working, maintaining the house, taking care of the kids when I could, and making sure everything ran smoothly. I no longer had time for me. I didn't matter anymore. I didn't exist. I gained weight. I went from one hundred twenty-three pounds to one hundred fifty-one pounds. I felt unattractive. I was depressed.

Since I was depressed and didn't have time for me anymore, I cut off my long shoulder length hair and wore a short natural. I loved it. It was a wash-and-go hair style. With my schedule, I didn't have time for anything else.

By December, I was stressed out to the max. I swallowed my pride and asked Carl to contribute more money. "Carl, you're making good money at Lockheed. It doesn't make sense for you to contribute only one hundred dollars a week. I need more money. You can easily give another fifty dollars."

"You don't need mo money. You're always trying to take my money. I ain't giving you shit."

He turned his back to me at the kitchen table after he said his piece.

"How can you sit there, making thirty-seven thousand dollars a year, and not contribute more to this household." I pulled up a chair adjacent to him at the table and looked him straight in the eyes. "What you are doing is a disgrace before God."

He pulled a cigarette out and lit it. His eyes evaded mine. "Don't put God in this. I give you money. Ask God for wisdom so you can pay the bills with what I give you. Ask Him to bless and multiply it."

"Don't you feel a responsibility to contribute more? I'm not asking for your whole paycheck, just fifty more dollars.

He threw up his hands. All right! All right! I'll give you fifty more dollars, starting next week. Will that make you happy?"

"I don't know what happiness is anymore. It will help pay the bills."

"I'm hungry. Why don't you start dinner?" he asked, finishing his cigarette and putting the butt out in the ashtray.

"I will in a few minutes. I had to ask you for more money first."

"Well, you have your extra money. Now go fix me something to eat. I'll watch the game while you cook." He left the table and went downstairs to watch TV.

While I cooked dinner, I prayed for strength to endure Carl's insensitivity. I reminded myself that The Lord was my shepherd. I shall not want. He supplied all my needs. In Him I put my trust. There is no help in man. I also knew God didn't like ugly. In my mind, Carl was destined to lose his job at Lockheed. He made too much money to contribute so little to his household.

My intuition proved to be right. The next month, January 1991, Carl got into a fight with a co-worker over a twenty-five cent cup of coffee. Witnesses said, Carl hit Buddy with a two-by-four with the intent to kill. Carl said, Buddy slapped him in his face after Carl poured Buddy's pot of coffee on the ground. To Carl, Buddy got what he deserved. Carl snapped and lost a good job because another man slapped him. Maybe now, he can understand how I felt being slapped for almost eighteen years. No man knows another man's sorrows. God knows. God cares.

# TWENTY

Carl's greatest strength was his ability to find a job. His greatest weakness was keeping it once he was hired. He was constantly in-and-out of jobs. Sometimes he worked one day. Often times he worked one month. Rarely did he work beyond three months on any job. No job satisfied him. None compared to Lockheed. He found fault with each new job.

Again, times were hard financially, but God was with me. The debt load was almost unbearable. My body could only work so much overtime. By this time, I was chronically fatigued. Another strategy had to be implemented before my body disintegrated. In March of 1992, a position came open on the midnight shift in the Emergency Clinic Lab. The shift differential was three dollars that meant earning two hundred and forty dollars more a pay check and six thousand more per year. The differential would allow me to work smarter, not harder. I applied for the position and got it.

Carl knew I applied for the midnight position although he strongly objected. It was okay for him to work any shift, but his wife could only work day shift. He felt nights were for husbands and wives, not work. Breaking the news that I got the position wasn't easy. I told him when he was most vulnerable.

We were in bed, talking, before we went to sleep. The lights were off. Our heads were nestled on our pillows. His right hand did the night walk to my side of the bed. When his hand reached my thigh, I grabbed it. I knew I had his undivided attention. He would do anything to continue his journey. "Not now. I have something to tell you first," I said, caressing his hand.

"What is it? Can't it wait till after we finish?" he said, placing his other hand on my breast.

"No. It won't take but a minute to say what I have to say." I clutched his hand on my breast and held it in my other hand.

"I'm listening. What is it?" He turned to face me then squeezed my breast while I held his hand.

"God answered my prayer concerning finances."

"I didn't know we had a financial problem." He squeezed again. He then moved half an inch from my lips. His left leg straddled my body.

I sat up in the bed to continue. "I've been working a lot of overtime."

"Will you please get to the damn point. My dick is hard as hell." He placed my hand on his erection. "I don't want to hear about no overtime, working or finances. I want some loving. A good old fashion fucking."

"Wait. Hold up. Let me say what I have to say first, then you'll get some loving." I removed my hand from his erection and my breast.

"Say it! For Christ sake, say what you have to say!"

"A door has opened up for me to earn more money without having to work as hard. You may not like it, but it will be for the best."

He put his arms around me, placed my head back on the pillow, and kissed me in the mouth. "Some loving will be for the best, right now. You can tell me later about the other thing," he said while getting on top of me.

I looked at him. His face was in mine. He kissed my lips and neck. His erection was so close to being inside of me. I tried to push him off, but he wouldn't budge. "Carl, let me finish," I moaned between kisses.

"Later." He kissed me and succeeded in penetrating me. "You can finish later."

He was right. I told him later in the morning. He didn't like the idea of his wife working at night. He felt my place was at home with him, in bed, in the wee-wee hours of the night. Reality overruled passion. Being in bed at night with Carl didn't pay the bills. Working the wee-wee hours of the night, making three extra dollars per hour, did. I worked Sunday through Thursday night.

There were several added benefits of working the night shift besides increased pay. One benefit was not having to pay for after school care. The boys had shorter days at school because I picked them up immediately after school. They also experienced me at my peak energy level instead of at my lowest. I slept while they were in school. When they came home, I was refreshed and not exhausted. It was a win-win situation, except for being a wife to Carl.

Keeping a roof over our heads became my number one priority. Taking care of the kids was second. Being a wife was no priority anymore because the first two priorities consumed all of my time and energy. There was only so much of me to spread around. There was none of me left for Carl or for myself.

Consequently, a gap formed between us. I no longer felt like a wife. I became the breadwinner, the cook, the maid, the baby sitter, and the bed warmer. Carl went out more with his single friends. Rarely did he take me out. When he did, I was too tired to go. The little free time I had, I wanted to spend it in my bed, sleeping, or relaxing at home. Therefore, he went out and I stayed in. We became roommates instead of soul mates.

Our marriage was empty. It was void of communication, love, companionship, vitality and fire. The brilliant flame of our early years was now a flicker on the verge of being extinguished. In our marriage, only the kids added chips to keep the flicker alive. Neither Carl nor I bothered to fuel the flicker. Our actions only diminished what the kids contributed.

For the most part, when were together at home, Carl was downstairs watching TV or entertaining his single friends. I spent my time upstairs in my bedroom reading. We seldom talked or spent time together in the same room. At home, he was in his world, and I was in mine.

My world shattered when Carl abandoned me a second time. The Friday after Labor Day, Carl walked out. I was sitting in my bedroom reading. The kids were in Carl's room playing and watching TV. I heard Carl come in the front door. He came up the steps, entered Carlos's bedroom, directly across from ours. That bedroom had two closets. One was Carlos's. The other one was Carl's. I heard him go through his closet. He came out of the room and left. My antenna went up. The way he came and left told me something was up. I went inside Carlos's bedroom and opened Carl's closet door. Empty clothes hangers filled the space. Carl was gone...again.

This time, I was not going to take his abandonment lying down. I refused to go through what I went through the first time. I called Mr. Smith, the attorney, the next day. We discussed divorce proceedings. His secretary typed the papers to be filed in the court. Carl and I had an appointment, Friday, two days later, to sign the divorce papers.

Ronald Smith Sr. had passed away since the last time I filed. He was in his late sixties when he died, last year. His son, Ronald Smith Jr., was thirty years younger. Although they had the same name, they were different as night and day. Ronald Sr. was a kind, gentle, and soft-spoken man. Ronald Jr. was heartless. He went for the jugular.

Carl and I were parked outside of Mr. Smith's office. Ronald Smith and Associates was boldly written in orange letters on the glass. The small office was one of six exact replicas on the street. Only the names on the window and street number made them different.

"Why are you doing this? I don't want a divorce," Carl said with both hands on the steering wheel looking at the window.

"I don't have a choice. You walked out on us again. I can't go through what you took me through the first time," I said with my right hand on the door ready to go inside. "Come on. Let's get this over with."

"No. Not yet." He held my arm. "Let's talk first."

I looked at my watch. "You have three minutes. I don't want to be late."

"What can I do to make you change your mind? You know I love you."

"There's nothing you can do. My mind is made up. You're not committed to this marriage. I will not sit around and let you leave me again."

"You're wrong. I am committed to this marriage. I wasn't thinking clearly when I left. I promise you, I'll never leave again."

"It's too late. Mr. Smith has our divorce papers written up. All I want you to do for me is sign on the bottom line."

"Is that what you really want? For me to sign the divorce papers and get the hell out of your life?"

"Yes, that's exactly what I want. You go your way, and I'll go mine."

He reached into his shirt pocket and pulled out an envelope. "You can have this whole check if you don't go through with the divorce. I'll straighten up. I'll do whatever it takes to make our marriage work. This check is my peace offering."

"Keep it. I don't need you or your check. Your three minutes are up. Let's go." I opened the car door and got out of the car.

Carl stuffed the check back into his shirt pocket. I waited for him at the office door. We entered together.

The office had a pecan leather sofa at the window which was directly across from the receptionist desk. A matching loveseat was perpendicular to the desk. Two pecan, leather high-back chairs were on the opposite wall of the loveseat and dark brown, oak coffee tables provided space for magazines.

Carl sat on the loveseat and picked up a magazine. I approached the receptionist desk. Her back was turned.

"Excuse me," I said as I looked at her stylishly cropped gray hair. She turned around from her bent position at the silver file cabinet. "My name is Vanessa Lewis. I have a nine o'clock appointment to see Mr. Smith."

Her deep, navy-blue eyes peeped over her spectacles. Her body appeared more youthful than her wrinkled face.

"Sign-in on the clipboard. Mr. Smith will be with you shortly. Please have a seat," she said, turning back around to continue what she was doing.

I sat down. Mr. Smith appeared a few minutes later and handed the receptionist a manial envelope.

"Mrs. Lewis is here for her appointment," she said, retrieving the envelope.

"Do you have her file?"

"Yes. Here it is," she said, handing him my file. "Call her back into the study."

Mr. Smith disappeared. The receptionist, Mrs. Henrietta Logan, called my name. "Mrs. Lewis, Mr. Smith will see you now. Go through the door and down the hall to the second room on the right.

I followed her directions. Mr. Smith was seated at the head of a long, high-gloss, dark-brown oak table.

"Have a seat, Mrs. Lewis." He motioned for me to sit next to him on his right. "I have all your papers ready. I will give you a chance to review them first before I summon Mr. Lewis to join us." He took the papers and explained them to me one-by-one. Afterwards he asked, "Do you have any questions?"

"No."

"I will call Mr. Lewis in. Once we get him to sign these papers, it won't take long for the divorce to go through. We are looking from thirty to ninety days, max." He ran his fingers through his coal-black, short hair. His left dimple indented as he smiled, revealing his badly coffee stained teeth. He winked at me with his olive green eyes. His protruded stomach growled as he left the office to get Carl.

When Carl entered the room, I was still examining the papers. Carl sat across the table from me. We both faced Mr. Smith as he sat down in the head chair.

"Mr. Lewis here is a copy of the divorce papers." Mr. Smith said as he handed Carl the stack of papers. "I will go over them with you, one page at a time. Stop me at anytime if you have any questions."

Carl placed the papers in front of him. "I'm ready, man. Let's get this over with."

Mr. Smith cleared his throat. "Mr. Lewis, please, look at the first page. It explains the divorce settlement your wife and I drew up. She is asking for $650 a month for alimony and child support.

"Wait a damn minute! I make $6.25 an hour, $250.00 a week, and $1,000.00 a month." Carl jumped up out of his seat. He paced back and forth. He pulled a cigarette from his shirt pocket and lit it.

"Calm down, Mr. Lewis. Let me proceed."

"Proceed my ass! You expect me to pay $650.00 a month in alimony and child support? What the hell am I suppose to live on? Pussy and air.Y'all trying to stick it to my ass."

"Mr. Lewis, these figures were derived from calculating the cost of maintaining the home and properly educating your children," Mr. Smith said, then drank from his coffee mug on the table. "The cost of living and inflation have also been included."

"Am I suppose to starve to death so they can live? What can I do with $350.00 a month?"

"The same thing you expect me to do with $300.00 dollars a month— EVERYTHING! Take it and buy your food, rent, utilities, insurance, clothes, gas, and entertainment. You think $300.00 is a lot of money. You have an extra $50.00 dollars for good measure. Go to the movies and buy some popcorn with it," I said, enraged.

"Johnny Taylor said, "It's cheaper to keep her." Now I see what he means. I might as well go striaght to the cementary when I leave here and bury my broke ass alive. I won't have a dime to live on. I'll be dead soon anyway." Carl sat down and lit another cigarette. Mr. Smith will you leave so we can discuss this privately."

"I will be glad to leave after you sign the papers."

"Man, you're crazy! I ain't signing no papers that will put a noose around my neck and make it impossible for me to live. I'd come out better putting a gun to my head and pulling the trigger."

"Sign the papers Carl. There is nothing to discuss. The marriage is over. You're wasting Mr. Smith's time."

"So this is what you want? This is how it is. I'll sign the papers, every last one of 'em." He proceeded to sign while Mr. Smith explained each one to him.

Mr. Smith gathered all the papers and placed them neatly in a stack. "Do you still want to talk?" he said, looking at both of us.

"No."

"Yes," responded Carl.

"I will leave you alone. I will give these papers to Mrs. Logan. Check with her before you leave for further instructions. Take as much time as you need." He left with the papers and his coffee mug. Mr. Smith closed the door gently behind him.

"Vanessa, let's get out of here. Go tell Mrs. Logan you changed your mind. Let's go home and make love like we never have before." Carl reached across the table for my hand.

"No, I'm not changing my mind. The papers are signed. We have thirty to ninety days to wait and this marriage will be all over."

"Vanessa, I love you. I don't want it to be over. Baby,come on. Let's go home." He gently held my hand. He looked me in my eyes and gave me his million dollar smile.

My heart sank. I don't want to do this, I thought to myself. Six hundred and fifty dollars is a lot of money for Carl to pay out. How WILL he live? I can't go through with this. I love Carl, and he loves me. "You're right," I told him, looking deep into his eyes. "Go tell Mr. Smith I changed my mind."

Carl kissed my hand. "You're doing the right thing. From this day on, I'll be the perfect husband."

"Oh, yeah. Give me the check," I said, holding my hand out.

He whipped it from his shirt pocket and handed it to me. "You can have this check and everything else I have. Let's go home. Let's get out of here." He got up and pushed his chair to the table.

Mr. Smith came in as I pushed my chair up.

"I changed my mind. I don't want a divorce."

"Since he has signed the papers, you should at least file them with the court. You will have thirty days or more to see if the marriage is working."

"No. That's not necessary. I'm not getting a divorce."

"Are you sure?"

"Yeah, man. We are sure."

"Well since you are sure about canceling the divorce, I can show you how to increase your income which will greatly improve your marriage and finances."

"What is it, man? We've tried every business there is."

"Amway."

Carl and I both laughed. "Amway. We've been in that twice. No thank you, man. We're out of here. Later."

What is the world coming to when you go to a lawyer for a divorce, and he wants you to sell soap. I thought as we left Mr. Smith's office.

# TWENTY-ONE

The Lord knew I was tired of struggling with Carl. He also knew I still loved him. Filing for a divorce wasn't an easy step for me to take. All I really wanted was for Carl to change, to listen to what I said instead of accusing me of nagging him. My words evaporated into the air while I banged my head against a wall to make this relationship work. Pretty soon, my head started hurting. Something else had to be done to get marital relief.

My method of dealing with Carl was both painful and ineffective. I promised myself the next time I filed for a divorce, I was going all the way with it. No more dipping and dabbling with this marriage. Everyone knows three strikes you're out and three outs completes an inning. I felt as if our marriage was in its last inning. Only God new for sure how many runs, hits, fowls, balls, strikes and outs were left to be played.

When we returned from Mr. Smith's office, Carl scored a home run. Our lovemaking made the game-worth playing without coming to an end. It seemed to be the only thing that kept the marriage intact. I thanked God for frequent home runs and doubles. They sustained the marriage.

For a short while, Carl was the perfect husband before he reverted back to being himself. In his days of perfection, he gave me his whole paycheck. I gave him a small portion of what was left over after all the bills were paid. We talked for hours about our future hopes and dreams. We went out together. We got back into each other. We became one again.

Everything was going fine until the Friday before Thanksgiving when the pendulum swung backwards. I was in the den watching TV with little Carl and Carlos when Carl came home from work.

"Daddy's home," shouted Carl when the front door opened. He leaped from the sofa and ran up the steps.

"Wait, Carl! Don't leave me," said Carlos, running behind him.

I trailed behind them into the living room. When I reached the top step, Carl was standing at the door with little Carl on his back and Carlos in his arms.

"Daddy, did you bring me something?" asked Carl.

"Daddy, what you get me?" Carlos asked, hugging Carl's neck and putting his dad's Braves cap on his head.

"Let me see." Carl reached into his back pocket to retrieve his wallet. He gave them each five dollars. "I didn't have time to buy anything. Here's five dollars to buy yourself something."

"Thanks, Daddy," said little Carl. "You're the greatest dad in the whole world." He hugged Carl's neck so tight he turned red.

"Damn, boy. I'm glad I didn't give you ten dollars. I'd be dead," Carl said, removing little Carl's tight grip from his neck.

Carlos fell butt first to the floor. "Ouch, Dad," Carlos said, rubbing his behind. "What did I do?"

"I'm sorry, son. I didn't mean to hurt you. I was only trying to survive. Sometimes an act of kindness can kill you quicker than an act of violence."

"Sometimes the ones you love can hurt you more than a stranger," I said, helping Carlos up.

"If that's true, I'm leaving while I'm still alive before I get killed in here with kindness and love," said little Carl, heading for the front door.

"Me, too," echoed Carlos, holding his behind. "Love hurts."

"Come here you two and give me a hug," I said, kneeling on the floor. "Your dad and I will never hurt you. We love you too much."

"That's what I'm afraid of—you'll love us to death. I'm outta here. Come on Carlos, let's go in my room and watch TV before Mama crushes us with one of her bear hugs," little Carl said running up the steps.

"It's my time to hold the remote control," said Carlos, running behind his brother.

"No, it's not. You held it last. I'm holding it today," little Carl said as he pushed Carlos to the floor at the top of the steps.

Carlos pushed Carl back."Don't push me!"

"Stop it this minute! Or I'll whip both of you," Carl said taking off his belt.

"Hurting one another is the only way to live. You said so yourself, Dad. Love kills. I want Carlos to live. Don't I brother," little Carl said while pushing Carlos again.

"Me, too," Carlos said, pushing little Carl back.

They continued to push one another until they went into Carl's room to watch TV.

"Come and sit next to me," I said, patting the sofa cushion.

Carl put his belt back on his pants. "No. I need to shower and change. I'm going out." He turned to face the steps.

"Carl, haven't you forgotten something?

"What?" he asked, turning to face me.

"My money. You gave the boys some money, but you haven't given me anything."

"I didn't forget. I'm not giving you anything this week. I have something I need to do."

"I don't know what you have to do, but you can't do it with the bill money. Give me my money then do what you have to do with yours."

"I'm fed up of working week-in, week-out, and not having any money for myself. I'm fed up with getting paid and still being broke. I'm spending my whole check on me this week."

"I'm managing the money, Carl. We have bills to pay. You can't spend your whole check on you."

"Yes I can."

"I can't spend my whole check on me. I have to pay the bills first. What ever is left over, if any, is my spending money."

"Well, that's how you manage money. I pay myself first. I pay the bills with what's left over, if any."

"But you're not managing the money. I am. Remember?"

"I remember you railroading me into the lawyer's office for a divorce. I agreed to let you handle the money then because it seemed like the right thing to do at the time because my ass was on the line. I would have agreed to just about anything. But, that was then and this is now. I'm going upstairs, take a shower, get dressed and have some fun."

"How can you call yourself the man of this house and take your whole check and spend it on yourself?"

"You won't let me be the man of this house. You want to be the man and the woman. You want to wear the pants and the skirt. Let me be the man for once, and I'll show you what I can do."

"You're showing me now. You'll take your whole check and spend it on yourself. That's why I could never give you my check to manage. We wouldn't have anything, no roof over our heads, no food, no clothes, no utilities— NOTHING."

"From now on, I'm not giving you my check either. You'll have to pay the bills the best way you can. Excuse me. I don't want to keep Lenny and Marlon waiting."

He went up the steps and closed the bedroom door. I sat on the sofa staring at the steps. If it wasn't for the kids, I would throw Carl out, head first. Out of love, of course, because love hurts. Those in your house can hurt you more than any stranger in the street, I thought to myself as I got up from the sofa and went back downstairs to watch TV.

The week of Thanksgiving, I had four consecutive days off. Those four days made me realize how much I had neglected myself. I needed to find me again. I looked in the mirror and didn't like what I saw, an overweight, unattractive, lifeless shell of who I used to be. I was going through the motions of life instead of living life to the fullest. I made up my mind that weekend that I would care more about myself.

By the third day, I had enough energy to press my hair straight. I had been wearing the short natural for over two years. I wanted my hair to grow back to my shoulders. I wanted to become the slim, long haired, attractive Vanessa I used to be.

I told myself, starting in January, I would take off one weekend per month. In April, I would start walking to lose weight. I kept my word. I had my one weekend off and I walked for one hour in my neighborhood three to five times a week. I lost sixteen pounds by September when I discontinued walking due to the cool weather. I discovered walking acted as a two-edge sword. It allowed me to lose weight and vent my frustrations. Walking became my solace, my therapy, my release mechanism.

When the walking ceased due to the cold weather, my mind developed another outlet. At night in my sleep, I dreamed of leaving Carl. I'd get on an airplane and fly to another city, alone. I didn't take the boys in my dream because I had promised little Carl I would never separate him from his dad anymore. I never promised, however, that I wouldn't leave.

The flights were almost daily. I'd travel here and there to different corners of the United States. I found happiness in my flights. They brought mental relief. I knew, I could never leave Carl physically until Carlos turned eighteen, eleven years down the road. I didn't know how I could endure eleven more years of this misery. God had to give me perseverance, somehow.

By February, the flights lost their relief effect. I suddenly realized how truly miserable I was. My life was passing before my eyes. I was quickly approaching forty. I knew beyond forty the grave was near. I asked myself, how on earth can I live ten more years of this life? I knew I wasn't living. I was merely existing, marking time until death came.

This doom-of-gloom was on me so strongly that I couldn't conceal it any longer. I remember sitting in the bedroom one Sunday afternoon with Carl. He was in the chair facing the bed, reading the Sports section of the newspaper. I was sitting on the bed facing him. Carl put the paper down after he finished reading it. I was sitting, thinking, smoldering from the inside. I looked at Carl with my arms crossed. Something momentarily came over me. I blurted how I felt without thinking. "I'm leaving you."

He gave me a puzzled look, wondering whether I was serious or not.
"When?"

"In ten years when Carlos turns eighteen."

He laughed. "You must be kidding. In ten years, you'll be too old to leave. You'll be forty-seven. Why leave then?" He laughed again.

"I can't leave before Carlos finishes high school. Our sons have been through enough. I can't take them through any more changes. I love them more than I love myself."

"Yeah, right." He pulled a cigarette from his shirt pocket, lit it, and pulled from it several times. "You're not going anywhere. This relationship will end when I say so. You must be tired."

"No. I'm telling you how I feel. This is the truth."

"I know. It's time for your cycle. You must be having PMS."

"I wish I was having PMS. I would P(ack) M(y) S(hit) and leave."

"I'll go downstairs so you can take a nap. Maybe when you wake up, you'll be yourself." He rose to leave the room.

"You don't have to leave. I'm not tired or having PMS. There is nothing wrong with me." I stood up beside him.

"Have you been smoking my marijuana? Are you hallucinating or something?"

"No. I'm telling you the truth. I refuse to live with you all of my life. I want to be happy before I die." I put both hands on my hips and looked him dead in his eyes.

"Woman. You're crazy! You can't live without me. We've been together practically all our lives."

"I know. But I'm still leaving you. I don't care how long we've been together."

"I'm getting outta here. I still say you're just tired. Lay down and take a nap. You'll feel better. I'll even cook dinner while you sleep." He closed the door before I could respond.

I took his advice and took a nap. I couldn't help it if he could not accept the truth. I was leaving him and that was the truth, not fiction or PMS.

The next week, a strange thing happened on the job. On one of my frequent trips to the ladies room, I met a correction officer in the hallway. He was on his way to the snack bar which was located across the hall from the ladies room. We stopped and talked."Hello," I said as we approached each other (The night shift was like one big family. We were very cordial to one another).

"Hi," he paused, "I have never seen you before."

"I know. I've never seen you before either. Have you been working this shift long?"

"Five years."

"I've been working it for two years. That's odd that we have never seen each other since it's just a handful of us working this shift. You see the same people night after night."

He leaned against the wall and crossed his legs. "I generally stay in my area except to come to the snack bar occasionally. I have to stay with my prisoners at all times."

"I generally stay in my area too except to go to the ladies room or snack bar. At this hour, there is not many places to go.

"Where do you work?"

"In the Emergency Clinic Lab." I had on my long, white, lab coat, but I guess it wasn't obvious. I pulled on it to make it more noticeable. My eye glasses were sliding off my nose. I pushed them forward with my finger.

"I have never heard of the Emergency Clinic Lab. Where is it located?"

"It's around the corner at the end of the hallway," I said, pointing to the right corner. "You can't miss it. It's next to GEC."

"I'd like to come visit sometimes. If that's all right with you."

"That'll be fine. I like visitors. Just come to the window."

"I won't get you in trouble will I?"

"No. It's just me and one other person who works this shift. She's cool."

"What is your name? he asked, looking at his watch.

"Vanessa. What is yours?"

"Zakee. Look Vanessa, it was nice meeting you, but I have to go to the snack bar and return to my area."

"I need to get back to my area also. I was headed to the ladies room, right here," I said pointing to the door directly across from us.

We parted ways. When we left, I had a grin from ear-to-ear. I hadn't felt that happy since the birth of Carl Jr.. While I was in the ladies room, I replayed the whole conversation again in my head. My heart pumped wildly. It felt as if it wanted to leap out of my chest. I told myself, I had just experienced love-at-first-sight. Nobody had ever affected me like that before. I felt an attraction so strong, it overwhelmed my senses. It consumed my whole being.

Zakee was very handsome, a ten in my book. He looked to be six-three. He towered over my five-foot, four and a half inch frame. He had the perfect physique, small waist, and extended chest. He looked like a person who lifted weights as opposed to a body builder with bulging biceps, triceps, and every other ceps. His smile was perfect with even, straight, white teeth. His short, brown hair complimented his mesmerizing eyes. His complexion was coffee brown with heavy cream. His navy blue pants and gray shirt fitted his well toned body like a glove.

To my surprise, he came to the lab window at 6:30 a.m.. I was sitting at the window accessioning blood specimens when he suddenly appeared out of nowhere.

"Are you busy?" he asked, standing in front of the lab window.

Startled, I replied, "No. I mean, sort of." His presence made me real nervous. Marlene had just arrived for day shift. I didn't want her and Jenny, my co-worker, to see him. What would they think? With me being a married woman, a Christian.

"Well, are you busy or not?" he asked a little short tempered.

"I am."

"I will come back another time," he said as he walked off.

I immediately turned around to see if anyone saw him. No one was looking. Everyone was preoccupied with getting set up for the next shift. I gave a sigh of relief. Afterwards, I wished I had talked to Zakee. Where did he go? Come back, please, I thought.

I went home feeling good about myself and life. I hoped Zakee would visit me again. I hoped I didn't scare him off. Whenever he looked at me, a spark ignited the core of my being. I felt alive again!

# TWENTY-TWO

The brief encounter with Zakee made me realize how wonderful a physical attraction felt. I vaguely remembered Jackie, my Georgia State University classmate, St. Joseph's associate, and Amway recruiter, talking about "chemistry" between two people. Jackie was still single at thirty-eight because she had to experience this "chemistry" before she considered marriage. I never felt "chemistry" before tonight. The only chemistry I knew of was in text books and laboratories which consisted of ions, chemicals and chemical reactions. I definitely was having a reaction, so what I felt must be "chemistry".

Maybe, this "chemistry" was what Tina Turner meant when she said, "Opposites attract. What's love got to do with it?" Did I feel love-at-first-sight, "chemistry" or the crazies? I don't know. All I know was, I couldn't get Zakee out of my mind. I wanted to see him again, tonight, I thought as I drove home from work.

My thoughts were of Zakee when I slept that morning, when I did homework with the kids that afternoon, when I cooked dinner that evening and when I dressed for work that night. I paid special attention to my hair and clothes. My hair had to be slamming. My clothes had to accent my body. I wanted to look good from head-to-toe, from tip-to-tail. My hair wasn't long enough for my favorite hairstyle—the Farrah Facett look. Instead I wore it with a full bang that swept the left side. I curled the back under and flipped the sides back. I chose a white skirt and navy blue, high-collar top that buttoned in the back. I stayed in the mirror an hour, making sure I looked good with every hair in place, everything intact.

Before tonight, I avoided mirrors. I used them only long enough to do my business. I didn't spend extra time making sure I looked good. I knew I didn't look good so what difference did it make spending extra time in the mirror—NONE!

Carl and the kids didn't notice the change. I guess it was too subtle. Mothers and wives were usually ignored anyway. As long as dinner was on the table and the wife came to bed ready for sex, nothing else mattered.

The time finally arrived for me to go to work. I had never been so happy going to Grady Hospital as I was that night. Lord, please let me see Zakee again tonight, I prayed as I drove on I-20 West. I knew it was no coincidence we met last night. There has to be more to this than one brief conversation.

This week, I worked the front of the lab and Jenny worked the back. Since I worked the front, I was responsible for accessioning the incoming specimens, running the chemistry analyzer—the Hitachi 717, processing the specimens, and answering the phone. Jenny ran the Coulter for hematology specimens, and performed the urinalysis and pregnancy tests.

Jenny was in her early fifties. Her gray hair was cut in a short, blunt style, which was perfect for her average height and stocky build. An avid reader, she always carried a paperback book in her lab coat pocket. When Jenny wasn't working or cleaning the lab, she was reading. What I liked most about Jenny was the fact that dust and dirt didn't stand a chance around Jenny. She cleaned everything from counter tops, telephones, and computer crevices. She was a great co-worker because she minded her own business and carried more than her share of the workload. Jenny and Norma at St. Joseph's Hospital were exact opposites although they were the same age.

That night, I was glad to work the front of the lab in case Zakee came by again. My constant stares toward the window greatly distracted me from my work. It was 2:20 a.m., and I had not seen a glimpse of Zakee all night. Where was he? Was he coming tonight? Will I ever see him again? Did I scare him away yesterday morning? Was it my imagination something happened between us? He was not coming, I kept thinking as I worked. I must get him off my mind. I'm a married, Christian woman.

My mind said, "Forget him," but my heart said, "I can't."The rest of my body said, "Shut up mind! You're brain dead. He brings the rest of us to life."

I heard a knock on the door as I put specimens in the centrifuge. Jenny must have forgotten her key, I thought as I went to open the door. The door was fully opened when I saw this tall, handsome man standing on the other side. My mouth and eyes opened wide. It was Zakee! He had not forgotten me.

"I thought you were Jenny."

"Are you disappointed?" he asked.

"Nooooo," I stuttered, "I'm pleasantly surprised."

"Are you busy?"

"No," I lied. I was busy as hell, but I wasn't ever letting him leave me again because of work. If he goes away this time, he may never come back, I thought. The work can wait. I closed the door and stood in the hallway with him.

"You looked strange when I came by yesterday morning. I started not to come tonight," he said, tucking a clipboard under his arm.

"Why did you come?"

"I wanted to see you."

My smile made it seem like 2:30 in the afternoon. Even my brain dead mind responded. "You go girl! You got a hook in his ass." My heart said, 'Thank the Lord.' The rest of my body said, "Leave it to us. We'll reel this brother right on in, hook, line and sinker."

"I'm sorry about yesterday. You caught me off guard when you appeared at the window," I said, moving from the door to the adjacent wall to let Jenny enter the lab.

Jenny went inside without saying anything. Her quick, I don't see anything glance, said it all—see no evil, hear no evil, speak no evil. That's my Jenny!

"Is she your co-worker?" Zakee asked when the door closed.

"Yeah, that's Jenny. She's great to work with."

"Most crackers are hard to get along with. You lucked out."

"Why do you talk like that? You have to take people individually. Some black folks will backstab you quicker than whites. It's not about the color of your skin, but the content of your heart. An evil heart, whether black or white, will commit evil acts," I said, reaching down to pick up a penny I saw on the floor.

"You are naive. A cracker is heartless. The injustices they have done to our people proves my point." His face turned red. His eyebrows arched high enough to fly off his face.

"What injustices? My closest friend is white. I've had numerous close white friends in the past. I went to integrated schools and worked side-by-side with white folks the whole time. Sometimes, I was the only black person in the bunch. I never experienced any injustices."

"You are the only black person who hasn't. Crackers have enslaved our people. They tampered with the Bible to make Adam and Eve white. The original man and woman were black, not white. Have you ever seen white dirt? People of color lived in the countries and civilizations of the Bible. Even Jesus was black. Crackers have taken the Bible and other books and altered them to exalt themselves. It is a plot to diminish us and other races in order to make themselves appear superior."

My eyes focused on his name tag when I adjusted my glasses as he spoke. It read, Zakee Abdul-Rauf. "You're Muslim?"

"Yes, I am. And as a Muslim, I have been taught the truth about our people, about our society, about crackers. Our people have contributed greatly to our society. Much of which have never been recorded or the credit has been given to others. There is no way you can take all our contributions over the ages and cram them into one month a year. Black History Month is a joke, an injustice to our people. The contributions we have made throughout the ages will take decades to learn." He grabbed the clipboard from under his armpit and fanned it in the air as he spoke. He missed my head by inches during his spiel. He didn't notice my head bobbing up and down to avoid being hit. He probably thought I was nodding in agreement.

"Carter G. Woodson started Black History Week in 1926 to coincide with the birthdays of Abraham Lincoln and Frederick Douglass. Later in 1976 to celebrate our bicentennial, his association expanded the week's celebration to include the entire month to provide time for programs, observances and celebrations."

"I know that. But it's still not enough time to learn about our forefathers. It's still an injustice of the white man no matter how you look at it."

"What the white man has done in the past does not compare to the injustices we are doing to ourselves today. When we murder our babies, sell drugs to our people, kill one another in our own neighborhoods, refuse to take advantage of the educational system we have, and lie and steal from one another, now that's real injustice to our people."

"We are oppressed."

"Only if we allow ourselves to be. Nobody has the power to oppress us if we submit our lives to our Creator who you mentioned is black. As a Christian, it doesn't matter to me if Jesus was black, white, green or blue." I paused momentarily while he tucked the clipboard back under his arm. "He is my Savior. Jesus came to deliver me and the world from our sins. Through His shed blood, our sins are forgiven. Because of His sacrifice, we can walk in newness of life and be at one with the Father. We are no longer cut off from the Father because of our sins."

We both looked toward the lab door as it opened.

"Vanessa, the computer is up," Jenny said, poking her head out.

"I turned and nodded to Jenny. "I'll be right there." I turned back to Zakee. "I have to go. When the computer comes up, I have to order everything and enter all my results."

He looked at his watch. "It's time for me to go anyway."

"Are you coming back?"

"I don't know. It depends on how busy I am."

"Have a good night," I said, opening the door. He walked off.

Jenny and I ordered the specimens that came in during the computer purge from 12:30 to 2:40 a.m.. We ordered and answered everything by 3:05. I thought about Zakee the entire time, especially, how much I enjoyed his company. It was something about him that made me click.

Zakee didn't return that night, but he came back the following night. When I heard a knock on the door, I knew it was Zakee. Jenny didn't say anything, but she knew something was going on. I answered the door and stepped outside.

"I was on my way to McDonald's. I stopped by since I had to pass this way," Zakee said with a smile on his handsome face.

"I'm glad you stopped by to see me," I said with a bigger smile than his. "Do you eat at McDonald's often?"

"No. I usually buy something from the snack bar to tide me over. But this is Ramadan. I fast from sunrise to sunset."

"I read an article, yesterday, in the Constitution about Ramadan."

"I read that article, too. It was very informative. It even mentioned that the first ten days of the fast is to receive Allah's mercy, the second ten days are for forgiveness and the last ten days are for redemption from judgement or hell fire."

"I didn't know Muslims believed in hell fire until I read the article. I guess a hell fire is a universal religious belief. If you don't live right in this life, you will be burnt up in the hell fire. The fire won't care if you are Christian or Muslim. The message is the same, live right now or burn later."

"True, undefiled, religion is not to save our own skin but to help and serve our fellow man," he said leaning against the wall.

"To love our neighbors as ourself."

"Exactly. To do good to one another. To be an asset to our community."

"What do you do for your community?" I asked, moving closer to the wall to make room for two people coming down the hallway.

He straightened up on the opposite wall to make room also.

"I feed the homeless every Wednesday morning."

"That's why you look tired? You fed the hungry instead of sleeping?"

"Speaking of feeding the hungry, my stomach just growled. I better go to McDonald's and feed myself," he said, looking at his watch.

"I need to get back to work anyway." I went back inside the lab, and he walked off. My body returned to work, but my mind was still with Zakee. I never knew a man who fed the homeless. As a Christian, that's what I should be doing, but I wasn't. Zakee is such a good man. Why is he single? I must ask him the next time I see him.

Zakee didn't come by the next night, and I was off the following two nights for the weekend. I thought about him the whole time I was off—every waking moment, every hour, every minute, every second of every day. I told myself it was idolatry the way I thought about Zakee, and it was. Nevertheless, I continued to think about him all the time. I just couldn't get him off my mind.

Friday in the mail, my Citibank credit card bill came. Inside was an advertisement for cruise discounts with Carnival Cruise Line. My heart skipped a beat when I read the insert. I had never been on a cruise before. I read the insert completely then called the 1-800 number listed. Since I had enough money for the deposit, I booked the three day cruise to the Bahamas for early October. We would go after my annual church trip in late September.

Carl and the boys were ecstatic when I told them we were going on a three day cruise to the Bahamas. It was like a dream come true.

The cruise and Zakee greatly lifted my spirits at home. They kept my mind off how miserable I was with Carl. I continued to stay in the mirror, taking pride in my appearance. I wanted to look good for Zakee. I started listening to the radio for love songs that reminded me of him. Before Zakee, the radio was a distraction. I preferred it off because it interfered with my Bible reading. Lately, I wasn't reading the Bible, so it didn't matter. I preferred to think about Zakee and listen to love songs.

Consequently, my spiritual life was going down the tubes. The combination of Zakee and the upheaval at church made me spiritually off balance. The pastor left with over half the congregation after headquarters made doctrinal changes. No longer were the Sabbath and Holy Days significant. Jesus Christ, alone, was to be revered. Everything else was secondary. Congregations from all over the world were affected by the change. I was affected too. Our Christian foundation had been changed from Sabbath-keeping and Holy Days observance to making Jesus Christ our only focus for salvation. It sounds so simple, but it's very easy for Christians to lose sight of Christ and get caught up in everything else.

Zakee and I had been talking for a month before the conversation changed from the general to the specific. He continued to visit me every night. I began to notice the way he looked at me. When I looked into his eyes something inside of me said, 'he sees something I don't see.' I felt beautiful! The spark, the glimmer, that came from his eyes made me feel this way. An incident later confirmed it.

We were standing outside the lab, talking as usual, when a question I had on my mind for some time came up.

"I'm a married, Christian woman, and you are a single Muslim. Why are you talking to me?" I asked, pushing my glasses up.

"I was raised a Christian although I am now a Muslim. I am at the stage in my life where I am ready to get married. I am looking for a wife who has an opened mind. She doesn't have to be Muslim as long as she can accept my beliefs." He stood back and gave me that spark stare. "Take your glasses off."

I took the glasses off as Zakee requested.

"Ah!" he said with a shocked expression on his face.

I was stunned by his reaction. He thinks I'm beautiful without my glasses. I must get rid of them. I would give anything to get that reaction from him again. I left my glasses off while we talked. I put them in my lab coat pocket. "You like what you see?"

"I am not saying." He paused with a stare of admiration. "I must go." He walked off.

I stood motionless watching him disappear down the hallway before I returned to the lab.

That evening, I searched for old photographs of me. I found one with my hair long in the Farrah Facett style. It was taken shortly after Carlos was born. Carl and I were holding hands at the base of the steps in the living room. The carpet was gold—the golden years when I looked good and felt good, when I was happy.

I took the photograph and stared at it. I told myself, I would get like this again. I'll let my hair continue to grow. I'll get my body back in shape. I'll look good from head to toe. I put the picture in my purse as a constant reminder. I'll look at it often to remember my goal.

The next day, I took the boys spring shopping. Carl wanted to shop at a discount outlet store near Belvedere. While waiting for the boys to shop, I found a booth with nice, affordable clothes. I did something I hadn't done in a long time. I shopped for me. I bought seven outfits that totaled over $350.00 dollars. One outfit was for the cruise. It was a black and silver sequined after-five skirt with an irregular hemline and matching top. Five outfits were dresses that could be worn to church. The last outfit was an olive-green, sleeveless, vested, pants suit. Amazingly, I looked great in every outfit I tried on. The walking had paid off.

The boys were not as fortunate as I were with their shopping. They found a few pieces to wear at the outlet store. We went to South Dekalb Mall to complete their shopping. We returned home excited about our clothes. I hung mine up in my closet with the price tags on.

I lay down afterwards on my bed and cried. *Lord, I care so much about Zakee. He's a good man. Why am I stuck with Carl? He doesn't mean me any good. He only wants to use me. I'm always being stuck with paying his debt. I'm now paying for three of his cars. When the house was refinanced, this month, in my name, I was stuck with paying for the Ford he purchased in '88 that was repossessed and the Lockheed loan from '90 that he never paid back. Those two liens on the house totaled over $6,000.00 dollars when I refinanced. Why is my load heavy and his is light? Why do I get stuck with his debt all the time? If it wasn't for Carl and Carlos, I'd be long gone.*

A still small voice replied in my ear, "Before you take the last price tag off, something will happen for the two of you to get together."

I sat straight up in my bed. The tears stopped. I thought about what I heard in my ear. The cruise! The last price tag will be taken off during the cruise. Something will happen between now and the end of September so Zakee and I can be together. Zakee will be mine—soon!

# TWENTY-THREE

Saturday, I wore the navy blue dress with the wide sailor collar to church. I carefully removed the price tag before putting it on. One mind told me to rip off all the tags except one to speed up the prophecy. My other mind told me that was not a wise thing to do. God had a plan He was working out in His own time and His own way. My position was to wait on the Lord.

Another prophecy was told to me soon after the first. The Lord laid it upon my heart to write my experience of Zakee in a book. He said, "This book will be written and it will be published." I was reminded of the book I started writing fourteen years ago but never completed. The book about Zakee, however, will be written to completion and published. The Lord also laid it upon my heart to begin this book shortly after my conception. The beginning of this book must correspond with my beginning. The end was not revealed.

I told Carl and the boys I planned to write a book next spring. The Lord placed it on my heart, the book will be started the end of April or the beginning of May '95. It was now the end of April '94. I trusted God to carry out His plan. He only gave me the desire to write. The abilities and skills He had to supply.

In addition to the prophecies, April '94 was a turning point month for me. I was standing in my bedroom, one evening, soon after both prophecies had been revealed. I was standing near my bed when I felt something inside of me well up and come out. It started from my abdomen and came out of my mouth. I didn't see anything, but I felt a sensation throughout my body. It lasted only a few seconds, but when it was over, I felt like a new person.

God revealed to me, I had been depressed for six years. The incident with Carl walking out in '88 was so traumatic, I was emotionally frozen to the event for six years. My anger was turned inward which resulted in the six years of depression. The love I felt for Zakee allowed the anger to subside then resurface, so I could deal with the pain. I was then able to forgive Carl for all the pain and suffering I had gone through. Through forgiveness, I was healed.

In my mind, I repeated the scene of him walking out on me over and over again. I couldn't move forward in my life because I was emotionally stuck in '88. No one knew but God how deep and painful my mental and emotional scars were. He knew. He cared. He delivered me by allowing me to experience love on a level I never knew.

God is love. Love is the most powerful emotion that exists. Love can heal deep, emotional wounds. This experience allowed me to love myself for the first time in my thirty-seven years of existence. I was reborn. I mattered. The new me, created by love, was UNCAGED to live my full potential!

The Lord revealed to me about the sky-blue carpet in all the rooms except the kids bedrooms. The blue carpet represented seven years of depression that followed the seven golden years. During the golden years, Carl Jr. and Carlos were born. The gold carpet throughout the house represented the joy they brought forth to our family and home. The blue carpet of depression was placed in all the rooms except the boys' bedrooms. The master bedroom was carpeted blue because the depression affected the occupants, the marriage, me. Next July would complete the seven years of depression. This year was a year-of-release. The carpet had to be replaced by then to end the depressed years and start a new era.

After my welling up experience and revelations, I went downstairs in the den. Carl was sitting on the sofa listening to his albums. I asked him to stand up and dance with me. When I put my arms around him, I felt nothing. The love I had for Carl was gone just like my depression. The two vanished together.

Before the song ended, I ran upstairs. The nothing feeling scared me. I knew I was now free to leave Carl. I was no longer emotionally bonded to him anymore. That night when we made love, I felt like I was being raped. The sex act confirmed, I didn't love Carl anymore. I turned over on my side and cried silently when it was over. Sex without love is rape.

Carl didn't have a clue what was going on with me because he was being satisfied sexually. He thought I enjoyed it like I had so many times before. I couldn't tell him I didn't love him anymore. I couldn't tell him I loved Zakee.

The welling up experience made me feel like a new person. All the years of abuse and wrong doings had been miraculously taken away. My cart-of-burden was empty, whereas, prior to the experience it was full to capacity. I couldn't take anymore. My cart broke from the weight of the heavy load. Instead of repairing the old cart, God gave me a new cart, one that was empty, without any burdens. The new cart represented the new me—burden free.

As I lay in my bed, Sunday evening, before going to work, I wrote a letter to Zakee inscribed on my heart. I knew I couldn't write him a physical letter with paper and ink because I was married. The inscribed letter was my way of saying what was in my heart to him. The words will forever be etched in my heart.

*Dearly Beloved Zakee,*

> *I love you with all my heart. Since I've met you, you have changed my life. I have never experienced a love as strong as the way I feel about you. Your gentle smile thawed my frozen heart. Your eyes, the way they look into mine, make me feel beautiful and special. The magnetism I feel between us when we*

*talk is electrifying. I can feel the aura of emotions that we share for each other.*

*Neither one of us can say with our mouths what we feel inside. The feelings are so strong and so real that our bodies emit our feelings like a light bulb.*

*Before I met you, I felt like a well-worn rag, full of holes and needed to be thrown away. You came along, picked me up off the ground, and placed me in your top pocket near your heart. You caressed my thin fibers with love. You took me home and mended my holes. I was something precious in your sight. To you, I was more than something to be bedded. Although I was worn and used, you cared for me as if I was brand new. I will always love you for making me feel brand new.*

*I want to be with you, but my marriage prevents it. Therefore, I must wait patiently on the Lord to deliver me from my marriage. I can't take matters into my own hands, such as seeking a divorce. I eagerly anticipate when we can get together.*

*Love,*
*Uncaged*

That night, Zakee visited me. I wanted to tell him how much I loved him, but I couldn't. I wanted to tell him about the price tag prophesy, but he would think I was crazy. I echoed the words of Pattie Labelle's song in my mind, "If only he knew."

He knocked on the door and I stepped outside to the hallway. I felt like a queen. My king had arrived.

"What have you done? You're bald!" I asked, shocked.

"I like to go bald when the weather turns. Don't it look smooth?" he asked, rubbing his hand on his bald head smiling.

I liked him better with hair, but he was so happy about his bald head I didn't want to burst his bubble. "It looks nice," I lied. He was still handsome to me without hair. It was something about the way he smiled.

"How is life at home?" he asked walking to the small ledge of the door that led outside to the air conditioner units. He sat down and looked up at me to answer.

"It's funny you should ask that question. This weekend, I discovered I don't love Carl anymore," I replied, pacing back and forth a few steps at a time.

"What happened?" His eyes widened.

"I put my arms around him and felt nothing. That never happened before."

"Am I the reason you don't love your husband?"

"I can't say. I think the main reason I don't love him is because I have gone through so much with Carl in the past that all the love I once felt for him is gone." I knew I couldn't tell Zakee the whole truth. I didn't want to scare him off.

"Why do you stay in the marriage? You've told me before how unhappy you are."

"I know. I even told Carl, I'm leaving him."

"When?"

"In ten years."

Zakee laughed. "In ten years, you'll be ready for the rocking chair."

"I can't leave before then because of the kids. I have to wait until my youngest son turns eighteen."

"It is no point of leaving then. You might as well work things out now."

"I have reasons to believe I will be delivered from my marriage before then, but I can't take matters into my own hands."

"You do. How so?

"When I tell you this, don't think I'm crazy." I stopped pacing and looked into his eyes.

"When I was twenty-four years old, almost fourteen yers ago, I went to a seer named Madame Lee. She told me, I was going to leave Carl. She also told me, I would have four children, two boys and two girls. I have the two boys already. What's happening in my life, right now, lets me know the time she was referring to will happen soon, before Carlos turns eighteen. I'm young enough to have more children. In ten years, I'll be too old."

"Maybe you will have more children by your husband."

"No. I don't want anymore children by Carl. He makes it too hard for me to rear them because he doesn't carry his fair share of the load. I knew after my first child, I didn't want anymore children by him."

"Why? How can you be his wife and not want anymore of his children?"

"Because, he doesn't have the father mentality of I am the provider, the bread winner. He doesn't understand his role is to nurture and mentor his offspring. He's more interested in hanging out with the guys, night clubbing, and getting high."

"You're saying he needs to grow up and be a man. He should put away the childish lifestyle and be a man, a father, a husband."

"Yeah. How did you know what I meant?"

"I hear it all the time. It happens everyday. Islam teaches men how to be a man. How to be the head of the house. I will work two jobs, if necessary, to provide for my family. My wife will not have to work. Her place will be at home with the children, to teach and care for them."

"Your family will be blessed because that is the way God intended for the family structure to be. A woman will be blessed to have you."

"I will be blessed when I find the right one. I have been single long enough. I am ready to get married." He stood up.

"How will you know when the right one comes along?"

"I'll know." He smiled and rubbed his head.

Your search is over, I said to myself. I'm the right one. Right here. I pointed to myself in my mind. I gripped the wall behind me with both hands to contain myself because I was ready to jump all over him. I pictured myself leaping into his arms.

"It's time for me to go," I said before I lost control.

"I must go, too. I need to go to the snack bar before I go outside to my car."

"I'll see you later." I entered the lab excited.

I am the right one. He's the right one for me. I never felt this way about anyone before in my life. The time for me to leave Carl is now while I'm young enough to have two of Zakee's daughters. He will be my next husband. He will!

My mission, now, was to convince Zakee his search was over, that I was the "right one". God will take care of my marriage with Carl. I will be delivered from one marriage and enter into another marriage with Zakee. I will have his two daughters. That was the plan—the mission.

I scheduled an appointment at America's Best Contacts and Eyeglasses when I got home. My appointment was in three weeks, the beginning of June. I remembered Zakee's reaction when I took off my glasses. I wanted him to see me that way all the time.

After I hung up the phone from making my appointment, I walked to the other side of my bedroom, near the window. I took off all my clothes and stared into the mirror to see how I could improve my body. I moved closer to the mirror when I noticed something strange. My eyes must be out of focus. I reached for my glasses. I must be imagining this. I stood directly in front of the mirror and put my hands to my chest. Lo and behold, I had breasts! Two big, succulent breasts!

I screamed! I jumped up and down. I couldn't believe it! How can you grow breasts at thirty-seven? Over the years, I thought my back was getting bigger when I changed bra sizes. I had gone from a 30A to 36B bra. It's like, God said, "Whoop, there it is! Wal-la, breasts.

"Lord my mission no longer seems impossible because you have given me ammunition to work with. I'm fired up! I'm ready to capture my prey!" I squeezed my breasts and strutted my stuff in my bedroom.

In my sleep, I had visions of walking down the aisle to marry Zakee in a beautiful church filled with guests. He was standing, tall and handsome, admiring me as I slowly strolled on the red carpet in my low cut wedding gown that emphasized my twenty-five inch waist and revealed my overflowing breasts. His first reaction was, "AH!", with his mouth and eyes wide opened at the sight of my beauty. I was his beautiful bride. He was my handsome groom. We would wed and be happy ever after.

I repeated the vision everyday in my sleep. The vision was so real. It made me extremely happy. The thought of being with Zakee the rest of my life made me exuberant.

Consequently, I became extremely excited about our relationship. I had written numerous letters to Zakee in my heart. The time had come to tell him how I felt. I couldn't contain myself any longer. I decided to write him a letter and I'd give it to him the next time I saw him. I wrote the letter while working in the lab, the end of June. The letter said:

*Dear Zakee,*

*I hope you don't take offense to this letter. In it is a lot of things I want to say. Your friendship is very important to me. I wouldn't do anything to jeopardize our relationship. I have written many letters to you in my heart. This letter is my first attempt to tell you how much you mean to me.*

*Knowing you made me realize the condition I was in. I felt like a dog, locked up in a cage with my two puppies. I was given food and drink but no love. I licked my wounds daily to keep them from getting further infected by those who mistreated me. I was left responsible for raising my puppies without the help of their father who only entered the cage to satisfy his sexual urges. After he was satisfied, he locked the cage door and left with the key.*

*I had been weakened over the years due to neglect and lack of love. I was content with staying locked up in my cage until both puppies were grown. I didn't have the strength to free myself from the cage, nor did I have the desire. I was content with being locked up until you came along. When you looked into my cage, a perfect stranger, the way you smiled at me gave me strength, courage, and hope to one day be free. I knew I no longer would be content to wither away in my cage, just waiting for the time to come for my puppies to grow up.*

*For the first time in years, I rose up, forgetting my wounds, and walked to the door of the cage. I pressed my face against the bars and smelled the fresh air. The sunlight hurt my eyes while I watched you disappear. I ran to the end of the cage and* barked when you were out of sight, but the leash around my neck pulled me back. I lay back down to lick my wounds, but they were healed.

In my weaken state, I was unable to break free from the cage. Your regular visits gave me the desire to be free. Since I have known you, God has strengthened me. One day when I went to the cage door, I tugged on the bars. Each day you came to see me, I tugged a little longer and a little harder. I never tampered with the lock because Carl had the key. He might notice something was wrong and interfere with me getting free.

The day finally arrived when the bars were weakened enough to match my God given strength. I pulled the bars back and broke free. I ran in the direction that you came to visit me, but my leash prevented me from coming to you. I now wait to be supernaturally freed from my leash. I want to be free to dwell with you all the days of my life.

Love,
Uncaged

# TWENTY-FOUR

I neatly folded the letter and placed it in my lab coat pocket. I walked to the telephone, grabbed the receiver and dialed Zakee's extension. Someone picked up on the third ring.

"Corrections. Thomas."

"May I speak to officer Abdul-Rauf, please?"

"He is at extension 7689."

"Thank you." I quickly dialed the extension. It rang twice.

"Detention. Officer Abdul-Rauf."

"Zakee. This is Vanessa. Can you talk?"

"I have a minute."

"I have something I want to give you. Can you come by and pick it up?"

"What is it?"

"A letter."

"Why don't you bring it to me? I'm in Yellow Detention. Bring me a Minute Maid grape soda and a small bag of peanuts from the snack bar. I'll pay you when you come."

"I'll be there in a few minutes."

I verified the five C.B.C.'s, complete blood counts, that had printed off. I answered the three negative pregnancy tests and started the dilutions on four positive patients before I left.

With grape soda and nuts in hand, I walked down the corridor to Yellow Zone Detention. It was a straight shot from the snack bar. Once I entered the emergency area, I turned at the first left. Yellow Detention was the second left.

Zakee was sitting at a desk alone. Five bloody, bandaged prisoners were stretched out on their beds.

"Come on in," Zakee motioned as I approached the entrance. He plopped a red grape in his mouth as I walked toward him. "Have a seat, right here," he said, pulling the chair next to him out.

I immediately sat in it. "Here's your stuff," I said, putting the soda and nuts on top of his Final Call Newspaper.

He reached in his front pouch. "Here's $1.50. Keep the change. It's your tip."

I picked the coins up. "Thanks for being so generous. Next time, I'll come on roller skates. Maybe, I'll get a bigger tip."

"Where is the letter?" he asked, opening the soda and chewing on the nuts.

"In my pocket."

"Do you want me to read it or not?" he asked, sipping and chewing at the same time.

"I do. I also want to talk about it later." I reached in my pocket for the letter and laid it next to his soda.

"I hope your letter is as good as my soda and nuts."

"It's better. The soda and nuts are physical foods. They will pass through. The letter is food-for-thought. It will stay with you forever."

A nurse came to monitor the prisoners. My chair was in front of a wide poll which blocked her view from the nurses station. Her back was to me when I entered the room. Her expression said it all when she saw me. Her dark-brown, shoulder length hair swung in her coca brown face. Her eyebrows were arched and ready to take off. The red-brown facial color told me her blood pressure was rising. The brown pupils in her eyes were red with flaming dots.

"Excuse me!" she huffed. "You're not suppose to be in here! No visitors are allowed." She looked at Zakee eating his grapes. "Some of us have work to do." She walked to the next prisoner and snatched his right arm to take his blood pressure.

"Wait a damn minute, bitch. Don't take your frustrations out on me. That's my damn arm you grabbin. If I wasn't strapped to this motherfuckin bed, I'd show you how it feel," said the prisoner with bloody bandages on both legs.

"Who are you calling a bitch? You are strapped down and wounded. Your life is in my hands. If you say another word to me, I'll take your life right now. Do you understand?" she asked stemmed.

He didn't say a word. Nobody did. I looked at Zakee, thinking he would intervene.

"Aren't you going to say or do something?" I finally asked.

"No. That is nurse Henderson. She has more venom than a cobra. She doesn't need my help to keep these prisoners in line. She doesn't like visitors either. She takes her job seriously."

I stood up. "I'm leaving before I become a patient. Call me after you read the letter."

"I will be by later if I get a chance."

I nodded and walked back to the lab. I felt good finally expressing my feelings to Zakee. The love I felt was too much to hold inside.

A lot of work came in while I was gone. I worked ninety miles an hour until it was time to go home. I didn't have time to think about Zakee or the letter. I was so busy, it didn't dawn on me, until I was driving home, that I hadn't heard from Zakee. I guess he was busy too, I told myself.

Since it was Friday morning, I wouldn't see him again until after the weekend. I wondered how he responded to my letter. Although the suspense was killing me, I had no other choice but to wait until the weekend passed.

When I got home, I ran to my closet, I had lost track of how many price tags were left. I counted them. Three tags remained. Tomorrow, I planned to wear the black, white, and shocking pink top with the long, black skirt to church. I wasn't sure when I would wear the other tagged dresses, probably soon.

As I slept that morning, I dreamed of how God would fulfill the prophesy. I repeated the words in my mind—"Before you take the last price tag off, something will happen for the two of you to get together."

In my dream, I was sitting in a graveyard crying, wearing my new, black, white, and shocking pink suit. Carl Jr. and Carlos were sitting beside me crying, too. Other people present consoled us. A white casket was being lowered into the ground as a tall, dark-skinned, white robed minister spoke and read from the Bible.

He said, "Dearly Beloved, we are gathered here today to pay our last respects to Carl Lewis who died a sudden and tragic death. As we place his body into the ground, let's remember his faithful and loving widow and sons, whom he left behind, in our prayers daily. From dust we were created and to dust we will return. Can I get an Amen? The Lord said in His Word, in I Thessalonians 4:13-18, *'But we would not have you ignorant, brethren, concerning those who are asleep, that you may not grieve as others do who have no hope. For since we believe that Jesus died and rose again, even so, through Jesus, God will bring with him those who have fallen asleep. For this we declare to you by the word of the Lord, that we who are left alive, who are left until the coming of the Lord, shall not precede those who have fallen asleep. For the Lord himself will descend from heaven with a cry of command, with the archangel's call, and with the sound of the trumpet of God. And the dead in Christ will rise first; then we who are alive, who are left, shall be caught up together with them in the clouds to meet the Lord in the air; and we shall always be with the Lord. Therefore, comfort one another with these words.'* Can I get another Amen for the reading of God's Word?"

The body was in its resting place when the minister finished reading the Scriptures. My eyes focused on the white casket then caught sight of one of the mourners standing far off. I wiped my eyes to see clearly. It was Zakee. He smiled and winked at me. I smiled back. My tears dried up. I was happy. Now, the two of us will be together, until death do us part.

The dream woke me up. "That's it!" I shouted. The Lord had revealed to me the fulfillment of the prophesy. Carl will experience a sudden and tragic death. I will be delivered from this marriage through Carl's death.

I was in the kitchen preparing dinner when Carl came home from work, excited.

"Vanessa. You'll never believe what happened to me on the way home!" Carl panted from the front door.

"Slow down, so I can understand what you're saying." I dropped everything and went into the living room.

"All right. All right," he said, slower but still fast. "I was driving on I-285, coming home, when a tractor trailer truck ran me off the road. I kept blowing my horn to get his attention, but he didn't hear me. I kept driving, and he kept coming over. Finally, his truck came all the way over in my lane. I drove onto the embankment, in a ditch, to get out of his way. I thought he was going to kill me, and he would have if I didn't get out of his way." Carl talked with his hands moving, reenacting the incident.

"Are you okay?"

"No. I'm still shook up. Look at my hands," he stretched them out for me to see, "they are still shaking."

"Sit down and relax," I said, nudging him to the sofa. "I'll get you something to drink. Sit down until your nerves calm down."

"Fix me a tall glass of straight liquor on the rocks," he yelled as I approached the kitchen.

"Carl. You survived the tractor trailer. Now, you want to kill yourself with Johnny Walker?"

"I'm too nervous. A tall stiff drink is the only way for me to relax. Besides, a little liquor ain't never killed nobody. Right now, I'd rather be alive and drunk than alive and sober."

"Did you get the license plate number?" I asked, handing him his tall glass of whiskey.

"No. I didn't think about no license plate number. My mind was on surviving, living." He swallowed his drink in one gulp. "Fix me another one," he said, handing me his empty glass.

"That was a lot of liquor. Don't you think you've had enough?"

"I still have the shakes. If you won't fix me another drink, I'll fix it myself." He reached in his back pants pocket."You just don't know what I've been through. I thought I was a dead man. My life flashed before my eyes. I cried at the thought of never seeing you again." Tears ran down his face. He wiped them with a used paper towel he pulled from his back pocket.

"I'll make you another drink. I'm sorry. I didn't realize how shaken up you are. I'll fix me a drink, too. I'm starting to shake."

Carl passed out on the sofa after he finished his fourth drink. By that time, he had either calmed his nerves or killed his soul. In any case, he was out like a light. The boys and I let him rest. Carl wasn't any company but at least he was alive.

For the rest of the evening, I thought about the incident. Carl barely escaped death this time. Will he be as blessed the next time, which was certain to come, soon? My answer was no. In my mind, Carl only had a few days, or weeks to live. His end would mark the beginning of a new life for me.

Another vision came to me in my sleep that night. I dreamed, Carl was fatally wounded at gun point by a masked gunman who carjacked his car. Carl was killed at the scene. His car was never recovered. The murderer was never identified.

The autopsy revealed the bullet pierced his heart, causing an instant death. Only one pint of blood remained in his body. The remainder of his blood covered the ground at the crime scene. The back of his skull ripped in two places due to the impact of his fall when he was forced from the car. The coroner stated in his report that Carl would have died from the head trauma if the bullet had not killed him first.

"Vanessa, Vanessa. Wake up," I heard Carl say while shaking me. "Wake up. You keep making funny noises."

"Carl, Carl, are you talking to me from heaven or hell?" I asked dazed and still semi-asleep.

"Wake up. Are you having a nightmare?" Carl asked, putting his arms around me.

"Uh?" My eyes opened. "You're alive! I touched his face with my right hand.

He took my hand and placed it on his erection. "Yes. We're all alive. You've seemed to have forgotten about us, lately."

I pulled my hand back, fully awake. "I dreamed you were murdered by a carjacker. He shot you in your heart and broke your skull."

"Damn! I almost got killed by a tractor trailer truck today. Now, you're killing me in your dream, tonight." He sat erect in the bed and placed his hand under his chin as though he was in deep thought. "I wonder if God is trying to tell me something?"

"Yeah fool. Keep your ass out of your car."

"No. I think He's trying to tell me something else."

"I know. He's telling you, to ride MARTA, it's smarter."

"Vanessa, if I died would you remarry?" he asked, looking into my eyes.

"Yes, if I met somebody, I wanted to marry. Would you remarry if I died?"

"Hell no. Once is enough for me. I don't think I could be happy with anyone else but you. I love you with all my heart." He kissed my left cheek and made a move like he wanted to get something started.

"Goodnight Carl." I rolled over on my right side. "I'm tired. I had a long day."

"Goodnight Doll." He moved back to his side of the bed.

Minutes later, we were both fast asleep.

The rest of the weekend, I pampered Carl. I cooked his favorite meals, served him breakfast in bed, and gave him some. Needless to say, he was a very happy man Monday morning.

Sunday night, driving to work, I thought about Zakee and the letter. Tonight, I will know his response. I hoped he understood what I meant. It was clear to me but sometimes men's minds are tilted. Stuff just rolls off which should sink-in and stick.

At three o'clock, I took a break outside the lab. I had not seen nor heard from Zakee all night. I was standing by the windows in the hallway, eating cut up watermelon, when he appeared. "How was your weekend?" I asked while putting a piece of melon in my mouth

"It was too short. I needed two more days."

"Did you read the letter?"

"Yes," he replied, staring at my container of melons.

"Do you want some watermelon?" I asked, putting a piece on my fork and pointing it at him.

"Yes. Feed it to me."

"You big baby. Here, you can have the rest of it," I said, handing him the container.

"I want you to put the pieces in my mouth, one-at-a-time." He opened his mouth wide, ready to receive the first piece.

"What about the letter? What did you think?" I questioned him while I fed him a piece of fruit.

"Wait until I finish eating. It is not polite to talk with food in your mouth. I do have manners."

"Didn't your mama teach you never to withhold information from a woman who is holding a fork in your mouth?"

"No. But she did tell me never to get involved with a married woman. You have me in a love triangle," he said, holding my arm, preventing me from feeding him.

"What are you going to do about it?"

"The right thing."

"Which is?"

"Finish eating your watermelon by myself." He released my arm, took the fork and ate the remainder of the watermelon.

# TWENTY-FIVE

I misinterpreted Zakee when he said, he was going to do the right thing. I thought he meant eating my watermelon. Later I understood, completely.

My love for Zakee was at a pinnacle. Since he admitted he was in a love triangle, I was determined to keep his angle intact. By removing Carl from the triangle, Zakee and I formed a straight line. No angles were necessary to have a fulfilling relationship with Zakee.

Zakee brought the best out in me. He had a way with me like no other man. His pizzazz drove me crazy.

Other men noticed the new, sexy, me. Everywhere I went, heads turned. Men talked to me more frequently. They gave me looks of admiration. Being uncaged definitely had its benefits.

The more attention I received, the more attention I wanted. I made sure I was slamming going to work in order to receive more attention. For someone who had been depressed for six years and thought of herself as unattractive, all the attention was mind boggling. And I loved every minute of it.

Frequently in the summer, I took the kids swimming. In the past, when I wore the short natural, I didn't think twice about going to work with my hair in that style. But now, that I was uncaged, I was ashamed of wearing my natural hair. I was accustomed to wearing my pressed hair in many nice looking styles. I couldn't go backward to the plain me. I wanted to be Vanessa, the beautiful, always, until the day I died.

I was in a dilemma. How do I continue to look good and go swimming at the same time? I can't press my hair every time I swim. Plus, I wouldn't have the time. What do I do? I thought for a moment but didn't come up with a solution.

One afternoon, in early July, the kids and I went to the pool. I worked that night and decided to wear my natural to work. To heck with what Zakee thought. This was my kinky hair, the way God made it. Something was wrong with me if I was ashamed of what God made.

I still wondered what Zakee's reaction would be. Would he think I'm attractive? Or would he lose interest? Tonight, I'd find out.

It was four o'clock in the morning. I hadn't seen Zakee all night. When I turned the corner to go to the ladies room, I spotted him coming down the hall.

Zakee smiled as he came closer. "What have you done to your hair?"

I kept walking toward him without replying. When we were at arms length, he reached out, gripped a handful of hair, yanked it up and pulled me down the hall like a bear with a cub.

"Do you like it?" I asked still under his clutch, not knowing what else to say.

"Yes, I do. I love short fro's. It looks good on you too," he said releasing my hair.

"I'm glad you like it. I wasn't sure what your reaction would be."

"Let me tell you something about me," he said, moving from the center of the hall to the wall. "There are two things I like in a woman, inward beauty and outward charm. The way you wear your hair is trivial to me. The inner integrity of your mind and heart are more important than your outward appearance."

"I noticed your visits have decreased since I gave you the letter," I said, changing the subject.

"You're not single like the rest of us," he said courtly with a serious expression.

"If I was single, would it make a difference?"

His eyes scanned my eyes and head. "Excuse me. I need to go to the snack bar and back to work." He walked off, leaving me standing in a daze.

Maybe it was the hair, I thought as I went to the ladies room. I've never seen him act icy.

On the way home, I had a bright idea. I would buy a wig and wear it to work on the days I went swimming. The idea excited me because I never owned a wig before. Being uncaged made me adventurous. That evening, I went to Royal Wig in the Wal-Mart Shopping Center on Wesley Chapel Road. The owner, a short, slim, middle aged, Asian female with short black hair, was sitting at the door when I entered. I was her only customer.

"Hello. May I help you," she said with a heavy Chinese accent.

"No. I just wanna look."

The place was small. A full length mirror covered the wall adjacent to the checkout counter. Wigs lined two walls and two counters that were in the middle of the floor. The wigs were an assortment of colors, lengths, and styles. They all were mounted on mannequin heads.

I looked at every wig. Finally, I decided on two. One was a whole-wheat-bread-brown, shoulder length with full bangs and curls that flipped under. The other wig was coal-black with wavy curls that reached the middle of my back.

I went to the mirror with both wigs. First, I tried on the brown wig. I experienced a sensation when I put it on. A type of euphoria came over me. I took the first wig off and tried on the other one. The second wig made me look like Diana Ross. I loved it! I placed some hair to rest on my breasts. I loved the way I looked in it. It made me feel beautiful, sexy, and devilish at the same time. "I'll take this one," I said, to the owner.

"That really looks good on you," she commented, nodding with approval.

I put the other wig back in its original place before walking to the counter to pay for my first choice. The owner reached for the price tag. "This will be

$36.98, with tax. Would you like earrings to go with your wig?" she asked, ringing up my purchase.

"No. I only have enough money to pay for the wig."

"Come back to see us." she smiled, handing me the receipt.

I wore the wig home. As I left the store, a car stopped in front of me with two handsome men inside.

"Hey, foxy lady. Do you need a ride?" asked the guy on the passenger side with short, wavy, black hair, smooth, jet-black skin and a Billy Dee Williams smile.

"No," I answered and smiled.

They drove off continuing to turn their heads back. This wig must make me look better than I think. I've never had that kind of reaction before. I'm going to knock 'em dead at work tonight, I thought as I walked to my car.

When Carl came home, I was in our bedroom, ironing, with the wig on. I heard him open the door and come up the steps. My back was to him when he entered the room.

Carl laughed. "What the hell is that on your head?" he asked, coming closer to inspect it.

"You know I'm uncaged. Expect the unexpected. (After the welling-up experience, I referred to myself as uncaged). Do you like it?" I asked, putting my ironed shorts on.

"Let me sit down to get over the shock," he said, reaching for the brown plaid chair next to me. Once seated, he looked up at me, studied the combination of me and the wig for a minute. "It's different."

"I'm different. I'm not the same person I used to be."

"I know. The new you don't fuck."

"That's because, I feel like I'm being raped when we have sex."

"You coulda fooled me. You're making that up. You act like you enjoy every minute of it to me."

"I have to pretend I'm enjoying it just to get through it. I turn over and cry when it's over. Look at my face. It's full of bumps. Since I've been uncaged, I've been on an emotional roller coaster ride. I used to be non-emotional. Now, I experience emotional highs and lows all the time. It feels really strange."

"It also feels strange not fucking but twice a month. I liked you better caged. At least you fucked."

"That's just it. You make me feel like a sex object. I feel, you don't love me as a wife. I'm just a "fucking" machine to you. Since I've been uncaged, I realized, I'm good for more than sex. I have high self-esteem. Before, I had none. I know beyond-a-shadow-of-a-doubt, 'I can do all things in Jesus Christ who strengthens me.' Without Christ, I can do nothing. With Christ, I can conquer the world! Hand me my walking shoes next to you."

He tossed me my shoes while I sat on the bed in front of him.

"I'm glad you feel that way. I quit my job today. You won't have any problems paying the bills with Christ helping you."

"That's right. How do you think we've made it this far? That was your fifth job this year. You've been in-and-out of jobs since you were fired at Lockheed in '91. I believe you don't want to work," I said, tying up my shoes.

"That's a lie. I want to work. You don't know how hard it is for a black man to find a decent job."

"The problem is not you finding a decent job but keeping a job once you are employed. You want every job to be like Lockheed, easy going."

"The jobs I get pay me peanuts for working my ass off. We may be off the plantations, but they want us to work like mules on the job. I ain't no fool. And I sho ain't no mule."

"I'm going to walk to vent my frustrations," I said, standing up.

"Are you walking in the wig?"

"No. Why?"

"The police might think you're working."

We both laughed. I took the wig off, combed my hair, and went walking. Carl watched TV.

I wore the wig to work that night. I didn't know if I would see Zakee or not.

Four-thirty in the morning, I heard a knock on the door. I answered it thinking it was housekeeping. When I opened the door, Zakee stood on the other side with his eyes bucked. I stepped outside, smiling, proud of my appearance.

"Your husband let you come out the house like that?" he asked with his eyes still bucked.

"Yes. He doesn't tell me what to do. I'm not a child."

"I wouldn't have it," he said, shaking his head in disapproval.

"You don't like it?" I asked, erasing my smile.

"You look like you're ready."

I am ready, I thought. I am ready to be with you. I turned around to show him the whole wig. "I love it!"

"Let me see it." He put his fingers all in it to examine it. "I don't like it. I don't like it at all," he said, getting upset. "I am leaving. I can't stand seeing you with that wig on." He walked off.

I still liked my wig even if Zakee didn't. I bombed out again, first the letter, now the wig. Every time I try to make things better, I end up making it worst. I went back inside the lab.

Zakee's sporadic visits came to a screeching halt, and because he changed posts every night, there was no way for me to located him. Besides, it wouldn't be right for me to track him down. Once when I saw him in the snack bar and waited for him to come out, he accused me of stalking him. I'm not a stalker. I'm a woman who is in love with a man she can't have.

As the days turned into weeks, I became obsessed with seeing Zakee again. Each time I went to the ladies room, I stared down the hallway to the Corrections Department, hoping to get a glimpse of Zakee either coming out or going in. I'd stand by the elevators near the entrance to the Corrections Department at eleven o'clock to witness the correction officers shift change, who came and went in groups. I stood there a few minutes to see if Zakee was in a group. Even if I didn't see Zakee, it was a sight to behold seeing all those gray and blue uniforms going here and there.

My obsession turned me into a mad woman. I got the telephone book to look up his name to see if it was listed. How many Zakee Abdul-Rauf's could be in the book, I reasoned? To my delight, there was only one name listed. I dialed the number. It was disconnected. I wrote the address down. I knew where his street was located. It was a ten to fifteen minute drive from my house.

The cruise was four weeks away. One price tag remained. Something was suppose to happen—soon.

I debated whether or not I should go to Zakee's place. I decided not to go. I went to sleep instead. I thought about the prophesy as I went to sleep.

As I slept, I dreamed of going to Zakee's place. I pulled up into the driveway, behind his car. I got out, looking good, wearing my sexy, green top that showed off my breasts, a short white skirt, and white sandals. I strutted to the door and knocked. Zakee opened the door, shocked to see me. His eyes lit up.

"What are you doing here?" he asked admiring my attire. "How did you find me?"

"Easy," I said in a very sexy voice. "I looked your name up in the telephone book. Are you glad to see me?"

"Of course." He smiled with desire in his eyes. He opened the door, drooling at the mouth. "Come in."

I went inside to the living room. We talked on the sofa. He suddenly pulled me close to him. We kissed. Our passions overruled our senses. We made passionate love on the sofa.

"I have been wanting you for a long time," he whispered in my ear when it was over.

"I've been wanting you, too. Every time I hear the song, My Body's Calling You, by R. Kelly, I think of you," I moaned.

"I can never let you go. I must have you for the rest of my life," he said while kissing me all over.

"I'm yours, till death do us part."

I then dreamed about our wedding and Carl's funeral. The prophesy will be fulfilled. Zakee will be mine!

The next day was Saturday. Usually, the kids went with me to church, but they went off with Carl.

Eli Woodson, my pastor, preached from the cafeteria stage. His six-foot, five inch, moderate built body, towered over the five-foot podium. Usually, I'm attentive and cleave to every word of his sermons. But today, my mind kept drifting in-and-out, more out than in.

"...Brethren, it's time for all the walls of division, of this world, to come down. We must be united by God's Holy Spirit that dwells in us. We must lay all prejudices aside and lay them at Christ's feet. Our fellowman, regardless of race, color, nationality, and yes, even creed, religious beliefs are our blood brothers and sisters in Christ. The same blood Christ made for the Christians, he made for the Jews, Muslims, New Agers, Buddhists, Atheists, and all others. Christ shed His blood for all mankind, for the forgiveness of their sins. We are commissioned to love all of God's people."

When pastor Woodson said, "...love all God's people", I thought about my love for Zakee. I agreed with him wholeheartedly. I loved him for his character. It didn't matter to me that we didn't have the same religious beliefs. Our beliefs were different, but we believed in the same God, the God of Abraham. The Muslims came from Abraham's son Ishmael, Sarah's Egyptian handmaid, Hagar's son. Christians came from Isaac, the son of Sarah, the son of promise. The Jews also came from Abraham, Isaac, and Jacob. Therefore, we worship the same God but are divided through our beliefs. There is only one God.

If these good Christians knew, I loved a Muslim, they would condemn me to the lake of fire. As I was thinking, my body was standing in front of the lake of fire. Satan and his demons surrounded me. Everything was dark except the light that came from the fire.

"Ah. What do we have here, fellow demons? Another backsliding saint," said Satan.

"Ha. Ha. Ha," roared Satan and his army of demons.

"You have committed spiritual adultery in your mind. You wicked backslider! I am merciless! Into the lake of fire you go to burn up!"

His demons lifted me up and threw me into the fire. As I burned, screaming in pain, Satan stuck a huge pitch fork into my heart.

"Here's another well-done saint."

"Ha. Ha. Ha," they all laughed again.

Satan scooped my ashes out of the fire and threw them into the air. They landed at Christ's feet, at His throne, in heaven. My ashes transformed back into my physical body. Christ was an illumination of brilliant light. His voice sounded like many waters.

"Why are you here?" He asked.

"Dear Lord, I was burnt up in the lake of fire for committing spiritual adultery. Please have mercy upon me," I pleaded.

"Your sins are covered by my shed blood. They are forgiven."

"Thank you, Lord. You are full of mercy and love. Lord, I am still guilty of loving a man that is not my husband. Lord, You said in James 3:6-8, "...The tongue is an unrighteous world among our members, staining the whole body,...no human being can tame the tongue..." Lord, I understand about the tongue, but who can control the heart?"

"You control your heart. You wrestle not against flesh and blood, but wickedness in high places."

"Dear Lord, several months ago, a prophesy was whispered in my ear. It said, "Before you take the last price tag off, something will happen for the two of you to get together." One price tag remains. That time is now. Will the prophesy come to pass?"

"Go your way. The prophesy is certain. It will come to pass in its time."

I was whisked off from Christ's presence like a whirlwind and placed back in my seat at church. I heard pastor Woodson's closing remarks.

"Remember brethren, there is neither black, white, Jew, Muslim, Christian, Buddhist, or Atheist. We are all one in Christ Jesus, our Lord."

When church was over, I took Zakee's address out of my purse. I'm going to his house now. I have to see him or I'll go crazy! I rushed to my car and drove to his address on Moreland Avenue. I looked at the address on the paper again. I looked at the address on the grocery store building. They were the same. Zakee lives in a store? But he talked about his dogs, his house, and his yard. My heart sank. Zakee where are you? Come back, you're mine!

# TWENTY-SIX

I sped from the grocery store with tears in my eyes. A car darted in front of me before I reached the I-20 East entrance ramp. I quickly changed lanes to avoid hitting the black Volkswagon Bug in the rear. The incident snapped me back to reality. This is a fast paced dog's world. The slow and weak don't have a chance. Driving on Atlanta's interstates is like driving on the Atlanta Speedway. You must exceed 70 miles per hour to keep up with traffic and prevent someone from running you off the road.

I cruised home at 75 miles per hour, thinking about Zakee the whole time. Things he'd said in previous conversations, I repeated in my mind. He spoke several times of his dogs. I never asked how many he had. But from his conversations about feeding them, he had two, possibly three large dogs. I never asked what kind either. Since I wasn't fond of dogs, the kind didn't matter to me. In my book, a dog was a dog.

Once he came to work wearing a glove. When I asked him, what happened? He took the glove off and showed me a gauze bandage that concealed eleven stitches. He accidentally cut his hand, the day before, when the sharp knife slipped while opening a bag of dog food. Needless to say, he was in a hurry and wasn't paying attention to what he was doing.

Zakee spoke about a fenced backyard. He enjoyed sitting on his back, screened, porch, in the cool of the evenings, watching his dogs, reading, and meditating. He often said his back yard was a quiet haven where he found serenity. His dogs laid by his feet as he reclined in his favorite white and green, outdoor recliner. Sometimes he ate his dinner outside because it was so peaceful.

I remembered those special occasions with his mother. On Mother's Day and her birthday, he either took her to a nice restaurant or prepared a meal especially for her. This past Mother's Day, he put his best white, lace tablecloth on his dinning room table. Covered it with fine gold and white china, crystal glasses, silver serving trays and two candles. He served her a meal of stuffed pheasant, wild rice, steamed asparagus, and Baked Alaska.

As I pulled into my driveway, I thought back on the grocery store. Maybe, I misunderstood him. Maybe, the dogs were watchdogs for the store. The fenced backyard was a fenced dog pen. His house was an upper or side room in the store. And the meals with his mother were pure fabrication.

Lies! Lies! Lies! I've been served a gourmet meal of lies. I felt like a bird stuffed with lies and ready to be served to the wolves. How could he be so deceitful? I always thought of Zakee as a kind, gentle, caring, honest man. I see, he's no different from the other dogs in the kennel.

Carl's car was gone. He and the kids were still out doing their thing. I decided, as I unlocked the front door, I'd grab a bite to eat then take a nap while the house was quiet

A turkey ham sandwich sounded good as I examined the refrigerator for my choices. I didn't feel like heating up my Sabbath dinner of barbecue chicken, string beans, squash, and macaroni and cheese. I was tired. I wanted to take a nap, as soon as possible, to rest my body and mind.

Zakee's address flashed in my head as I closed my eyes. The dogs, the store, the yard, the Mother's Day meal, all churned in my head. Finally, I dozed off to sleep.

In my sleep, I dreamed of Carl, Carl Jr., and Carlos walking in a graveyard. They were crying and stopped at a gravesite. My name was carved on the headstone. It read, Mrs. Vanessa Grant Lewis, August 18,1956 to August 23, 1994, Uncaged and Free.

"Your mama is free now," said Carl, drying his eyes, consoling the boys. "She is in her final resting place, waiting the resurrection of the dead."

"Mama told us about the resurrection many times," said little Carl, placing a bouquet of red and white roses on my grave. "She said everyone who has ever died will live again in the resurrections."

"Yeah, Dad. Mama told us about three resurrections in the Bible. I acted as if I wasn't paying Mama any attention, but I remember her saying, the first resurrection was for the dead in Christ. They will rise first and meet Christ in the sky at His second coming."

"Your mama will be in the first resurrection. She was baptized and had God's Holy Spirit."

"Mama said, when we are older and fully understand God's Word, repent of our sins, and wanted to live God's way, we can be baptized, too. Right now, we are too young and don't fully understand God and His truth," little Carl said, touching the headstone.

"What else did your mother say about the resurrections, Carlos? It makes me feel good to know you were paying attention. She always thought she was wasting her time with y'all. She didn't think you were listening."

"The second resurrection is for the people who died not knowing Christ. They will come back to life and be taught by Christ, how to live."

"Mama, always said, those in the first resurrection had spiritual bodies like Christ. While those in the second resurrection had physical bodies. She read, Ezekiel 37, the valley of dry bones, to explain the second resurrection," little Carl added.

Talking about the resurrections made them stop crying. I believe they were comforted in knowing, I would live again. That one day, we would be united again as a family.

"Y'all get an A+ today for explaining the resurrections. Do you feel better knowing your mother will live again?"

"Yes, Dad, I do," said little Carl. "Mama explained it to us because she didn't want us to grieve over her death or your death when y'all died. She said, "Your dad and I won't be with you always. When we die, don't grieve because we will live again. Jesus Christ, your Savior and elder brother, will never fail you or leave you. He will be with you until the end.""

"Wow. I can't believe y'all remember so much of what your mama said. I'm really impressed. Your heads are not as hard as I thought."

"There's one more resurrection, Dad," interrupted Carlos.

"Which one is it, son?"

"The third resurrection. It's for the wicked who lived but refused to obey Christ. They knew Christ and His truth but refused to obey Him. They will be resurrected to be thrown into the lake of fire. Their ashes will be on the soles of the righteous feet."

"Which resurrection do y'all want to be in?" asked Carl.

"The first!" they shouted.

"Me too. Y'all said that loud enough to wake the dead. Let's get out of this place."

They walked to the next gravesite on their way out.

"Look Dad!" shouted little Carl, pointing to the grave. "Look at the name. That's the same person who died trying to save Mama out of the burning car before it exploded."

"Can you pronounce his name? I can't."

"Sure Dad. His name is Zakee Abdul-Rauf, November 30, 1951 to August 23, 1994."

"He was a very brave man for attempting to rescue her. What a shame. They both died together. Now, they rest together, in their graves, side-by-side."

"Dad, I'm hungry. Can we go to the Old Country Buffet as our reward for paying attention to Mama?" asked little Carl.

"Only if you can tell me what book in the Bible explains the resurrections?"

"That's easy, Dad," exclaimed Carlos, giving little Carl a high-five. "Revelation 20."

"Y'all know how to break me. The Old Country Buffet sounds good. I'm ready to eat, too. Let's go. This place is giving me the creeps," Carl said, scratching all over.

"Bye Mama," the boys said, waving. "We'll see you later."

They left me to rest with Zakee next to me.

I woke up crying, realizing the death of Zakee and me was the fulfillment of the price tag prophecy. I was saddened and relieved at the same time. If I couldn't have him alive, I'd gladly have him dead, resting by my side, until the resurrection.

Carl and the boys were standing over me when I opened my eyes.

"What's wrong with you? You were moaning so loud when we came home, we thought you were being attacked," stated Carl, sitting on the bed. "You're crying. Did you have another nightmare? Did you kill me again?"

"No. This time, I killed myself."

"Mama. Do you want to die?" asked Carlos, handing me a wad of tissues from a box of Kleenex on my dresser.

"No, son. Not yet." I wiped my eyes and blew my nose.

"If I did die, what will happen to me?" I asked, seeing if they would respond like they did in the dream.

"Your body will rot and worms will eat it up," said Carlos proud of his answer.

"Little Carl, what will happen when I die?"

"You'll be reincarnated. Bring me some money when you come back. I know I'll be broke living with Dad."

"Let me get up. I can't die yet. Y'all don't remember what I taught you, about death in the Bible, concerning the resurrections. Sit down. We will have a Bible study, right now," I said, reaching for my Bible at the head of my bed and turned to Revelation 20.

"I'm leaving," announced Carl, standing up. "It's a double header on TV that I came home to watch. I'll leave you and the kids alone to have a Bible study."

I saw little Carl ease out the door ahead of his dad.

"Little Carl, come back here!" I shouted, placing my feet on the floor, ready to run after him.

"I'll go get him, Mama. I won't let him miss the Bible study," Carlos said, running out the bedroom door.

Suddenly, I heard the front door slam. I ran down the steps and opened the front door. Carl was pulling out the driveway with the boys.

"Come back here! Where are you going?" I yelled from the front door.

Carl stuck his head out the window. "Old Country Buffet. We decided to get something to eat while you have your Bible study."

"Bye Mama," the boys said, smiling, as they waved from the car as it pulled off. "We'll see you later."

I returned to my room and had my Bible study alone. Only in my dream did my family know the truth. In real life, they didn't know squat. They didn't know, and they didn't want to know.

"Lord, I can't die yet. I have work to do," I said as I began my Bible study.

After my Bible study, I walked through the house, noticing how run down everything was. When I was depressed, the condition of the house didn't matter. But now, since I've been healed of my depression, I wanted everything in my life right. Everything broken must be either fixed or replaced. My house, in its present condition, was depressing.

I took a notepad and pen from the top kitchen drawer and made a list of what needed to be done. I divided the list into three categories, urgent, ASAP, and later. Things I needed to purchase after the cruise I put in the urgent column. The majority of the repairs, however, had to wait until next year when I had time to save some money.

First, I noted what needed to be done on the outside. In the urgent column, I put gutters, grass, and replacing the three outside and inside doors. Painting the front porch and back deck were ASAP.

Second, I noted what needed to be done in the living room. In the urgent column were: painting the walls, replacing the badly soiled blue carpet, replacing the soiled and torn yellow sofa and loveseat with stuffing coming out of the arms, the cracked glass in the coffee table needed to be replaced, a hole in the wall behind the front door needed repairing where the door knob went through it one day. ASAP was replacing the fourteen year old drapes with new vertical blinds.

The kitchen was next. It had two urgent things that needed to be replaced— the damaged floor with several holes in the tile, and a new table with chairs. The original chairs to the table had been damaged over the years. We were using metal chairs instead. ASAP was replacing the low hanging light fixture with a ceiling fan. In the later column, I put new stove, dishwasher, microwave oven, and possibly converting the deck into a dinning room.

I went upstairs to the bedrooms. I noted the hall bathroom needed a new floor, ASAP. My room urgently needed, painting, new comforters with matching curtains, blinds, carpet and a new bathroom floor.

I opened little Carl's bedroom door. He needed a new bedroom suit, urgently. He was sleeping on the bunk bed I bought twelve years ago. New carpet was also on the list.

I closed the door to little Carl's room and entered Carlos's room. He urgently needed a bedroom suit, comforter and curtains. His bed was propped up on one side with telephone books. As I examined his room, I noticed his bed was leaning to one side. The sag in the middle was sagging more. I went to straighten the bed. I took the three telephone books out and pulled the bed over. Out of curiosity, I opened the white pages and turned to Zakee's name. To my surprise, a different address and number were listed. I grabbed the book, ran to the phone, and I dialed the number. It rang. A man answered.

"Hello, may I speak to Zakee?"

"Speaking."

"Zakee, this is Vanessa."

"I am working on a report. I don't have much time."

"I haven't seen you in a while. I was wondering what was going on?"

"I am getting married."

"When?"

"In two weeks."

"How long have you known her?"

"Six weeks."

"Do you love her?"

"Love is an ethereal feeling. A concept I can not comprehend."

"Don't get philosophical with me. Do you love her or not? Yes or no?"

"Yes."

"That's all I want to know. Goodbye."

Click.

I stared at the phone. I couldn't believe what I heard. Zakee was getting married in two weeks. So that's the fulfillment of the prophecy—"Before you take the last price tag off, something will happen for the two of you to get together."

Lord, I know You work in mysterious ways, but I don't understand the connection. How can I gain Zakee by losing him? He is suppose to marry me, not her.

# TWENTY-SEVEN

Zakee was getting married. While his fiancee was scoring home runs, I couldn't come up to bat. Based on the score, I wasn't in the ball game. I wasn't even near the field. She was scoring with Zakee while I was tied up in another game that was almost over. It was illegal to start a new game without finishing the old. Losing Zakee made me, more than ever, want this old game with Carl to end—soon.

Carl and I were in the bottom of the ninth. One more out would end this marriage. Losing Zakee made me realize where I was with Carl in our game. Our sex life had hit rock bottom. He had to intoxicate me before I gave it up because I refused sex when I was sober. I couldn't pretend anymore that I enjoyed sex with him. Sometimes I was so drunk, I didn't remember anything. Carl told me, the next morning, things I did and said the night before.

Luckily, the cruise was approaching. It lifted my spirits. The anticipation gave me a mental boost. I spent the remainder of the time left preparing for our September 20, vacation and September 29, cruise.

The time finally arrived to pack. As I surveyed my closet, deciding what outfits to wear, I slowly pulled out the black and silver sequined dress. The price tag dangled in the air as I clutched it in my arms. Tears streamed down my face as I remembered the price tag prophesy. Losing Zakee, broke my heart into a million pieces. Emptiness and pain enveloped me. Lord, please give me the strength to endure this dark, dark, hour.

Without removing the price tag, I placed the dress in the garment bag with the other six new outfits. The high I felt when I purchased them had been replaced with a low, sinking feeling. The anticipation of Zakee one day seeing me in the outfits was now an impossibility just like our dream wedding.

This particular time in my life marked an impasse with Zakee. I didn't know what the future held but for the present time our journey was over. I must now concentrate on piecing my heart and life back together. I couldn't afford to look behind, instead, I must tread forward, one-step-at-a-time.

I thought of the cruise as a transition period of my life. Just like I crossed the Atlantic Ocean and set foot on unfamiliar soil. I must take my mind, my life on a different journey—a journey that far transcended anything I've ever experienced or imaged.

The cruise itself was wonderful! We dined first-class for dinner and piged out the rest of the day with the numerous buffets. The highlight of the cruise to all of us was definitely the food. Next was the entertainment. There was not a dull moment during our entire waking hours. We watched movies, live shows, shopped, gambled, took a bottom glass boat cruise and the boys snorkled. The worst part, unquestionably, was having to spend so much time with Carl. At the end of the day he was ready for sex, and I still couldn't handle it. I discovered new ways to avoid him. Having the boys in the same room, helped out a lot. By the end of the cruise, we were not ready to come back home.

My first order of business, after the cruise, was getting my house in a livable condition again. I purchased as many items as possible on the urgent list then started with the ASAP column. Bringing the house up helped lift me also. I felt broken inside, and I was sure the broken, soiled, cracked, torn furniture, damaged walls, carpet, and floors contributed to my mental despair.

The second order of business was writing books. Not only did I want to write a book about my life and Zakee, but I wanted to write children's books. I planned to take a basic writing course in January and start writing "Uncaged" in April or May.

I knew the Lord would help me to accomplish both. Therefore, I committed them into His hands. It was now His responsibility to get them done. In the meantime, I went on about my business.

Immediately, after I returned from the cruise, events started happening. Before my vacation, I browsed through a *Good House Keeping* magazine on the job. I read it halfway through. When I returned from my vacation, I picked the magazine up again to finish reading it. Inside was an advertisement card from The Institute of Children's Literature to request a writing aptitude test. I cut the application card out, filled it out, and mailed it in. The next night, I went to get the same magazine, but it was gone. I never saw it or another advertisement again.

The week I received the aptitude test, a newspaper flier from Atlanta Metropolitan College arrived in the mailbox. This was the first time in thirteen years, since I lived at my address, that I received a flier from them. Inside contained information on a basic writing class that started in two weeks. I registered. The class was almost canceled due to lack of participation. The teacher was even absent the first day of class. Six students enrolled by the second week to enable the class to proceed. Halfway through the class, the aptitude test was due. I sent the completed test back and was accepted. I enrolled for the January session.

The week of Thanksgiving, I bought Carl Jr. a black lacquer, queen size, bedroom suit, curtains, comforters, and sheets for the three bedrooms, and blinds for my bedroom. I asked Carl to paint Carlos and our bedroom for his contribution to the remodeling. It was his responsibility to buy the paint. Everything else would be done later.

One day in October, soon after the cruise, I was standing outside the lab when Zakee came down the hall. He was grinning from ear-to-ear. When he reached me, he stopped.

"I wanted you to know, I got married," he said, beaming.

"I know. You told me on the telephone, you were getting married in two weeks, the last week in August."

"Oh, that was you I was talking to. I thought you were another Vanessa I know."

"What day was your wedding?"

"September 10th. We just returned from visiting her people in Detroit."

"Congratulations. Marriage agrees with you. I've never seen you so happy."

"Thanks. I just came by to tell you I was married," he said then walked off.

I stared at him until he disappeared. I was truly happy for him. If marriage made him beam like that, he must really be happy.

The beginning of December, I saw Zakee again in the hallway outside the lab. His beam was gone. I noticed the spark returning for me in his eyes. He stopped to talk.

"How is everything with you?" I asked while chewing on my apple. I had just taken a big bite when he appeared.

"Not too good. Every time I look around, my wife has the dinning room full with her suitcases and other things. She's left seven times and is threatening to leave again," he said, looking distressed.

"What are you doing to your wife to make her want to leave?" I asked, taking another bite.

"Nothing. I think she's immature," he replied, resting on the wall.

"Why you say that?"

"She's twenty-nine. I think she needs to grow up."

"Twenty-nine! I repeated almost choking on the apple. "You're forty-three. Why did you rob the cradle?"

"I like young women. Any woman past thirty-three is too old for me."

"I remember, you thought I was thirty-two when we first met."

"You didn't look thirty-seven...I guess I just don't understand women."

"You're still newlyweds. You're just going through a period of adjustment. Hang in there."

"Technically, we're not."

"Why not?" I asked puzzled.

"We're not legally married. We had a Muslim ceremony, but I never filed the marriage license in the courthouse because she started acting funny and packing her things two weeks after we said our vows."

"Wait-a-minute. You're not really married?"

169

"No. And the way she's acting, we won't be together long. I haven't filed the license, and I don't intend to as long as she keeps packing her things."

The apple became tasteless, I discontinued eating it for fear of either choking on it or spitting the residue in Zakee's face. The news of his marital status made my knees buckle. I needed to return to the lab before I passed out.

"I need to go back inside. My break is over."

He looked at me but didn't say anything.

I went inside throwing the apple core into the nearest trash can. I repeated our conversation in my head over-and-over again. Zakee wasn't married after all. Before I took my last price tag off, on the cruise, the relationship was in trouble. Does this mean, he will someday be mine? The possibility of still being able to be with Zakee excited me.

I ran into Zakee again, the following week, in the hallway going to the ladies room. He had on a navy blue, pullover sweater, blue pants, and gray shirt. He looked better than ever. We stopped to talk.

"What's happening?" he asked, smiling.

"You tell me. How is your wife?"

"Everything is the same." He paused. "Maybe, worst."

"Why you say that?"

"She got mad at me the other night for going out alone."

"So, you're in the doghouse," I said, folding my arms.

"I have been in the doghouse ever since I have been married. I can't take much more," he said, lowering his head, looking at his black shoes.

"Hold your head up. What do you plan to do?"

He lifted his head but lowered his voice. "I don't know. I am waiting to see what she does. She's in my house with her five year old daughter. She even gets mad if I say anything to the little girl."

"I'm taking a writing class to write a book about us," I said, changing the subject.

He looked at me questioningly. "You act like we had an affair."

"No. We never had an affair. We have never touched each other except for the time you grabbed my arm when I fed you my watermelon. We've only talked. But you have changed my life."

"How?"

"I tried to explain it to you in the letter, but I don't think you understood. The way I feel about you brought me out of a six year depression. You make me feel alive again. Before I met you, I was going through the motions of life, existing but not living."

"What did I do to make you feel that way?"

"I felt something between us. Do you deny it?"

"I'm not saying."

"Do you think I'm a fatal attraction?"

"I have considered it?" he answered laughing. "It's a real possibility."

"Well, I'm not. Sometimes it's not how a person feels about you but how you feel about the other person."

"I feel wrong for talking to another man's wife. People are crazy today. They are subject to do anything. You read about people being blown away everyday because of marital affairs."

"That's not true in our case. We've never had an affair. I do feel a very strong attraction between us, even if you deny it. I see it in your eyes."

"You see sleep and hunger in my eyes. I need to get something to eat and lay my head down a few minutes before my lunch break is over."

"Okay. Be funny. One day you will admit it."

"That day is not today. Excuse me," he said, moving past me. "I must leave before my break is over."

He went to the snack bar, and I went to the ladies room. One day he will admit it, I thought as I opened the door to the ladies room. In the meantime, we must go our separate ways.

I took the week after Christmas off to spend extra time with the boys for Christmas break. I decided to use some of the time to clean closets and drawers. As I cleaned, all I thought about was how unhappy I was being married to Carl. I wanted a divorce, not because of Zakee but because of me, my mental health and well being. I realized, I was still angry with Carl for leaving me in '88 and all the injustices he did to me since that time. The memories of the $5,857.92 check which he gave me $100.00 dollars for myself and $250.00 dollars for the kids. The nasty attitude and little support I received when payday came. The fact that I always got stuck with his debt, such as, his three cars I was presently paying for. I paid GMAC $25.00 dollars per month for the over $4,000.00 dollar balance of the repossessed Grand Prix in '88. The over $3,000.00 dollars for the repossessed Ford Mustang that had a lien on the house when I refinanced it in my name this year. And the $900.00 dollars for the 1981 Chevrolet Chevette he bought when I refinanced my car last year. Not to mention, the $2,000.00 dollar Lockheed loan, his job instability since '91, our total communication breakdown and the feeling of being raped during intercourse. I was tired of being used. I couldn't take anymore.

Old photographs were stashed on the floor of my closet in a large plastic bag. I pulled them out while removing my shoes and other belongings from the closet floor. I stopped cleaning and started looking through the pictures after I opened the bag and discovered what was inside. Most of the pictures were of the boys when they were small. Carl was in a lot of the pictures, holding them, giving piggyback rides, or playing in the sand by the beach. They were all of joyous occasions. Everybody was smiling, looking so happy. I cried as I continued to look at each picture. I had completely forgotten about the good times of long ago. They included times in the park, flying kites, picnics, family gatherings, funtimes at home, and when we worshipped together. Each picture captured a smile of joy of those times before and after '88.

I sighed long and hard when I looked at the last picture. I had been wrong about Carl. I had completely forgotten about the good times. They far outweighed all the negative memories and injustices I had been inflicted with. I repented, right then, and decided to make a go of my marriage. I decided, it was worth salvaging.

I returned all the pictures to the plastic bag. I thought about Carl, his favorite meal, making love to him without being drunk. A warm, loving feeling came over me as I finished cleaning the closets and drawers. I felt good all over.

The telephone rang while I was cooking Carl's favorite meal of fried chicken, cream potatoes, baked spinach, and can biscuits. I answered it. It was a salesperson who did home repairs. I scheduled an appointment for Thursday, January 12.

Carl came home as soon as I hung up the phone. Seconds after the front door closed, I greeted him with a kiss.

"Am I in the right house?" he asked, hugging me. "You look like my wife, but you're acting like someone else."

"Silly. It's me," I said laughing, hugging him back. "You're at the right house."

The smell of fried chicken filled the room. He inhaled a long, hard whiff.

"Do I smell fried chicken or is my nose playing tricks on me?" he asked, releasing his hug and walking to the kitchen.

I trailed behind him smiling. The biggest grin spread across his face as he saw his meal on the stove.

"What's up?" he asked, facing me. "Something is going on. You greet me with a kiss at the door. Then you cook my favorite meal. Are you pregnant?"

"No. I'm not pregnant. I just realized, today, how much I love you. How much you mean to me and how happy I am to be your wife."

He walked towards me, put his arms around me and we embraced. He kissed my head then passionately kissed my lips.

"Do you mind if we skip dinner and have dessert first?" he asked after we kissed.

"We don't have any dessert."

"Yes, we do," he said, placing his hand between my legs. "This is the best dessert on earth. It's sweet and satisfying."

"What about the kids? They're downstairs watching TV."

"No problem. We'll go upstairs to our room and lock the door. We'll be finished before they know what's going on. Come on, whoever you are," he said as he pulled me towards the steps, holding my hand, "before you turn back into the old Vanessa."

We entered the bedroom, locked the door and enjoyed dessert.

Dessert became a nightly treat. Carl and I were one again. No longer did I feel like I was being raped when we made love. I didn't need alcohol either to enjoy sex with Carl. All I needed and wanted was Carl.

Our twentieth wedding anniversary, January 10, was also a joyous occasion. We survived the many trials and tribulations of the former years. The future appeared promising. Surely the worst was over and the best was yet to come.

# TWENTY-EIGHT

Reaching our twentieth anniversary gave me an unsurpassing thrill. It enhanced the renewed zeal of our dying love. However, after the candles were blown out and the champagne was gone, the excitement disappeared like the smoke and the fizz. Another photograph, of a once joyous occasion, was the only permanent reminder of the event.

I asked myself, the next night, will we be together in '96 to put another candle on the cake? My answer was, only if our cake of marriage is frosted with love, decorated with roses of happiness, joy, respect, balanced financial support, and hope for a better tomorrow. It must have candles of communication that illuminate light of our aspirations and dreams. Their light must increase in time and never wean. Then and only then will this marriage survive another year.

Thursday, January 12, Nelson Roberts came to give Carl and me estimates of my list of home improvements. We wanted estimates for three inside doors, three exterior doors, a new kitchen floor, gutters, wall-to-wall carpet, and re-cementing the front right corner of the foundation. His estimate was $7,000.00 dollars. We asked, what could he do for $3,000.00 dollars? He said, his company didn't do jobs under $5,000.00 dollars. We told him, our finances couldn't go above $3,000.00, and we thought his prices were inflated. He thought we were wasting his time. We knew he was wasting ours. Carl politely showed him to the door although his initial, friendly, disposition was gone. He definitely was not our great-white-hope to get the job done.

I prayed to the Lord when Mr. Roberts left. *Lord, I don't know how I will get the home improvements done. My resources are limited, but Yours is limitless. Please, make a way for me to repair and purchase everything on my list. In the name of Your Son, Jesus Christ, I pray, Amen.*

Carl and I tried to think of other alternatives to get the repairs done. However, none of our ideas were feasible at the time. We decided to let the matter rest and enjoy TV with the boys until it was time for me to go to work.

That night, I saw Zakee. We were both standing at the ground floor elevator next to the new Emergency Clinic Lab. I had just gotten off the elevator, and he was waiting to get on.

"Hi. It's good to see ya. Long time no see," I said, stepping off the elevator.

His eyes searched my face. "Your face has cleared up. Are you and that brother getting back together?" he asked, staring me in my eyes. "Your face was full of bumps, but now it's clear."

I looked into his eyes. I wanted to say, yes, but nothing came out. I couldn't say, no, because then I'd be lying. His eyes never left my face as he waited for my reply. Consequently, he left when a third elevator came. I put my hands to my face to feel the smoothness. I hadn't noticed the disappearance of the bumps until he mentioned it. I never knew he saw them since he never committed on my face before.

I walked quickly to the ladies room to inspect my face in the mirror. As soon as I locked the door, I stared into the mirror. Sure enough, my face was clear. The ten month battle with my complexion had cleared overnight without me realizing it. It disappeared in the same manner it came—subtly.

Oh my God! I thought as I examined my face. What am I doing? Reality hit me like a ton of bricks. If I get back with Carl, I'll lose any chance of getting with Zakee. I asked myself, is getting back with Carl what I really want to do? I pondered the question. Afterwards, a discontented feeling engulfed me.

The incident with Zakee disturbed me tremendously. I knew I had to answer his question. Therefore, I wrote him a letter upon my arrival to the lab.

*Dear Zakee,*

*When you asked me if I was getting back with my husband, I couldn't answer you then. However, allow me to answer you, now, in this letter. Yes, I am.*

*Over the Christmas holidays, I found old photographs that captured happy times of our twenty year marriage. For the past six years, my mind was completely bogged down with all negative events. I had totally forgotten about the good times. I repented of wanting to divorce Carl and made a go of my marriage. The subsequent weeks have been blessed. On January 10, we celebrated our twentieth wedding anniversary.*

*I categorize my marriage into three divisions: The first was a six year honeymoon where we thrived on each other's love. The second was seven golden years when we purchased a house, had our two children, traveled to the Caribbean, and was the beginning of getting ahead financially. The third category was six years of depression with a year of release. These depressed years resulted in the disintegration of my home and family. We suffered separations, continuous job losses, financial difficulties, communication barriers, and depression.*

*Before I saw the photographs, I wanted a divorce. I was very unhappy and wanted the misery to end.*

*Meeting you ended the six years of depression for me because I loved you like I have loved no other person in my life. I remembered a prophecy given to me when I was twenty-four.*

*The seer, Madame Lee, prophesied I would have four children, two boys and two girls. She also said, eventually, I would leave my husband. When I met you, I thought you would be my next husband, and the father of my two daughters. I was waiting for God to deliver me from my marriage so we could be together.*

*Enclosed are two photographs. The picture with my short hair was taken during the depressed years. The picture with my long hair was taken during the seven golden years. I keep them as reminders. My goal is to return to the way I was during the golden years of my life, only this time it will be everlasting.*

*Yours Truly,*

*Uncaged*

I removed the photographs from my purse. The picture of me with long hair showed Carl and I standing at the base of the gold carpet steps holding hands with Carl's left arm wrapped around my waist. I was wearing a knee length, black dress with white vertical stripes. Carl had on black pants, a gray sweater, and black shirt. I reached for the scissors on the desk to cut Carl out of the picture. His left hand was still visible on my waist. The short natural picture was at a church dinner dance. I had on a black sequined, formal dress. I was sitting at a table for eight, alone with a devious smile on my face. I stuffed the two pictures in the letter before I sealed it.

I heard Jenny talking to someone at the window.

"Vanessa, you have a visitor," she yelled from the window.

"Who is it?" I yelled back annoyed, not wanting to be disturbed by officer Isaiah Avery, a married security guard who had an obvious crush on me and visited me regularly.

"Your boyfriend."

I went to investigate. It was Zakee. I didn't think Jenny noticed anything was going on between us because she never said anything before. I opened the door to talk outside.

"What brings you to my neck of the woods?" I asked Zakee smiling, holding the letter in my right hand.

"You didn't answer my question at the elevator. Are you ready to answer it now? he asked, looking pissed.

"If I didn't know better, I'd swear you cared about me."

"Well, are you and your husband getting back together?" he demanded.

"I have the answer in this letter," I said, handing him the letter.

"Why can't you tell me with your mouth?"

"I'm a writer. I express myself better in the written language. Besides, I have more to say than to answer your question. There are certain things I want you to know about me."

"I could write a book about the things you don't know about me," he said, placing the letter inside his top shirt pocket underneath his sweater.

"Maybe one day, we'll be able to read each other's book. I hear my clock going off to start up the Coulter. I need to go."

"All right," he said, walking off as I opened the lab door.

While putting the controls on the Coulter, I realized I had finally gotten over Zakee. It didn't matter to me about either of the prophecies—the one given by Madame Lee concerning the two daughters, or the finality of the price tag prophecy, being able to get together with Zakee. My focus was on Carl and my marriage.

Over the three day Martin Luther King weekend, I noticed something was still wrong with our lovemaking. Although I didn't feel like I was being raped, I didn't fully enjoy it. For some reason, I couldn't put my whole body into it. My mind wanted me to relax, forget the past, and enjoy the moment. My heart was still hurting from being broken. It needed more time to mend. It kept giving signals to the rest of my body to hold back, don't submit completely.

My body said, hold up broken heart. Carl is rocking our world. Get-in-gear heart because we are loving it.

As a result, I felt empty, dissatisfied, and violated when we finished. Something was missing in our relationship, but I couldn't put my finger on it.

Wednesday, after the holiday, the mailman came to my door with two certified letters from IRS for me to sign. One letter was addressed to Carl Lewis. The other letter was addressed to Carl & Vanessa Lewis. I opened the letter with both names on it and read it.

DEFAULTED INSTALLMENT AGREEMENT - WE INTEND TO LEVY RESPOND NOW!!
*** THE AMOUNT YOU OWE IS $1,253.24 * *
AVOID ADDITIONAL INTEREST: PAY THIS AMOUNT IN FULL IN 10 DAYS

This is a formal notice of our intent to levy (seize) your property, or the rights to it, to pay the tax you owe. Our records show you are not meeting the terms of your installment plan and we will collect the entire amount of your tax liability if you don't MAKE YOUR PAYMENTS AS AGREED.

To prevent this, you must BRING YOUR PAYMENTS UP TO DATE BY 01-26-95.

If you don't comply with the terms of the agreement by 01-26-95, we may issue a Notice of Levy on 02-15-95 without further notice to you. This means the law allows us to seize (take) property (for example, automobiles, and business assets) to collect the amount you still owe. We also may take your wages, bank accounts, commissions, and other income. See the enclosed publication for additional information.

I was so angry with Carl after I read the letter because it was his responsibility to pay IRS $100.00 dollars per month for back taxes. Carl was notorious for not paying his bills, but he had gone too far this time. This IRS letter signified the last out of our marriage. I was furious with Carl and wouldn't take anymore. He was O-U-T! O-U-T of the marriage. O-U-T of my life! O-U-T! O-U-T!! O-U-T!!!

The '92 tax was the final thing in both our names. Ever since '89, we filed our taxes separately, except for one year, '92. After the walkout in '88, I refused to sign anything with Carl. Refinancing the house in my name last year put an end to any legal document with joint ownership.

While waiting for Carl's arrival from work, I seethed, simmered and stewed. I couldn't wait to give him a piece of my mind. When he arrived home, I was in our bedroom. I heard him enter the kitchen first before coming up the steps. I waited like a cat ready to pounce upon its prey. Carl entered the room. I had both letters in my hand. "Here's your mail," I said, handing him the certified IRS letters while sitting on the end of the bed. He took the letters, sat in the chair in front of me, and read the one I opened. I was fully cooked when he finished. "What do you plan to do about the letters?" I asked with my arms crossed and obviously agitated.

"Do you have three hundred dollars I can have to pay them with?" he asked, putting the letter in his lap.

"No," I replied, giving him a disgusted stare. "I can't believe you're asking me for money to pay IRS. You give me $150.00 dollars a week. I have to pay $650.00 dollars for our mortgage, $325.00 dollars for groceries, $150.00 dollars for utilities, $35.00 dollars for the telephone, $230.00 dollars for life and health insurance, $80.00 for piano lessons, $63.00 dollars for the orthodontist, $60.00 dollars for karate classes, and $50.00 dollars for GMAC—it went up in January. These are bills we should pay together. Plus I have my personal bills such as $330.00 dollars for my car note, $250.00 dollars for my investments and $1,000.00 dollars a year for my car insurance. Not to mention tithes and offerings."

"If you won't help me, I won't be able to pay them. Can't you rob Peter to pay Paul so I can pay the IRS?"

"You don't have to worry about the one with both our names on it. I will mail the full amount tomorrow. This will be the last time I'll get stuck paying your debt because I plan to get a divorce. I have had it with you. I can't take anymore. Every time I get two steps ahead, you set me four steps back."

"Divorce! Don't you think you're overreacting? Three hundred dollars will straighten this out. You'll divorce me for three hundred, measly, dollars?" He stood on his feet in a rage.

"It's not the amount of money that's the issue, it's the principle. You have shunned your responsibility for the millionth time. Consequently, I'm stuck paying your debt. I'm not spending my life struggling with you. I can do bad by myself."

Carl stooped down to pick up the letters that fell to the floor when he stood up. He threw them on the bed next to me.

"I want to pay my bills," he said, sitting back down. "I just haven't had the money."

"That's a lie! If you can play golf every Saturday and most Sundays, Cash Three everyday, Fantasy Five and The Lotto, then you can pay $100.00 dollars a month to IRS. You do those things last, not first."

"I play everyday so I can win, in order to pay my bills. I can't help it if I'm economically challenged," he said standing up, turning his pockets inside out. "Look I'm so broke, I don't even have pocket lent."

"I'm economically, emotionally, spiritually, and mentally challenged being married to you. I've given you twenty-five years of my life. I refuse to give you anymore. If I could sum up our marriage in one word, it would be FRUSTRATED! You frustrate me to no end! I'm not happy and I'm tired of being frustrated. I feel my life is off track. Getting a divorce will give me a fresh start and put my life back on track."

"You've been wanting a divorce for sometime. Go ahead and get a divorce if you're not happy with me. I'm tired of you keep throwing divorce up in my face every time something happens. Damn it! If a divorce will make you happy," he took the IRS letters and threw them across the room, "get a damn divorce!" he shouted as he stormed out the room.

"I will, Carl Lewis. I will," I muttered, sliding my wedding rings off my finger.

# TWENTY-NINE

"If you're tied up, you'd better stay tied up," are the words of Johnny Taylor's song, "It's cheaper to keep her." I say, "If you're tied up and in an unhappy relationship, it's better to become unleashed before the relationship strangles you to death." If both parties are happy and the relationship is working, by all means, stay tied up until death do you part.

I know I married Carl for better or worst, for richer or poorer, in sickness and in health until death do us part. I also know, I lied. The worst was too much and the poorer was more than I could take. Twenty years ago, I had no idea what those words really meant. At the time, I thought, I could easily live up to my vows. We were young. Life was fun and carefree. Later came trials, children, financial burdens, infidelity, communication barriers, abandonment, and loss of love. When these things happened, the good times were forgotten. The negative memories lingered, leaving deep mental scars.

Now that my scars are healed, I can not allow them to re-open. I must protect my sanity, my well-being, at all cost. Even if it means reneging on my marriage vows to save myself from more hurt.

I didn't have any money for a lawyer. But I wasn't letting the lack of funds deter me from getting a divorce. January 26, was my next payday. I'd have to alter my budget to pay for the divorce. Considering Ronald Smith was out of the question. The last ordeal with him was too much. This time, I'll select someone else.

Thursday, January 19, I started calling different lawyers from the yellow pages. The prices ranged from three to five hundred dollars for an uncontested divorce. I already informed Carl, I wanted custody of the boys and ownership of the house. I felt like they were mine since his walkout in '88 when he specifically gave them to me in his goodbye letter.

Telling the boys was my greatest challenge. How could I chose the right words, the right time, the right place, to tell them I'm divorcing their dad? Since I couldn't figure it out, Carl and I agreed not to tell them until the divorce was final. We both felt it would be easier saying, we're divorced, than saying, we're getting a divorce. I also felt like it was too early in the school year to tell them. The later they found out, the better for their grades.

In the meantime, Carl and I continued to act the same. We pretended nothing had changed between us. We slept in our bed as usual although we discontinued having sex. We did everything exactly the same for the sake of our sons.

Friday, January 20, I had an appointment to get my oil changed and investigate the noise underneath the car I had been hearing for five months.

When I drove into Southlake Buick, Volvo, and Subaru Service Department, Mike Taylor, a Service Consultant, assisted me. The service department had two service consultants, Mike and David Ruffin. Mike's desk was at the entrance of the two lane garage, on the left side. One lane was for entering and the other lane was for exiting. David's desk was at the end of the entrance lane. The cashier window, entrance to the waiting room, and soda and snack machines were to the right, in that order.

I canvassed Mike as he approached the car. His long sleeve shirt and khaki pants complimented his medium framed physique that could pass for a man in his thirties. But his balding, dark-brown hair and aging face told his age of forty-something. His large, round, dark-brown, friendly eyes glistened against his golden brown skin as he spoke.

"How may I help you," he said, swerving from his chair, four feet away.

"I'm Vanessa Lewis. I have an eight o'clock appointment for an oil change. I also need you to investigate the noise coming from underneath the car," I said, getting out of the car, handing him the keys. I stood beside Mike. He was a few inches taller than me. I estimated his height to be five-foot ten.

"What kind of noise do you hear?" he asked, placing his ballpoint pen behind his small round ear as he sat in my car.

"I can't describe it."

He cranked the car. "Is it a grinding, scrubbing, screeching, or knocking noise?"

"It's all of those except the knocking."

"I see," he said, holding his chin then rubbing the back of his head. "My mechanics will thoroughly check your car to find the problem. Is there anything else?" he asked, writing my mileage and serial number down on his note pad as he closed my door.

"No."

"Come over to my desk. I'll make a work order for your car."

"How much do you think it will cost?" I asked, trailing behind him.

"I won't know until my mechanics find out what the problem is."

"Can you give me a rough estimate?"

He laughed. "Roughly, from $50.00-$1,500.00 dollars."

"That range is too wide. What about a close approximation?"

"Relax, it won't cost you you're first born to get your car running like new again," he said, typing on his keypad. "Now, I need your name, address and telephone number."

"Vanessa Lewis."

"Miss or Mrs.?"

"Ms," I interjected. "Actually, I'm Mrs., but I'll be getting a divorce soon."

"How soon?"

"As soon as I get the money to pay for a lawyer."

He glanced at my hands. "I see you're not wearing a wedding ring. I thought you were single."

"I will be shortly. I took my rings off when I decided to get a divorce."

"Is that so," he said, looking up from his terminal. "Let me take you out to dinner after your divorce."

Speechless, I looked at him stunned.

"You're not against men are you?"

"No, I'm not. I'm shocked. I've been in a twenty-five year relationship. I've never been asked out by a man." I paused for a moment before I continued. He looked at me waiting for my reply. "I'll be delighted for you to take me out to dinner."

"Good. Now, since that's settled, what is your address and telephone number?"

"I can't give you that information yet. I'm still married."

He laughed again. "We have three Vanessa Lewis's in the computer. I want to make sure I have the right one," he said, pressing keys on the keypad, looking into the monitor.

"My address is 8956 Lockheart Dr., Decatur, Ga. 30032. My telephone number is 555-9663."

He removed the newly printed work order from the printer.

"I need you to sign at the X," he said placing his pen down on the work order, pointing to the X. "Your car will be running like new. You'll have a new car. And a new man to go with your new life," he said with a mischievous smile.

I signed at the X and handed him the paper. "The new running car and the new life I'll take. But I don't need a new man. I just need to get rid of the old one."

"Have it your way, Ms. Lewis..."

"Vanessa," I interrupted.

"Vanessa," he said, smiling. My dinner invitation still stands. I'll give you more time to think it over. Have a seat in the waiting area while I take your car to my technicians. Unless of course, you rather wait here until I get back."

"No. I'll wait inside and take a nap while I wait for my car. I'm tired since I came here straight from work."

"If you change your mind, I'll be here," he shouted as I walked away. He then drove my car to the garage.

I walked toward the waiting area, opened the door and found a vacant chair to the left of the door. Five people occupied the small area which contained eight sky-blue, cushioned chairs with dark brown armrests. Six chairs faced the twenty-five inch, color TV mounted on a pecan brown console. An elderly couple were helping themselves to the free coffee next to the TV. The chair I chose was one of two not facing the TV. I threw my black leather coat over my head and fell asleep.

At 11:23 a.m., I came back to life. I glanced at my watch while my head was still buried underneath my coat. Trying to be inconspicuous, I slowly pulled the coat from over my head to inspect the waiting area. Four people were waiting. Three I recognized from before I went to sleep. All eyes were glued to the TV.

In an effort not to draw attention to myself, I quietly went to the restroom located behind the six chairs. Once inside, I splashed my face with water, combed my hair, used the toilet and popped a peppermint in my mouth I had gotten earlier from the small table next to my chair.

While inside the restroom, I heard my name being paged to come to the front desk. I took one last look in the mirror to make sure everything was in place. Feeling confident that I looked smashing, I went to the front desk. Mike was sitting in his chair talking to another patron. I patiently waited for five minutes until they completed their conversation. The well-built, thirty-something, attractive, black female with long, past the shoulder length hair, strutted her stuff to her gold, late model Volvo. Although she captured my attention, Mike didn't seem to notice her beauty.

I reached his desk as she pulled off. "Did you page me? I heard my name over the loudspeaker in the lounge," I asked, popping another mint in my mouth for safe measures.

"Yes, I did. Your car is ready," he said with admiration in his eyes.

"How can you look at me that way when a fine fox just left your presence and you acted like you did not even notice her beauty?"

"Haven't you heard, beauty is in the eye of the beholder? Outwardly, Astra is a very attractive woman. She's an intelligent, warm, hard working, vivacious woman. She's got it going on. But she's not for me, and I'm not for her. It works both ways."

"Have you ever asked her out to dinner?"

"No. And I probably never will. Do you think I ask all my single clients out to dinner?"

"I guess so since you asked me the first time we met."

"It's something about you I like. I feel a connection, a certain vibe," he said leaning back in his chair, placing both hands behind his head, smiling. "I'm attracted to you. I'm not attracted to Astra. Besides, I feel she has too many wolves roaming at her door."

I looked at him, not sure what to say. "Since I've been out of circulation for so long, I don't know the rules of dating. Come to think of it, I never really dated anyway."

"You got married without dating? Did you have a shotgun wedding?"

"No. I prematurely left my parents nest. I was suddenly propelled from my home into my marriage within eight days. Maybe, you could call it a slingshot wedding."

"How long have you been married?"

"Twenty years."

"That's a long time. You hurried into it, now you can't wait to get out of it."

"You might say that."

"I know I couldn't get out of my second marriage quick enough. My ex-wife totaled my car, emptied the savings account, charged three thousand dollars of merchandise on our charge cards that I ended up having to pay back. And the bitch, pardon my expression, used up all the money in the checking account. That's one woman I couldn't get out of my life quick enough. But that's another story," he said leaning forward, clutching my work order.

"What was wrong with my car?"

"The front and rear bearings were badly worn. We replaced them. Fortunately, they were still under warranty which expires March 20, of this year."

"How much is my bill?"

"$30.59 for the oil change."

"Thanks, Mike. You're an absolute jewel."

"No. You're the jewel. I'm just an ordinary gem," he said, picking up the ringing telephone on his desk.

I walked to the cashier window across the driveway. Mike had gotten off the phone and had my car parked in the exit lane by the time I paid my bill. He was standing beside my car with the door opened, anticipating me getting inside.

"Don't forget to let me know when your divorce is final. I want to take you out to dinner," he said, closing my door as I nestled inside.

Pressing the power window button, I rolled my window down.

"After my divorce, I plan to write a book. I won't have much free time. I plan to get my life back on track, first, before I enter a new relationship."

"I understand. But you also have to eat. A nice dinner will add a little spice to your life. We'll call it a new-lease-on-life meal. Maybe, you can include it in your book."

"I may or may not mention the meal, but you will be remembered. I must go now," I said, rolling my window up and driving off.

The car drove like new. It was wonderful not hearing the screeching, scrubbing noise. Two exits from the dealership, my exuberance came to an screeching halt when I heard a loud noise from under the car. Suddenly, the car veered to the right. I clutched the wheel tightly to keep from losing control. The right tire drove as if it was flat. I nervously pulled over in the far left lane near a fork of a joining expressway. Hastily, I got out of the car on to the busy expressway to inspect the tires. Surprisingly, no tire was flat.

I got back inside the car and entered back onto the busy freeway. Shaking like a leaf, I managed to get on the far right side before the next exit. Still shaking inside and praying all the way, I made it safely to the dealership. Mike was there and looked surprised when I drove up. I got out of the car shaking. "Something is wrong with my car!" I nervously exclaimed to Mike.

"Calm down," he said consoling me, putting his arm around my shoulder. "What happened?"

"I heard a loud sound then the car was hard to steer. I didn't think I was going to make it back here in one piece," I said almost at the point of crying.

"I don't understand," he said rubbing the back of his head. "I was sure my technicians located and fixed the problem. There must be something else wrong with it. Let me take your car to the garage. I'll inspect it myself. Give me your keys," he demanded, looking upset.

He quickly drove off after I handed him my keys. I waited by his desk for fifteen minutes until he returned.

"I'm sorry, Vanessa, but I have to keep your car for awhile. The problem is your front axle. We don't have the kind you need in stock. I have to special order one for you."

"If you keep my car, how will I get home and back and forth to work? I don't have money for a rental car."

"Don't worry. I'll get you a loaner car to drive while yours is being repaired."

"That'll be fine," I said, giving a sigh of relief.

"I'm sorry for the inconvenience. Wait here while I get you a loaner car," he said as he walked off.

Mike came back not with just any loaner car, but with a brand new, 1995 red, fully loaded Volvo with leather interior and sunroof. I heard one of his associates say, it was not a loaner car. I smiled and Mike ignored him by handing me the keys then showing me all the features of the car.

"I'll call you when your car is ready," he said, closing the door. "It may take a week to get the part in."

"As long as I have something safe to drive, I don't care how long it takes. It's getting late. I need to leave before my sons get home." I drove off feeling calm and good inside. During the drive home, I thought of Mike, how nice he was to me. I thought about, how I did nothing to deserve his admiration. It appeared to be natural for him.

Although Mike was nice, I felt nothing for him. Maybe it was too soon, I convinced myself. Starting a new relationship was the last thing on my mind.

Getting my life together, repairing my house, figuring how to be more of a parent to my sons, and writing my book, were foremost on my mind.

I prayed as I continued to drive home:

*Lord, You know my heart. You also know the heart of every man. Lord, I can only judge by outward appearances and what the person reveals to me. My knowledge of another person is only in part, in bits-and-pieces as they reveal themselves to me. Heavenly Father, You know the whole person from the inside out. Father, let me not lean to my own fragmented understanding but to Yours.*

*Father, I propose to establish a sign to identify the person You have chosen for me. Father only You know my complete character makeup. Only You know who and what I need.*

*Father, I am reminded in Your Word of two occasions where You honored the signs of men that You were with them. I too need the reassurance that You have chosen my next soul mate for me.*

*The first incident in the Bible is in I Samuel 14:9-12. It was regarding Jonathan, the son of Saul, and his armor-bearer who went up against the Philistines. He asked for this sign:"If they say to us, 'Wait until we come to you,' then we will stand still in our place, and we will not go up to them. But if they say, 'Come up to us,' then we will go up; for the Lord has given them into our hand. And this shall be the sign for us...And the men of the garrison hailed Jonathan and his armor-bearer, and said, 'Come up to us, and we will show you a thing.' And Jonathan said to his armor-bearer, Come up after me; for the Lord has given them into the hands of Israel."*

*The second incident is in Judges 6:16-17, 36-40. Gideon, the son of Joash, asked for a sign that You was with him. "And the Lord said to him (Gideon), 'But I will be with you, and you shall smite the Midianites as one man.' And he said to him, 'If now I have found favor with thee, then show me a sign that it is thou who speakest with me.'...Then Gideon said to God, 'If thou wilt deliver Israel by my hand, as thou has said, behold I am laying a fleece of wool on the threshing floor; if there is dew on the fleece alone, and it is dry on all the ground, then I shall know that thou wilt deliver Israel by my hand, as thou has said.' And it was so. When he rose early next morning and squeezed the fleece, he wrung enough dew from the fleece to fill a bowl with* water. Then Gideon said to God, '...let it be dry only on the fleece, and on all the ground let there be dew.' And God did so that night; for it was dry on the fleece only, and on all the ground there was dew."

Father, this is the sign that I have chosen to identify the next man in my life. The man whom I hope to spend my last days with. The man who will treat me like I want to be treated. The man who will cherish me. The man who will build me up and not tear me down. The man who will love may mind more than my body. The man who will be faithful, and devoted to me until death do us part. The man who fears You and walks in Your ways. The sign is: As long as I am single, I will never ask a man for money. But the man of my life will give me $50.00 dollars or more, voluntarily. When he gives the money to me, I'll ask him, "What is this for?" his reply will be, "This is for you because I am your man." And indeed he will be from that day on. Amen."

# THIRTY

Meeting Mike made me realize I needed to get the divorce ball rolling. The first thing I did when I got home was call several lawyers from the yellow pages. I chose Mr. Joseph Wear because of his rapport over the phone. His fee was five hundred dollars for an uncontested divorce. My appointment was the day after my next payday, Friday, January 27.

Prior to seeking this last divorce, I saw Carl for who he truly was. I felt like his character makeup was chiseled in stone. As a result, my heart and mind had been destroyed from the chiseling process. However, since I told Carl I wanted a divorce, I noticed a change in him, but I refused to be swayed the other way no matter how much he "changed".

On the evening of the 22nd, Carl came into our bedroom while I was sitting on the bed writing out the bills to be paid. I needed to know what bills would or would not get paid in order to pay Mr. Wear. When I finished writing checks for all the essential bills, I had $102.78 left over. Carl was sitting in the chair in front of the bed watching me write the checks.

"You know, I've been thinking a lot lately," Carl said with his chin in his left hand."I'm not the kind of man you want. You want somebody who is responsible and who will sit you down. I haven't been that kind of man for you. You need this divorce so you can be happy," he said, lighting a cigarette.

I stared at Carl wondering who turned his light on. It was hard for me to believe that he finally got the message. Why now? "Are you high?"I asked.

"Why is it when a man searches his inner-self for answers to his problem, he's thought of as being fucked-up? No, I'm not high. I've been soul-searching," he said, inhaling his cigarette.

"Does this mean you have accepted the fact that our marriage is over?"

"I still don't want a divorce," he paused to exhale, "but I will not stop you from getting one. I still feel you're making a terrible mistake."

"Do you know a cheap lawyer? I don't have enough money to keep my appointment Friday."

"Look in this Creative Loafing Newspaper I picked up today," he said, tossing it on the bed from his lap.

"Thanks," I said, opening the paper, looking in the advertisement section.

"You've let Satan in our home. I've noticed you don't read the Bible like you used to. You used to be a fine Christian woman. But something has happened to you lately," he said, going to the bathroom.

While he was doing his business, I spotted several ads for under $100.00 dollars. One ad for $69.00 dollars really caught my attention. I wrote the information down on the back of the gas-bill envelope along with two other ads. Since it was late Sunday evening, I'd call them first thing Monday morning. When Carl returned to his chair, I picked up the conversation where we left off.

"The only thing that has happened to me is I am uncaged. I am free to be me. I am no longer a victim of my past. My deep mental and emotional wounds have been healed. You see a new creature who loves herself for the first time in thirty-eight years. And because I have self-love and high self-esteem, I won't allow you to treat me like a rag anymore."

"Self-love is demonic. You're suppose to love God and your fellowman, which includes your husband, instead of yourself."

"Self-love is not demonic. You have to love yourself before you can love anyone else. Even the Bible tells us, to love others as we love ourselves."

"There you go quoting the Bible. The Bible also says not to divorce. You pick-and-chose what you want out of the Bible."

"Yes, God hates divorce. But He also hates two people who have entered the institution of marriage to profane it by not cleaving to one another. You have not cleaved to me. You have put family, friends, jobs, golf and everything else before me. By your actions, you have put me last in your life instead of first."

"You are first to me. As a-matter-of-fact, you're very special to me."

"That's funny, I don't feel special to you. We are more like roommates living under the same roof. There is a big difference between husband and wife and roommates."

"Yeah, the difference is husbands and wives have sex. Roommates talk."

"No. The difference is God. The couple not only want to please each other but God as well. They live by God's way 100% of the time. They have forsaken their will for His divine will in their lives."

"I don't need a sermon. I need a wife. Why don't you call off the divorce? We can work on our marriage. It's not that bad."

"Sorry, Carl. This marriage is over for me. For a long time, I thought the Carl I loved died on the operating table in '88. But, now, I know beyond-a-shadow-of-a-doubt, the old Carl didn't die then. I am convinced, the same man who went down came back up. The difference was my blinders were removed when you walked out. Without the blinders, I saw the true you who depressed me for six years."

"You're not making any sense," he said getting up, heading for the door. "I feel, you're making a big mistake. Don't you see how you are breaking up our family? Please, don't separate our sons from me."

"Don't accuse me of breaking up the family. You devastated us when you walked out in '88. But you can't see that."

"That was then—seven years ago. Don't keep throwing shit up in my face that happened seven years ago. Today, we're together as a family."

"But, I'm stuck in '88. In my mind, I keep going back to the day you left me. My body is in '95 but my mind is in '88."

"Fuck it! I'm going to kick-it around for awhile. Keep living in '88. I'm living in '95," he said, storming from the room.

"Thanks for the paper!" I shouted to the back of his head. "I see several divorce ads for under $100.00 dollars. Call it your contribution to the cause," I mumbled to myself.

Monday, I called several of the ads. My first choice was Legal World because it had the lowest price of $69.00 dollars. The earliest, available, appointment was two weeks away, on Monday, February 6, at 1:00 p.m..

After making my appointment with Legal World, I canceled my Friday appointment with Mr. Wear. I didn't mind waiting another week and a half to save over $400.00 dollars.

Mike called the following Monday and informed me the part for my car was in. However, his technicians were backlogged. My car wouldn't be ready until Friday or Monday at the earliest. I told him not to rush with my car because I wanted it fixed right. He agreed. We both felt Monday, February 6, would be the best day to pick up my car. I liked that arrangement since the dealership was in the general area of Legal World.

On February 6, when I pulled into the dealership, Mike smiled, sporting a dark gray suit with a complimentary splash of color tie. He looked very nice. Realizing who I was, Mike proudly pulled on his tie as if to say, this is for you. His jest was flattering. Mike had a way of making me feel special.

"Did you enjoy the Volvo?" he asked with a wide grin, opening my door.

"It's a beautiful car. My kids wanted me to keep it forever,but I explained how my car was almost paid for and I didn't want to start over with a new car note," I said, getting out of the car.

"I will put this car back and bring your car to you," he said, getting into the driver's seat.

"Thanks, Mike. Please hurry. I don't have much time. I'm going to get my divorce papers as soon as I leave here."

"Ahhhh, that excites me," he said, grinning, rubbing his hands together. "I'm coming to your church after your divorce. You can tell everyone you are my fiancee."

"Wait-a-minute, Mike. Let's take this thing one-step-at-a-time. First, I must get my divorce papers. Second, I must get my divorce. Third, we must get to know each other..."

"Fourth and last, we must get married," he interrupted. "We are wasting time. Let me hurry up and get your car so you can get started on the first step, then two through four will follow. Or better yet, we can combine three and four. We can get to know each other after we are married."

"You're crazy! Do you know that? Go get my car. It's almost time for my appointment."

"Your car is coming up!" he exclaimed as he left.

Mike returned with my car within the next five minutes. We said our goodbyes and I drove off. He reminded me of our dinner date. I assured him I would not forget. The drive to Legal World was fifteen minutes away. I looked at the car clock. The time was 12:40. I pulled into the office complex off Highway 85 at 12:55. A vacant parking space was located in front of building F-3. A small black and white sign hung over the door. It read, Legal World, Butch Humphreys, Paralegal, 555-0945.

Hastily, I grabbed my purse, locked my car door and entered the door without knocking. A balding, middle aged, white man sat behind a desk to the left of the door, using a computer. Two solid brown chairs were next to the door. An olive-green, low back sofa, matching chair, and end table were to the right.

"Have a seat. I'm Butch Humphreys. I will be with you in a few minutes," he said, continuing typing in the terminal.

"I'm Vanessa Lewis. I have a 1:00 o'clock appointment. I'll stand if you don't mind. I sit all the time."

As I stood, I observed what Butch was doing. He had a small stack of papers on his right that he used to type information into the terminal. When he completed the stack, he opened his upper, right, desk drawer and retrieved a cassette tape. With the tape in hand and papers from another stack, he left the terminal.

"Excuse me. I will be back in a few minutes. I have a client in another room who should be finished," he said as he went into another room across from the green sofa.

Butch came from the room a few minutes later with a stout, ash blonde woman who's hair was cut short and frizzy on the ends. Her small round eyes were red as if she had been crying.

Butch escorted her to the door. She had the items in her hand that Butch took into the room. Slowly, she scooped up a small pile of her belongings near the green chair.

"Mrs. Lewis, I am sorry to keep you waiting. Mrs. Cofield's husband left her for another woman. She's distraught about raising their two small children alone. Although she is initiating the divorce, she is taking it very hard. How are you today?" he asked extending his hand for me to shake.

"Fine, thank you."

"I get so much business after New Year's that I work ten hour days, six days a week until April. Springtime, lovers meet, and fall in love. Some get married in the summer. They realized they made a mistake in the fall but it's too close to the holidays to break up. Then BANG!" he said, clapping his hands together, loudly, "the holidays are over and they are calling me up to get them out of their mess."

"I've been married twenty years."

"Some messes last longer than others."

"I don't consider my marriage a mess."

"Are you happy?"

"No."

"Do you want your marriage to continue?"

"No."

"Do you feel you will be happier divorced?"

"Yes."

"Is your marriage a mess?"

"Yes-s-s," the word slurred out of my mouth.

"Now that we have come to an agreement that your marriage is presently a mess, and you want it to end, we can proceed. By the way, I'm in my third marriage. That's how I BANG!" he clapped his hands again, "got the idea to become a paralegal and start this business. I was paying lawyers too much money to get me out of my messes. With that said, let's get started with yours," he said, sitting behind the desk.

Butch gathered papers from his desk. His small, potbelly rested on the top drawer. The overhead light reflected on his large bald area in the back, making it shine like glass.

"I believe, I have everything I need. Come with me, Mrs. Lewis," he said, getting up going to the same room he came out of with Mrs. Cofield.

"Butch, if you are so busy during this time of the year, why am I the only one here?"

"Because it's only one of me. I allow one-on-one time with each client."

We walked in the back room which contained a large round, brown, wooden table, and four chairs. A half pot of coffee with all the condiments were on a separate table near the door.

"Help yourself to coffee. It's free," Butch commented after noticing the direction of my eyes as he pulled up his chair next to mine.

"No, thank you."

"Mrs. Lewis, as a paralegal, I prepare your divorce papers to be filed in the Superior Court of your county. Since I am not a lawyer, I will not represent your case. You will represent yourself before a judge who will finalize your divorce. After you pay a $65.00 dollar filing fee and wait at least thirty-one days, you can go to the courthouse for your divorce."

"My husband and I can go to the courthouse anytime after the thirty-one days without a specified date or time?"

"Your husband does not even have to show up. Once he signs the papers, his role in the divorce has ended. You can kiss your marriage goodby. Do you have any children?"

"Yes. I have two sons."

"What county do you live in?"

"Dekalb."

"Dekalb County requires both you and your spouse to attend a class for divorce parents. When you file your divorce papers, ask for information regarding the classes. These classes are mandatory. You will not be able to get a divorce without attending one. Do you have any questions before we proceed?"

"Under what circumstances can I be denied a divorce?"

"The judge's discretion is to either grant or deny you a divorce, but they usually grant at least ninety percent of the divorce cases."

"What kind of case falls in the ten percent category?"

"You have to realize judges are human. Some are pro-marriage and not pro-divorce. They may use their position to save a marriage instead of dissolve it. In which case, the judge probably would suggest counseling instead of a divorce. Are you ready to get started?"

"Yes."

"Since you are having the divorce papers drawn, you are the plaintiff. Your husband is the defendant. I need your first and last name, and middle initial."

"Vanessa A. Lewis."

"Your spouse?"

"Carl Lewis."

"What is his middle initial?"

"He doesn't have one."

"Do you know how you want your assets divided?"

"Yes. I keep the house. I'll give him whatever he wants out of the house. It's all junk that needs to be replaced anyway."

"Have you decided on who gets custody of your children?"

"I will."

"Have you thought about child support payments? By law, you are eligible to receive 23-28% of your spouse's income for two children."

I got my calculator out of my purse and figured, $8.50/hr X 40hrs/wk = $340/wk X .25 or 25% = $85.00. "I want $85.00 dollars per week for child support."

"Let's make it an even number—$86/week because I have to halve the number of each child. Your child support payment will be $43/week/child."

"That's fine. I'm not trying to hurt him or prevent him from being able to live."

"Do you want alimony?

"No. That won't be necessary."

"I have a few more questions to ask you in order to prepare your divorce papers."

Butch asked his questions then left the room while I listened to the tape, "How To Do Your Own Divorce": By Attorney Elmer H. Young III. He slipped it into the tape recorder before he left. All I thought of while the tape was playing was, it's almost over. Soon, I'll have my divorce papers in my hands— something that has never happened before. This time will be different from the other two times. This time, I'm going all the way.

Butch returned with the completed divorce papers within twenty minutes.

"Mrs. Lewis, you're all set to get out of your mess. Don't do as I did—get out of one mess and BANG!" he said, clapping his hands, "get into another mess."

"I won't. I have a sign to identify the right man for me. If I ever get married again, it will be unto death do us part."

"Right. My fee is $69.00 dollars."

I wrote Butch a check for $69.00 dollars. He removed the tape while I wrote the check. We exchanged tape for check. Butch tucked the check into his shirt pocket then discussed each page of my divorce papers.

"Mrs. Lewis, your husband has to sign in three places." He proceeded to show me the three places. "Two of his signatures have to be notarized," he placed a large X by the two places. This page just needs his signature," he said, pointing to a place on another page. "You're all set, Mrs. Lewis," he said, handing me my divorce papers stuffed inside a large brown envelope. "Good luck."

"Thanks. It's been my pleasure."

I grabbed my papers, tape, and other belongings and left. When I entered the car, I popped the tape into the tape player. Nothing, except an act from God, would change my mind this time. I knew, my greatest challenge was getting Carl to sign the papers. Once they were signed, the marriage would be over in thirty-one days.

# THIRTY-ONE

On the way home from Legal World, I remembered passing a pawn shop on Highway 85 with a sign that read, We Buy and Sell Gold. I thought, surely, I could get enough money from my wedding rings for a nice lunch to celebrate and buy an outfit or two with the change. Suddenly, I made a U-turn at the intersection of the pawn shop then parked in its tiny lot.

Guitars, keyboards, VCR's, TV's and boom boxes lined the walls. Two glass cases filled with an assortment of jewelry were on both sides of the narrow passageway that led to the short, petite woman in the back of the room. Her smiling face and the abundance of jewelry assured me I was in the right place. Maybe, I'd treat myself to Red Lobster, I thought, as I approached her.

"How can I help you?" the woman asked as I reached the back counter.

"I have two gold rings I'd like to sell." I took the rings from my purse and laid them on the counter. "What can I get for these?"

"I have to weigh them first. She placed the rings on a small scale behind her. "I can give you $12.00 dollars for your rings," she said with her back to me.

"Excuse me. Did you say, $12.00 dollars or $112.00 dollars?"

"Lady, you heard me right," she said, facing me placing the rings on the counter. "$12.00 dollars."

"Why so low?"

"You have 10K gold that weighs twelve ounces. We pay one dollar an ounce."

"That's okay," I said, picking up my rings. "I paid over $400.00 dollars for these rings. I'm not giving them away," I said, politely walking out of the store.

I couldn't believe the pawn value of my rings. Twelve dollars amounts to less than one dollar per year of marriage. How can a real marriage last when the symbolic rings are worthless? Now, I understand why the kids laughed at my diamond and said, it was the size of a speck of dust. Little did I know, it had the same value.

I left and continued my drive home. I prayed as I drove:

*Dear Heavenly Father,*

*I pray, You grant me favor with Carl. Father, please remove any stumbling blocks that will prevent Carl from signing the divorce papers. Father, I know you hate divorce, but I am miserable with Carl. Father, even though my mind and heart are set on leaving Carl if it is Your divine will that we remain married, then I pray You prevent the divorce from going through. Let Your will be done in my life, always. I ask this in the name and glory of Your Son and my Lord and Savior, Jesus Christ. Amen.*

The prayer eased my mind, knowing whatever happened with my marriage was according to God's will. I presented the divorce papers to Carl, after dinner, when we were in our bedroom.

"Carl, I have the divorce papers for you to sign," I said, removing them from the brown, oversized envelope on my nightstand.

Carl was sitting in the chair reading the paper but quickly dropped it on the floor when I handed him the divorce papers.

"So, you're going through with this?" he asked, looking at me with a blank expression, holding the papers.

"Yes. I am. There are three places you need to sign," I said, showing him the places. "These two places with the X need to be notarized. This place just need your signature," I said, pointing my finger on the signature line.

"You can have your divorce. I hope it'll make you happy. Tomorrow, I'll get these signed."

I smiled. Not wanting to appear exuberant, I turned my back to him and beamed. "I appreciate your cooperation."

Carl read the divorce papers while I ironed my clothes for work. We didn't say anything to each other because we were in our own separate worlds.

Our worlds came together, however, when it was time for me to get dressed. Lately, Carl enjoyed watching me get dressed as if I was performing on stage. He silently sat in the chair and watched me put on every stitch of clothing, smiling throughout the show. At the completion of my performance, I went to work.

The hustle and bustle at work didn't prevent my regular friends from visiting me. I told each one, I was getting a divorce. Shortly after Rodney Daniels, a funny, young, security guard friend, departed a new visitor appeared from nowhere. My new visitor was a security guard whom I'd never seen before.

"I overheard you talking to the other officer about getting a divorce," he said, positioning himself in front of the lab window, leaning forward.

"Who are you?"

"Bryson Collier. I have spoken to you several times in the hall, but I never stopped to talk. You always spoke."

"Why did you stop tonight?"

"I don't know. I just did." He paused with an expression on his face as if a cat had his tongue. "I'm divorced too. Let me take you out?" he finally asked, standing erect so I could see his whole profile.

Bryson was charcoal black with perfect white teeth. His very low haircut and clean shaven face gave him a very neat appearance. His rectangle, gold, wire rimmed glasses complimented his face. The fullness of his extended chest filled his white uniform shirt to the point of bursting.

"You can't take me out. I'm still married. I only received my divorce papers today. Why did you divorce?" I asked Bryson who was staring at me smiling.

"My wife kept leaving me in the beginning of our marriage. Every damn time I looked around, she kept going back home to her mother. Each time she left, I brought her and our oldest son back home. The last time she left, I refused to go get her. I told her, I didn't take your ass to your mother's and I'm not bringing your ass back. After I refused to get her when she left, she stopped damn leaving."

"That happened at the beginning of your marriage. What happened to end the marriage?"

"I couldn't get her to do a damn thing for me," he said, beating his chest like Cheeta. "I cooked all the meals, did all the repairs around the house, and did every damn thing for our two sons. She didn't do shit but fix her plate and watch TV."

"How long were you married?"

"Sixteen long ass years. It was over in three years, but we dragged it out for sixteen years. My marriage taught me the real meaning of the word commitment—commit my ass to the mental institution."

I laughed at Bryson. He reminded me of the old Carl when he made me laugh all the time. "What type of repairs do you do?"

"You name it. I can do it."

"I need repairs done on my house. Would you be interested in the job?"

"Do I get to take you out first?"

"I can't make a date while I'm married. Ask me after I'm divorced."

"You're on." He pulled an ink pen from his shirt pocket. "Let me have a piece of paper from your pad?" he asked, pointing to the pad on the counter. "What type of repairs do you need?"

"I need my walls painted, new carpet, new kitchen and bathroom floors, gutters, a hole repaired in the living room wall, new inside and outside doors installed, mini-blinds installed on the windows and ceiling fans put up."

"I can do everything you need with no problem. When do you want me to start?"

"That depends on how much you charge?"

"I won't charge you an arm and a leg, just a finger and a toe," he chuckled. "Don't worry about how much I charge. We'll talk about my fee later. I need to know when you want me to start?"

"After my divorce, during spring break, the first week in April. I'm taking off that week to be with my sons. My husband and I agreed to stay together until the Friday before spring break begins. That's the day we plan to tell our sons we are divorced. Then they will have a whole week out of school to let it sink in."

"I'll make sure I'm available that week even if I have to rearrange some things on my schedule."

"Thank you Bryson. You don't know how much this means to me," I said, looking intently into his eyes.

"I knew I stopped at this window for a reason."

"Yes, you were definitely, God sent, an answer to my prayer."

He smiled a devilish smile, showing his pretty teeth.

"How long have you been married?" he asked scratching the back of his head as if he had fleas.

"Twenty years."

"Why are you getting a divorce?" he asked, placing his hands on the window ledge. He obviously was through scratching his brains out.

"There's a lot of reasons, but the main reason is I'm not happy. And I refuse to live the way I'm living for the rest of my life. I've given my husband twenty-five years of my life. I can't give him anymore of my life to waste. I feel like it's time to move on and get my life back on track. Getting the repairs done to my house is part of the process."

The Emergency Clinic Blue Zone dropped off specimens as I finished my sentence. The courier clocked in the requisitions where Bryson was standing. He stepped back because he was in the way. Moments later, the courier left and Bryson assumed his position in front of the window.

"I can't talk now. I need to accession these specimens." I grabbed a plastic bag, removed the stamped requisition and enclosed tubes of blood.

"Sure. I was answering a call when I stopped anyway. I'll go answer it." He walked away as I continued accessioning the specimens.

As I worked, I thought about Bryson. His subtle charm and devilish smile captivated me. He reminded me of the old Carl. Inside, I felt a chemical reaction. Although it wasn't as intense as with Zakee, it did exist. He appeared to be a good man. I'd never met a man who did everything. I didn't know they existed.

The more I thought about Bryson, the more I thought, what's wrong with me? I'm not over Zakee. Secretly, I hoped we could get together after my divorce to fulfill the last part of the price tag prophecy—something will happen for the two of you to get together. The first part—before you take the last price tag off—had been fulfilled. Now, with my pending divorce and possibly with Zakee's divorce or near divorce, we can finally get together.

Throughout the night, I kept looking at the window for Bryson's return. I wanted to see him, but I didn't want him to know how I felt. The shift ended without my seeing Bryson again. I was beginning to think I was becoming man crazy, or worst—uncaged and unglued. My reaction to him really disturbed me.

On the drive home, I thought about the divorce papers. I hoped Carl would not change his mind but have the papers signed. After the encounter with Bryson, I realized I needed this divorce because I no longer thought of other men as being off limits. Mentally, I was already a single woman.

That evening when Carl came home from work, I was in my room reading. He immediately went into the bathroom after he entered the bedroom. I discontinued reading because all I could think about was getting my hands on my signed divorce papers. Fortunately, Carl only took a minute to do his business.

"Here's your signed papers," Carl said, tossing them to me with his right hand while he zipped his pants with his left hand.

"Where did you get them notarized?" I asked, retrieving them from the edge of the bed.

"Bank South. It's free if you have an account."

I opened the envelope and turned to the pages that were to be signed. I smiled when I saw the signatures and the notarized seals.

"Thank you for your cooperation. I really appreciate not having to fight you for my freedom."

"I'm sick of you throwing divorce up in my face all the time. Besides, I wouldn't be doing either one of us any good by keeping you in a relationship you don't want to be in."

I held the signed papers close to my heart. I exhaled then closed my eyes. Carl rambled on about something, but I was in my own world, my utopia. Realizing I wasn't listening anymore to what he was saying, he left the room. As the door closed, I kissed the papers over and over again. I smiled as I thought of Dr. Martin Luther King's famous words, "Free at last. Free at last. Thank God Almighty. I'm free at last!"

Wednesday, February 8, the first day I could file my divorce papers, inclement weather shut the city down. I called the courthouse to see if, by chance, they were opened. To my disappointment, it was closed according to the telephone recording.

Wednesday night, Bryson came back to the window. I was on the phone giving a report to the doctor while he waited until I finished. He handed me a piece of paper as I gave him my full attention. Written on the paper were his first name along with two work numbers and his home number.

"Call me when you're ready to get started working on your house," he said, smiling.

"I told you, I won't be ready until the first week in April."

"I take referrals. Somebody else might need my services. You never know."
I stuffed the paper with his numbers in my lab coat pocket.

"Are you divorced yet?" he asked, laughing. "I can't wait to take you out."

"I have my signed divorce papers in the car. The courthouse was closed yesterday because of the snow. I'll try again today. Everything should be opened, don't you think?"

"Sure. The streets are clear. We didn't have much snow, but it doesn't take too much to close Atlanta down."

"I know. How are things with you?"

"I'm having problems with my friend, Helen. She wants a baby, and I can't have any children. We're having a hard time over this baby thing. She knows I've had a vasectomy. The thought of having another child makes me itch," he said, shaking all over like bugs were crawling on him.

An alarm went off in my head as Bryson spoke. The fact that he had a friend didn't disturb me as much as he couldn't have children. How can I have two daughters by a man with a vasectomy? The fact that he couldn't father children proved Bryson was definitely not my man. Zakee was still number one. Mike Taylor was a nice man, holding the number three slot.

"I must go now. I have work to complete," I said, abruptly.

"Call me at this extension when you get some free time," he said, writing a number on a piece of paper then handing it to me.

"Okay." I said, placing the second piece of paper in the same pocket. As I stood up to leave, he left. While working, an alarm rang loudly in my head. How foolish of me to be attracted to Bryson when he's involved with someone else and shooting blanks. I appreciated his honesty. He didn't have to tell me about his friend. The fact that he couldn't have children still bothered me. It did not silence the alarm.

I decided to write Bryson a letter. I could tell he was interested in me. But he was Mr. Wrong. I needed to nip this in the bud before it bloomed. I also didn't want him hanging around the window, spoiling my chances of possibly getting with Zakee. Although Zakee was out of sight, he was not out of my mind. Nothing and no one would ever come between us if I had anything to do with it. I wrote the letter at the first opportunity.

*Dear Bryson,*

*I regret to end our relationship before it has started. But you mentioned tonight, you have a vasectomy. The next man in my life must be able to father children because it was prophesied to me fourteen years ago, I would have four children, two boys and two girls. I already have my two sons. The fact that I'm*

leaving my husband confirms to me that I will have my two
daughters. Please discontinue further communication with me.

*Vanessa*

I took the piece of paper with his Grady work number out as I placed the folded letter inside the same pocket. I quickly dialed the number. Bryson answered.

"Bryson, this is Vanessa. I have a letter for you. Can you pick it up when you come this way?"

"Read it to me."

"Okay," I said, then read the letter.

"That's a sad letter. I'm coming to get it. I'll be there in a few minutes."

"Okay. Bye."

In less than five minutes, Bryson appeared at the window. I took the last tube of blood out of the centrifuge, took off my gloves, then handed him the letter.

"Are you sure about this?"

"Yes. You're the wrong man for me."

Bryson took the letter and left. I felt good ending the relationship before it got started. I knew I did the right thing. Our relationship was not meant to be— no sperm, no daughters, now way Jose.

My good feelings didn't end with Bryson. I also felt extremely good going to the courthouse when I left work. Once I cleared the metal detector, I went straight to the directory on the wall at the elevators. Quickly scanning the directory, I located the Superior Court on the second floor.

I waited for the next available elevator and followed the signs to the Superior Court. A young, white, female clerk assisted me when she finished with the middle aged gentleman ahead of me.

"May I help you?" she asked after returning to the counter from taking papers to the back of the room.

"Yes. I came to file my divorce papers."

"The filing fee is $65.00 dollars. You must go to the first room on the right, pay the fee then return here with your receipt."

"Do they take checks?"

"Yes."

I followed her instructions then returned to the counter.

"I have my receipt," I said to the same clerk.

She copied my receipt and took my divorce papers.

"Go to the last counter for further instructions."

I carried the papers to the last counter about twenty feet away. A short, round, brown sugar, black clerk came to help me after I waited five minutes watching her and others go to-and-fro doing nothing.

"What can I do for you?" she finally asked while picking her yellowed, crooked teeth with her long, red, press on nails.

"I was told to come here for further instructions. I filed my divorce papers at the counter at the other end."

"After thirty-one days have past, return to this counter to appear before a judge in his chambers. You can come anytime, Monday through Thursday from 8:30 until 1:00 p.m.. If you have children, you must attend a mandatory class for divorced parents. The cost is thirty dollars per parent. The classes are held every first and third Wednesday from 9:00 until 1:30 p.m. at the Decatur Library on Sycamore Street. I will give you information and an application to attend the classes. You do not have to attend the class with your spouse, but you both have to attend. Do you have any questions?" she asked, getting the divorce parent information and application from her desk three steps away.

"Is it true that my spouse does not have to be present if I am the plaintiff?" I asked when she returned to the counter.

"Yes, that's true. Here is the information I promised you," she said, handing me a packet of papers.

"All I have to do now, is wait thirty-one days and attend the class for divorce parents?"

"Yes, that's it. Of course, you know not to have sexual relations with your spouse during the waiting period."

"Yes, I do. Thanks for your help. I'll see you in thirty-one days."

I left the clerk's counter with a new walk. I was practicing my new walk of freedom. Although it wasn't official yet, it felt good all the same.

# THIRTY-TWO

With each step walking out of the courthouse, I thought of Bryson. The more I thought about him, the more he seemed to be everything I wanted in a man. I especially loved his uncanny sense of humor which reminded me of Carl. I also loved the fact that he was a handyman who knew how to do everything which made him unique from Carl. I asked myself, how can I allow a good man like Bryson slip through my fingertips because he can't have children? Didn't God grant Carl the blessing of fathering two sons even though he was once sterile? Can't the same God bless me with two daughters by another man who is also sterile? God is no respecter of persons. What He did for Carl, He can do for Bryson.

While driving home, I couldn't believe how attached to Bryson I had become. For him to come anywhere close to Zakee frightened me even more. Tonight, I'll tell him I've changed my mind about us not seeing each other. Suddenly I remembered, I was off tonight. Therefore, I wouldn't see Bryson again until Saturday night. The next two days off will allow me more time to give the matter more thought.

When Carl came home, I didn't tell him I filed the divorce papers. I waited until we were in bed, instead. We had our heads on our pillows ready to fall asleep. "I filed the divorce papers today," I said with my eyes staring at the ceiling in the dark room.

"I'm sure this is the happiest day of your life," Carl said, turning to face me.

"Before the divorce can be final, we each have to attend a mandatory class for divorcing parents. The classes are every first and third Wednesday from 9:30 to 1:30 p.m.. We have to go on March 1, because the February 15, session is already filled. I'll even pay your $30.00 dollars for the class. I plan to mail the application and check tomorrow."

"That's very kind of you to pay for my class. But, I'm telling you now, I'm not going. Don't waste your money on me. Save it for something really important like buying you a couple of drinks after the divorce to celebrate."

"Carl, I'm not kidding. The classes are mandatory. You have to attend whether you like it or not."

"What happens if I don't attend the class?"

"I don't know? I was told they are mandatory. I'm still mailing your fee with mine tomorrow. You won't have any excuse not to attend except for your own stubbornness."

"When will the divorce be final?" he asked, propping his pillow up at an angle.

"Monday, March 13, is the first day we can get the divorce. We have to wait thirty-one days after the papers have been filed. Sunday, the 12th, is the thirty first day."

"I don't want to talk about this anymore. Is there anything else you want to talk about before I go to sleep?"

I turned to face him. "I want you to know, I have been faithful to you throughout our twenty year marriage and five year courtship. With the exception of Rocket, I have never kissed or touched another man."

"Your faithfulness really makes me feel like a winner when I'm losing you. Look, Doll," he said, facing me, "even though you've filed the papers, you don't have to go through with it. We can forget the whole thing and rebuild our marriage. We don't have to divorce," he spoke with his voice cracking.

"I'm sorry, Carl. It's too late to rebuild what has been completely destroyed. There is nothing left of our marriage except the legal papers that say it exists."

"No, you're wrong. My love for you will never be destroyed. I will love you until the day I die," he said weeping loudly, wiping his eyes with the bedcovers.

I made no attempt to comfort Carl. I prayed silently instead:

*Dear Heavenly Father,*

> *Please comfort Carl because I'm unable to at this time. I know the right words to say to stop his heart from breaking but won't say them. Over the course of our marriage, Carl has snatched my heart out from my chest, with all the love I had for him and crushed it in the palm of his hand. He then took his foot and stomped my heartless remains into a fine powder. I pray before You, tonight, heartless and stomped. My only regret is that I didn't divorce him seven years ago, the first time I filed. During the past seven years, he has placed numerous emotional scars on my mind. The memories continue to linger in my mind and have become instant replays of the past. Father, although I have forgiven Carl for every trespass against me, I'm unable to forget. Please send Your Comforter, Jesus Christ, to console him.*
>
> *Father, I've been faithful to Carl throughout our marriage. But I know of one incident when he was unfaithful to me. In my heart, I feel like there were other instances of infidelity, but I can't prove it. Father, You know all things. I pray each time Carl was unfaithful to me, it takes him the same number of years or relationships before he finds the right person for him. In Jesus Christ name, I pray. Amen.*

The dreary night turned into a dreary day and continued throughout the weekend. My only solace was seeing Bryson when I returned to work, Saturday night.

Saturday night at work, the anticipation of Bryson made me stare at the window constantly. Zakee passed by the window around 1:30 a.m.. I caught a glimpse of Zakee walking by, slyly looking inside. His eyes were turned toward the window while his head remained straight. I had a mind to say something to him, but I wanted him to think, I didn't see him looking at me.

As Zakee strolled out-of-sight, Bryson came to the window. He stood straight up with a blow pop in his mouth. From a distance, he looked like a black Kojak. I was anticipating him to say, "This is for you, baby," while taking the candy out of his mouth.

"What are you doing at my window?" I asked, walking toward him from the chemistry analyzer. "I thought, I made myself perfectly clear that we will discontinue any further communication."

He swirled the blow pop around his mouth before biting into the gum portion. Finally, he spoke after taking another big plug, leaving only the paper stem.

"You say one thing in your letter, but your eyes tell the truth. I can see the sparkle from here. Your letter made a great slam dunk in my circular file where it belonged. I even discarded some gum on it before it made its finale. So your letter was good for something," he said, swallowing the gum from his blow pop.

I hit the green exit button next to the door and walked outside to where he was. "I've changed my mind about us. I've been miserable these past few days thinking we couldn't start a relationship. I can't believe I'm attached to you in such a short period of time," I said, walking toward him, penning him into the corner.

Bryson gave me his devious smile which told me, he was glad for my change of heart.

"What made you change your mind? Let me guess. It was my irresistible charm?" he asked, giving me a Kojak moment.

"No."

"My unmistakable good looks," he said, profiling.

"No."

"I give up. What changed your mind?"

"You remind me of the good things I loved about my husband. Namely your personality and sense of humor. Along with the fact that you know how to do everything. Somehow, I find you intriguing."

"Why would you be interested in a man who reminds you of your husband? I know, I wouldn't be interested in any woman who reminded me of my ex. I might have a flashback and kick her ass."

"Are you a violent person?"

"When it comes to my ex, I'm subject to do any damn thing. Do you still love your husband? I think you do. Maybe, you should give your divorce more consideration. If I remind you of your husband, then why not stay with him? You know how he is. I am an unknown."

"At one point in my life, I loved my husband more than anything and anyone in this world, including God and myself. Later, I found out, I was in love with a mirage—a figment of my imagination. He was a person whom I created in my own mind to satisfy me. I know now, I could never be happy with the real man. You on the other hand, have piqued my curiosity. I want to learn more about you."

"Is that so? I will call you later to talk more about us. I must go now because I am the relief man tonight," he said, looking at his watch. "It's time for officer Fisher to take his break." He walked off, and I went back inside.

Bryson kept his word and called me later. At 3:15 the telephone rang. Jenny answered the phone.

"Vanessa, line 5032 is for you," she shouted to the other side of the room.

"Emergency Clinic Lab, Lewis speaking," I said, picking up the receiver.

"Hey, are you busy?" asked Bryson.

"I have a few more results to enter into the computer. I should be finished in less than five minutes."

"Meet me in the second floor conference room by the cafeteria when you finish. I am here taking my break. I will be waiting."

"I'll be there in five minutes."

"Good."

Click went the phone before I said, goodbye.

Quickly, I entered the last of my results into the computer then told Jenny, I was taking a break.

The elevator opened as I pressed the up button. No one was on the elevator or the deserted hallway leading to the conference room. I quietly knocked on the conference room door, hoping only Bryson heard my knock. The door opened, immediately.

"Come in," Bryson said, smiling.

The door closed behind me as I stepped forward. The dimly lit room made me feel eerie. I sensed trouble but didn't say anything. My eyes instantly focused on three large sofas positioned in a semi-circle. One faced the wall of windows located on the opposite side of the door where we were standing. An array of chairs lined the remainder of the space, up to three feet from the door. To my right were several tables and chairs.

"Why did you invite me up here?" I don't like being isolated like this," I said, feeling and acting uneasy.

"Relax. I am harmless. I wanted us to talk in private. Sit here," he said, walking to a chair close to the door. He walked to another chair by the wall. Our chairs faced each other. "I wanted us to talk without being distracted. I often come here to be alone when I want some quiet time," Bryson said, leaning back in his chair with his hands in his lap.

"What do you want to talk about?"

"Something has been bothering me concerning your divorce, I want cleared up. I have a friend who was in a similar situation as yours. She had been married for seventeen years and had only been in one sexual relationship. She divorced her husband, had several flings, then went back to him. After her flings, she decided her ex was the best thing she ever had. No other man loved her the way he did. They are together to this day. I understand that you have only been with your husband, too. Are you divorcing him because you are curious to see how it may feel to be with someone else?"

"No. My circumstance is different from your friend's. I'm not interested in having sex with another man, until I remarry. Unlike your friend, I don't believe in pre-marital sex. As a matter-of-fact, I have a fear of being with another man, sexually."

"Tell me again. Why are you divorcing your husband?"

"Because all the emotional, mental, spiritual and sexual bonds have been broken in my marriage. The sex bond is the hardest to break. It is the first bond formed and the last bond broken. Once the sex bond is broken, the marriage is over."

"Are you absolutely sure you want to leave your husband?"

"Yes, I'm sure. I tell myself, I can admit I'm miserable so I can be happy. Or I can pretend I'm happy and be miserable. I admit, I'm miserable being married to my husband. My decision to get a divorce, therefore, has nothing to do with another man. I need the divorce for my own peace-of-mind, my mental health, my happiness—for me." I stood up to leave. "I must go. It's busy in the lab. I don't want to leave Jenny by herself for too long."

Before I could make a step, Bryson had his arms around me, rubbing my back, holding me close to his full chest. He lifted my head to kiss me, but I pulled away.

"I'm still Mrs. Lewis," I said, walking to the door, closing it behind me, leaving Bryson frozen in his tracks. I returned to the lab, thinking of Bryson. That was the first time I been in the arms of another man since Rocket. Bryson's embrace lingered with me. Although his lips didn't touch mine, I wondered how his kiss felt. Maybe, after the divorce, I'll find out, I thought as I worked.

Bryson and I started taking breaks every night in the waiting area of the small pharmacy at the Pratt Street entrance. We grew closer everyday. Our conversations were centered around our failed marriages and our four sons. His sons were 13 and 11; mine were 13 and 8. We discovered a lot of common ground to discuss.

The days leading up to the divorce passed smoothly. Carl started attending church with us, something he hadn't done in years. He seemed to be "born again". Suddenly, he became religious and family oriented. He even gave up his all important, all day Saturday, golf sessions to attend church with his family. The first Saturday, February 25, when Carl went to church with us, it threw me off guard.

I had just left Carlos's room after deciding what he was wearing to church when I entered our bedroom. Carl's only light-gray suit, pink shirt, and black, blue and brown tie were on the bed. He was in the bathroom taking a shower. Instantly, my antenna went up. What meanest thou by this, I asked myself? Clad in his briefs and T-shirt, Carl opened the bathroom door. He smelt loudly of Bruit after-shave and cologne. While I was standing near the door ironing my navy blue and beige checkered dress, he grabbed me from behind and kissed my cheek. His freshly shaven face glided across my face.

"Stop it, Carl, those days are over," I said, squirming from his embrace. "What are you up to anyway?"

"You're still my wife, Mrs. Lewis," he cheerfully said, smiling. "You'll always be Mrs. Lewis. You might as well get this divorce thing out of your head. You're mine today and forever!" He picked up his pants and started getting dressed.

"Where are you going? Are you playing golf in suits these days?"

"I'm going to church with my family. I've been reading my Bible and want to hear more of Christ's Word, today. The only way I can be a better husband to you is by becoming a better man," he said, tightening his tacky, flowered tie around his neck.

"Ouch!" I yelled, burning my finger with the iron, shaking it in the air, then kissing it. "You look like Carl, but you sound like somebody else."

"You heard me correctly. I'm a God fearing, church going husband and man. Our marriage will be better than its ever been."

"Our marriage is over," I said, facing him with my thick white housecoat on, holding my pressed dress in my hand.

"Is that right? If our marriage is over then call Carlos and Carl in here and tell them we are getting a divorce," he said, smiling as if he had my neck in a noose that I couldn't get out of without complying with him.

"Carl, we agreed not to tell them until the Friday before spring break begins. We wanted them to complete as much of this school term as possible without disturbing their grades."

"Those are your plans. I say, tell them now or call the whole thing off."

"If you love your sons, you'll wait."

"Either call the divorce off, or I'm going to call them in here and tell them the truth," he looked at me, tightening the noose to an unbearable notch.

I glared into his eyes. "Do as you please. I'm not calling off the divorce no matter what you do or say."

"Have it your way. Carl and Carlos come here!" he shouted. "I have something to tell you."

The boys hurried into the bedroom.

"You called us Dad?" they both asked at the same time.

"Your mama and I are getting," he paused and looked at me.

I stared at him with the intent to kill. My eyes said, how dare you stoop this low.

"a new car soon," Carl continued.

"When Dad?" exclaimed Carl.

"How soon?" questioned Carlos.

"I don't know. Why don't we look at cars after church today?"

"Wait-a-minute, Dad. We're not going to Plucker World or Plucker Town to buy a car this time are we?"

"Yeah, Dad. We're tired of riding in plucker cars. Why don't you buy some smooth wheels like a Benz or BMW?" added Carlos.

"Carlos, I think I will buy a BMW—Better Moving Wheels."

"Hurry up and get dressed for church so we won't be late," I cut-in.

"Okay, Mom. I just have to brush my teeth," said Carl.

"I'm ready too, Mom. I just have to comb my hair and put on my shoes," Carlos said, running out the door.

"Dad, were you kidding about buying a new car and getting rid of the Chevette and Mustang pluckers?" asked Carl.

"No, son. The plucker days are numbered. Go on and brush your teeth."

"Okay, Dad," Carl said, leaving the room.

Fully dressed, I looked at Carl when they left. "Thanks for not telling them."

"When I saw their innocent faces, I didn't have the heart to tell them. I love them too much to break their hearts like you're breaking mine."

"You did come up with an excellent idea. Your two pieces of cars should be replaced with one reliable car. We'll look at cars after church and eat at The Old Country Buffet. We'll call it our last supper out together since our divorce is two weeks and two days away," I said, grabbing my purse and Bible.

# THIRTY-THREE

As the divorce drew nearer so did my excitement to end the marriage. Shortly, I would be a single woman—something I knew very little about. In the past when Carl and I went through our many changes, I never thought of being single. This time was different, however, because I felt totally separated from Carl. No longer were we one but two distinct entities. The oneness was over and so was the marriage.

Monday, February 27, I stood in front of the credit union door, waiting for it to open at 7:15 a.m.. Usually, I am the first person in line because I get to the door twenty to thirty minutes before it opens. Oddly, on this particular morning, a slender, golden-brown female with long dreadlocks was sitting on the floor at the door. We waited silently for a few minutes before she spoke.

"They should open at 7:00 o'clock," she said with a northern accent, pushing her oversize, brown glasses to her small, oval face. Her mahogany eyes focused on me while she squatted on the floor, holding a book she was reading.

"That's too much like right. The night shift always get shafted."

"I made a special trip to come here on my night off. I thought it opened at 6:30," she said, adjusting her black, travel case purse on her small shoulders.

"Ha. Six-thirty! You really haven't been to the credit union in awhile. They've always opened at 7:15," I said, opening my book, "Writing for Children and Teenagers," from my correspondence course.

"I completed my third manuscript four months ago," she said after adjusting her glasses to read the title of my book.

"What a coincidence. I plan to write children books and a novel about my life. I've never met anyone who writes. What's the name of your last manuscript?"

"Mind Shock."

"That's an unusual title."

"It is an unusual book. I sent the manuscript to several publishers. One wanted me to pay for over half the cost of publishing in which it amounted to several thousand dollars. I wrote and told them to return my manuscript. I will take my business somewhere else."

"I don't blame you. You want the publisher to pay you for writing the book, not you pay the publisher."

"Exactly! I will continue to send it out until I get a publisher who is willing to pay me and publish my manuscript at their expense."

"I know that's right. What is your manuscript about?"

"The absolute futility of an under stimulated mind due to the absence of colloquial subliminal messages in the visual receptors of the brain. This knowledge is especially relevant to our black heritage. Most of our minds have been deprived of the proper stimuli which enables us to reach our full potential in life. I want my readers to be aware of the various stimuli, use them and shock their minds into Zion or the ultimate fulfillment of their destiny."

"I will make sure I read your book when it's published. I know my mind needs stimulating." Frankly, I wanted to say, "Dah-h-h?" But being a writer, I needed to be more expressive. Although I didn't understand what she said, I wanted to say something.

"I am with the I.B.W.A, the International Black Writers and Artists, Inc.. As a matter of fact, I attended their monthly meeting this past Saturday. If you are interested, I can give you the number of the founder, Edna Crutchfield. You can call her for more information."

"Thanks. Write her number in my book," I said, handing it to her.

She searched feverishly in her purse for the number but to no avail.

"I can't find her number, but you can have mine. Call me later, and I will give you Mrs. Crutchfield's number. I know, I have it at home."

"That sounds good. I'll make sure I call you later."

The credit union door opened as I glanced at her name in my book. It was spelled Maisha.

"How do you pronounce your name?"

"My-e-sha," she said, standing up to enter the credit union.

That night, I called Maisha. She gave me Mrs. Crutchfield's number who promised to send me a membership packet. She informed me the next meeting was Saturday, March 25, from 2:00-5:00 p.m., in the Federal Government Building, downtown. I wrote the information on my calendar. That was one meeting I knew I would attend. In my heart, I felt God allowed Maisha and I to meet in order to accomplish the task of writing my novel.

I felt like one hurdle had been passed. Now, my next hurdle was the divorce class, this coming Wednesday, March 1. The problem was not me attending but making sure Carl went.

Tuesday evening, before the class, Carl came into the kitchen from the den while I was eating a slice of chocolate cake.

"The class is tomorrow," I reminded Carl, lifting a piece of cake from my dish into my mouth.

Carl opened the refrigerator, took the two liter Coke bottle out and poured himself a glass full.

"I'm not going," he said, putting the bottle back, closing the refrigerator door.

"You have to go tomorrow because it's the last one before the thirteenth."

He smiled as he walked from the kitchen. "Don't worry about me. I'm not going to the class. I'm not getting a divorce either," he said as he walked down the steps to the den.

The next morning, I went to the class alone. Carl's bullheadedness was sure to catch up with him, I thought, as I listened to the speaker who confirmed the class was mandatory for a divorce.

Carl returned home, that evening, in an especially good mood. He kissed me on my cheek, as he entered the bedroom, while I sat in the chair reading a book.

"How is my lovely wife?" Carl asked, sitting on the bed directly in front of me, grinning.

"Why are you so happy? Did you get a raise?" I asked, putting my book down, wondering what precipitated his disposition.

"No. I got something better than a raise."

"What? A three month evaluation?"

"I got my family back."

"How did you come up with that conclusion?"

"The divorce class was today. Right?"

"Right."

"I had to attend this class before we got the divorce. Right?"

"Right."

"I didn't attend the class today, therefore, we wont be getting a divorce. Right?"

"Wrong. I don't know what will happen to you, but I shouldn't get penalized because you refuse to attend the class," I said getting up to give him the handouts I received. "I brought some information home."

"Fill me in on what was discussed."

"The two main things it emphasized were not letting the children be caught in the middle of the parents and not to equate child support with visitation rights."

"Explain what you mean."

"Parents should discuss matters among themselves instead of relaying messages from the child to the other parent. The second point was if the noncustodial parent does not pay their child support payments, they still have a right to see their child. Nonpayment is a legal matter that will be handled by the courts."

"You mean to tell me, if I don't give you a dime in child support, you'll still let me see my boys?"

"Yes. That's exactly what I mean. Our boys are the ones who will suffer. As for me, I rely on Jesus to supply all my needs. He is my Shepherd. I shall not want," I said, sitting back down in the chair.

Carl watched my every move. "I've been noticing, you've been acting strange lately."

"What do you mean?"

"You've been wearing perfume. You bought new panties and bras. You seem to be totally distant from me."

"As a matter of fact, I am. I'm talking to someone at work who God sent to repair the house."

Carl's grin turned into a frown. "So soon?" he asked with a cracked voice.

"I wasn't looking for anyone. It just happened."

"It just happened, my ass!" he said, reaching in his shirt for a cigarette.

"Calm down."

Carl leaped from the bed and hovered over me.

"I bet you've been seeing that Nigger all the time! That's why you want to divorce my ass!"

"No. That's not true. I met him the day I received my divorce papers. We struck up a conversation about marriage, divorce and repairing the house. I told you, I can't continue to live my life in a shambles. I want everything fixed that's broken, including me."

"God didn't send you no man to break up our home. Satan sent you that repairman. Can't you see that?"

"No, I can't. You're just upset because I found someone."

"You're wrong. I'm upset because I've been a jackass! I thought, I had me a good woman. I see now, I didn't have shit!"

"Well since you feel like I'm shit, I have something else I want to tell your jackass."

The veins in his head and neck were ready to burst. Carl reached for another cigarette. He seemed to be eating them instead of smoking them. Pacing, back and forth, he listened while I spoke.

"Last February, after I told you I was going to leave you, I met a Muslim man who I fell in love with. It was love-at-first-sight for me. We never kissed or touched in any way. We only talked at work. The love I felt for him delivered me from six years of depression that started when you walked out in '88. I even thought, one day, we would get married."

"You actually thought that man was going to marry you?"

"Yes."

"I see, you been dogging my ass out for a long time. I can't believe this shit! My wife with other men! This is too much. I can't stand to be in the same room with you anymore," he squealed as he stormed out the door.

Stunned, I sat motionless in the chair for a few minutes then laid on my bed and listened to the radio. While in a quasi, trance like state, Carlos suddenly came running into the room.

"Mama! Mama!" he shouted, standing over me. "Daddy said, you are divorcing him."

"Yes, son. That's true."

"Where are your tears, Mama? Daddy had tears when he told us."

"I don't have anymore tears. I've use them all up a long time ago. I'm happy about the divorce," I said, reaching to give him a hug.

With his head buried on my breasts, he muttered, "I love you and Daddy."

"We love you too, Carlos."

"Mama," he said, raising his head up.

"Yes, Carlos."

"Will Daddy be my dad?"

"Of course, son. He'll always be your dad. Nothing can change that."

"Will I see him again?" he asked, sitting up.

"Of course, son. You'll see him a lot. The only difference between now and after the divorce is your dad won't be living with us."

"There's another difference, Mama."

"What?"

"I'll get one spanking for doing something bad instead of two."

"What do you mean, two spankings. Your father doesn't spank you. He talks with a switch in his hands then walks away."

"But if he was here, he might use the switch one day. See ya, Mama," he said, kissing me on my cheek. "I'm going back downstairs to watch TV."

"Bye, Carlos. I love you."

Little Carl came in later to verify the divorce. His biggest concern was if he would be able to get enough money for spring shopping. His next concern was getting a Six Flags season pass which I had promised him for several years. I even told him, I would give him his own phone. Little Carl was delighted and looked forward to having his own phone.

Carl had a beeper, therefore, he would only be a telephone call away. The boys were older and could easily contact him whenever they wished. I believe, Carl's beeper, coupled with the boys being older, made the biggest difference in their reaction from previous times.

The kids knowing about the divorce made it seem more a reality. Carlos response surprised me because I thought he would be all torn up. The reaction of both Carlos and little Carl quenched my anxiety of them finding out about the divorce. Now, that the truth was revealed, I was glad they knew.

# THIRTY-FOUR

The same night at work, March 1, I told Bryson the events that happened at home. He was surprised I told Carl about him and Zakee. I was amazed Carl had not figured something was going on earlier. Maybe his lack of attentiveness was another sign we were no longer husband and wife but roommates.

The next night, at work, Zakee stopped at the window while I was accessioning specimens.

"Well, well, well. What wind blew you my way?" I asked Zakee as he stared at me.

"Tonight is my last night working here. I will be working at the police station, starting Sunday. I came to say goodbye."

"Thanks for stopping by to say goodbye. By the way, how is your family?"

"My wife left me in January."

"She did. I wondered if you were still with her."

"How is everything at your home?"

"I told my husband about you yesterday. How you changed my life. You know, I still plan to write a book about us."

"You and your book," he replied, smiling.

"I haven't talked to you for awhile, but I am getting a divorce on the thirteenth of this month."

"He's letting you go?"

"He doesn't have a choice. I am divorcing him. I told you when I first met you, last year, I was going to leave him."

"Yeah, in ten years, remember?"

"No. I said, it would be sooner because of the things that happened since I met you, remember?"

"Give me your number."

I picked up a notepad, wrote my number down and handed it to Zakee. "Give me your number, too," I said, handing him a piece of paper.

"Don't you have it?"

"I found it in the telephone book the last time. I want you to write it down for me."

He wrote his number down on the paper and gave it to me.

"You look so good," he said, admiringly.

"I thought, I would never hear you say those words," I said, grinning from ear-to-ear.

"It's time for me to go. I just stopped to say goodbye. I will call you after your divorce," he said, putting the paper in his sweater pocket, walking off.

I finished accessioning the specimens, smiling the whole time. The thought of being with Zakee excited me. Finally, the "Price Tag Prophecy" will be fulfilled, I thought.

Carl came home, that evening, smelling like gasoline. His blue jeans and brown leather jacket were covered with oil.

"What happened to you?" I asked when he came into the house. I was at the kitchen table eating a bowl of ice cream, facing the door.

"My damn car conked out. It spittered and sputtered for half a mile then died," he answered, closing the door while taking off his oily jacket.

"What did you do?"

"I got out the car, raised the hood, checked the oil and other fluids then started wiggling things around to see if anything was loose."

"What did you find out?"

"I don't know a damn thing about cars," he said, wiping his jacket with a towel that was on the counter. "I ended up calling a tow truck to pull that piece of shit away."

"How did you get home?"

"I called Terry. He picked me up and dropped me off."

"How did you get so nasty?"

"After I closed the hood, I crawled under the car to see if anything was leaking. When I started feeling around, oil leaked all over me. Lately, I can't win for losing," he said, going to the sink to wash his hands.

"Is the Chevette running? I know you've been having problems with it, off-and-on," I said, eating the last of my ice cream.

"If I'm lucky, it might take me back-and-forth to work. But the way my luck is running, I probably won't get it out the driveway." He reached into the cabinet to his liquor stash and poured himself a drink.

"Are you going to look at it today to make sure it runs?"

"As soon as I get a good buzz going. I'll take a look at it."

"Why do you need to get high first? It seems to me, you could do a better job sober."

"The liquor will help me concentrate on what I'm doing. The buzz will help block all this other shit, that's going on, out my mind."

"You know, Carl," I said, getting up from the table to put the empty bowl into the sink. "This divorce was meant to be. Madame Lee told me fifteen years ago, I was going to leave you. But she never said, you were going to leave me. I've never quite recovered from that to this day. Our relationship hasn't been right since then."

"I was thinking today, when we first started talking as teenagers. How we teased each other about not receiving the child support payments for our children.

216

Remember, how I came up with countless excuses for not giving you your money?"

"I know. It was like an omen. Don't you think? The fact that we always referred to them as our children and not our child. And knowing the way you handle your finances, you won't be paying me my child support payments, but you will come up with numerous excuses instead."

"No. You're wrong. I'll pay you on time. I love my sons."

"We will see. Although, I know I'm right. Our teasing twenty-five years ago was an omen. I feel very strongly about it. It was funny then, but it won't be funny now."

"Since you know everything, give me an omen about my cars."

"I'm no psychic. But any fool can tell you, you need a new car. Your two pluckers have plucked out."

"I'm the fool for thinking I had a loving, faithful wife."

"I haven't been unfaithful to you. I've only talked to other men. You're the one who's been unfaithful."

"Yeah, right. Look Vanessa, I'm not that teenage kid you first met. I'm a grown ass man. I know what's going on," he said, finishing his drink. "I'm going outside to make sure the Chevette will get me to work tomorrow." He put his jacket back on then went out the front door.

I went downstairs to watch TV with the boys who were still taking the news of the divorce well.

Carl finished working on the car just in time to watch me get ready for work. His presence unnerved me, but I didn't know how to tell him.

I continued to see Bryson every night at work. I sensed feelings were developing between us. He confirmed my feelings, Wednesday morning, March 8.

Bryson walked me to my car after waiting on me at the Butler Street entrance. When we reached my car on the third floor parking deck, we stopped to talk. I stood in front of my car while he leaned on the car next to mine on the passenger side.

"I feel really blessed to have met you," Bryson said, folding his hands in his lap as he blocked my path. "You make me feel like I did in high school."

"I know. I feel the same way. It's scary. Don't you think?" I asked, looking into his penetrating eyes.

"All I know is, I want you to be mine."

"Bryson, you know, I'm still married. I can't talk like that yet. Excuse me, please," I said, walking past his body barricade. "I think, I better get in my car before I get in trouble."

"You're all ready in trouble."

He blocked my path, momentarily, but later allowed me to pass. Once I was seated inside my car, I locked the door then pushed the button to roll the window down.

"Thanks for walking me to my car," I said, smiling.

"My pleasure," he said, smiling back, staring intently into my eyes. "You're in more trouble than you can ever imagine."

"I don't know exactly what you mean, but I think, I better leave," I said, rolling up the window.

Bryson quickly reached over the window before it went all the way up and pushed the button which made the window roll back down. He stuck his head inside and put his tongue half way down my throat.

"I told you, you were in trouble," he said as he walked off grinning.

I couldn't believe what had just transpired. Bryson kissed me. It wasn't just any kiss. I felt a warm glow flow throughout my body and especially between my legs. "Oh, my God!" was all I could say as I sat with my mouth and legs wide opened and my eyes bucked. Bryson was right. I was in trouble.

My body had never responded to anyone like that before. From my reaction, I knew, I couldn't handle it, either. In a-state-of-shock, I drove home thinking of Bryson and his kiss the whole time.

I called Bryson at MARTA, his full time job, when I woke up. I told him my reaction to his kiss. He laughed. "I told you, you were in trouble," he reminded me. He suggested we talk about it at Exchange Park, the next morning, when I got off work. I agreed to meet him at 8 o'clock. Although Bryson didn't know where I lived, I thought it was odd for him to select a location so close to me. The park was around the corner from my house.

I drove to the park Thursday morning at the designated location, near the picnic tables. A dark green van was parked at the predetermined spot. I parked two spaces from the van. Bryson sat in the driver's seat and motioned me to come inside the van. His eyes watched me as I strolled to the van wearing white pants, sneakers, a black turtleneck sweater, and a long black leather coat.

"Get in," Bryson said as he opened the passenger door.

Bryson with his quick hands pressed the lever of the passenger seat to make it horizontal as I laid my head back.

"Get me up!" I yelled, trying to sit up. "Get me up this minute!"

All right. Don't panic," he said, adjusting the lever, laughing. "But, if I ever get you down, I'll never let you get back up."

"I came to talk, Bryson. Therefore, don't try anymore shenanigans with me. Understand?"

"All right. Let's talk," he said, still laughing, with his eyes glued to my turtleneck sweater.

"Let's talk outside. I don't trust you inside this van because you're too quick with your hands."

He grinned his devilish grin.

"All right. If that's what you want."

We walked to the picnic tables, a few feet away. He held my hand as we walked. Stopping at the last table, near the water fountain, he held me close to his wide chest then raised my head to kiss me. Snapping my head back down, I buried it further into his chest.

"We came to talk and nothing else," I said, looking into his mesmerizing eyes. "I'm still married. Yesterday, you caught me off guard. I can't let that happen again."

"I keep telling you, I want you to be mine. I don't have anything else to say," he said, squeezing me lovingly. His body felt good next to mine. I melted in his embrace.

"Bryson, what are we going to do? Your kiss, yesterday, blew me away. I feel out of control."

"Relax. There's plenty more where that came from."

"That's the problem. I find myself wanting more. It scares me because I shouldn't be feeling this way. I am a married woman."

"Your marriage will be over in four days. Besides, you are human. We both are."

"Why does it feel wrong?"

"Because your husband is the only man you've been with. Your feelings are different, not wrong."

"I guess you're right. This is new for me since I've only been with one man."

"Can we kiss on it?"

"No, not yet. I don't feel right being here with you like this. I really should be leaving."

"I'll be glad when your divorce is final so you can relax," he said, walking me to my car.

"I will be too, for the same reason. I'm glad we came today. I feel in control again since I didn't give in to your advances."

"Ha! You might control me at the park, but you won't be able to control me in the house."

He opened my car door after I unlocked it. We said our goodbyes and left. I was out-of-sight before he entered his van.

I went home feeling good. Bryson was sorely needed in my broken life. I'm sure it was no coincidence he repaired things. My greatest need was for me to be repaired—to be made whole again. Bryson was just the man to do it.

# THIRTY-FIVE

The thought of ending my relationship with Carl and starting a new relationship with Zakee and/or Bryson made me even more eager for Monday to arrive. I don't know what Carl had up his sleeves but mine were empty of any malice. I simply wanted my freedom, to go on with my life, and to get my life back on track.

As for Carl, I wished him well. I prayed, he would be happy. I'm sorry our marriage did not go the full distance—until death do us part. The relationship, as it was, was killing both of us alive. Reflecting back on our twenty-year marriage, I was giving Carl what he's wanted since we married in '75—to be single.

My good mood, of being with Bryson, lasted the whole day. I took the boys shopping. They were out-of-school, and I felt like splurging. And besides, since I knew I was in control of my feelings, I could afford to be a little out-of-control with my spending.

That night, Carl was in the kitchen with the boys when I started getting ready for work. I locked the door to prevent Carl from watching me while I dressed. Since his presence unnerved me, I didn't want him spoiling my good mood.

I had just put my underwear on when I heard Carl turning the knob of the door.

"Let me in!" he screamed, pounding on the door.

"No! I'm getting dressed."

"Do you have something to hide? Is that why you won't let me in?"

"No."

"Are you marked up?" he demanded, as he continued to beat on the door.

"No! I just want some privacy. Can't I dress in private!" I shouted, annoyed.

"I'm coming in there! You are hiding something from me."

I heard Carl run down the steps. Moments later, he was at the door, picking the lock. I continued to get dressed as if nothing was going on. When he finally picked the lock, I was in the bathroom, brushing my teeth, fully dressed in my pink jumpsuit.

I heard him enter the room and walk to the bathroom without stopping.

"You and your men!" he uttered as he pushed me into the bathtub. My body sprawled inside the tub after my head hit the facet. Grabbing the collar of my jumpsuit, Carl lifted me up with one hand..

"I'll kill you," he said, with clenched teeth and his fist touched my nose.

Motionless, I looked him dead in his eyes. I knew, if I moved or said anything, my life would be over. Instantly, a peace came over me. I did not fear for my life.

"Daddy! Daddy! The telephone," little Carl yelled outside the bedroom door.

Releasing his grip on my collar, Carl stood up from his kneeling position to answer the phone. I thanked Christ for intervening at a crucial moment in my life. With a long sigh-of-relief, I pulled myself out of the tub. Carl came back inside the bedroom as I finished getting ready. He sat on his side of the bed talking to himself, obviously, disturbed. I didn't say a word to him. Walking toward the door, I grabbed my purse and went to work. Fortunately, the boys weren't aware of what happened.

I drove to work nervous and upset. My head ached from the impact. I felt a large, sore knot below my left knee. My left hip felt bruised. I couldn't complain about my injuries. I was glad to be alive.

By the second hour into my shift, I had regained my composure. I was glad I didn't have to face Carl when I went home because he would be at work. I knew these last few days would be rough. I prayed, that God would see me through.

Since the boys were out of school, I took them and a few of their friends to Dave and Busters. When we returned home, Carl's house key was on the kitchen table. I went upstairs to confirm what I suspected—Carl had moved out. I told the boys later their father was gone for the last time. Carl called to inform me he had moved in with a co-worker. He felt it was best. I agreed and was relieved.

Saturday, Carl picked the boys up because he wanted to spend the remainder of the weekend with them. As soon as they left, I called Bryson. I'm home alone, was the message I left on his phone. A few minutes later, the phone rang.

"Hello," I said, picking up the phone, hoping it was Bryson.

"So, you're alone. If you give me directions, I'll keep you company."

"Aren't you working?"

"Yes. I am on the lines, today. No one will miss me if I come to see you. Don't worry about me. I am interested in you, especially, since your episode with Carl the other evening. I just want to put my arms around you and make sure you're okay."

I gave Bryson directions to the house. "How soon can you get here?" I asked, anxious to see him.

"Twenty minutes. Ten, if I break all the speed laws."

"Try fifteen. Drive like a maniac instead of a speed demon."

"By the way, how long will they be gone?"

"Until tomorrow."

"I am on my way."

"Okay. Goodbye."

"Click."

Ten minutes later, the door bell rang. I answered it, hoping it was Bryson. It was. He was dressed in his navy blue uniform, grinning from ear-to-ear.

"Come in," I said, with a matching expression.

He came inside and we kissed passionately at the door. His hands glided up and down my buttocks, slightly lifting the beige, knee-length skirt I wore to church.

"You look nice," he said, between kisses.

"Thank you," I responded, holding him closer.

"I missed you so much. It seems like ages since the last time we talked," Bryson said, holding me, rubbing my back. "I am glad you called me. I've been thinking about you all day."

"I've been thinking about you, too. Even during church, today. Would you like to go downstairs to the den and listen to the radio?"

"Sure, that sounds good."

We embraced as we walked down the steps to the den. His hands clutched my beige jacket as we entered the den. Together we walked to the radio. I turned it on and we started slow dancing and kissing. As we danced, his hands moved all over my body. His kisses became demanding.

"Bryson, stop," I moaned, as I pulled away from his embrace, before we get in trouble."

"That's not what you really want," he said, as he continued to kiss me, passionately. "I want you, and you want me."

"That's true but not now. Not today."

"Tomorrow is not promised to us. Today is all we have," he said penning me against the wall.

"No. Stop it. I really mean it."

"All right. Have it your way," he said, walking in a circle, trying to get his erection down. "If you change your mind, I won't be responsible for my actions."

My curiosity and PMS were getting the best of me as I watched Bryson. My swollen, sore breasts, were begging to be caressed. In my mind, I wondered how his hands would alleviate the soreness from my aching breasts. Carl was good at relieving the soreness. I wondered, how good Bryson would be.

I walked over to Bryson, put my arms around him and kissed him fervidly.

"You better stop while you're ahead," he said, pushing me away. "I told you. I won't be responsible for my actions."

"I know. But I will be responsible for mine," I said, kissing him again.

"All right! I told you to leave me alone," he said, picking me up, and hurling me on the sofa.

Before I could blink-an-eye, my panties, and stockings were pulled down. My skirt was over my waist. Bryson was on top of me, completely inside, going to town. He pulled my jacket and bra up and started sucking on my breast like a baby. Although I did not have an orgasm, he felt wonderful!

Bryson sounded like Tarzan as he climaxed. Afterwards, he laid on me like a limp dishrag.

"You couldn't leave well enough alone. I told you, I wouldn't be responsible for my actions," he said, getting up.

We got ourselves back together, talked and kissed for an hour before he received a call over his work radio. Riddled with guilt, after he left, I went to my room and dropped to my knees.

*Dear Merciful and Benevolent Father,*

*Forgive me for I have sinned. I have profaned the blood of Your Son, Jesus Christ, who died for me.*

*His shed blood, washed all my sins away. Now, I have sinned, dishonoring His sacrifice for me. He died without sin so that I, a sinner, could be justified before You and live in righteousness.*

*Lord, in I John 1:8-9, You say, "If we say we have no sin, we deceive ourselves, and the truth is not in us. If we confess our sins, You are faithful and just, and will forgive our sins and cleanse us from all unrighteousness."*

*Lord, David committed adultery with Bathsheba, yet he was a man after Your heart. He cried out to You in Psalms 51 regarding his trespass. These are his very words and they apply to me:*

*"Have mercy on me, O God, according to thy steadfast love; according to thy abundant mercy blot out my transgressions. Wash me thoroughly from my iniquity, and cleanse me from my sin!"*

*In Jesus Christ name I pray. Amen.*

Feeling forgiven of my trespass, I studied God's Word for an hour, thanking Him and praising Him, before drifting off to sleep. Sunday, I continued praising God and thanked Him for the sacrifice of His Son, Jesus Christ.

The boys came home that evening happy and full of life. We enjoyed the rest of the evening together, talking, playing UNO, and watching TV. They reluctantly went to bed, at ten, not wanting the evening to end.

On Monday morning, March 13, D-Day, I came home from work before I went to the courthouse to make sure the boys caught their school bus. Carl told me when he dropped the boys off yesterday, he planned to be at the courthouse. I excitedly drove to the courthouse in anticipation of the divorce. As I approached the courthouse intersection, an image of a baby, wrapped in a blanket, appeared through the windshield.

"I'm coming. I'm coming, baby girl. Mama's coming, soon," I said to the image before it disappeared.

Pulling into a vacant parking space, across the street from the courthouse, I suddenly remembered, I only had fifteen cents. I stared at the expired meter as I parked the car. I gave the boys all the other money I had for their lunch. I said a short prayer then got out of the car. A car parked next to me as I locked my door.

"Excuse me, sir. I don't have enough money to put in the meter. Do you have any spare change?"

He smiled, then reached into his pants pocket and handed me two quarters and a dime.

"Thank you, sir," I said, taking his coins, putting them into the meter. He walked off without putting any money into the expired meter in front of his car.

I praised Jesus Christ on the way to the courthouse. He won one battle for me. I knew He would win the rest.

Going directly to the second clerk's desk on the second floor, I told a clerk my name and purpose.

"Have a seat, ma'am. Someone will be with you, shortly," said the heavyset, long nailed clerk, I met a month ago.

I waited on the wooden bench, beneath the desk, for fifteen minutes before a young, short, dark-skinned woman called my name.

"Mrs. Vanessa Lewis?" she asked, questioningly.

"Yes." I replied, standing up.

"Please come with me. I am Shinquilla Thomas. Let me take you to begin your divorce proceedings."

We walked to the elevators and waited with several other people. She motioned to get on the elevator going up. We exited and went to a room across from the elevators.

The room was decorated with expensive leather sofas and chairs. A large, oak desk was near the door. Shinquilla asked a stout, short, blonde woman for my file. It seemed like I waited hours, but it was only twenty minutes before Shinquilla announced, it was time to see the judge.

"You have Judge Clarence Peeler, Jr.," Shinquilla said, as we walked to his chamber. "I will stay with you throughout your case. Do you have any questions?"

"What kind of judge is he?"

"That depends. He has good days. And he has bad days. You're his first case, so I don't know what kind of day he's having."

"Do you know if he is pro-marriage or pro-divorce?"

"He's definitely pro-marriage."

"How do you know?"

"You'll know as soon as you set foot in his chamber," she said, opening the door leading to his waiting area and secretary's desk.

"Judge Peeler is expecting you," the secretary said when Shinquilla told her my case.

We walked around the corner to his chamber. He sat in his oxblood red chair, reading, as we entered the room. Judge Peeler was white haired, medium framed, in his seventies. Pictures of his family filled the room. An old photograph of him and his wife was on his desk, turned for visitors to view. His only piece of jewelry was his wide, gold, wedding band. Shinquilla handed him my file as he motioned us to be seated into the two leather chairs facing him at his desk.

He opened the file and read its contents. Looking up over his black, horn rimmed glasses, he asked, "Mrs. Lewis, is the defendant, Carl Lewis present?"

"No sir."

"Has Mr. Lewis agreed to comply with the division of property and child support payments?" he asked, looking at me with his gray, piercing eyes.

"Yes sir."

"What reasons do you have for filing this divorce petition?"

"Mr. Lewis and I have irreconcilable differences which makes it impossible to function as man and wife. We no longer have a marriage. If our relationship continues, it will be to the detriment of one or both of us," I said, very sternly, feeling the pain from my head, side, and leg.

He flipped through the pages of my file. "I see you attended the seminar for divorce parents, but Mr. Lewis did not."

"Yes sir, that's correct. Will I still be granted the divorce?"

"Since Mr. Lewis is not present to refute any charges against this petition or plead to save his marriage, I hereby grant the judgement and decree of this divorce, due to irreconcilable differences between the plaintiff and the defendant. Mr. Lewis will be required to attend the Seminar for Divorcing Parents within thirty days. I will write the stipulation on the divorce decree," he said, writing on a paper in the file. He took an ink stamp and stamped the papers several times.

I exhaled a long sigh of relief. I was divorced. The marriage was over. Thinking back on what had just happened, I realized how God had supernaturally delivered me. Carl and I had planned to come before the judge together. God knew, but I didn't know, the divorce would not have been granted if we came together. The bathtub incident was God's way to get Carl out of the house so I could come alone and the divorce granted. Romans 8:28 came to my mind:

*"We know that all things work for good for those who love him, who are called according to his purpose."*

God truly works in mysterious ways! Judge Peeler handed Shinquilla the stamped file.

"Mrs. Lewis, we can go now," she said, standing up to leave.

I stood up and led the way out of Judge Peeler's chambers. We passed his secretary who was talking with an older white couple. They were obviously the next case.

"You may go into Judge Peeler's chamber, now. He is ready for your case," the secretary said, as we left the room.

"What's next?" I asked Shinquilla while we walked down the corridor.

"That depends on whether you want your name changed or not. If you change your name today, it will be free. If you change your name later, it will cost you $65.00 dollars."

"I will keep Lewis. I don't have a problem with the name. It was the man with name that I had a problem with."

"In that case, we will return to where I picked you up. You can get a copy of your divorce paper for twenty-five cents."

"I don't have any money."

"I will give you a quarter," she said, reaching into her pants pocket.

"Thank you, again."

We rode the elevator down to the second floor. Shinquilla handed the clerk behind the counter my file and told her I wanted one copy. I was told to go back to the room on the right to pay the quarter then come back with the receipt.

While waiting on my copy, I remembered the thirty dollars for the divorce seminar that Carl didn't attend.

"Is there any way I can get a refund for the divorce seminar my ex-husband did not attend?" I asked when the clerk gave me my divorce paper.

"Yes. Here's the location on this form," she said, handing me another piece of paper.

"Thank you."

I looked at the location on the form. It was located inside the courthouse. I took an elevator up. After locating the room, I inquired about my refund. At first, the woman waiting on me couldn't find my application. Fifteen minutes later, she came to me with a check for thirty dollars.

"You can go to the bank across the parking lot to cash this check."

"Thank you. I will," I said, leaving.

I went to the elevators, exited the courthouse and walked to the bank. Being divorced already had its benefits because I had more money after than before.

The parking meter had five more minutes left. I unlocked the car door and headed home, ecstatic.

Thoughts filled my head while I drove. I thought about my mother barking when I was born. To me, the barking was an omen—a sign, that characterized my life up until the divorce. It signified that I would be treated like a dog most of my life. The divorce started a new era that ended my dog days.

As I drove, another image appeared before my face. I was very pregnant, at the point of delivery. A large book was in front of the pregnant image of me. A voice spoke to me and said, "Your book will be published first before you deliver. There will be a question about your name. It will be changed before the work goes to print." I took what I saw and heard, to heart. I knew they were true. I also knew, in their own time, they would come to pass.

The telephone rang as I entered the house.

"Hello," I said, as I picked up the receiver.

"Vanessa, I want you to know, I tried to be there today," Carl said, on the other end.

"What happened?"

"Both cars stopped running. I called my dad to pick me up, but he got lost and went back home. Then I called Terry. He picked me up and we went to the courthouse. Every place we went, they said, we had just missed you. I even went to the Divorce Seminar office and they said, you had just left. Terry is taking me to get a new car today as soon as I get off the phone. By the way, I have a copy of the divorce decree," Carl said, crying. "Vanessa, I want you back."

Goosebumps popped up all over my body. "Carl, you were never meant to be with me today. It was meant for me to be alone. Because, if you had been with me, we would not have gotten this divorce. But by the grace of Jesus Christ, I am UNCAGED and UNLEASHED!"

Click.

"Arf! Arf! Arf!"


To be continued with: *The Bearer of the Sign*

# The Bearer of the Sign

Lord, You know my heart. You also know the heart of every man...My knowledge of another person is only in part, in bits-and-pieces as they reveal themselves to me...Father, let me not lean to my own fragmented understanding, but to Yours.

Father, I propose to establish a sign to identify the person You have chosen for me...Father, I am reminded in Your Word of two occassions where you honored the signs of men that You were with them. I, too, need the reassurance that You have chosen my next soul mate. The first incident in the Bible is in I Samuel 14:9-12. It was regarding Jonathan,the son of Saul, and his arm-bearer who went up against the Philistines. He asked for this sign: "If they say to us, 'Wait until we come to you,' then we will stand still in our place, and we will not go up to them. But if they say, 'Come up to us,' then we will go up; for the Lord has given them into our hand..."

The second incident is in Judges 6:16-17, 36-40. Gideon, the son of Joash, asked for a sign that You were with him. "And the Lord said to him (Gideon), 'But I will be with you, and you shall smite the Midianites as one man.' And he said to him," If now I have found favor with thee, then show me a sign that it is thou who has speakest to me.'...Then Gideon said to God, 'If thou wilt deliver Israel by my hand, as thou has said, behold I am laying a fleece of wool on the threshing floor; if there is dew on the fleece alone, and it is dry on all the ground, then I shall know that thou wilt deliver Israel by my hand, as thou has said.' And it was so. When he rose early next morning and squeezed the fleece, he wrung enough dew from the fleece to fill a bowl with water..."

Father, this is the sign that I have chosen to identify the next man in my life. The man whom I hope to spend my last days with. The man who will treat me like I want to be treated...The man who will build me up and not tear me down. The man who will love my mind more than my body. The man who will be faithful, and devoted to me until death do us part. The man who fears You and walks in Your ways. The sign: As long I am single, I will never ask a man for money. But the man of my life will give me $50 or more voluntarily. When he gives the money to me, I'll ask him, "What is this for?" his reply will be, "This is for you because I am your man." And indeed he will be from that day on.

# ABOUT THE AUTHOR

I, Deeva Denez, was born and raised in Atlanta, Georgia. I am the second of three siblings. In 1977, I graduated from Georgia State University with a B.S. Degree in Medical Technology. I've been a medical technologist since 1977, but started my writing career in 1995 with my first novel, "Uncaged."

"Uncaged" is the first of a three book series. The second novel, "The Bearer of the Sign" is completed and is a continuation of "Uncaged." The third book, "The Image—A Prophetic Birth" will be written next year. Because of my writing experience and my desire to help other writers, I formed my own company, The Literary Connection. It promotes and facilitates with other writers. I also publish other writers.

I have been interviewed on several radio stations in the Atlanta, Columbus, and Macon areas. I have had numerous book signings and have been featured at both The Black Arts Festival and Sisters' Only in Atlanta. I am presently married and live with my family in Decatur, Georgia.

Printed in the USA
CPSIA information can be obtained
at www.ICGtesting.com
LVHW081614311023
762279LV00005B/32